"Great. Why a ... , Ms. . . ." She glanced at the card again as the words printed in bold black letters penetrated through her confusion.

". . . World Federation of Monarchists?" The words squeaked out of her throat, strangled by the realization that her grandmother had been uncharacteristically quiet on the Ibaranian royalty front. She'd never pressured Makeda about it, not even a nudge, which Makeda had attributed to her newfound irritability, when in fact something else was far more likely.

"My name is Beznaria Chetchevaliere," the woman corrected with clear amusement, pulling Makeda's attention from the disbelief that was shifting to understanding. "The World Federation of Monarchists is the organization I work for. I'm taking pictures of you to add to the file I'm creating for you. You may not believe it, but stodgy old monarchists require reams of paperwork, and if I'm going to prove you're a princess, we're going to need an excessive amount of documentation."

"Prove *what*?"

By Alyssa Cole

ALYSSA COLE

HOW TO FIND A PRINCESS

❖ RUNAWAY ROYALS ❖

AVONBOOKS

An Imprint of HarperCollinsPublishers

Excerpt from *When No One Is Watching* copyright © 2020 by Alyssa Cole.

First Avon Books mass market printing: June 2021

Print Edition ISBN: 978-0-06-293400-0
Digital Edition ISBN: 978-0-06-293399-7

Cover design by Nadine Badalaty
Cover photography by Shirley Green (couple)
Cover images © kotina - adobestock.com (background); © Vasya Kobelev/Shutterstock (type frame)
Dress by Trofina Joy

For Corey.

Acknowledgments

As always, my thanks to Erika Tsang and the Avon staff, and my agent, Lucienne Diver. Special thanks to copy editor Chris Wolfgang and everyone who helped make this story better.

How to
Find a
Princess

Chapter 1

Makeda Hicks was used to delivering quality customer service with a smile no matter how bad she felt, but as she rushed into the manager's office of GrabRite Supermarket #074, Atlantic City, New Jersey location, out of breath and sweaty from surviving a gauntlet of needy customers, disappointment tugged at the corners of her mouth.

As she sat down, she already knew what her manager, Mr. Romano, was going to say from how he kept wiping at his mustache with thumb and forefinger though no trace of his lunch remained. She was good at anticipating people's needs and desires, and Mr. Romano currently desired to be done with whatever he had to tell her.

I didn't get the promotion I wanted, she thought.

The promotion you deserve, the little voice that occasionally shouted from the help-y abyss of her soul called out.

The promotion she *needed* to begin to chip away at the debt that had just emerged from nowhere—no, not from nowhere. From her foolishly thinking that doing something nice couldn't ever come back to bite her in the ass.

"Ballsy being late to our meeting," Mr. Romano said gruffly, though there was a familiar teasing in his voice.

"Sorry," she said, lacing her fingers together. "Customers kept stopping me to ask questions and—"

"And you kept letting them stop you, like you always do," he finished for her. He shook his head and gestured toward her with both hands. "Makeda. You know I think you're a wonderful human. But the assistant manager position requires the ability to say no, to delegate instead of just taking everything on yourself, the ability to . . . to . . . not be you."

He paused, then waved a hand. "Sorry. I'm sorry, that sounded meaner than I meant."

"No, it's okay," she said, her lips stretching tightly over the familiar frame of her reassuring smile. "I know how I can be. I'll work on that and maybe next time, I'll be ready for the promotion. Don't worry. I'm not upset."

Inside she was shriveling up like the earthworms she used to find drying in the sun after a rain shower when she was a kid. She'd rehydrate them, then drop them back into the grass, keeping herself busy while her mom slept off her hangover. Her mother had gotten sober eventually, but Makeda had continued to be everyone else's watering can.

Drip, drop.

"Is Lindsey going to get the promotion instead?" she asked without a trace a venom, even as she thought about how her coworker spent most of her time smoking out back, never memorized the weekly sales circular that Makeda designed, and still called aisle seven "ethnic foods" even though Makeda had renamed it "International Tastes."

Mr. Romano nodded, his gaze darting to the side as if he felt her willing him to at least give her the respect of eye contact.

She ran her thumb over the ring on her middle finger, a rounded gold band covered with finely etched fish scales, the familiar texture beneath the pad of her thumb a reminder of how quickly a good thing could go bad.

Makeda had busted her ass studying retail store design and customer psychology in her precious downtime, researching the healthiest products to stock for customers using WIC, the most expensive products with the highest profit margin to stock for tourists and big spenders. She'd thought the promotion was in the bag, that if she worked hard enough, kept her nose to the grindstone, she'd maybe end up in corporate one day. Instead Lindsey would probably fail her way up to smoking in front of headquarters instead of behind GrabRite #074.

"I'll have to congratulate her," Makeda said with perfectly measured politeness.

"And . . ." Mr. Romano's mustache trembled and he exhaled, his gaze finally meeting hers. "Damn, I hate this so I'm just gonna say it. I have to let you go."

Makeda stared at him, her forgiving smile pasted on her face even as her thoughts whirled wildly. Maybe she was misunderstanding.

"Go where, Mr. Romano?" She was blinking too quickly but couldn't help it. "Are they finally opening the GrabRite location in Linwood? The commute would be a bit much, but you know I'd love to help build—"

Mr. Romano held up a hand and cut her off before she could finish. "The new location went over budget, and sales have been down with the drop in tourists and so many people out of work. Corporate brought in some people to figure out how to streamline things."

"But I'm the one who streamlines things," she said through the smile she couldn't seem to let go of—she didn't know what would happen if she stopped smiling right then. It was like the support structure holding up a rapidly crumbling building. She huffed a laugh, a panicked sound strained through cheer. "Streamlining is what I do. For little money. And no promotion."

Drip, drop.

"Well, that little money was too much for headquarters. They decided to cut several full-time positions and yours was one of them."

"But—can't we figure something—" Makeda pressed her lips together. She was helpful, and part of that helpfulness was being able to anticipate responses and quickly assess situations so she could best deal with them. She already knew that even she couldn't fix this.

Listing everything she'd done for GrabRite over the last few years wouldn't change what was currently happening, and it'd only hurt Mr. Romano, who was a good enough guy even if he did overorder wholesale toilet paper for the employee bathroom so he could bring some home.

Thoughts of how she'd pay her bills made her fake smile falter.

"Do I get a severance package?" she asked calmly.

She'd never been fired before. She was too useful to be fired. She was competent, too, but that wasn't her appeal—she was *useful*, doing the things no one else wanted to do, fixing things before others acknowledged they were broken, organizing without making anyone feel they'd made a mess. If you were useful, then people were less likely to get rid of you. But, somehow, useful hadn't been good enough this time.

"I got you two weeks," Mr. Romano said, rolling a ballpoint pen back and forth on his desk. "I asked for two months, but they denied it."

She was almost glad when she saw the sheen of tears in his eyes and heard the waver in his voice. It allowed her to push her own pain aside and tend to his guilty conscience instead.

"Don't feel bad. It's not your fault and I'll land on my feet."

She was certain she heard the sound of her grandmother sucking her teeth, as the old woman always did whenever Makeda went out of her way for others.

"Don't you know what happens when you give all your own sweetness without saving any for yourself?" Grandma Ora, or Grandmore as she preferred to be called, always asked whenever she caught Makeda in an unprompted act of kindness. *"You get left with*

nothing but the bitter. You gonna mess around and end up like me."

Makeda wouldn't call Grandmore bitter, but the woman was tough. She'd once threatened a guest at the B&B for calling Makeda a *sentient welcome mat*, though the woman hadn't meant it as an insult. Sometimes Makeda wished she were more like her grandmother, who did what she wanted, said what she wanted, and had a flair for adventure and drama that caused dustups to this day—dust that Makeda swept under the proverbial welcome mat that was herself.

No adventures, no drama, and always there to lend a helping hand, even when her hands were full, that was Makeda. And that usually worked out just fine for her—until it didn't.

After giving Mr. Romano a pep talk and going through all the initiatives she'd been working on that would likely never be finished since Lindsey would just let them gather dust, she made her way to the employee lounge. The thought of everyone knowing she'd been fired—including Lindsey, who always teased Makeda for being too eager to please and had managed to not only keep her job but walk away with a promotion—made her stomach churn, so she grabbed her belongings and slipped out before any of her shift buddies noticed. She didn't want to upset them or, worse, have them try to console her.

It felt a bit deceptive, but they'd find out soon enough and she'd message them her goodbyes later.

When she walked out into the parking lot, the overcast morning had turned into a beautiful, warm early spring day; the clear blue sky might have been mocking if she didn't decide to take it as a sign of better things to come. It was possible that it just hadn't sunk in that she was, for the first time in her adult life, jobless. She'd already heard from Steph, who'd been hunting for a new job for weeks, that prospects were terrible so she wasn't looking forward to doing the same, though maybe it would help them reconnect after a rough couple of months. She also wasn't looking forward to having her grandmother inevitably ask the question she'd never quite been able to answer: *what do you want to do with your life?*

Makeda was a planner, with a never finished to-do list of work tasks, projects at her grandmother's B&B, requests from friends, and even requests from strangers, but one section of the list was always conspicuously blank—the part where she should have set down her own hopes and dreams. She'd just helped Steph make her five-year plan, and regularly gave advice when people seemed stuck, but she never took the time to do the same for herself.

What do I want to do with my life?

The first thing that came to mind was "be gainfully employed" and the second was "make Steph that casserole she likes" and she wrinkled her nose. Well, no one would ever call her exciting, and that was just fine with her.

Excitement was overrated.

She drove the short distance to the studio apartment she shared with Steph on autopilot, steadfastly ignoring the strange noise coming from under the hood of her old-ass Honda Civic. She'd take it to

Roger, her mechanic, who wasn't the greatest but who she was too loyal—or guilty—to abandon for greasier pastures. Or maybe she'd use her new free time to look into learning car repair so she could fix things herself.

She spent the short ride soothing herself by creating work for herself. She'd spend an hour each day watching car repair videos on YouTube and narrowing down her own car's problems. Four hours submitting job applications, split into two-hour blocks. Evenings she would keep free for quality time with Steph—maybe there were some YouTube videos that would help her repair that situation, too.

Despite the bad news that she hadn't allowed herself to truly accept, her planning calmed her, and she had a little bounce in her step when she opened the front door to her apartment building and walked in. That bounce bottomed out when she saw Steph turn down the rundown stairwell in her jeans and a T-shirt. She came to a halt when she spotted Makeda, stiffening as she looked down at her from the landing. The giant hot pink suitcase at her side was a stomach-churning beacon against the peeling beige paint and cheap brown linoleum.

"Oh. You're not at work," Steph said, sounding annoyed, then tucked a shock of curly black hair behind her ear. Her other hand gripped the suitcase handle resolutely.

"Neither are you," Makeda said.

Steph shrugged, seemingly unconcerned even though Makeda had never missed a shift in their two-year relationship and was more likely to be late getting home after agreeing to cover for some-one else.

"My last day was yesterday actually," Steph said, frowning down at her from the landing. "I got to thinking while filling out those worksheets you made for me and I decided I'm moving back to Cincinnati. I wanted to have all my stuff out of your place before I told you."

Your place. Steph had been living there for a year.

"Your last day? Cincinnati?" Makeda blinked up at her. "And you were just going to . . . leave?"

"No, I was trying to get my stuff out so we could talk after. It would've been easier that way." Steph sighed. "Now you're going to look at me with kicked-puppy eyes but still offer to help me carry this." She jiggled the suitcase handle.

"I mean, yeah. Of course I'll help you," Makeda said as calmly as she could manage. Maybe if she just acted like she always did, Steph would get with the program and go back to how she'd been, too. "Did you pack using the rolling tech-nique I showed you, to fit more stuff and so your clothes don't wrinkle? Those travel containers are in the storage box under the bed. I can repack for you if—"

"Are you kidding me?" Steph flung a hand in the air and then shoveled it through her hair. The question was an accusation, sharp even if it wasn't loud, and it cut right through all the excuses Makeda had been making for her partner lately.

It wasn't frustration with work, or a bad day, or hormones. It was disdain.

"Sorry," she said quietly.

"This is why—ugh, I can't with this." Steph shook her head, dislodging the strands she'd tucked behind her ear a moment ago, and exhaled deeply.

"You're mad that I want to help?" Makeda asked, focusing on that instead of the fact that Steph was leaving, for good. No more cuddling on the couch, no more sharing funny memes. God, was she never going to kiss Steph again? Feel her cold feet under the blankets, or make her special treats to take to work?

"I'm mad that you think *helping* is a personality," Steph bit out. "I can't do anything without you butting in and trying to do it for me. This morning, you took my cereal spoon *out of my mouth* because you had washed my favorite one."

Drip, drop.

"But you love the little cereal spoon. It was our joke. I thought . . . I thought . . ." Makeda's eyes burned. She'd thought she was brightening Steph's morning, but she'd been laying down the straw that broke their relationship's back instead.

Steph began dragging the heavy suitcase down the stairs toward Makeda, a loud thump echoing in the hallway as the rolling wheels hit each step. Some desperate part of Makeda hoped that Steph would fall so she could catch her. Then they would laugh, remembering all the things they loved about one another, and the moment would pass and—

Steph grunted as she dragged the suitcase down another step and then another. "Living with you isn't even like having a roommate at this point. It's like having a robot that was programmed to be helpful but has no concept of boundaries so it's constantly asking, 'What do you need? What do you need?' but never really listening."

She lugged the suitcase down the last step and stood in front of Makeda, her angry expression crumpling into sadness as tears sheened her eyes.

"I'm sorry, okay? You're great, but it's overwhelming—it's like if I told someone I liked mozzarella sticks and they kept shoving them down my throat every time I opened my mouth, whether I was hungry or not."

Righteous resentment flashed through Makeda. "Okay, I get it. You didn't seem to mind when it benefited you, though."

Steph nodded and kicked the toe of her Converse against the wheel of her suitcase. "Yup. You get to throw all the shit you've done for me in my face when I'm not grateful enough, too, and I have no ammo to lob back because I'm not constantly trying to win the perfect special helper award."

A tear trailed down her cheek, passing over the scar from when she'd walked into the revolving door at the Borgata when they'd gotten tipsy on their third date. Makeda had patched her up with the Band-Aids she carried in her purse in case of emergency.

"Okay. I can work on that," Makeda said, despite the mild protest from her sense of self-respect. She ignored it. "I can change."

"I think I'm done," Steph said. "Because most of all, I'm tired of knowing that I could be absolutely any-fucking-body and you'd treat me the same way. It's the fixing that makes you happy, not me. And that's not something you can work on. It's how you are."

Something shriveled in Makeda at this second reminder that being *her* was bad somehow, when all she ever did was try to be good.

"That's not true," she replied, blinking back her own tears even though she was still in the *this can't really be happening* zone. "It's not. I love you, Steph."

Didn't she?

Steph's brow wrinkled. "Maybe you do, in a white knight kind of way. But hey, you'll love the next person you turn into your personal fixer-upper project, too," she said, then began pulling the suitcase.

Makeda reached for the door of the building to hold it open for her, out of habit, and Steph's shoulders went to her ears.

"Don't! Makeda, I'm leaving you. Let me struggle a little!"

Steph pulled the door open herself and shouldered her way through it, but the wheel of the suitcase got stuck on the jamb. Makeda reached out and held the door against the wall so the suitcase would fit through. Steph didn't say anything, but as she walked off her shoulders heaved the way they did when she cried in earnest.

Makeda watched as she turned and walked down the street without looking back.

"What a day," she said quietly to herself, then pressed her teeth against her trembling lower lip.

What a day.

Chapter 2

"What do you want me to say? Fuck that girl," Grandmore drawled through the phone on the pillow beside Makeda's head—the pillow now served as a phone cradle and she had no roommate to complain about speakerphone.

Two days had passed since the breakup. Steph had come back once, on the evening she'd left. She'd needed to retrieve her social security card, which had been in Makeda's things since she'd recently helped Steph do her taxes. They'd had sex. Then she'd left again, wiping her shoes on Makeda's newly revived hope on her way out.

"Good riddance," Grandmore went on, starting to get worked up, and Makeda could just imagine her lightly wrinkled face scrunching up like she smelled something bad. "Never liked her ass, anyway."

Makeda chuckled out a sob and pulled her duvet around her in the nest she'd made on her bed. When she responded, her voice was thick. "Yes, you did."

"Well, she made you cry, and now I don't like her retroactively." Grandmore sighed. "Why don't you move back in here and help run the Golden Crown this summer? I'm getting too old to do all this cleaning and smiling at these tourists, and I keep forgetting to book reservations and update spreadsheets—you know, the shit you love to do. Besides, the guests and Kojak are happier when you're here at the B&B, and I think you are, too. I don't know why you moved out to begin with."

Makeda had moved out to please Amber, the girlfriend who'd dumped her a week before she'd met Steph. Amber, who was currently ignoring her since sending her last text.

> You're the one who offered to cosign the loan. You made the business plan, even when I was doubtful. You kept saying it was no problem and we'd figure it out. Well, now it's *your* problem.

Makeda thought of how eager she had been to help when Amber kept hinting she needed advice. How she'd used all the small business knowledge she'd acquired helping Grandmore launch her B&B. Most of all, she thought of how she'd ignored her qualms about Amber's ability to actually run a business and whether there was demand for an event planner for pets. Remembering the launch of Party Puppers LLC made her groan aloud.

"Come on now. Chin up, Keda," Grandmore soothed.

"I'll move back in," she said, pushing the thoughts of debt aside. Working at the B&B wouldn't help her money situation much, but she could save on rent, gas, and utilities while she figured something out. "My lease is month to month anyway, and I wouldn't want to disappoint Kojak. Thank you."

"I'm sorry about your job and your woman, but I wasn't calling about none of that." There was a pause, and in the brief silence, Makeda already knew she was about to regret whatever came next. "I'm calling about your royal lineage."

Makeda felt the nausea that had been nudging at her stomach since Steph had left return with a vengeance.

"Grandmore, *no*." She snatched the phone from the pillow and dashed her thumb across the speakerphone widget on the screen before pressing it to her ear.

There was one subject she had a short fuse about; it was the tall tale straight out of a kid's movie—the story that had consumed her mother with its fairy tale allure and spat her out.

"Please don't start," she said, shutting her eyes as if that would block out memories of her mother's disappointment and her classmates' jokes. "I'm already stressed enough without this nonsense."

"What nonsense? The kingdom your grandfather was from is looking for its long-lost royal heir."

"My grandfather was from Newark," Makeda said firmly.

"I love Melvin Smith, God rest his soul, and that's why I didn't mention any of this to your mother until after he passed. He loved both of you so much, and Ashley is his daughter, period." Grandmore sighed. "But your *biological* grandfather—who disappeared before he knew I was with child—came from the Kingdom of Ibarania. I'm the one who's supposed to be forgetting things, not you with your young brain."

"I haven't forgotten," Makeda huffed, then recited one of the facts she'd been forced to memorize. "'Ibarania is a former monarchy on an island in the Mediterranean Sea. The modern culture reflects a heritage influenced by African, Phoenician, and Sicilian influences—'"

"—and it produced at least one man finer than Teddy Pendergrass and with a voice as sweet," Grandmore cut in. "*Oh*, he was handsome."

"I thought we agreed not to talk about this anymore," Makeda said, hating the tight pleading in her voice.

"I didn't agree to shit, Keda. I'm just living my truth, which is also your truth."

Makeda sighed in frustration at rehashing an argument that was supposed to have been dead but had zombie shuffled back into her life at the worst possible moment.

"Is it true though?" she asked, kicking her covers off and sitting up in bed.

"You calling me a liar?"

"No. Just pointing out that nothing ever came of my mother's trying to make something of this, and I don't plan on following in her footsteps."

Her mother, Ashley Hicks, had always been a daydreamer who imagined something more awaited her in life than working the casino floor, but after Grandmore had revealed her supposed royal lineage, her imagination had gone into over-drive. It had started off as a thrilling secret. Two secret princesses living among the boardwalk rabble. For Makeda, the magic had been in the possibility. For her mother, the obsession had been in proving her worth.

The difference had ruined everything.

"I'm sure it's easier for you to think I'm easily fooled or flat-out lying," Grandmore said. "But the truth is, your grandmother had a freaky-deaky summer tryst with a runaway prince and got knocked up. I sometimes bend the truth, but I have never lied about this—me and Prince Keshan humped our way from Chicken Bone Beach to Margate that fateful summer weekend. You know the prince and the pauper? It was more like the prince and this pus—"

"Grand! More!" Makeda jumped up so that she was standing in the nest of sheets. "Enough! Why are you like this?"

Grandmore laughed, the familiar mischief in the tone making Makeda laugh in response despite her annoyance.

"I'm a Hicks. I was born this way, baby."

Makeda rolled her eyes. "Okay. Let's say the eff-boy who told you he was a prince to get into your draws was actually telling the truth. So? You want me to be like your daughter, so obsessed with the possibility of a fairy-tale life that she ruined her reality?"

And mine, too?

Grandmore cleared her throat delicately. "Keda."

Makeda didn't want to accept that Grandmore's summer fling had really happened. Because if it had, all her mother's silly striving dreams for herself and Makeda, the ones she'd dashed against slot machines and then floated in liquor bottles until finally passing them off to the offering plate, wouldn't be the nonsense Makeda had convinced herself they were.

Panic awoke to join the sadness as she imagined her mother throwing everything away, again, to chase this ridiculous dream now that it might actually be within reach. Her mom finally had her life together and had found a sense of peace and fulfillment. Makeda finally didn't have to worry about her. This couldn't start all over again.

"I hope you didn't mention this to her," Makeda said.

"I talked about it with her already. She prayed on it and decided that she's doing her thing and she'll keep doing her thing. We both agree that's best," Grandmore said, assuaging Makeda's fear a little but not completely. "She has her a nice family, a nice house, a nice congregation in her nice town. You, on the other hand . . ."

Makeda guessed her grandmother wasn't trying to be cruel, which was why, for once, Grandmore didn't finish saying what she was thinking. Makeda was great at filling in with context, though, so Grandmore didn't have to.

"*. . . you don't have anything.*"

"She thinks it could be good for you."

The liquid in Makeda's inner watering can rippled as an old anger shifted in its depths.

"Yeah, that makes sense. Everything that happened last time we opened this Pandora's box was great. Oh, wait, no it wasn't." Makeda ran her hand over her faux locks—she'd been mostly in bed for three days without a bonnet on and was sure they looked a mess.

"I know what happened with your mother was bad, but—"

"You don't know," Makeda said, surprised at how angry she sounded. No one knew how bad it was, because Makeda had handled the stumbling drunkenness and the obsessive visits to the Ibaranian embassy by herself. "You were down South with Grandpa's family for the worst of it."

Grandmore cleared her throat. "The only reason I'm bringing it up is there's money. Apparently, a royal bank account that's been gathering interest for decades is funding this whole heir search, so it has to be a few stacks at least, right?"

Makeda's practicality pushed her reluctance aside. She was unemployed and shouldering a high-interest debt that wasn't hers. Could she afford to totally blow this princess thing off because of some bad memories?

Yes, yes she could.

She'd sworn off royal fantasies long ago, along with the idea of someone showing up from Ibarania to claim her and her mother. She'd figure out how to pay the debt without getting tangled up in bad memories and worse ideas.

"Where did you even hear about this?" she asked, trying to move away from the money talk. "How do you know it's not some scam?"

"My friend Deborah forwarded me a text and—"

"Is this the same friend who told you 5G towers were summoning demons?" Makeda asked.

"She was just looking out for me. If you can't count on your homegirls to warn you about demons, they're not really your friends."

"A text chat forward about cash offered for missing royalty. Sounds legit," Makeda said.

"All you have to do is fill out a form to start the inquiry process. It wouldn't hurt, would it?"

"Grandmore." Makeda gripped the phone in her hand tightly, remembering what happened to girls like her who had the audacity to think they might be something special, even for a minute. "I don't want to argue about this, okay? I'm too old for this nonsense, just like your daughter was, except I have sense enough to know the idea that someone like me could be a princess is laughable."

"No, it isn't," her grandmother said, sounding a bit wounded. "That's what I hate about this. Not that you don't believe me, and not that you're mad about the past. The fact that somewhere along the way you stopped even thinking it was possible."

"I grew up. I *had to* grow up. I'm just Makeda Hicks, nobody special, and that's good enough for me." She tried to ignore what she'd learned as the gulf between her and her mother had widened over the years—that she wasn't good enough for her mother. She sometimes wondered, if she'd been the kind of girl who waited for someone to save them like the princesses in stories instead of saving people herself, would her mother have kept loving her? Maybe more than booze and gambling, even?

She knew addiction didn't work like that, and was glad her mother was better now, but part of her still felt hurt that the recovery had had nothing to do with her, even though she'd been the one suffering alongside her mother. Her mom had removed alcohol from the pedestal of utmost importance in her life and replaced it with church, leaving Makeda wondering what she could ever do to be as important as either. Her mother had eventually met a visiting pastor, remarried, and moved to Virginia, leaving seventeen-year-old Makeda behind with Grandmore so she could start a new life without excess baggage.

That hadn't been her mother's explicit intention—she hadn't known school was hellish for Makeda and decided against making her move—but it was what it'd felt like.

Makeda stepped down from the bed and headed toward the bathroom—wallowing time was over. She'd shower and then clean the apartment until no trace of Steph remained. Until the dust that had been kicked up in her memories settled down, too. "I have to go, but I'll come over to make dinner tonight."

"I'll make *you* dinner, you're the one going through it," Grandmore said, then paused for a few beats. "I had a dream. You were on the *Titanic*, wearing a crown made of seashells."

Makeda sighed. "Crucial question—was Kate Winslet there, and if so, which one of us got to float off on the door when the ship sank?"

Grandmore sucked her teeth.

"There wasn't an iceberg. Global warming, I guess. There was a storm, but the ship didn't sink."

Grandmore made the sound in the back of her throat that meant she was getting emotional. "Everything turned out fine and you were so happy once the storm had passed—happier than I've ever seen you. It was a good dream."

Her grandmother enjoyed spinning yarns, but her dreams—the *dream* dreams—never lied.

"Well, maybe it means I'll take a dinner cruise that has a seafood buffet," Makeda mumbled.

"Can't you just put yourself out there with this Ibarania thing and see what happens?" Grandmore asked, her frustration rising to the surface. "What would it hurt? You're always so ready to do something when it's for other people, when it means you get nothing but a smile and a nod, if that. Do this one thing for yourself."

"How is it 'for me' if I don't want it?" she countered.

"I wouldn't be on you about it if I hadn't watched you put your dreams behind everyone else's until you forgot you had them," Grandmore said. "You used to crave adventure and all that stuff you read about in books. You used to think you deserved them."

Makeda refused to think of how she'd been before the world had recalibrated her ambitions. "Things change. I'm thirty-one, Grandmore."

"Do you think that means you're grown?" Grandmore cackled, and Makeda felt anger well up where understanding would have once immediately rolled in. Yes, she was grown. She'd been the one taking care of everything her mother slacked off on before anyone else had even noticed there was a problem.

Grandmore sighed. "I'm seventy-five, and I still want things for myself. Love and excitement and new challenges. You don't stop wanting nice things, or hoping, because some magazines say life stops at thirty like this is Medieval Times or some shit. You best believe if I was in your shoes, I'd be on a plane to collect my tiara."

Yes, she would be. Because Grandmore, and Makeda's mother, didn't think about what came after they up and did things, like buying a house to turn into a bed-and-breakfast or telling everyone who would listen that you were royalty from some made-up-sounding country.

"Can we not talk about it right now?" Makeda asked, then added, "Please."

"Fine. We won't talk about it."

Makeda waited for Grandmore to start in with her usual follow-up round of pressure, but instead the old woman told her to hurry up and come over, and then hung up.

Makeda sighed as she turned on the shower to skin-melting degrees Fahrenheit, tugged on her shower cap, and stepped in to boil away her breakup funk and the memories the word *princess* had dredged up.

She'd lost her job. And her girlfriend. She was going to have to pack up and move back in with her grandmother. And now she had to feel guilty about stonewalling Grandmore about the princess bullshit that had made her life unbearable for years—that had stolen her confidence and her relationship with her mother.

Grandmore probably thought she'd eventually give in. Makeda *always* gave in to other people, sometimes before they even asked. What had that gotten her?

Whenever bad things happened, she always bounced back, returned to her cheery self once her watering can of kindness refilled. But there was apparently a vault of anger beneath her watering can, the place where she'd been shoving all her frustration and pain for most of her life, and it was seeping into her usually endless supply of caring.

Makeda wondered what would happen if she kicked the can and opened the vault instead. She wouldn't try to be a princess, *ever*, but she'd try being selfish on for size—it would be a much more comfortable fit than any frilly gown.

Chapter 3

$\mathcal{A}$s Beznaria Chetchevaliere genuflected before the throne of Algernon Shropsbottomshire-burrough, Lord Higginshoggins of Hogginshiggins, Director General of the World Federation of Monarchists and the second-worst person she had ever worked for, she mulled over the possibility of launching herself through the second-story glass window of WFM headquarters without breaking any bones, and then running off into the British countryside.

The giant leather-and-wood chair in the receiving area of Lord Higginshoggins's office wasn't exactly a throne, and a curt bow wasn't exactly genuflecting, but that was semantics. Beznaria had learned in her several years at the WFM, located in a British manor house that was crumbling beneath the ivy that clung to it, was that there wasn't much difference between a man who fancied himself a king and a man who wanted to be a kingmaker—literally.

Algernon Shropsbottomshireburrough, pronounced Smith, was both.

He wore the turquoise heraldic colors of the Kingdom of Hogginshiggins—a monarchy created by his father that had existed only from 1943 to 1945 on a European territory smaller than the square meterage of Vatican City. This forgotten monarchy, was, like the WFM headquarters itself, the product of a mediocre man's inherited wealth and ability to buy land; it had briefly found purchase during the turmoil of wartime politics as a haven for shady characters, but its legacy was Lord Higginshoggins, a completely common British man with the unfounded belief that he was somehow innately superior.

Like the outlandish accent he'd cultivated, the outfit distracted from his oceans-deep ordinariness. It wasn't at all the right color for his skin tone, though he hadn't appreciated being informed of that. Bez had been the unfortunate informant.

He fixed her with slate-gray eyes that weren't at all shrewd—he wasn't a clever man. He was only a questionably rich one, who had convinced other rich fools who wanted to be kingmakers and make themselves kings as well to join him.

"Junior Investigator Chetchevaliere," Lord Higginshoggins drawled in his exaggeratedly posh tone that made Bez's teeth press together. This acknowledgment was the signal that she could stop straining her back in the service of pretending he was important.

"Director General Shropsbottomshireburrough," she responded by rote before straightening.

"Your Grace," he replied.

"I am but a simple island girl, not a member of the nobility," Bez replied. "Though I do appreciate that you finally see my inner noblesse. I have always—"

"I am Lord Higginshoggins of Hogginshiggins, thus *I* am to be addressed as Your Grace," he cut in, a small vein on his forehead standing out from his skin. Bez often had that effect on boring people.

"Right." Her gaze strayed away from him, over the imperialist hoard that decorated the office—carved African masks, statuettes from the South Pacific, vibrant South Asian fabrics—wistfully landing on the Tudor-style window. She pushed her large, round glasses up the flat bridge of her nose, running a few numbers through her mind, and decided against the tactical window smash-and-dash. She'd just purchased a new suit for work; she wasn't going to shred it, and perhaps her body as well, just because she wanted to escape her yearly work evaluation like a clam wanted to lick salt.

She much preferred being ignored and overlooked by her superiors at the WFM. In a way she counted on it. When people took you seriously, they paid attention to what you were doing and asked all kinds of invasive questions. At moments like this, when people actually paid attention to Bez's track record, they were likely to find a few discrepancies in how closely she followed the organization's goals of fostering the growth of monarchies worldwide as opposed to her own moral imperatives.

"You may be seated, Junior Investigator Chetchevaliere," Lord Higginshoggins said with BBC enunciation. She assumed that his Henry IV melodrama accent was an attempt to distract from the fact that he was absolutely average in appearance, with graying blond hair, a long face, a long nose, and a medium-dad bod. She was taller than him and fairly certain she could deadlift him. He seemed to be aware of this, too, which contributed to his dislike of her.

She wanted this meeting over with. Mercifully, it would be her last evaluation. Her contract would be up in a few months, and she'd be free to return to Ibarania and her family for good, even if she hadn't achieved her goal of clearing their name.

"I will remain standing, Your Grace," Bez said, automatically folding her hands behind her back and standing at ease.

"Of course, you will," he said with a grimace and shake of his head. "Your problem with authority is one of the *many* notes in your evaluation."

"I don't have a problem with authority," Bez clarified, then thought on the point a bit more. "No, that's not correct. I have a problem with those who have authority but not the fortitude to wield it over me. In Ibarania, we call this problem *xettru flaccide*—flaccid scepter. It was a phrase coined by Queen Malia, daughter of Queen Lalla, when the Knights Hôpitalier attempted to invade and—"

"Junior Investigator Chetchevaliere!"

Bez startled, confused as to why he was yelling her name as if she was across the room instead of right in front of him. "Yes?"

"We will begin the performance evaluation now." He pulled a thick file from the table beside his faux throne—Bez was surprised he hadn't had the complaints against her printed on a scroll.

She knew what it would say; she'd been receiving the same comments since she started school.

Too quiet. Too loud. Too scattered. Too focused. Too friendly. Too withdrawn.

Bez was simply too much for most people. Her parents had wondered if her neurodivergence was the issue, but Bez resented the implication. She was quite happy to be "too much" because the alternative, in her eyes, was to be too little.

"The erratic, bizarre, and frankly disastrous manner in which you've handled your every mission has landed you at a ranking of ten out of ten amongst junior investigators, simply because we can go no lower," Higginshoggins began. "You simply do not follow any rules."

"I follow rules when they are reasonable," she replied, though she was already losing interest.

"Rules exist for a reason," he said.

"So do platypuses. They're much more mysterious and exciting, though."

His brow creased. "What?"

That was a common response. Generally, her thoughts flittered about in her head like fireflies of varying dimness. There was an order to their flittering, and a rationale behind their brightness, but when it came down to it, she grabbed at the most radiant one and generally that worked out for her even if it didn't always make sense to others.

"Nothing. Continue, Director General Higgins-burrough."

He gave her a reproving look and continued with his review. His lecture in bootleg iambic pentameter faded to a drone somewhere on the periphery of Bez's attention as her thoughts returned to the story of Queen Malia, who had repelled Crusaders with an inventive use of olive oil. It had been one of her favorite childhood stories, one her grandmother told with great flair, and a young Bez had even semi-successfully recreated the infamous olive oil slide that saved the kingdom, to the dismay of her parents and siblings.

"Do you have anything to say?" Lord Higginshoggins asked, his voice cutting into her musing. He was looking at her with an expression that revealed she was supposed to be contrite.

She raised her brows. "About the olive oil? Don't use the expensive kind your mother saves for special occasions, that's all I'll say."

"What olive oil?" he asked, that vein beside his eye ticking again.

"On the drawbridge," she explained.

Lord Higginshoggins grimaced more deeply. "About the three hundred pounds worth of cabbages on an unauthorized mission to Njaza a few months ago! Does that ring a bell?"

Bez glanced to the side as she searched through the various thoughts flitting about in her mind.

"Oh yes." She nodded. "Three hundred pounds on cabbage, which was a rather bold markup, but a small price to pay for a kingdom that is currently beginning to flourish for the first time in decades due to my intervention."

He grimaced.

"Your unauthorized intervention. We had been monitoring the Njaza situation since the creation of this organization. Thirty years!" He slapped her folder closed. "We've been trying for years to find a way in, to set up dialogue and make sure the right kind of monarchy was established there. One with the right kind of ideals."

"And I managed that in one trip!" Bez preened a bit. Since her transfer from the archival research group to the junior investigation team, which carried out more sensitive and physically strenuous missions, praise had been hard to come by. Of course, an organization entrenched in the past didn't always appreciate outside-of-the-box thinking, and Bez's thoughts always scurried far and fast from the confines of what other people might deem proper.

Lord Higginshoggins dropped the folder onto the table angrily, signaling that somehow her triumph in Njaza wasn't admirable.

"What you managed was to upend all of our plans in one fell swoop. The first Njazan vulnerability in years, the first opening for the WFM to get in and make sure they learned to adhere to our rules, and it closed before we could even set up a meeting, all due to your unapproved meddling."

Bez ignored the underlying meaning of his chastisement—her employer often suggested strategies like bribing officials and fomenting coups, but she preferred to pretend those things weren't

part of her job description. Forgetting things that
didn't match her worldview was one of Bez's great
strengths. Memorizing the fine print was another.

"Your Grace, according to my employee contract,
I am authorized, nay beholden, to follow up on any
match I facilitate on our RoyalMatch.com marriage
site. I was preapproved to travel to Njaza, as it was
part of standard operating procedure," she said. "A
scandal linked to our subsidiary site would draw
unwanted attention to the organization as a whole,
would it not? If you're unfamiliar with this, may I
direct you to article three in the contract for junior
investigat—"

"Enough!" Lord Higginshoggins rubbed at his
left temple, his eyes closed. "Suffice to say, your
evaluation is decidedly unsatisfactory."

Bez shifted her stance a bit. "Very well. I accept
that. I will now begin my performance evaluation
of *you*. To start with, your role has no clear tasks,
apart from drinking tea and taking meetings with
men who believe they are important. When you do
take the time to attempt to organize or plan, the
results are subpar. Your secretary handles the ma-
jority of your workload and receives a fraction of
your pay. I believe my first question would be what
purpose do you serve, exactly, and how can you
actually . . . serve it?"

His face went from pale to a deep puce that
matched better with his livery than his usual skin
tone.

"Junior Investigator Chetchevaliere. That is not
how evaluations work. I am the one who does the
evaluating."

"Who evaluates you, then?" Bez asked, wiggling her nose so that her glasses stopped sliding down.

"I am the director general." There was a long pause, during which Bez wondered if she would be able to construct the olive oil drawbridge trap using only objects found in Lord Higginshoggins's office.

"Is my evaluation over?" she asked when he didn't say anything further after a long moment had passed.

He folded his hands as he looked down at her, which seemed to be an unfortunate indicator that it was not over. Bez resisted the urge to stare back, having been reprimanded for her staring contest reflexes. Sweat beaded at her hairline, threatening her silk-pressed bob; Lord Higginshoggins blinked first.

"You are Ibaranian, yes?" he asked.

Bez reflexively moved her stance from at ease to attention. "I was born of the island best and most beautiful among all those extant. Yes."

"And you have shown particular interest in the fall of the Ibaranian monarchy and the rumors that Queen Aazi survived, have you not?"

"I have," Bez replied, wrangling her full attention to focus it on him. He leaned back in his overlarge chair in response to the sharpening of her focus.

"And you have put in several requests to be allowed on to the recently organized Ibaranian hereditary heir investigation? And been denied, each time."

She hadn't thought it was possible for him to look more smug, but Bez was occasionally wrong.

"Yes. Though I am the foremost scholar on the Ibaranian monarchy among the investigators, due to my family's background. I've been told that due to my rank as a junior investigator—"

"—as lowest ranking junior investigator—"

"—as the bedrock of the junior investigators, that I couldn't be approved to join the investigation team."

"Your interest is driven by your grandmother's role in Queen Aazi's disappearance, and the accusations that have followed her for years."

He regarded her for a long moment, and she blinked, furious that she had lost their stare down, however brief, and that she had done so because he dared jab his long nose into her family's shame.

She gave a terse nod, not trusting herself to say more. She was impulsive, but not in matters of family honor.

Lord Higginshoggins leaned forward in his seat and she thought about how easy it would be to grab him by the cravat and flip him over her shoulder.

"Jeta Maria Chetchevaliere was the Grand Dame of the Royal Order of the Ibaranian Guard at the time of Queen Aazi's disappearance. Until this dereliction of duty, the Chetchevaliere name was synonymous with the Royal Guard." He leaned forward, malicious glee sparking in his eyes. "We've tracked the unauthorized research you've been doing in the Federation archives. You've followed up on every reported sighting of Queen Aazi in our records."

"All usage of Federation archives was authorized under section 6 d of my employment contract," Bez said. This was a lie, but she was sure the man had no idea what the contracts even looked like. "And, yes, historically Chetchevalieres were knights of the Royal Order of the Ibaranian Guard for generations, until Queen Aazi disappeared under my grandmother's watch. It wasn't dereliction of duty, though. And you should refrain from saying so again." She smiled, showing her teeth, but from the way he blanched she knew her point had been made.

"Well what was it then?" he asked, and Bez hesitated.

Henna Jeta had only directly spoken about the day the queen disappeared once, and that was to say that the queen, newly widowed after the death of King Emilio, had been separated from her at a bustling dock in Sicily and disappeared without a trace. A vanishing queen had intrigued the world briefly, and sightings popped up sporadically, but the monarchy of a tiny island nation hadn't held widespread international interest. Henna Jeta had been persona non grata in many places in Ibarania, but she'd never cowered, and her children and grandchildren had inherited her ability to ignore criticism. They hadn't really needed to, not for monarchy-related reasons at least, until the recent surge of interest in Ibarania's past and the resulting search for Aazi's heir.

Beznaria, the youngest of five children and her grandmother's constant companion, had developed an obsessive interest with the royal guard, begging to be trained as Henna Jeta had, to be told stories of palace life, and to know exactly what had happened that day. Her grandmother had only indulged two of those wishes.

"*Do not worry about the past, Bezzie. I wish I hadn't failed in my duty. But Ibarania has moved on, and so should you.*"

Bez had understood that her grandmother's guilt was likely why she refused to speak of what happened, and had decided to relieve her of that burden.

"*I'll find her one day, Henna. I am your squire and that is my pledge!*"

Henna Jeta always told her not to worry and to look to the future, but Bez took her promises very seriously, which was why she was willing to work for a meddling monarchist like Lord Higgins-hoggins.

"Is discussing my family history part of the evaluation?" Bez asked.

"No. It is part of your next assignment."

Bez's heart thumped harder in her chest. "Please provide more detail, Your Grace."

"Our top investigators on the Ibaranian heir team have been swamped with claims. These are the ones we've received from the United States alone." He picked up another folder, this one double the thickness of her employee file. "We've managed to narrow them down a bit—quite easy to do since many of them were confused as to what kingdom they even claimed to be heir to."

"Hmm," Bez replied. Part of her work before becoming a junior investigator had been reviewing claims of heritage for the WFM and marriage profile applications on their app, RoyalMatch.com. There was almost no one in the world as well-versed as an American royalty enthusiast.

"We do not believe any of these claims to be true— and we don't particularly want them to be, but protocol requires they be looked into," Lord Higginshoggins said. "We have ample evidence on the disruptive nature of American royals on a *pure* monarchy. They are a menace. I'm sure you're aware of how we have been disrespected by Thesolo's new princess, who didn't even allow our observers at their royal wedding. Do you understand what I'm saying?"

Bez didn't understand but nodded confidently regardless. She'd figure that part out later. She was too busy trying to manage her growing excitement.

"Good. Now, none of our other investigators wants to waste their ti—ah, are available to travel to America at the moment. Thus, your next mission is to go to the United States, investigate these frivolous claims, and return to file your report when you have found that none of them have merit." He held the folder out but pulled it slightly out of reach when she grabbed for it. "Do you *understand*?"

"Of course, Director General Your Gracehoggins," she said; all of her attention was focused on the folder he waved in front of her, an excitement she hadn't felt in years short-circuiting her communication abilities.

He handed it over, and she snatched it. He was saying something about her budget, deductions for previous expenditures, and reiterating the undesirability of the possibility of an American heir, but Bez paid him no mind.

The reason she'd even decided to work for the WFM had come to fruition. She was going to search for the lost heir of Ibarania—she was going to keep the promise she'd made Henna Jeta all those years ago.

"Thank you for entrusting me with this mission, Your Grace," Bez said. "I will do my best, as I have on all of my missions."

"That's what we're hoping for," Lord Higginshoggins said with an uncharacteristic smile. "You may go."

Bez considered the smash-and-dash again, just out of pure jubilation, but instead jogged out of the musty office before Higginshoggins could change his mind. She would find the lost heir and clear her family's name—and her grandmother's conscience—or she wasn't a Chetchevaliere.

Chapter 4

*M*akeda used to hum when she cleaned, but she was silent as she sprinkled Comet around the bathtub of the honeymoon suite at Golden Crown B&B two months after moving back in. There was a dark brown ring in the vintage clawfoot tub she'd installed herself, and she truly hoped it was mud from off-roading because the room's occupants had helpfully tracked the same substance into the carpet and streaked it on the bed linens.

In the past, she would have been slightly put out but hoped the guests had had a good time. Right now, she was seething, fighting the urge to call them and demand they come back and clean up after themselves. She soothed herself with the fact that there was a lull in bookings and there would be no guests for the next few days; this should have been distressing, but she was just glad she wouldn't have to slap on a smile to interact with strangers.

It'd been two months since Steph had dumped her, and Makeda's watering can hadn't refilled yet—

there was a little something in there, but it wasn't sweet. She'd always thought Grandmore had been exaggerating when she'd warned her to stop giving away her sweetness, but maybe Makeda *had* used up all her kindness, and all she had to show for it was a stank attitude and a sore back.

Usually, she'd bounce back to her cheery self a few days after yet another crushing disappointment, but "sentient doormat" had become too accurate a description—she felt flat and grimy, like too many people had wiped their shoes off on her. She'd withdrawn from all of the activities that had once given her purpose because nothing seemed to matter. And it wasn't because Steph had left or her job had let her go, but because she'd worked so hard at keeping them both and all her effort had been for nothing in the end.

Makeda now lived her life by the schedule she had put in place to get through each day: wake up, drink coffee, clean. Do accounting, chat with guests. Make necessary repairs. Watch stories with Grandmore and Kojak. Play games on her phone before bed. Sleep.

Her cell phone rang, and she pulled it from the pocket of her shorts and answered in case Grandmore needed a ride home from aqua aerobics. Apart from warranty scammers, few people called anymore since Makeda had stopped volunteering her time so freely.

"Hello?"

"Mak? It's Linds."

Makeda suppressed a groan. Unfortunately, Lindsey wasn't one of the people who'd lost

Makeda's phone number, mostly because Makeda still couldn't say no to GrabRite. The woman who'd gotten promoted over Makeda couldn't seem to figure out how anything at the store worked without a reminder—the same reminders Makeda had given her for years, except she was no longer paid to do it. But if she stopped now, the other employees would suffer and the shoppers would, too.

"What is it, Lindsey?"

"We're having another problem here at the store and since it's, um, something related to what you used to handle . . ."

"You mean the things that are part of your job description now?" Makeda asked.

"I need the password for the employee payroll site," Lindsey said, ignoring the question. "And also the graphic design site for doing the circulars. Really, this is stuff you should have taken care of before you left."

Makeda wanted to hang up, but instead spent the next fifteen minutes swallowing her anger, reminding Lindsey about the password manager, walking her through how to make the circular—Makeda had made the last two as a favor to Mr. Romano—and generally doing Lindsey's job from afar. She hung up feeling both hollowed out and bursting with anger that didn't have an outlet. She wanted to rage, to explode, to be a Lindsey or a Steph or anyone who didn't just grin and bear it. She'd managed not grinning but was still bearing it.

Kojak hopped onto the edge of the tub, meowing as if she owed him something, and she placed him on the floor and ushered him out as she rewet the cleaning powder that had dried while she talked to Lindsey and scrubbed the ring of mystery substance from the bathtub.

She returned to the bedroom to strip the sheets from the bed and continue her systematic cleaning. Some people might have been frustrated by scrubbing bathtubs at the B&B, but Makeda wasn't. The Golden Crown was her baby, too, and most of her early twenties had been spent helping get the place off the ground; she'd become handyperson, housecleaning staff, bookkeeper, sous chef, barista, tour guide, and shuttle driver to help make Grandmore's dream come true.

Besides, cleaning was a satisfying outlet for her help-y inclinations. It made her feel accomplished, generally had immediate results, and a bathtub would never ruin her life after she'd invested her time and energy into caring for it.

Okay, that isn't fair, she chastised herself as she threw the linens in the hallway and pulled the old upright vacuum into the room. People, much like bathtubs, didn't *ask* for her to dedicate time and elbow grease into making them shine. On the flip side, bathtubs didn't dump her or default on loans they had sweet-talked her into cosigning for them.

The buzzer at the front door sounded, startling her. There were no guests booked for today and no deliveries scheduled. Maybe it was Lester, the mail carrier. The buzzer rang again, and *again*, and—no, this wasn't Lester's energy. Any other delivery person would have left the delivery and kept it moving to meet their quota by now. Whoever was at the door, they were rude, impatient, and likely to be a pain in the ass.

Makeda was done dealing with pains in the asses; she flipped on the very loud vacuum and continued cleaning the mess that previous pains in the asses had left behind.

The person BZZZZTed again; three long, nerve-jangling presses that cut through the sound of the vacuum's motor.

She fought the rising anxiety that came from ignoring a clear bid for her attention—for some reason, this felt like a battle of wills. She was tired of people just expecting her to drop everything and do what they wanted. She was ashamed that, without actual effort to resist, she was the kind of person who would.

The buzzing stopped and Makeda grinned triumphantly, putting a little more oomph into the push and pull of the vacuum. It was pathetic that ignoring someone at her door felt like any kind of victory, but she'd take it.

"Hello," a voice called from behind her a moment later, and Makeda gasped and spun around, vacuum gripped by the handle and hefted, ready to bash whoever had sneaked up on her.

A woman was standing in the doorway—tall and brown-skinned with a straight blunt-cut bob that rested on her shoulders in a silky wave, like she'd just unwrapped the perfect doobie. Her hazel eyes, a stunning contrast to her dark skin, were magnified by comedically large round-lens glasses perched on her nose. The lenses were smudgy with fingerprints and the sight of them would have made Makeda spray her in the face with Windex if she wasn't so shocked by her presence.

The woman sported a black suit that managed to accentuate her broad shoulders and long, muscular body despite its clearly untailored fit. Makeda wasn't judging, but it reminded her of the cheap polyester tuxedo uniform of restaurants she'd worked at, worn to project a false sense of professionalism. Was she a traveling saleswoman? Not common, but people did show up trying to sell things from time to time.

The green button-down shirt and skinny tie beneath her jacket pulled the look together into a disheveled chic, like the fashion editorials models in oversize asymmetrical outfits, although this woman was far from the waif-thin looks of any couture spread. She was solid and muscular and Makeda's face went hot just from looking at her.

The woman scrunched her face as she examined Makeda, as if trying to increase the magnifying power of her glasses. People usually didn't look at Makeda with this much interest—she was the type who won people over with her usefulness and reliability, not by grabbing their attention. The woman's full lips spread in a smile to reveal a gap between her two front teeth.

"Excellent reflexes," the stranger said with an approving nod, speaking loudly to be heard over the vacuum that was sucking at the air between them. Makeda turned the power off, but the woman still shouted her next sentence. "You've no idea how many people sense someone creeping up on them and turn without grabbing for even a butter knife."

"You creep up on people often enough to know that?" Makeda asked. Her arms started to ache, so she lowered the vacuum but kept a tight grip on it in case she needed to deliver a suction-free beatdown.

"Not often, no." The woman clasped her hands behind her back, her gaze drifting off to the side, as if she were trying to remember something. "Wait. Perhaps often, but not *regularly*. It is a skill, not a habit or a hobby."

There was a husky musicality to her voice, an accent that might have been Italian or Arabic.

"Usually people trying to sell things wait outside," Makeda said in the least hospitable voice she could muster, which was still far too warm but only because her cheeks were burning. "Is there something I can do for you?"

"I believe there is," the woman said. "I'm looking for a woman named Makeda Hicks. Are *you* Makeda Hicks?"

Makeda wasn't an accent ho, but hearing that voice wrap itself around her name sent a shiver of delight through her. The woman made the three syllables sound exciting. Full of possibility.

"I—I am," she said, gripping the handle of the vacuum even more tightly. "I'm Makeda Hicks."

The woman's gaze sharpened. She didn't move, but it somehow felt as if she'd closed the space between them. It reminded Makeda of when Kojak stalked her as she cleaned, staring at her from across the room one moment, then pouncing at her ankles from beneath her the next.

The woman continued to stare, seemingly having no intention of blinking or need to do so. Sweat beaded on Makeda's upper lip as the panic of sudden and incredibly inconvenient attraction overtook the adrenaline that had kicked in moments ago.

No. This wasn't attraction of the sexual kind; it was just cleverly disguised as such, like it had been so many times in the past. Grandmore had her dreams that gave hints about the future, but Makeda had a help-y person's intuition . . . and as she withstood the full blast of the woman's attention, she understood that the tug she felt was actually a warning beacon from her watering can.

Chaos radiated from this stranger, the kind that appealed to Makeda's innate urge to *fix*, and if she wasn't careful it would suck her right in. Worse? She'd like it.

"It's been quite the adventure tracking you down. You're not at all what I imagined," the woman said matter-of-factly as she looked Makeda up and down. "Much shorter than expected of al-Hurradassi stock, and lacking in obvious menace. You're about as intimidating as a sea snail."

Oh.

The woman hadn't been staring because she liked what she saw, but because she was making a list of Makeda's faults. Like Steph had. Like people had for most of her childhood. Like Makeda did to herself.

The woman whipped a cell phone out of her pocket, the movement so fast it was startling, and began taking pictures of Makeda. There was a kind of glee in her eyes that should have been off-putting but was somehow alluring—

No! Makeda mentally snapped at herself. *Don't let the chaos vibes pull you in.*

"They didn't exactly sanction this final investigation, but the search team will be won over by this for sure. The Cinderella angle! Do you understand what an easy sell the Cinderella angle is?" She stopped taking pictures and squinted at Makeda. "Perhaps you do, which is why you rudely continued cleaning instead of coming to see who was at the door? Maybe you wanted me to find you toiling away?"

"I didn't expect a stranger to break into my house just because I didn't answer the door," Makeda said, growing more frustrated as the situation continued to spin out of her control. Grandmore would have hustled this woman out of the house already but Makeda was letting the woman cha-cha slide over her doormat self.

"I didn't break in. The door was unlocked."

Makeda was fairly certain she'd locked the door behind her grandmother when she'd left for aqua aerobics. She narrowed her gaze. "Even if it was, most people have enough home training not to waltz in uninvited."

"I do lack that," the woman conceded. "And I apologize for insinuating that you were acting like something you weren't. I can see that such artifice is beyond you. You truly *are* a shabby ragamuffin in your heart of hearts."

"Shabby? Ragamuffin?" Makeda looked down at the dolphin shorts and old T-shirt she was wearing, and then at the stranger. "You have some nerve coming in here with your 1920s insults, wearing a too-big Burlington Coat Factory sales rack suit."

Beznaria shrugged, as if settling her jacket more comfortably. "There is no need to besmirch my fashion sense or my frugality, Ms. Hicks. I'm simply doing routine follow-up, and this will go much more smoothly if you comply."

Makeda's patience snapped. "What are you talking about? Why are you taking pictures of me? And who are you? Can you answer at least one of those questions?"

"Ah. Right. Proper introductions! I always forget the introduction, but to be fair, when I'm on a mission the goal is generally for the person I'm observing *not* to know who I am. This is a habit, and not a skill."

"That's . . . not making things any clearer," Makeda said.

The stranger unbuttoned her jacket with one hand and reached for an inner pocket, then handed Makeda a card. "Here."

Makeda snatched the card—as much of a snatch as she could muster, though it was more of a tug—and felt no more informed about what was going on after she read it than before.

BEZNARIA CHETCHEVALIERE

JUNIOR INVESTIGATOR

WORLD FEDERATION OF MONARCHISTS

That last name seemed familiar for some reason.

"Great. Why are you here, Ms. . . ." She glanced at the card again as the words printed in bold black letters penetrated through her confusion.

World Federation of Monarchists.

". . . World Federation of Monarchists?" The words squeaked out of her throat, strangled by the realization that her grandmother had been uncharacteristically quiet on the Ibaranian royalty front. She'd never pressured Makeda about it, not even a nudge, which Makeda had attributed to her newfound irritability, when in fact something else was far more likely.

Grandmore wouldn't go behind my back . . . Well, yeah, she absolutely would.

"My name is Beznaria Chetchevaliere," the woman corrected with clear amusement, pulling Makeda's attention from the disbelief that was shifting to understanding. "The World Federation of Monarchists is the organization I work for. I'm taking pictures of you to add to the file I'm creating for you. You may not believe it, but stodgy old monarchists require reams of paperwork, and if I'm going to prove you're a princess, we're going to need an excessive amount of documentation."

"Prove *what*?"

Makeda was generally not prone to panic, but at this sneak attack of what was, in a way, her worst nightmare, her mind blanked and she sprinted past the woman, heading out of the room.

Beznaria trailed beside her, undeterred. She wasn't sprinting because her long legs covered more ground with each stride. "To answer your first question, I'm talking about the fact that even the most talented public relations person wouldn't be able to stage something as perfect as stumbling across a possible long-lost heir to a throne as she cleans unidentified brown substances in a run-down B&B in a rundown town in *New Jersey* of all places. The Cinderella angle."

Makeda's newfound indignation flared, and she stopped mid-getaway and whirled to glare up at Beznaria. "You can say whatever you want about me, but not Jersey, not Atlantic City, and for damn sure not the Golden Crown."

Beznaria lifted her cell phone and tapped the screen. "Investigator Chetchevaliere logging video evidence of the infamous al-Hurradasi fury." She held up her phone's camera so that she was getting an even more aerial view of Makeda, and whispered her next requests. "Can you scowl more? And perhaps threaten me with your Hoover again? Brandish it like a scimitar."

"No, I will not scowl or brandish my vacuum for you," Makeda said, jumping up to bat at the phone. "I'm sorry, but you need to leave. Now."

"And *I'm* sorry, but I haven't finished my work here, so I can't," Beznaria said, still recording. "I mean, truly, what kind of investigator just leaves when they're told to? A bad one. I regret to inform you that I rank in the top ten junior investigators at the WFM. I will not be deterred."

Makeda tilted her head. "How many investigators are there in total?"

Beznaria lowered the phone and blinked. "The total number of investigators is classified information. My point was that I can't leave just yet. If you knew what I'd gone through to get here, you'd be a bit more compliant."

Compliant. That was what everyone expected her to be, even this tall, fine-ass stranger who may or may not have broken into the B&B. She'd had enough; if she was a doormat, she was one with spikes, and this Beznaria Chetchevaliere had just activated them.

"Fine. You leave me no choice."

Makeda was quaking in her house slippers as she marched up to Beznaria, but she grabbed her by the sleeve and tugged anyway. Then tugged again.

"What are you doing?" Beznaria asked with that annoying amusement in her tone.

Makeda walked around Beznaria, placed a palm on each shoulder blade, and began to push at her back—her very sculpted and muscular back. Makeda surged up with all the power her legs could muster. Beznaria didn't even rock forward.

I really need to work out more, Makeda thought as she began to push with one hand and then the other.

"Can you do that a little lower? And toward the center, between my shoulder blades? American commuter train seats are quite uncomfortable, and there is a knot I can't reach—aaaahhh, yes, right there."

The woman let out a low moan that was simultaneously anger-inducing and lascivious. Makeda's libido, which had been dormant for months—apparently waiting to be reactivated by the right combination of chaos, confusion, and carnality—belly flopped not into her watering can but another suddenly moisture-logged area.

"Enough," Makeda gritted out, stopping her attempt at pushing and heading back around to tug hard at the woman's jacket sleeve. "Please just—"

She watched in horror as the sleeve tore apart along the seam, lengthwise, the shredding sound cutting through whatever temporary fury had gripped her.

"I—I—" She jerked her head up toward Beznaria, who'd stood calmly while Makeda pushed and pulled her. She released the fabric, and it flapped pitifully against the woman's side, and Makeda scrunched her face in contrition, overwhelmed by the confusing turn of events. "Attack a stranger" hadn't been on her schedule for the day. "I'm not the kind of person who rips people's clothes off. I'm sorry."

Beznaria grinned. "I must say that knowing I'm the first person who inspired this kind of behavior in you has gone straight to my ego. However, you shouldn't apologize for standing your ground against a perceived interloper. It shows weakness that might be used against you."

"Great, now even burglars are telling me what I need to change about myself," she said, inhaling sharply through her nose.

Kojak chose this moment to reappear, yowling plaintively as if he hadn't eaten just a couple of hours ago.

Makeda threw her arm up to gesture at Beznaria. "You come here demanding food when you slept on guard cat duty?"

One moment her hand was being used to shame a cat, the next it was ensconced in the warmth of a much larger one. Beznaria pulled her behind and stepped in front of Makeda like a protective shield.

"Be gone, demon!" Beznaria began herding Makeda back with one hand and dramatically shooing the air with the other, as if she'd generate enough wind to sweep the unamused cat out the door.

Makeda darted around Beznaria and gathered up the cat, who did look kind of like a wrinkled little demon, into her arms. "Are you . . . afraid of cats, Ms. Chetchevaliere?"

"That's not a cat," Beznaria said, eyeing Kojak like he might sprout wings and fly across the room. "I enjoy the company of cats. *This* is clearly a hell spawn that has found its way into your humble lodgings."

Makeda twisted her mouth—had to get that *humble* in there, didn't she? "He's a cat. And you're scared of him."

"I'm not scared of anything," Beznaria said with a shrug, though she was still walking backward. "In fact, that creature is cute. That's right. Adorable. I love it. Perhaps I'll steal it from you and make it my familiar." She stopped an inch from the wall and stared at Kojak as if he might fly toward her, claws out and ready to attack.

Makeda had no trouble imagining what a jerk would do in this moment and she used it to form what she loved best: a plan. She was going to use

Kojak to herd this weird woman, who had planted her foot directly onto Makeda's sorest of sore spots, out of her house, out of her life, and make sure Makeda was never bothered about Ibarania again.

She held Kojak out in front of her, *Lion King* style. The cat didn't struggle, as if he knew the pose was one of adulation and thought it was natural for him to accept this from the human who served him.

"Oh, you're not scared?" she asked in her customer-service voice. "Do you want to hold him, then?"

Beznaria scampered back. Makeda, feeling very unlike her old self, smirked and took a step forward, swinging Kojak gently back and forth. He purred appreciatively.

"Maybe I can drape him around your neck," Makeda said brightly. "Like a little kitty cat scarf."

Beznaria squeezed her eyes together and stopped her attempt at escape, her body going rigid. "All right."

Makeda paused and Kojak looked back at her, disgruntled. "Wait. What?"

A shudder moved through Beznaria's tall, sturdy frame before she steeled herself again. "If you want to asphyxiate me with your demon kitty, I submit to your will."

Makeda stared at the woman, who stood with her arms at her side, jacket sleeve ripped, and her face tight with reluctant anticipation, and Makeda's stomach turned.

No one had ever given in to her without pushback. Makeda was the giver, the acquiescer, the one who, figuratively, would allow themselves to be choked out by a demon cat just to please someone else.

She'd thought she wanted to be on the other side of the situation for once, but it felt terrible to see someone offer themselves up to her like this. Terrible and wrong. She didn't feel empowered. She felt like a bully.

She lowered Kojak.

"What are you doing to my baby?" Grandmore's aggravated demand echoed in the hallway.

Both Makeda and Beznaria whipped their heads in the same direction as the stairs creaked loudly and her grandmother's close-cropped curls and suspicious expression came into view.

Makeda pointed at Beznaria. "This woman broke into the Golden Crown, started taking pictures of me, then tells me she's here because—"

"Not you! My *baby*." Grandmore held out her arms.

Kojak wiggled free and dropped lightly onto the ground to pad toward Grandmore, then glanced smugly at Makeda when he was scooped up against the old woman's bosom.

Grandmore narrowed her eyes at Makeda. "I know I've encouraged you to embrace your freaky side, but you and your new lady friend are up here talking about choking on demon kitty cats. Kojak is a sensitive creature and doesn't need to be exposed to all that, you hear me?"

Makeda blinked a few times as her grandmother's meaning fully sank in.

"Oh my god, why are you like this?" Makeda whined. "The demon kitty *is* Kojak, and this isn't my lady friend."

"Dame," Beznaria said, stepping into the hallway and bowing regally before Grandmore. "I'm her damefriend."

Makeda looked at her grandmother, who was beginning to show a particular interest in Beznaria. Panic set in as she realized what would happen if the two began to talk.

"You are not my damefriend. You're a stranger, and you are leaving."

She grabbed Beznaria by the hand this time before tugging, ignoring the warmth of the woman's palm. However, the shock that went through her when Beznaria's grip tightened around hers stopped Makeda in her tracks. Beznaria's index finger, long and not slender, smoothed over the back of Makeda's wrist. She glared up at this woman who was about to wreck her life but made her body tight with unwanted desire.

"Keda! I've never seen you be so rude before. Even when you tried it all summer, the best you could manage had 'please,' 'thank you,' and 'I'm sorry' attached. Now you're snatching people up?" Grandmore smiled conspiratorially, then chucked her chin toward Beznaria. "You. Dame. Who are you?"

"Dame Beznaria Chetchevaliere, Junior Investigator, World Federation of Monarchists." She bowed regally, and Makeda imagined her hopes for a speedy end to this situation being crushed between Beznaria's abs and thighs. "I presume you are the enchanting Ora Hicks, who wrote a spellbinding account of her encounter with a man who called himself Prince Keshan."

Excitement shimmered in Grandmore's eyes. "Yes, I am. Come help me make some coffee."

"I'm happy to help, though it's a bit late for caffeine for me. I'd love tea or decaf if you have it."

Makeda knew this was a lost cause but gave one last shot at running interference. "But, Grandmore—"

Her grandmother shook her head. "You can join us after you finish cleaning."

Makeda felt like a kid again.

"I will clean the room," Beznaria said.

"No you won't," Makeda and Grandmore said at the same time, for different reasons.

Grandmore looked at their uninvited—or possibly invited—guest and jerked her head toward the stairs. She began her descent, chin up, and Beznaria followed behind her, throwing a wide-eyed gaze over her shoulder before she reached the bottom landing.

That look made Makeda tense up, and not from anger like it should have. She took a deep breath and told herself not to panic. She'd been waiting for an opportunity to prove she wasn't a sentient doormat anymore and now she had it.

Chapter 5

Bez had a rotating list of things she was sure of in life. Her current surety was that, in less civilized times, Makeda Hicks would have run her through with a scimitar without a second thought.

It was an oddly arousing thought, and not the first that had sprung to mind since she'd creatively entered the B&B—lockpicking was an art after all—and stumbled upon Makeda and her hell Hoover, demon cat, and soft, warm body that'd fit snugly against her own.

Makeda sat across the table from Bez, freshly showered and dressed in an outfit that made her look like a character from the nineties American television shows that had been syndicated in Ibarania.

Her long dark locks were pulled into two buns on either side of her head and held in place with pink scrunchies. A few locks had been left down to frame her face, and she wore a hot pink button-down shirt with a cactus pattern, straight-leg jeans cut off at the knee, and pink slippers. She picked up a mug that had the words I WILL CUT YOU written in glittery black text, and her finger—the one that wore the ring that had brought Bez here—tapped on the word CUT.

Bez wasn't the greatest at picking up hints, but she understood the message, and she ignored it.

She still couldn't believe that this woman was possibly the key to her family's redemption and her grandmother's peace, but the more she looked at Makeda, the less doubt there was. She'd stared at Lalla al-Hurradassi's face every day growing up—if not the painting that hung in her family home's entryway, then the murals and banners and money emblazoned with the Pirate Queen's image. The similarity was faint, but it was there. The wide set eyes. The jut of her jaw and breadth of her forehead.

"Maybe if you cleaned your glasses every now and then you wouldn't have to stare so hard. Is there something on my face?" Makeda scowled.

Makeda's annoyance might also be evidence, as the al-Hurradassi temper was legendary, but if everyone who got mad when Bez was around was a descendant of Queen Aazi, then the missing queen had been quite busy in the postwar years.

"Yes," Bez answered, then she turned her head to look around the dining room for the hundredth time, taking in the framed pictures and lived-in furniture that reminded her so much of her own family home that she'd been avoiding for the last few years. "There is a patch of lighter skin just below your left ear. Where your neck meets your jawline."

Makeda placed her hand over her neck; Bez knew that her palm was rough from scrubbing and her fingers were strong with blunt cut nails.

"It's a birthmark. My mom has it, too," Makeda said, then jolted upright, her expression tensing with worry. "You didn't contact my mother, did you?"

"No. I didn't call anyone because I prefer the element of surprise in my investigations. That, and your grandmother's email made it clear that Ashley Hicks shouldn't be contacted."

Bez saw a bit of the tension leave Makeda's body, though the worry remained in her eyes.

"And the birthmark is a love bite, actually," Beznaria said, bypassing discussion of any family issues until she could investigate further. "Or that is what it has always been called. 'Lalla's Kiss,' after Lalla, the first queen of Ibarania. The legend states that she wasn't born with it, though all of her descendants have been; it appeared on her skin the morning after she killed her husband."

"That wasn't in the *Encyclopaedia Britannica* when I was a kid," Makeda said, then caught herself, wiping the interest from her face. "Not that it matters."

"Queen Lalla," Ora said. "Keshan had mentioned her when he gave me the ring, but that was all so long ago and I never got as interested as my daughter did."

"She was a pirate queen who ruled Ibarania, and the first al-Hurradassi," Bez said, straightening in her seat. "She was brought to old Ibarania as an enslaved child—she'd been kidnapped from a tribe in North Africa, it's said, though she talked very little about her past. At some point she led a revolt and escaped, stole an Ibaranian ship, and took to plundering pirates like the ones who had stolen her from her family. She became the scourge of the Mediterranean."

"Ooo, this is better than a History Channel show," Ora said, tapping her granddaughter on the arm.

"Can you get on with this?" Makeda asked, unmoved.

"Her fleet was so bloodthirsty in their decimation of slavers, and so ruthless in their quest to liberate those who had been stolen for profit, that even the most feared pirates avoided them at all costs," Bez said. "When the King of old Ibarania finally caught her, he offered her marriage or death, and surprising everyone, she chose marriage. Then she killed him on their wedding night, led an uprising of the various enslaved peoples of Ibarania, and created her own unified monarchy on the island. She said it was her wedding gift to herself."

"Yes!" Ora clapped. "Now why don't they make *this* into a movie?"

"The love bite comes from the legend that the old king let his guard down as she sucked at his neck in their marital bed. She bit down to hold him in place as she shoved her blade into his guts and disemboweled him."

Bez caught herself midswing of her imaginary knife, just before she knocked over her mug. She grabbed a cookie from the plate in front of her instead, bringing warm chocolate chip delight to her mouth. She'd helped Ora slice and bake the premade dough while they waited for Makeda to clean.

When she glanced at Makeda, the woman was trying to appear unmoved, but Bez saw the hint of another al-Hurradassi trait that overwhelmed all attempts at submission by outside DNA—the dimple of doom, so named because it was the last thing many saw before being run through by their pirate queen.

"That was a thrilling reenactment, but I don't see what any of this has to do with me," Makeda said.

"Since I've told you multiple times now, I'm going to have to assume this is some form of deflection? An attempt to throw me off?" Bez smirked and poked her glasses up her nose. "It won't work. You cannot hide from me, Makeda Hicks."

"I'm not hiding, I'm sitting here telling you to your face that I want no part in this, like I've been telling my family for most of my life." Makeda turned to look at her grandmother, furrows of worry stretching between her brows. "Did you really send those forms in on my behalf? When I asked you not to, and everything that I already went through?"

"You didn't ask me not to send the forms, you said you didn't want to talk about it anymore," Ora said, moving back and forth in her seat. Bez's grandmother called that movement *getting bitten in the pants by the guilt ants.* "I sent the forms in on *my* behalf, as a witness who'd known, in the biblical sense, a man claiming to be Prince Keshan, the lost heir to the throne," Ora continued. "But I did point out that you were my granddaughter."

"Correct," Beznaria said. "Her story was corrob-
orated by reports of a musician in a band called
Keshan and the Golden Crown Players. He
claimed to be the son of a queen who'd lost her
memory while away from her homeland and, after
regaining it, decided to continue living a normal
life. Ora Hicks mentioned you, as was necessary,
and attached a very becoming photograph of
you with a dab of paint on your nose."

And a ring on her finger.

The ring was the main reason Beznaria was
there, two months after she'd started her mission in
the US and one month and three weeks after she'd
realized Lord Higginshoggins had given her a file
of clearly bogus claims when he'd sent her off. The
man was terrible at his job, but Bez's brief foray into
the classified files of the higher-level investigators
had revealed a dozen leads that were more promising. When she'd gotten word from her father about
how upsetting the search was becoming for Henna
Jeta as people began to dig into how exactly the
queen had been lost, Bez had decided she couldn't
leave until she'd investigated every claim that the
WFM hadn't. Each of them had turned out to be as
false as the original files she'd received.

It had only been a few days ago, as she prepared
to head back to WFM headquarters in defeat, that
she'd found Ora Hicks's email, with the attached
photo. That was how this covert operation had
started—covert in that her superiors at the World
Federation of Monarchists hadn't approved her
request to investigate Makeda Hicks. In fact, they
had issued what an easily swayed person might

have considered a denial, but Beznaria hadn't been able to ignore what her instincts were telling her— and she couldn't ignore her promise to Henna Jeta.

"How do we know this Keshan dude was telling the truth? How do you even know *she's* telling the truth?" Makeda's question was almost a plea, and the look in her eye was crestfallen. "I love my grandmother, but you can't take anything she says at face value. She lies about her birthday to get free cake at restaurants. She has multiple email accounts so she can keep using free trials. She tells everyone she sang backup for the Supremes during their residency here back in the day, when really she was working concessions!"

"You ungrateful heifer," Ora muttered, reaching out to move the plate of cookies away from Makeda and toward Beznaria.

Beznaria rocked back in her chair, balancing on two spindly legs.

She didn't know what to make of this woman. In her years at the WFM, she had never come across someone desperate *not* to be royalty. WFM investigators were beset by con artists and scammers of all kinds, though more often just everyday people clinging to the possibility that there might be something more to their lives—to themselves intrinsically. Makeda looked like she would rather swallow sea hag slime than discuss this any further.

Bez actually felt a twinge of regret at having to push this, but this was the only promising lead she'd ever stumbled across that hadn't immediately led to a dead end.

"Ms. Hicks. My job is to investigate claims that have merit, and in my professional opinion, what

Ora Hicks submitted does. I am, of course, still investigating. That is my job. The trail of the man who called himself Prince Keshan disappears sometime around 1972—the summer after your grandmother received him carnally."

Makeda frowned. "Don't say that ever again, thanks."

"As thrilled as I would be to find the so-called Prince Keshan, who would be the direct hereditary heir, right now I'm here to see you. Now that I've assessed you, I believe there's enough evidence to start the second phase of the investigation, but to do that, I'll have to bring you with me to Ibarania."

How she would do that was the issue, but she'd cross that bridge when she got to it. Bez knew she'd get the woman to come with her, but she hadn't been prepared for her stubbornness.

"I understand you may have some questions," Bez said, trying to sound professional. "Feel free to ask anything."

"You a lesbian?" Ora Hicks asked, squinting in her direction.

"Grandmore!" Makeda placed both hands over her face. "Don't just ask strangers things like that!"

"I was asking for you! She's a fine-looking woman. I'm looking out for you."

"I meant questions specifically about the search for the missing heir," Bez said, feeling her ears go warm for the first time in years. "I'm queer. I use the term pan, in part because it captures my puckish nature, but I prefer and have only dated women, with the exception of an unfortunate two-week debacle with my high school best friend Steven."

"Pan. Okay then." Ora's grin broadened and she glanced at her granddaughter and then back to Bez. "*Someone* has been moping since she got dumped. She's always bringing home these girls who don't appreciate her, and I'm tired of it! Now a more on topic question: what happens now? Does she get a crown and all that good stuff?" The woman nudged her granddaughter.

"Well, there are a few steps between my investigation and her receiving the title," Bez said. "The first step would be coming to Ibarania with me to be presented to the review board."

The actual first step was making the WFM aware that she had, in fact, followed up on her lead and would be bringing Makeda to Ibarania for consideration. Lord Higginshoggins wouldn't be pleased that the heir had turned out to be American, and even less pleased that said American didn't seem to even want the role, but it would all work out.

"What are the other steps?" Makeda asked, pulling her chair back so that Bez's legs no longer stretched alongside it. "Not that it matters since I won't be traveling to a foreign country with a total stranger, but you know, since you are talking about me, you could maybe fill me in."

Bez wanted to ask when she'd stopped filling her in, but that wouldn't help matters.

"Prospects and their claims will be interviewed by the review board. If chosen, the selected heir will be provided clothing from Ibarania's top fashion designers and a room in the royal wing at our five-star hotel, though if chosen they'll be assigned a more permanent residence for their visits to the country for events. They'll also be given social media accounts where they can post images of their exploration of their possible new kingdom. There will be a ball at the brand-new seaside resort and events center to announce the heir."

Makeda's eyes narrowed, and Bez, who was usually maddeningly opaque to other people, had the disturbing sensation of being seen through like the waters of Lalla's Lagoon.

"So this whole thing is a tourism campaign for the island, is what you're saying," Makeda said. "You're sitting here trying to ruin my life over a scheme from the Ibaranian tourism board."

"Since when did you become so skeptical?" Ora chided. "And since when did you have a life?"

Makeda rolled her eyes.

Bez cleared her throat. "While this initiative was prompted by the World Federation of Monarchists, the Ibaranian government's focus is the benefit an international royalty search and monarchy will bring to the country's tourism industry, in addition to revenue that might be raised by the sale of merchandise."

"Trust me, I know," Makeda said. She turned in her seat, just the slightest motion, and Bez looked over her shoulder at the area she'd turned away from. A China cabinet with shelves lined with commemorative plates and bobbleheads.

"Those are from my daughter's old collection," Ora said when she followed Beznaria's gaze. "Figured we might as well use them to go with the whole Golden Crown thing we have going on."

"So I get to be on a plate and wear some clothes that I don't want, that's what you're offering?" Makeda cut in.

"All official prospects are compensated for their time even if they don't win," Bez added. "Compensated well."

Bez said this as casually as she could, but she had taken a peek at Makeda's credit report, that odd American tradition of holding their citizens hostage via debt and, even more oddly, the lack of it. It had shown a lifetime of meticulous care for her financial situation, and then the recent appearance of an uncharacteristic and substantial amount for a business loan.

Makeda began to work her bottom lip with her teeth, and Bez went in for the kill.

"You will be paid a handsome fee. You will get an all-expenses-paid vacation to an island paradise where you get to live out a true princess fantasy. Ball gowns! Everyone staring at you and talking about how amazing you look! Attendants to provide your every whim, within reason! It's a dream come true, yes?"

For just an instant, Bez thought she had won. Makeda's eyes went glossy; of course she might get misty-eyed as she realized the enormity of the luck that had befallen her.

Then Makeda blinked and the soft sheen was gone, replaced by a rock-hard resolve. "I get it. You probably need some comic relief for this thing, but I'm not the one. I want nothing to do with this. I refuse to be paraded around so people can laugh and judge whether I'm princess material."

"Why would people laugh?" Bez asked.

Makeda's gaze dropped away like a kicked seaside stray, and Bez had her answer.

People had laughed at Bez when she'd said she was going to be dame of the guard when she grew up. They'd laughed when she said just about anything. Bez had never liked the laughter—she found it grating—but she also had never assumed that she herself was laughable. Not everyone was like Bez though, with a hard head and thick skin and innate knowledge of her general worth, nay, superiority, as a human specimen.

"Do I look like a princess?" Makeda asked.

"No, you don't actually," Bez said. She stood, shucking her jacket as she did and unbuttoning the top buttons of her shirt, revealing the white tank top she wore underneath.

"Hey now," Ora said. "Is this some Magic Mike shit? Don't think we're gonna give you money just because you start shaking your ass."

Bez was still looking at Makeda, whose gaze had jumped back up to hers, anger and hurt showing in the strain around her eyes.

"Personally, I think you look like a queen. But princess is better for the WFM's marketing purposes." Bez knelt before Makeda, as she had playacted so many times as a child, and then stripped her shirt down her shoulder partially revealing the tattoo that covered her arm from epaulet to elbow. If Makeda had known anything about her Ibaranian heritage, she would've recognized the motif of waves cresting below the fish scale armor—the pattern as ubiquitous in Ibaranian art as the vendetta blades tattooed below the epaulet on her shoulder. Instead, the woman had grown up in this city that had nothing in common with Ibarania apart from the sea that lapped at its shore.

She took Makeda's hand, the one with the fish scale armor ring, and placed the warm palm and warmer metal of the ring against her exposed skin. She stared into Makeda's eyes, willing her to accept the truth of the situation.

"You wear Lalla's ring, fish scale armor crafted by Ibaranian royal artisans, gifted to your grandmother by Prince Keshan. I have the armor of the Royal Guard on my skin because it is in my blood. I believe you are the lost heir, and I am willing to do anything to bring you back to Ibarania because it is your place, and my duty."

Makeda stared at her for a long moment, a moment in which Bez felt something bright and hot crush her whole body in its grip. Was this dizzy, heady feeling the blood oath sworn by Chetchevaliere to al-Hurradassi generation after generation kicking in? Or was it something else? Whatever the sensation was, for the first time ever Bez felt a response to the call to honor and protect that she'd been searching for first in the military and then in the WFM.

She tried to remember how her grandmother had described the sensation of pledging fealty to Queen Aazi in the Piazza Regiana before the minarets of the palace.

Makeda dragged her fingertips over Bez's arm, seemingly tracing the design, leaving a tingling trail in the wake of her gentle touch. Then she pulled her hand away and shook her head, as if clearing it. "No. I said no. I'm not a princess, no matter who my grandfather was, and more important, I don't want to be one."

"You don't want to be one." Bez blinked, trying to process what had been said though it made entirely no sense. Someone who refused to be a princess was utterly confounding to a person who had grown up longing to protect one.

"That's it?" Ora asked, disappointment clear in her voice.

Makeda raised both brows at her grandmother. "That's it. Shouldn't you be proud that I'm not such a pushover anymore?"

"Oh, you were never a pushover when it came to *this*," Ora said, shaking her head in disgust.

"What is 'this'?" Makeda asked.

"Not letting yourself have anything good, anything just for you. You're ready to give and give to everyone else but have the nerve to get mad if anyone asks you to give to yourself," the old woman said. She turned to look at Bez. "She thinks she's changed. Only thing changed is she doesn't smile while depriving herself."

"How is something just for me if I don't want it?" Makeda looked at Bez and stood up. "And I have changed. If I hadn't, I wouldn't be kicking her out right now. Time to go."

Bez had to bring the heir to the throne back. She couldn't fail her grandmother, and leaving without Makeda Hicks would mean failure. But she hadn't imagined the heir would be completely resistant.

She began running contingency plans in her head.

The problem was, she didn't have any—this was what she relied on her brain fireflies for. When it came to Makeda Hicks, she wasn't yet sure what was driving her decisions: instinct, or a subliminal message being transmitted by the brain fireflies interfering with her main objective.

Beznaria's gaze rested on Makeda for a bit, then slid to Ora. "Actually, I'm stuck in town for a few days and need a place to stay until I can finalize my travel arrangements. I understand that the Golden Crown is the finest accommodation in the city. Do you have a room available?"

"No," Makeda said. "There are cheaper rooms at the big hotels, and you can gamble there, too. Maybe win some money and make this trip worthwhile."

"I can help with some of the repairs if I stay here," Beznaria added, her earnest gaze still on Ora.

"We don't need help with repairs," Makeda said.

"Hush," Ora said, tugging Makeda's shirt to pull her back down into her seat.

Beznaria pushed her glasses up the bridge of her nose, her gaze locking onto Ora. "I noticed that tiles in the bathroom need recalking, and there are cracks in the walls and ceilings of several rooms that could be easily fixed. A few shingles on the roof are loose, too. I'll need something to keep me occupied until my passage back to Ibarania is confirmed."

Makeda jolted in her seat and looked at Beznaria askance. "Wait. When were you in the other rooms, or out on the roof?"

Beznaria's eyes darted to Makeda, but only for a millisecond before returning to Ora, who was the only other person invested in Makeda going to Ibarania.

"You would do all that for free?" Ora asked innocently, though there had been no mention of nonpayment.

Beznaria grinned and leaned in a bit like she was getting ready to haggle at a swap meet. "I'll do it in exchange for meals and a room. I like to keep my hands busy, and casinos don't appeal to me. If I take risks, it's only because the odds are in my favor."

"We don't need or want your help," Makeda cut in, but Ora was in deal-maker mode.

"Can you do plumbing? Something is wrong with the sink and Makeda only made it worse when she tried to fix it."

Bez nodded, and Ora turned in her seat. "Take your damefriend's bag that's out there up to the terrace room."

"But—"

"But what? You already turned down an opportunity of money for nothing that literally walked into our B&B. You have repair money I don't know about, or should I turn that down, too?" Ora raised an eyebrow.

"No."

"That's what I thought."

Bez watched Makeda stalk off and wondered what it would have been like to meet her without the burden of convincing her to do something she clearly didn't want to do. A chance encounter at a coffee shop, or in a dark club with music throbbing through them both. A place where Makeda wouldn't frown at her and see her as the enemy.

She didn't often wonder about people in this way. She enjoyed a good fling, but her romantic musings were so few and far between that her father had sat her down and given her a list of rules after she'd broken yet another woman's heart with seemingly no compunction.

One, if something pisses her off, do the opposite of that. Two, if YOU piss her off, apologize. Three, if she likes kissing, kiss her a lot. Four, when she talks, pay attention to the details.

Bez wasn't trying to date Makeda—though she imagined rule three could be quite fun with her—but maybe those rules would also help her woo the woman into doing what she needed her to do. She couldn't do the opposite of what was pissing her off, but she could apologize.

She followed her to the entryway in time to see Makeda give her duffel bag a light kick. Something about the restraint in the kick—enough to show anger but conscious not to break anything fragile in the bag—tugged at that sense of loyalty that had flared in her when Makeda's palm had rested on her arm.

Bez went over to pick up the bag. "I apologize," she said.

"For coming here and trying to ruin my life?" Makeda asked without looking at her.

"No, for taking you with me when I leave." She pushed her glasses up. "I don't leave jobs unfinished unless it's one I don't feel like doing. Unfortunately for you, I've been waiting for most of my life."

"And I've been running from it. You plan on kidnapping me?" Makeda asked. "Because that's the only way I'll be leaving with you."

Bez had considered that option but decided against it. She placed an elbow on the reception desk and leaned against it so that she was slightly closer to Makeda's height. When the woman finally turned her way, Bez smiled. "I have no need of chloroform—I can be very charming when I have to be. You'll come with me, and it will be your own decision."

Makeda's long lashes fluttered a few times as she blinked, then she shook her head. "I think you mean very annoying."

"Being annoying is also a useful tool in getting people to do what you want." Bez leaned down a couple of inches closer to Makeda and dropped her voice. "I let nothing in my arsenal go to waste, sea snail. Not a single thing."

Most people were unnerved by a Chetchevaliere stare down, but Makeda tilted her head and held her gaze, not backing down an inch. Bez was suddenly reminded that she found nothing more attractive than a woman whose head was as hard as her own. Makeda knew what she wanted and what she didn't want, and Bez's determination was momentarily blinded by a brain firefly flashing the message, *What would it be like if she wanted you?*

"Nothing in your arsenal can go up against deep-rooted, intense, and unfaltering aversion to being a princess," Makeda said, her voice cool and rigidly controlled. "You might think I'm a push-over like everyone else does, and maybe I still am. But not with this. Don't waste your time thinking you'll change my mind."

Makeda slipped past her, the fabric of her T-shirt brushing a static charge against Bez's cheap suit as she headed up the stairs.

Bez turned to watch her go, noting her reaction for future reference and ignoring how snugly her shorts fit. She was about to follow after Makeda when the demon cat stalked down the stairs, stopping to stare.

Bez blinked.

"Fine. You win this round," Bez said, and then went back into the dining room. She'd regroup, and then she'd convince Makeda to leave with her, no matter what the stubborn American thought would happen.

There was no other possible outcome. She had promised after all—her first and most fervent oath. She might lie through her teeth in the line of duty, but she didn't break promises to people she cared about.

She'd bring the lost heir to Ibarania and clear her family's name.

Chapter 6

Makeda's plan was to avoid Beznaria for the duration of the woman's stay. It wasn't a detailed plan, like booby-trapping the B&B and catapulting the meddling investigator into the sea, but she was relying on her most valuable skill: patience. She only had to deal with the uninvited guest for a day or two, and when it came to the art of ignoring her own discomfort, Makeda had put in more than the required ten thousand hours of study to become a master.

Despite this, by the second day her patience was already beginning to wear thin.

It shouldn't have been so difficult to keep her distance when the Ibaranian was the only guest at a B&B with creaky stairs and multiple unoccupied rooms to hide in, but the woman seemed to have a preternatural sense of where Makeda would be and the ability to get there a few steps before her or creep up a few steps behind.

If Makeda went to the kitchen for coffee? Beznaria was there, either already brewing a cup or preparing a delicious snack in her continued wooing of Grandmore. As Makeda had repaired the suit jacket she had ripped using Grandmore's trusty Singer, Beznaria had stood guard to prevent pin pricks and help her feed the fabric through the machine. When Makeda tried to work through her to-do list, Beznaria showed up, smoothly co-opting each task from her or looking over her shoulder and giving *suggestions*. Earlier that morning, Makeda had driven to the grocery store on the other side of town, since she now avoided GrabRite like she would any of her many exes, and she'd sworn she saw Beznaria jogging behind her car, T-2000 style, in the rearview mirror.

Makeda was starting to understand Steph's parting shots at her a little better. Having someone offer to handle the most basic tasks made her want to scream, and she'd only been dealing with it for approximately thirty-six hours.

She could pour her own coffee—she was the only one who knew the exact proportion of cream and sugar; she could sew by herself; she could make her own plate; she could fold her own laundry; and she most certainly hadn't appreciated Beznaria's offers to tuck her into bed.

She absolutely hadn't been up half the night thinking about that last one either. Insomnia was natural in times of stress.

But the new levels of aggravation she was feeling had made her realize something: for the last few months she'd told herself that she was some new, angry version of herself, but that wasn't true. It turned out all she'd been was numb.

She hadn't changed. She'd gone from help-yness turned up to eleven, to help-yness with some cheap noise-canceling headphones thrown over it. She'd never really gotten mad at Steph. She was still giving free labor to GrabRite. She hadn't even raged about being stuck with a debt for a dream that wasn't hers—she'd quietly accepted it and continued to pay against the interest. Makeda had confused not feeling the overwhelming drive to give, because she wasn't feeling anything at all, with being a new, independent version of herself.

She hadn't known the difference until Beznaria Chetchevaliere had broken into the Golden Crown—Makeda was sure she hadn't left the door unlocked—and shown her just how wrong she'd been. Now Makeda was tingling all over, like circulation returning to a limb that had fallen asleep, and feeling all kinds of uncomfortable things. Panic and terror and resentment that she'd have to be the girl she'd once been—smiling awkwardly at school as classmates sneeringly called her "Princess" and hounded her mercilessly, and smiling anxiously at home as her mother lovingly called her Princess and poured another drink as she flipped through travel guides to Ibarania. Fear that her mother would get involved in this mess. Annoyance that even when she minded her business, other people's desires still managed to seek her out and overshadow her own—and that she wasn't sure that she even had any of her own anymore since her top priorities were the B&B and paying Amber's loan.

It was like the investigator had smashed the lock on the vault of Makeda's pent-up frustration at just the right angle and now the lid was off. The way Beznaria simultaneously tried to force Makeda to give in to her while treating her with a strange deference, made Makeda feel a different throb, which was a problem. Her whole body had gone hot just from laying a hand on the investigator's admittedly well-sculpted biceps. What the hell had that been? Grandmore had been sitting right there, and Makeda had still been momentarily ready to risk it all.

Makeda wasn't a risk-it-all person; she generally lost by consistently hedging her bets.

She worried that she would give in, not because she'd suddenly want to be a princess, but because Beznaria's chaotic presence would eventually wear down her resistance.

On the third day, after a morning of successful evasion thanks to Kojak's yearly vaccination, she waited until she heard Grandmore launch into one of her stories about her past boardwalk adventures and sneaked out of the house. No one could break the thrall of Grandmore's reminiscences, and she decided to take advantage of it by going on her weekly boardwalk stroll.

It was something she'd started after she'd moved back in with Grandmore. She didn't always walk the entire stretch of boardwalk, miles of wide wooden planks; usually just enough to get her steps in for the day and tire herself out a bit. She sometimes stopped to chat with storeowners and picked up food and water to hand out to some of the unhoused people she'd become friendly with over the years, but mostly she practiced being alone.

People-watching by herself didn't feel as good; she kept wanting to point out funny things but had no one to point them out to. She would stop for coffee or a cherry-flavored Italian ice and force herself to sit on benches or sand dunes instead of heading back to the B&B to clean and do busywork. She didn't like being alone, and that was why she forced herself to take these weekly walks. It was practice, or sometimes she thought maybe it was punishment. Not wanting to be alone was what had made her seek out the Stephs and Ambers of the past, what had made her stay long past when she should have gone.

At the bottom of her watering can of sweetness was the shadowy creature fed by her desire to give: loneliness. With her can mostly empty, the creature breached the surface more and more, and was choosing now of all times to do it again.

Makeda remembered sitting on the dunes with her mother, Grandmore, and Gramps when she was a kid, before they'd found out about Prince Keshan and all her energy had turned toward containing her mother's obsession. So many years had passed, but sometimes she felt like she was still searching for those perfect days when her biggest worry had been menacing seagulls and not monarchical fantasies.

Her phone vibrated in her pocket, and her stomach jolted with a sudden fear that it was her mother, but when she pulled it out, the number from GrabRite showed on the display. Her annoyance surged as she answered, and this time there was no seal on the vault to keep it locked in.

"Lindsey?"

"Mak? There's an emergency."

"There were never this many emergencies when I worked there," Makeda said. "Wonder what changed that you're calling me every other day with a new problem."

"What?" Lindsey's voice was strained with indignation.

"What now?" Makeda asked.

"It's just, I'm going through the files and I think you messed up this spreadsheet tracking seasonal—"

"I didn't mess anything up," Makeda said. The words just slipped out, instead of her usual placation. She leaned into the satisfaction, much preferring this to having to give her time and energy to someone who didn't deserve it. "You don't know how to use Excel, but you lied on your résumé and said you did. That sounds like *you* messed up."

There was a pause, which was understandable since Makeda had broken script. She was supposed to give in, to just do what needed to be done even if it wasn't to her benefit.

Not today, GrabRite.

"Mak, come on, if I don't fix this, the store will suffer and—"

"And I don't work there anymore."

"But . . . but if you don't help, there will be trouble this week at the store."

Makeda started to slide back into help-y mode, but pulled the emergency brake.

"I don't work there anymore, and what happens there is no longer my responsibility," she said.

"Don't call me again unless there's a job opening. Also, you can find Excel tutorials on YouTube."

She hung up and stared at the phone and her slightly shaking hand, her ears ringing a bit behind the sound of crashing waves. Guilt surged, but so did an unfamiliar pleasure. She'd put her foot down, without apologizing.

Maybe the annoying investigator's presence did have some value—Makeda was learning to say no and mean it. And she'd keep saying no until the Ibaranian understood and left.

She decided to go somewhere that hadn't been around when she was a kid, given all the memories the princess stuff was pulling up—the Ferris wheel at the Steel Pier. She hated the Ferris wheel in the summer, with the sticky heat and the pier teeming with people and the line to get on the wheel almost as far back as the boardwalk. Now, in the pre-season before the shore was overrun by tourists, there was a refreshing breeze and the warmth was dry, not oppressive. The crowds were sparse, and when Makeda got on, she could expect to have a car to herself and not be stuck with a bickering family or amorous couple.

From the window of the trendily designed car, she could look out over the wide possibility of the ocean and feel that stirring that had once been familiar to her. She'd lost it, down on the ground where reality had started pressing in on her early and often, but the Ferris wheel lifted her up into that sensation every now and again, the one of being overwhelmed, not with bills or worry for other people and the obligations she'd made to them, but with possibility. With all the places she could imagine out in the world, and all the adventures she'd once imagined she'd have. When the ride was over and she placed her feet back on solid ground, she would leave all those fantasies in the air, where they belonged.

There was no wait when she arrived, and the young white guy who worked there took her ticket and guided her on board. Makeda felt herself unclench as she stepped into the car, ready for approximately fifteen minutes of reprieve from a life that had suddenly become a minefield of everyone else's hopes and dreams, and the realization that she didn't really have any of her own.

"Miss, you have to wait for the next car," the Ferris wheel worker called out from behind Makeda. "The next one will be empty. Miss!"

Makeda's senses pricked as she turned, picking up on Beznaria's chaos vibes before the aggravating investigator stepped into the car behind her. The woman grinned down at her and Makeda knew what mice saw last before Kojak sent them on to the great cheese platter in the sky.

The tension that had been relieved by shutting Lindsey down clamped her in its vise again. "You—"

"I am but a tourist trying to see your fine city along the Atlantic," Beznaria said, hamming up her accent. "This Ferris wheel is said to have a good view that's best enjoyed with good company."

Makeda should have jumped out just before the Ferris wheel worker shut the door, like a heroine sliding into an airlock at the climax of an action movie, but Makeda was not final-girl material. No matter how much she wanted to change, she was the person who stood there as a xenomorph approached, and perhaps petted the tiny alien tongue and offered it a snack before it disemboweled her.

The Ferris wheel started to move, and she sighed, annoyed with herself, and dropped onto one of the benches. Beznaria sat down right beside her, close enough that Makeda could smell the sweet grass scent of her lotion—close enough that anyone watching them would think they were a couple.

Beznaria pushed her glasses up, depositing another fingerprint to the smudge menagerie that was killing Makeda softly.

"Can you even make out the view through those things?" Makeda resisted the urge to pull them off and rub them with the microfiber cloth she kept in her purse. "You could at least give them a wipe if you're here to see the sights."

Beznaria appeared not to be listening. She jumped up, startling Makeda, and started walking all over the car—she examined the railings, stared at stains on the seats, and even did a jumping jack or two, making the car swing back and forth.

Then she dropped back onto the bench, even closer to Makeda than she had been.

She leaned down in that annoying way tall people had of making it clear that there were a few inches of distance between your shoulder and theirs.

"How many people," she asked, "do you think have had sex in here?"

"What?" Makeda's voice came out in a high squeak. "Why would you ask that?"

"It just seems that when in a small semiprivate space, fornication becomes a challenge of sorts for many people. The Ferris wheel's nature adds the bonus of a time limit to whatever amorous intentions one might have, and the additional bonus of the threat of discovery. How long does a rotation take? Twelve to fifteen minutes, is it, before that door will open?" She moved her face directly in front of Makeda's and squinted. "Are you coming down with something? Your cheeks are a bit—"

"I'm fine!" Makeda stared straight ahead, hoping Bez couldn't hear her heart beating wildly or see the sweat gathering at her hairline. Maybe the smudgy glasses would work to her benefit. "I just don't want to think about whether there are sex germs covering the surface of the small metal box I'm stuck in for the next few minutes."

Bez leaned back in her seat.

"Fine. We can talk about Ibarania." Subtlety was not the investigator's strong point. "We don't have a Ferris wheel like this there, but my sister, she works for the ministry of tourism, she says they want to build one if the new ceremonial monarchy increases the island's profile. The Ruota Royale. Maybe they can name it the Makeda Royale if you become princess."

Makeda's shoulders locked up. "I came here for peace, not to talk about the royalty thing, okay? I can't even relax in my own home because you're there, at least let me have a few minutes to myself."

"You don't relax in your own home, though," Beznaria pointed out. "I've seen your to-do list, and it's in no way compatible with relaxation."

"Doing things is relaxing for me, but not with people looking over my shoulder and constantly trying to offer their advice." She cut Bez a look from the corner of her eye.

Beznaria slumped back, spreading her long legs wide. Her suit was a rumpled mess, but it managed to look artfully shabby even though Makeda knew the wrinkles had formed because Beznaria threw it onto a chair instead of hanging it up.

"I'm just making conversation and getting to know you," Beznaria said. "While some investigators might need to rely on the 'corner your quarry on a Ferris wheel and force your agenda onto them' trick, I am above that."

"Then why did you follow me here?"

"I'm implementing a variation. The 'corner your quarry on a Ferris wheel and flirt with them' trick. That is my preferred method, in this instance."

"Has anyone ever told you that you're incredibly annoying?" Makeda bit out, still feeling empowered by hanging up on Lindsey.

"Most people don't say it outright, but you did the day we met," Bez said cheerily. "I find it rather refreshing. You'll become accustomed to it. Like a sea snail in climate-change-warmed seas."

Bez didn't seem bothered by the insult; she seemed oddly flattered. Makeda wondered if it was possible for the woman to care about anything but achieving her own objectives. There was something intriguing about Beznaria's single-mindedness when Makeda's life had become so aimless.

Beznaria stretched her legs out and then drew them back toward her; her gaze was out over the ocean.

"I haven't been home for five years."

Makeda looked around for the invisible person who'd asked when the investigator had last been home, and then remembered her superpower of drawing people's sob stories from them just by breathing in their vicinity. She heaved a sigh.

"The World Federation of Monarchists has headquarters in London, and the travel required has meant not even being there most of the time," Bez continued. "I was flirting, but I was also just talking about home because you're the first person I've been able to talk about it with for some time."

Makeda crossed her arms and leaned back. "What is that like? Never being at home." She didn't want to indulge the investigator, but she was genuinely curious. She'd never left home, and the thought of spending years away made her chest hurt.

"I try not to think about how it feels, but I would have to say it's been lonely. My family is very close, so I'm happy to be going back." Bez glanced down at Makeda. "I'll be happier if you come with me."

Makeda's chest grew even tighter. She hated that it was a stranger saying this to her—as a joke, to get what she wanted—when none of the people she had longed to hear those words from ever had. They'd left her behind instead.

"Why do you care? Does the WFM give you a bonus if you bring me in?"

"Yes, there'd be a small bonus, and it would be helpful considering my contract is up and I'll have to find new work after this," Beznaria said. "But my happiness wouldn't be about the bonus. You saw my tattoo. I am a Chetchevaliere. You are an al-Hurradassi, if you are truly Queen Aazi's great-granddaughter. It is my duty to bring you home. My duty to my country and family. And to you."

Makeda stared at Bez, dismay roiling her stomach because this didn't feel like manipulation. The brightness in the investigator's eyes, the set of her jaw and sudden puffing of her chest—that kind of earnestness couldn't be faked.

"Why is it your duty?" Makeda asked.

"Probably for the same reason you're even entertaining going to Ibarania now. Have you read about the disappearance of Queen Aazi?"

"I did a long time ago, but there are so many different accounts of what happened that I really don't remember," Makeda said. "World War II was over and Ibarania had resisted invasion but lost their king. He was the descendant of Lalla right?"

Beznaria nodded. "Yes. He was the first male hereditary heir, but he found a fierce match in Aazi."

Makeda glanced at Beznaria. "Most of the stories mention that the head of the Royal Guard was with her when she disappeared. Some said that maybe she . . . she . . . You know."

She made a slitting motion across her own neck.

"I know all about what people say." Bez laughed ruefully. "That guard was my grandmother."

"Oh! My bad. I didn't mean to insinuate that she was a killer." Makeda grasped for something to step this back because while she was leaning into jerkiness, grandmothers were off limits.

Beznaria smiled, amused. "She was the head of the Royal Ibaranian Guard, so she can kill a person in more ways than either of us can imagine—but she didn't turn those skills on the queen. I know this. I need to bring you back with me so that everyone knows."

Makeda rubbed her finger over the fish scale ring—she knew what it felt like to carry the burden of mistakes that weren't yours, and the way the desire to fix them could blot out your own dreams. What would Beznaria be doing if her grandmother hadn't lost a queen? Probably not stalking a random American and trying to drag her back to Ibarania.

"You really believe this. That I'm royalty and you're, what, my bodyguard?" She remembered the sensation that had gone through her when she'd pressed her palm to Beznaria's tattoo, the crackle like lightning passing over her skin.

"Of course, I do. In regular circumstances, I'm not in the habit of pursuing women across the world, even if they do look like you."

Makeda's stomach lurched even though the Ferris wheel continued at its regular pace. "I assure you that in regular circumstances, no one pursues women who look like me, domestic or international."

Well, that wasn't exactly true. People were able to track her down when they needed something.

She could tell Beznaria was looking at her and fought the urge to hunch her shoulders.

"Ah, so the American romantic films are correct," Bez said, her voice full of amused wonder. "Beautiful women really do sit around lamenting how unattractive they are. Do you also trip over random objects and eat pints of ice cream when you're distressed?"

Makeda inhaled sharply. She was cute—that was what people said if they commented on her looks, and even that was a stretch given how many people had invested time and energy into making her know she was far from it. But Beznaria had called her beautiful, so casually.

"You're just saying what sounds good," Makeda said.

Beznaria laughed. "That is actually one of the few things I'm *not* skilled at. I'm saying that if you aren't pursued on a regular basis, the circumstances must be irregular."

Makeda's resistance began to slip. Could she believe that Beznaria was saying this because she meant it?

No.

"Flattery will get you nowhere," she retorted, inwardly cringing that she couldn't come up with a cooler put-down.

"I don't flatter you to get myself anywhere, but . . ." Beznaria was looking deeply into Makeda's eyes, and that tingling sensation started in her body again. Her gaze dropped to Makeda's mouth and in the space of that brief ocular movement, the particles between them seemed to burst into millions of microscopic flames.

Makeda's libido had already made its appearance known, but for once she had an impulse that seemed driven by greed and greed alone. "But what?"

"Are you sure it wouldn't?" Bez asked, her voice softer and lower.

"What wouldn't?" The microscopic fire particles seemed to slip out from between them to focus their weight behind Makeda's head, pushing it toward Beznaria's.

Beznaria ran her tongue over her lips. "Flattery. Would it not get me anywhere with you?"

Something moved over Makeda's body in a quick velvet wave.

Pleasure. That was pleasure. She leaned into it, just as she had with her annoyance with Lindsey.

"Probably not, but you seem like the type who enjoys a challenge."

Their faces were very close now. The sun streaming in through the car's windows showed each individual fingerprint on Beznaria's glasses, but also the clear honey brown of her eyes and the smooth skin of her cheeks, and her full lips. Makeda wasn't sure what she was feeling because she was too busy thinking that she wanted Beznaria Chetchevaliere—chaotic nuisance and attempted life-ruiner—to kiss her.

It would be okay, here in the air where she allowed herself her fantasies, she reasoned. A princess and her lady knight—the kind of fairy tale she'd always wanted, if she had to be a princess. Not the one her mother had imagined for her. With the way Beznaria was looking at her, gaze full of wonder like she already believed, Makeda could allow herself to believe, too, even if just for the remainder of a Ferris wheel ride.

Their lips were a breath apart when Makeda's senses crashed into her like a wave razing sand-castles at the beach; the heated particles surrounding them fizzled out. She pressed her lips together as she pulled out of the forty-five-degree angle that had brought her so close to Beznaria's mouth.

Beznaria blinked, then jerked her gaze back to the ocean. She added at least four more smudges to her glasses as she pushed them up, even when they reached the summit of the slope of her nose. "I suppose I shouldn't flatter myself either."

"No, you shouldn't."

It didn't matter. Beznaria was going to be gone soon, and Makeda's life would go back to how it usually was.

That was what she wanted.

The usual.

She peeked at Beznaria without turning her head.

"I must admit that it's hard not to think about having sex in a Ferris wheel car when I'm not talking about Ibarania and not flattering either you or myself," Beznaria said, as if she'd felt Makeda's glance. "Are you sure I shouldn't continue with one of those topics as a distraction from the sex thoughts?"

"Oh my god, fine." Makeda huffed in disbelief. "Talk about Ibarania all you want."

"Ibarania. Right, let's go with that." Beznaria sounded slightly disappointed. "Well, the reason they want to restart the monarchy is to promote tourism, but also to cultivate a sense of national pride and to spark interest in our rich history."

"Shouldn't you find someone from the island, then? So it's not some outsider coming in?" Makeda asked despite her resolution not to get involved in this mess. "Like, if you work somewhere and they promote someone from within it's more inspiring than just bringing in some random person. There are all kinds of ways you could have your new monarchy without involving me, a person who's never set foot on the island and wouldn't have the slightest idea of what to do as its princess."

"I believe that was another proposition," Beznaria said. "But it's a much less exciting news story than finding a long-lost heir halfway across the globe, wouldn't you say?"

Makeda couldn't argue with that.

"Tell me why you don't want to be involved," Beznaria said. "You won't have to do the hard work of making laws and all of that. You'd just be a figurehead. Haven't you given any thought to the ways this might benefit you, even if it's just having a bit of fun?"

Makeda's irritation flared up. Yes, she had. She'd once thought that being a princess would be an amazing adventure, until she'd been made aware that princess adventures weren't designed with girls like her in mind. The thought of being paraded out in front of a group of people—of how they would laugh when they were told *she* was their princess—wasn't her idea of fun. It made her jaw tense up and her shoulder muscles tight.

"That's the girl who thinks she's a princess? Her?!"

She gripped the bench seat with her fingertips. "Why don't you figure that out yourself, Miss Top Ten Investigator? I said we could talk about Ibarania, not me."

"Very well, though I'd prefer to talk more about you."

Beznaria launched into more facts about the island, and Makeda chatted politely until the ride came to a stop. When the door to the Ferris wheel car opened and they stepped back onto the solid ground of Steel Pier, her resolve hadn't changed.

"I'm going to take care of something. *Don't* follow me."

"All right," Beznaria said easily—too easily—and then turned and walked in the opposite direction.

Makeda kept looking back over her shoulder and when she arrived at the other end of the boardwalk, where she'd walked aimlessly, she was furious—not at Beznaria, who hadn't followed her, but at the fact that she was a little disappointed by it.

MAKEDA SLUNK BACK home that evening in time to hear a shriek from the kitchen. She ran in, heart thumping in her chest, to find Beznaria spinning pizza dough in an elaborate routine for Grandmore's enjoyment.

It was like a scene straight from the fantasies of how she'd imagined family fun nights could be—how things had been when her grandfather was still alive and her mother hadn't fallen into the abyss of royal obsession. She'd always tried to integrate her girlfriends into her life with Grandmore, but most of them found it frustrating that she wanted to spend so much time with her. Now here was Bez, having a casual hang with the old woman.

It didn't help matters that she was in slacks and her button-down shirt, looking like the living embodiment of Makeda's dream woman: shirtsleeves rolled, forearms artfully dusted with flour, and strong hands working that dough in a way that let Makeda *know* that if she'd given in to her urges in the Ferris wheel it would have been the best ten minutes of her sexual life.

"Dinner's almost ready," Beznaria said easily, as if she were an old friend of the family and not a total stranger who had forced herself into their lives. "I'm making my dad's homemade pizza. After tasting a slice on the boardwalk, I thought maybe you'd like to see what you're missing out on. Ibarania has the best pizza in the world."

Bez's familiarity, and the reminder of why she was being so friendly, forced Makeda back on the defense. Staying out all day had achieved nothing because the stress and confusion caused by Beznaria's presence resumed from where she'd left them, like she'd returned to a video game save point.

"I was going to cook," Makeda said stiffly. She stopped in the entryway next to Kojak, who knew better than to involve himself in kitchen business and was sulking as his gaze tracked the spinning pizza disc.

"I thought you decided you were being selfish now. Cooking for other people isn't selfish, is it?" Grandmore asked. "Besides, your pizza is always dry. The crust gets stuck all up in my throat."

Grandmore was still mad at Makeda, it seemed.

"Okay," Makeda said. "I'll go set the table while you two have your pizza-making date."

"I already set it," Bez said cheerily. "Why don't you sit? I can pour you a glass of wine."

Makeda frowned, hating the parts of her that wanted wine and wanted Beznaria to be the one to pour it. Grandmore cooked for her all the time but she couldn't remember the last time someone she was capable of having impure thoughts about on a Ferris wheel had tried to wine and dine her.

She has an agenda, she reminded herself. *She told you flat out that she does.*

"No, thanks," she said coolly. "There's silverware to—"

"Did it," Bez said.

Grandmore glanced at Makeda with a pained expression. "A tall, fine woman who does all the chores is cooking for us and offering you wine and you're sitting there pouting instead of locking that down. I have failed in my duties as your grandmother."

Makeda rolled her eyes and then leaned against the doorway, standing beside Kojak as they both watched Beznaria work.

"What am I supposed to do now?" Makeda sniped. "Just sit around?"

"That's an option. Do you ever do that?" Beznaria asked.

"Just sitting around is the least relaxing thing I could imagine," Makeda said. Doing things kept her occupied, and made her feel useful. If she wasn't useful, then what was left?

She shifted against the wood, standing up a bit straighter.

"Ah, some people are like that, I suppose. How was your day?" Beznaria asked as she effortlessly spun a disc of dough. "After our turn on the Ferris wheel?"

The spinning disc wobbled—Makeda wouldn't have noticed if she wasn't staring at it so hard to avoid looking at Makeda's flour-dusted forearms and strong hands.

"Fine," Makeda said, and then because it felt too rude not asking, "How was yours?"

"It was excellent. I went to the arcade, where I won many prizes. I also stopped in at a casino to try a slot machine." She frowned as she worked the dough. "I had a slight altercation with a worker, who tried to blame me for breaking the arm off a slot machine. I told them that it wasn't my fault that they use machines that rely on pressing a button but they still attached an arm to pull."

Makeda pressed her lips together, refusing to laugh, though she could fully imagine Beznaria wielding a slot machine arm like a sword as she made a daring escape through the casino floor.

Bez sighed. "I may be on some kind of casino's most wanted list, so I'll have to lay low until I leave."

Makeda took the opportunity to reassert her rudeness. "Great, so you're heading to Ibarania soon?"

Beznaria should have been annoyed by this, but the look she tossed over her shoulder was not only indulgent, it was familiar—as if after just a few days Beznaria already had Makeda's number. Like they were friends. Like this whole comfortable scene wasn't just an act to make Makeda lower her defenses. And like Beznaria had meant it when she'd said, *"I'll be happier if you come with me."*

"We are," Bez said without the slightest bit of doubt, and Makeda pushed off the door frame and stalked off. She'd meant to head to her room, but ended up going to the dining room to straighten Bez's place settings, and then sitting because she wouldn't hide anymore after wandering around the entire day. If that meant she had to share dinner with the investigator, she'd survived worse.

Makeda held onto her coolness as the pizza was served and wine was poured, and even as she tussled with Beznaria, who tried to tuck a napkin into Makeda's collar; she held on as if her life depended on it, because it did. She'd faltered in the Ferris wheel, but she had to be steadfast against the pull of the investigator's chaotic charms. It was the only way to keep herself safe.

The pizza, with a spicy homemade tomato sauce, perfect crust, and delicious mixture of mozzarella, parmigiana, and haloumi, was the second best she'd ever tasted, but she didn't compliment the chef.

She didn't join in the dinner conversation, even when Beznaria and Grandmore talked about their travels, and she had questions about places like Ghana and Italy and London. Grandmore loosened up and tried to prod Makeda into joining the discussion by talking about her charity work, but eventually rolled her eyes and gave up after getting grunts in response. Beznaria talked about her job at the WFM and made it sound mysterious and intriguing, but didn't look directly at Makeda over the course of dinner.

Makeda sipped her wine and wondered why her newfound boundaries felt even lonelier than giving everything for nothing. After dinner, Beznaria went to her room, likely to look up more ways to annoy Makeda, and Grandmore took her tablet to the living room to video chat with her friend in Georgia. Makeda opened her email on her phone, but when she saw the numerous volunteer requests that marked the start of summer, she sighed and put it away.

She still wanted to help, but the strangest fear seized her—that if she agreed to do one thing, she had to agree to do them all. It had been the same at work and in her relationships. The same with her mother. Makeda felt guilty about not responding, but her near-empty inner watering can left her without the energy to do more.

When the B&B's phone rang, she jogged over to the reception desk to answer it, glad for something to do besides feel sorry for herself.

"Golden Crown Bed-and-Breakfast, Makeda speaking. How may I help you?"

"Hey, Keda. It's me." Her mother's voice, speaking in that familiar but tentative tone she'd been using since Makeda was a teenager. The hoarse strain of someone who'd messed up speaking around the enormity of what had happened instead of just hocking up something more than a trite apology. "You doin' good?"

"Hey, Mom." Makeda heard the flutter of panic in her voice and swallowed. "I'm okay. What's up? You don't usually call this late."

"My mother told me about the investigator," Ashley Hicks said with a tight laugh. Makeda hated that laugh; it was more of a vocal tic than an expression of amusement. "Kinda funny that they ignored me for years, but now apparently someone just showed up on the doorstep looking for you?"

More tight laughter.

"Yeah," Makeda said bleakly. "Funny."

Her mom cleared her throat. "I—I debated about whether to talk to you about this, prayed on it with Bill, and . . . I wasn't always a good mother, but I'm still yours, and I wanted to see how you were doing."

Makeda sighed. "You mean 'see what I'm going to do'?"

A pause. A guilty chuckle. "I guess that, too."

Fear filled Makeda with a fizzy dread, like when someone knocked over a soda display at the GrabRite, pushing at the cap of her calm. Her mother sounded off in a way that she hadn't for years, and even though Makeda was a grown-up now, it was terrifying to finally let herself imagine all the ways in which Beznaria Chetchevaliere's arrival might send her mother careening back into obsession.

Their shared secret that had once filled Makeda with joy had played out like a fairy tale, but the ones where the protagonists ruined their lives chasing what wasn't meant for them instead of being happy with what they had. Her mother had thought herself a Cinderella, but she'd been the evil stepmother, willing to sacrifice anything to the altar of royal recognition—even her daughter. And now here she was, dipping her toe back into the obsession that had ruined both of their lives.

"It wouldn't be smart or healthy to get involved with this. For either of us," Makeda said firmly. "I know that this kind of thing isn't for me; I've had years to think on it and even more to come to that conclusion. And we know what happened with *you* last time. You don't need to be thinking or praying on this. You need to forget it and focus on the good stuff you have going on in your life right now."

There was a pause and then her mother launched into her sales pitch, a familiar aggressive frustration in her tone. "It's just . . . the princess stuff isn't that big of a deal, is it? Things are different now; you're grown and nobody's gonna tease you."

"Mom."

"Couldn't you use the money? The chance to get out and see the world? It's not like you have anything tying you down."

Having something that should have tied her down hadn't stopped her mother from doing what she wanted, but Makeda didn't say that.

"Let's not talk about this," Makeda said. "We haven't for years, and when we did before it never ended well."

"I just don't think you're thinking this through," her mother pushed, ignoring Makeda's request. "This is what we wanted, isn't it? All those trips to the consulate, all our research? And I know you're not religious, but if this is happening now, don't you think that means it's *meant* to happen? Why turn away a blessing?"

"We have different ideas of blessing," Makeda replied, trying to keep her cool as heat pressed at the corners of her eyes. "This is more like a curse to me."

One that had faded away but clearly had not been broken.

There was a long pause.

"Are you rejecting this because you think it'll hurt me?" her mother asked in a small voice.

"I did wonder how you'd feel," Makeda admitted, tapping her toe against the wood siding of the desk. "Since you were the one who cared about being a princess. But that's not—"

"No, I mean are you refusing to follow up on this as some kind of . . . revenge against me?" her mother asked, and Makeda felt the question like a fist in the stomach. "Are you throwing this chance away because you still haven't forgiven me for the—the difficulties we went through all those years ago?"

"You think I'm the kind of daughter who would do something explicitly to *hurt you*?" Makeda's voice was rough and incredulous and she tried to even out the troughs of pain. "After everything, that's what you think of me?"

A tremor moved through her and didn't stop, leaving her shaking with rage.

She'd done nothing but help her mother. Listen to her daydreams. Supported her when everyone else watched her fall apart just because there might be a damn tiara waiting for her in some far-off land, and then helped pick up the pieces. No one bothered to check if Makeda had any fractures herself; she was supposed to just go on as if nothing had happened.

She hadn't even been a burden afterward by asking for money or time or attention—or an apology. And now she was being accused of being the one causing pain?

She wasn't sure she'd ever been so angry. Usually she stuffed it all down, but it wouldn't stay where it was supposed to. All her usually repressed feelings finally pushed politeness out of the driver's seat.

"I can't believe you would say that to me," Makeda bit out. "Forgiving you doesn't mean I need to go on some wild quest after a heritage I don't even care about, but the fact that you think it does isn't surprising. You always put this imaginary royal version of me ahead of the real me who just wanted you to—to—"

Makeda clamped her mouth shut. She was angry but she still had that internal shutdown valve that stopped her from hurting someone too badly. She didn't know what her mother would do if she heard the unvarnished truth—that Makeda had just wanted her to be a good mother. That she still wanted her to.

"No, that came out wrong. I didn't mean . . ." Her mother sighed. "I always mess everything up when I try to be close with you. It's something that should connect us but . . . Look, I just don't want you doing anything to hurt yourself because you want to hurt me."

"The only time I hurt myself was *helping* you, but thanks for your newfound concern," Makeda said, not recognizing the acid in her tone.

"I'll let you go, baby," her mother said in that tired, forlorn way that would keep Makeda up later when the guilt set in. "Didn't want to bother you or bring up the past. Just wanted you to think about your future."

"Trust that I am. I've always been the one thinking and planning for the future in this family because if I didn't no one else would. Bye, Mom," Makeda said, then sighed and added, "Love you."

"Love you, too."

Makeda placed the portable phone on the cradle, blinking away tears of frustration. She was supposed to see this princess thing as a gift? A blessing? It was a curse that would never loosen its grip on her family, that could surge up and destroy everything.

Hearing that thread of hope in her mother's voice made the precariousness of the situation much too real. This chapter of the obsessive fairy tale needed to be closed, permanently, and she would do the closing.

She scraped together the rudeness she'd been cultivating as she marched up the stairs, and then knocked loudly on Beznaria's door. She'd barely removed her hand when the door swung open.

The investigator, still dressed in her slacks and dress shirt with the sleeves rolled up, took a step forward, leaned against the door frame, and looked down at her. Her hair was tucked behind her ears, and her eyes were more serious than Makeda had expected behind her smudgy glasses lenses. Makeda regretted having installed the vintage light bulbs that threw a soft, luminous highlight over Beznaria's cheekbones and full mouth.

"I thought you didn't want to be bothered, but here you are at a strange woman's door just before bedtime." Beznaria's grin spread slowly, revealing the gap in her teeth, but her gaze was still probing. "Did you change your mind about being tucked in, or did you need something else?"

"What I need to know is when you're leaving," Makeda said. "This is getting out of hand."

"What exactly is out of hand about my staying?"

"You're a stranger."

"In a strange land, yes," Beznaria mused. "Though a kind woman did tolerate my presence for at least fifteen minutes today."

Makeda flexed her fingers in agitation. "You showed up out of nowhere trying to convince me to go to Ibarania, and now you're just here fixing things and chatting with Grandmore, and following me out to the boardwalk." *And almost kissing me on Ferris wheels*, her brain unhelpfully added. "This is way out of hand."

"Do you only allow people you know to pay or barter for a room? That doesn't seem like a very sound business plan."

Makeda gritted her teeth. "Can you just tell me why you're here?"

If the investigator left, Makeda could tell her mother there had been a mistake. That they'd found out Keshan had just been some dude from South Jersey running a grift to get women into bed. She hated lying, but she would do anything to prevent her mother from backsliding, and Ashley Hicks was currently at the tipping point.

Beznaria wiggled her nose as if resetting her glasses. "I believe I've been quite clear about why I'm here."

"I mean why you're still here. Why you think you can convince me to go with you when I said no." Her neck hurt from glaring up at Beznaria, but she refused to take a few steps back or go get a step stool. "I can't be that important to you as a princess prospect. Can't you just grab someone off the street? What's the difference?"

Beznaria tilted her head to the side in that owlish move that Makeda found simultaneously endearing and enraging. "If I were, *hypothetically*, capable of grabbing someone off the street, perhaps by injecting them with a sedative or slipping one into food I had prepared for them . . ."

Makeda swallowed hard and wondered if she should have eaten that fourth slice of pizza as she pretended to ignore the dinner conversation.

"If I were going to expend the tremendous energy that goes into the takedown and . . . legally questionable transport of another human, I would be quite sure to grab the person I believe to be the actual heir. That's you. Are you suggesting I grab *you*, sea snail?"

Beznaria asked the disturbing question in a benign tone, but her mischievous gaze was a warm caress against Makeda's skin.

"You know that's not what I'm suggesting," Makeda said, ignoring the nickname and the throb of expectation at the idea of Beznaria touching her, pulling her close . . .

"That's too bad because I *will* do what you ask of me, within reason," Beznaria replied.

Makeda pushed through the haze of innuendo. "You mean if it fits your agenda. I've asked you to leave twenty times and you haven't."

"Leaving behind the probable heir when my mission is to find the probable heir isn't reasonable," Beznaria said, pushing up her glasses—adding another smudge to the collection that had been paining Makeda since Beznaria's arrival, and something in her snapped.

This was one irritation that could be easily remedied, unlike the ninety-nine other problems in her life.

"Hand over your glasses," Makeda said.

Beznaria whipped them off and handed them over without question. Apparently, this request was reasonable. Makeda marched over to the side table in the hallway, pulled out a microfiber cloth to swipe over the lenses, and then marched back. When she got to Beznaria, she didn't just hand the glasses over. She walked right up to her, close enough to feel the heat of her body, and reached up with both hands to place the glasses onto her face.

She told herself that she was exhibiting her dominance, like an animal nipping at an interloper's ear to remind it of its place in the hierarchy. The problem was that if she were acting on pure animal instinct, she wouldn't have wanted to chase Beznaria away.

The investigator was stock-still as Makeda placed the glasses on her face, except for the deep rise and fall of her chest. Her exhale was a brush of warmth against the skin on Makeda's inner elbow and that warmth spread through her, mixing with all the confusing and conflicting feelings the strange woman inspired.

She started to pull her hands away, but Beznaria reached up to catch her wrists and hold them in place.

"What are you doing?" Makeda asked, trying to sound annoyed but the word came out husky and low. She could feel the race of her pulse where Beznaria's fingertips pressed lightly against the sensitive skin at her inner wrists.

"I'm adjusting," Beznaria said, blinking at her. "Do you know why I don't clean my glasses often?"

"To torture me?" Makeda asked.

"No, but that is duly noted as an effective method of torture." Beznaria tilted her head a little, her grip on Makeda's wrists tightening a fraction and then loosening. "It's because there is a tiny bit of magic in the moment when my glasses go from dirty to clean, where everything is crisp and clear and beautiful."

If what had happened on the Ferris wheel was a near kiss, Makeda didn't know what to call this. She'd never thought dirty glasses talk was her kink, but she was discovering new things about herself all the time.

Every part of her wanted Beznaria to pull her into the room and close the door. To pull her into the bed and fuck her until she couldn't think, couldn't care about Ibarania or her mother or any of the mess of the past that was trying to drag her back in, even though Bez was the epicenter of that mess's resurgence.

"If you cleaned them more often, you could have those moments all the time," Makeda somehow managed, not even sure she was making sense.

Beznaria leaned close to Makeda's ear. "I'm very good at denying myself pleasure. I find it makes it much more satisfying when I finally give in. What about you?"

"I'm good at denying myself, but I've never given in," Makeda said in a low voice.

"Try it," Beznaria urged, and this was one thing Makeda wouldn't say no to.

Instead of overthinking, she tilted her mouth toward Beznaria's and went for it, just as Beznaria did the same. It was wonderful for the millisecond that their lips brushed, that spark jumping between them again and the anticipation of what was to come making her lightheaded. Unfortunately, all of the need throbbing through Makeda that had propelled the impulsive motion didn't allow her to pump the brakes in time; her bottom lip smashed right into Beznaria's front teeth, the sudden pain pulling her to her senses just in time for regret to flood in.

She pulled away from Beznaria, bringing her hands to her mouth. "Ow!" Her tongue swept over the ragged cut on her inner lip and she tasted iron.

Beznaria was looking down at her, eyes wide and hand over her own mouth.

"Oh god," Makeda whispered again, this time in humiliation. Of course, she'd busted her own lip while trying to be sexy and impulsive. It was better this way. She definitely should *not* be kissing this woman, and maybe some higher being was making that clear. "I'm so sorry. I shouldn't have—I'm sorry!"

Beznaria moved her lips back and forth, then shrugged. "I'm fine. What about you. Are you hurt?" She raised a hand toward Makeda's face. "Let me see."

Makeda jerked back, her hand-eye coordination suddenly spectacular. "Why, so you can see how ridiculous I am with your new 4D vision? So you can laugh at my swollen lip? I'm fine." She dropped her gaze to the ground and stared at Beznaria's sock-clad feet, then sighed and lowered her hands.

Beznaria didn't touch her face, but she knew the woman was examining her from a few feet away. "Put some ice on it."

Makeda rolled her eyes. "I know."

She'd marched upstairs to finally take control of the situation, and somehow this was the result. Standing like a fool with a self-inflicted injury while replaying the moment she'd crashed mouth-first into Beznaria over and over again.

"Who laughed at you?" Beznaria asked quietly. "Who made you think you were laughable?"

Makeda didn't think she could be any more embarrassed, but now Beznaria felt sorry for her.

It wasn't as if the taunts from the past suddenly filled her head, but the shame that she had felt then returned, as did the shame she felt for never having moved past the bullying and having somehow invited it. At having supported her mother for all these years only to be asked if she was trying to spite her. At having tried to kiss the woman who'd brought all this back up to the surface.

"It doesn't matter," Makeda said, taking a few steps back and shoving her hands into her pockets.

"It does," Beznaria said, frowning. "They've made my goals much more difficult to obtain."

Of course that was why she wanted to know. Her regret sharpened into a spike of humiliation.

"Thanks for your concern." Makeda started to walk to her room.

"Hypothetically," Beznaria called out behind her. "If I were hypothetically capable of grabbing someone off the street and engaging in certain activities that are legally gray but morally righteous, like explaining to someone how wrong they were to laugh at a young girl for thinking she might be a princess, having their names might make such a hypothetical task easier."

Makeda whirled around. "Wait. Are you telling me that leaving me alone is unreasonable but tracking down my bullies over a decade later isn't? That's ridiculous."

"Yes," Beznaria said. She was still again, but not in anticipation as she had been a moment ago. This was the stillness of repressed motion. "It's quite reasonable. I have a rubric and it falls dead in the reason zone. There isn't a statute of limitations on making someone aware of their bad behavior. If it's still hurting you all of these years later, why shouldn't they hurt a bit, too?"

Makeda's throat went rough. Her mother and even Grandmore made it seem like Makeda should just . . . move on. *Leave the past in the past.* The fact that her mother thought she was trying to get revenge for said past had made her feel ill. Beznaria was here ready to roll up on Tonya Smith from third period algebra, who probably didn't even remember Makeda had ever existed, and show her what's what because she didn't think it was bad to make people pay for hurting you.

Pleasure worked its way into her system. Not sexual, but a kind of light, all-over tingling, as if Bez's words had just exfoliated away a layer of Makeda's distress.

She's just trying to win you over.

Are you really this gullible?

Maybe a little, if not enough for Bez to get what she wanted.

"Please don't go legally ambiguous on any of my old classmates," Makeda said.

"Classmates," Beznaria said. "I see. And you went to Atlantic City High School . . ."

"I'm serious," Makeda said. "Don't."

Beznaria sighed as if not being allowed to track down and harass Makeda's tormentors was the pinnacle of unfairness, and then nodded. "Fine. Is there anything else you need?"

Makeda briefly allowed herself to think of how a careless and selfish person might respond to a beautiful woman framed seductively against the backdrop of a four-poster bed asking what they needed. The desire that kept getting mixed up with her newfound anger flared in her again.

She ran her tongue over the painful cut in her mouth and thought about all the things that could be done that didn't require use of her own mouth.

"Keda! Who was on the phone? Was it your mother again?"

Most careless and selfish people thinking about seduction weren't in their grandmother's house, and Makeda was grudgingly glad that she was. If not, she might have been all in on whatever honeypot ruse Beznaria was trying to pull with her.

"Good night," she said to the still staring investigator. "Hopefully you'll be gone tomorrow."

"That depends on you," Beznaria replied, and shut the door, leaving Makeda in the dark hallway.

When she opened her own door, she noticed something hanging on the doorknob and remembered Bez mentioning winning a prize at the boardwalk. God, it was probably a princess plushy or a tiara or . . .

It was a scrunchy with a little plush snail on it and it made Makeda's sour mood start to rise when it should have made it plummet.

Beznaria was right, Makeda realized.

This did depend on her.

She was already giving in to the call of chaos, Ibaranian edition. She'd come upstairs to kick the investigator out but ended up sharing personal information and almost losing a tooth instead.

This was over.

No more cleaning glasses or getting Action Park in the panties from the overtures of a woman trying to seduce her into giving in.

She was definitely getting rid of Beznaria Chetchevaliere, and closing the door on the princess situation once and for all.

Chapter 7

As she lay on her back under the kitchen sink trying to remove a rusted lug nut, Bez gained a new item for her rotating list of sureties: home repair was a punishment sent from the abyss, despite all of the American TV shows that tried to make it look like fun.

She was adequate at making small repairs, but the things she'd been working on were a bit above her pay grade—she fervently hoped nothing she fixed ended up costing more due to Bez's handiwork. She was at least sure that the roof tiling she'd pulled up had been replaced correctly.

She was willing to repair every leaky pipe and cracked wall in the Golden Crown if it helped convince Makeda to return to Ibarania with her. Bez had just finalized how they would get there, working with a negative travel budget and lack of WFM support, and she was more than satisfied at what she'd managed to pull together.

Apart from her desire to restore her family's honor, Bez wasn't one for long-term planning; she generally leapfrogged from idea to idea, hoping she landed on lily pads large enough to support the weight of her current goal. She'd succeeded with finding a route home, but after her previous day with Makeda, with one near kiss and one bumbled one, she was beginning to wonder if she'd made a mis-hop.

The Ibaranian house music playing in her wireless earphones suddenly shifted to the sound of an incoming call—for a second Bez thought it was part of the song, then she fumbled with her phone in her pocket and pressed the button to accept the call.

"Beznaria Chetchevaliere, at your service," she said, returning to her work on the pipe.

"Yes, I know this," a gravelly and slightly aggrieved voice said. "I gave you this name, and I called the number to speak to you, of course it's Beznaria Chetchevaliere. You think I don't know this?"

Bez almost jumped up and hit her head against the pipe, but she slid out from under the sink instead, sitting in a crouch as she had when she was a girl listening to Henna Jeta's stories.

"Oh, it's you," Bez said. "I wish I hadn't picked up! Bah, you know I hate it when you call. It's terrible."

"Well, I love talking on the phone as much as I hate you." Henna Jeta laughed.

"I hate you, too, Henna," Bez said, her chest warm.

Bez was the only one of Jeta's grandchildren who still played the love/hate reversal game with her—everyone else found it exasperating, trying to figure out whether the old woman was joking or not, but Bez and her Henna always understood each other.

Almost always. Except when it came to Bez's unrelenting fascination with the past glory of the Chetchevalieres.

"I'm calling because that man has been sticking his nose around here," Henna Jeta said. "Hoghigs. Your boss."

"What?" Bez's brow creased. "He called you?"

She was somewhat surprised. She had skipped out on her return flight home to follow up on Ora Hicks's email, despite having been told not to, but her calls and emails to the WFM had been going ignored for days.

"A person can't stick their nose through the phone, Bezzie, come on," Henna Jeta scoffed. "He came here to our house. Talking down to me like I haven't bled better men than him on the end of my blade."

Bez's hands froze on the wrench. "Why did he come to the house? To look for me?"

"He said you didn't return to London and that you were officially classified as 'missing in action.' And me? What did I think? That this starfish-brain granddaughter of mine just emailed me a selfie from New Jersey. But I didn't tell him that." Henna Jeta paused. "I didn't tell him about anything. He kept asking about Aazi, too. And the day she disappeared. I told him he could read my official report since I'm old and can't remember."

The idea of Algernon Shropsbottomshireburrough interrogating her grandmother, a woman he wasn't fit to dust sand from and a warrior who'd fought invaders to preserve Ibarania while the Higgins-hoggins family had reaped the spoils of war in its temporary kingdom, made Bez consider leaving for Ibarania immediately just to demand a duel.

"I will talk to him," she said tightly. "And tell him to back off."

How she would manage to talk to him when he wasn't answering her calls was something she'd have to figure out, but this had gone too far now.

"It's not just him!" Henna Jeta said, aggrieved. "Everyone is asking now that they started this campaign. I'd made my peace with dishonor and these urchins clinging to old grudges. But now even the young people are starting to come up with theories on their social media. John came to ask me if it was true that I killed the queen."

Bez had never doubted her grandmother, but she was an investigator—she understood why other people did. Her grandmother was the only witness to the queen's disappearance, and her explanation was too vague even for Bez.

"Henna," Bez said. "It's okay. People don't blame you, they just don't understand that you would never do that."

"Yes, they do. And even if they don't, I blame me," Henna Jeta said. Her voice didn't waver, it didn't rise, and it was the strength in her tone that shook Bez. Her grandmother was putting effort into staying composed, which meant that she was more distraught than Bez had ever heard her.

"Everything will be okay," Bez said awkwardly, not knowing exactly how to console anyone, but particularly not the toughest woman in the known world. It was Henna Jeta who'd taught her to fight, both the stylized battle of the Royal Guard and the desperate no-holds-barred style of the Ibaranian docks. She'd taught Bez how to wield a sword, a knife, and any sharp object within reach. But those skills couldn't help stop gossip—they were the reason for the gossip. When a woman is known for her deadly skill and her ward goes missing, people only remembered how many ways she knew to kill someone, not that she'd honed those skills under an oath to protect.

"I'll fix everything," she said. "I promise."

"Ah, here we go. I know things are bad when I get pity from my grandchild who was just in diapers." Henna Jeta sighed. "My Bezzie, there is nothing for you to fix. I have told you this since you were small. My burden is not yours, understand?"

Bez rolled her shoulders. "And I have told you since I was small that I will never let you carry this alone. I'm not small anymore, Henna Jeta. I *will* help."

Bez heard footsteps coming down the hallway— light and cautious, the tread of a person always on the verge of hopping up to do things for others.

Except for me.

"You think you can beat me or something, talking to me like this? You're soft, with all these promises. I will have you on your ass and a knife at your throat before you know what hits you." Henna Jeta's voice was disgruntled, but in her usual way, so Bez allowed herself to chuckle in relief.

"I have to go, but don't worry," Bez said. "Don't forget that a Chetchevaliere never breaks a promise."

She'd bring Makeda back home with her and prove Henna Jeta was innocent.

"What does that mean, Bezzie? You know I hate this nonsense mystery talk. And what are you doing in New Jersey?"

"Picking up a souvenir for you," Beznaria said as Makeda walked in, chin up and bristling with a renewed aura of annoyance.

"Bezzie?"

"See you soon!"

She disconnected her call, then tugged out her earphones and tucked them into her pocket. She was still troubled by her grandmother's distress, but the sooner she talked Makeda into going, the sooner Henna Jeta would feel better.

"*Bonmera*," she called out to Makeda, receiving a grunt in response.

Ora Hicks kept trying to convince Bez that her granddaughter was a soft-spoken person who hated confrontation and could be easily convinced, which matched what Bez's own background check had pulled. But one reason Bez always tried to do her investigations in person was that data and secondhand accounts often had only a slight correlation to reality.

Makeda was stubborn—at least when interacting with Bez. She had softened during their previous encounters the day before, but she was back to active antagonism now. Good. Bez wanted to spar after hearing about Higginshoggins visiting her home, and she could take a few verbal jabs from Makeda as a distraction.

"I'm surprised you're not a morning person," Bez said. "Your grandmother keeps telling me you're kind and thoughtful and selfless, like some kind of Disney p—"

Makeda fixed her with an icy glare.

"—Ah, like a person who enjoys waking up early to sing to birds and feed stray kittens." Bez lay back down to get at the resistant nut under the sink, gripping the wrench hard.

"You don't have to be a morning person to do those things," Makeda grumbled as she stomped an unnecessary circle around Bez's outstretched legs. "Who wears a suit to fix pipes?"

"I do," Bez said.

"Do you prefer I wear something else?" Bez asked.

"I don't care what you wear and I don't care if you ruin it," Makeda said.

Bez smirked as her wrench slid off the lug nut yet again.

"You cared about my glasses enough to take them off and clean them yourself, it's only reasonable to assume you care as much about my clothes." Bez stopped fidgeting with the wrench. "Not that I'm implying you would take my clothes off to clean them like you did my glasses. Though if my jacket is any indication, your first instinct *is* to rip the clothing from my body."

A loud grinding sound filled the kitchen, and the scent of coffee mingled with the slightly moldy undersink smell.

"I could take it off," Bez mused loudly, speaking over the noise of the coffee grinder. "But that would mean working in my underwear. Your grandmother did invite me to treat the Golden Crown as my home while I'm here, I understand that Americans are very prudish about that sort of thing."

The pulses of the grinder became one continuous drone. Makeda seemed determined to ignore her and Bez didn't like it for reasons that had nothing to do with her need to bring Makeda back with her.

"How is your mouth?" Bez called out even more loudly. "Is your lip healing okay?"

The coffee grinder apparently had more settings than Bez's favorite vibrator because the noise grew even louder; the coffee had to be so fine it was no longer visible to the human eye at this point.

The grinder finally stopped. "I'm sorry about that. I shouldn't have just . . ."

"It was fine," Bez said, wrinkling her nose as rust flaked down on her from the lug nut that refused to budge. She probably should have given up on this repair, but a Chetchevaliere didn't stop just because something was impossible. "Well, not you splitting your lip, but the intention was perfectly understandable. I'm rather hard to resist."

She waited for a cutting response, and when she didn't get one, looked out from under the sink, catching a glimpse of Makeda's bare legs. Dainty feet, solid ankles, thick calves—Bez's view cut off at the hem of the yellow shorts hugging the smooth brown skin of Makeda's thighs and the hint of cheek beneath them. Above that, she already knew there was the flare of wide hips, the curve of a belly, and—

Bez tore her gaze away and focused on the lug nut, redirecting her energy toward the task at hand and not the ass that made her think *damn*. Bez wasn't one to abide by rules, but Makeda was technically off-limits to her, by the rules she'd set for herself and, if Makeda was truly the heir, by the blood oath sworn by Chetchevalieres through the ages. Still, even a stone-cold dame of the guard couldn't ignore that Makeda Hicks was thicker than a bowl of Henna Jeta's seaweed stew.

And they had almost kissed twice.

And Bez wouldn't mind if it almost or actually happened again, even if it was another semi-headbutt.

"Let's not talk about it anymore," Makeda said.

"All right," Bez said. "Though as you learned yesterday, telling me not to think about something makes me think about it all the more."

Makeda stepped over Beznaria to place something in the sink, and when Bez looked out from under the sink she saw that she was between Makeda's thighs. The lug nut she had been loosening suddenly twisted free, ricocheting in the confined space of the cabinet as the pipe came loose and drenched her in cold, stagnant water.

"Mutanna min diu!" Bez spluttered as her reflexes kicked in. She dropped the wrench and slid out from under the sink, landing on her knees right in front of Makeda for the second time since her arrival. When she swiped the sink water from her speckled lenses and looked up, Makeda was watching her with wide eyes. She held a polka-dotted

dish towel in her hands, which she was wringing reflexively.

"Your shirt is drenched."

It was among the more civil things the woman had said to her in the last four days, but there was nothing civil in the way she stared. Bez's wet shirt clung to her chest and Makeda's gaze followed suit.

A new surety rotated in—when a beautiful woman looked at you like *this*, it meant trouble. And this wasn't the first time Makeda Hicks had looked at her like this.

"It is, indeed. With unpleasant-smelling pipe water. Maybe I *will* have to work in my underwear." Bez plucked at the top button of her shirt, and Makeda squealed and threw the towel into her face. Bez was slightly disappointed she hadn't thrown herself again, but a towel was useful.

"Wait," Makeda said. "We sell T-shirts. I'll bring one for you."

Bez pulled the towel off her face in time to watch Makeda and her perfectly fitting shorts jog out of the kitchen, her long locks bouncing against her back. She returned a minute later holding a black cotton shirt. She held it up, the length of it reaching her mid-thigh. In yellow words emblazoned on black, it said Golden Crown B&B, with three small crowns stacked next to *B&B*.

"I think this is the right size," she said as she handed Bez the shirt.

"This is quite stylish. Thank you." Bez pulled her promise knife from her pants pocket, flipped it open with a flick of her wrist, and stabbed it through the shirt's fabric.

"What are you doing?" Makeda squealed, stepping back.

"You're very excitable when you stop scowling," Bez noted, then tuned Makeda out as she worked, paying attention to the path of the sharp blade. When she was done, she held up the two sleeves she'd just removed, making sure to flex her biceps as she did. "You see what my arms look like; if I'm not wearing a suit, I might as well give them breathing room. I'm going to remove my wet shirt now, avert your eyes if you wish."

Makeda hurried over to the coffee machine as Bez unbuttoned and removed her shirt quickly, slipped the T-shirt over her head, then ran a hand through her damp hair, which had waved up a bit. "All done."

Makeda turned with two mugs in hand. Her gaze zipped from Bez's hair to the tattoo covering her right arm from shoulder to elbow.

"I can put the shirt in the wash with the towel if you leave them there," Makeda said, stretching to pass a mug to Bez as if she didn't want to get too close. "It's decaf."

Beznaria was still kneeling on the floor and scuttled over to a dry spot on the floor to sit, crossing her legs comfortably in front of her. The mug had ceramic flowers on it, and the shape of them pressed warm into her palm. She clutched it tightly to make sure she didn't need to perform yet another shirt switch.

Makeda had listened two days ago when Bez had expressed her dislike of caffeine to Ora. Bez took a sip. And apparently the day before, too, when she'd mentioned liking hot chocolate packets mixed into her coffee if she did drink it. She was paying attention to Bez's details, rule four. Did that mean anything, other than Makeda was naturally observant of things that Bez generally didn't pay the slightest attention to without explicit instruction?

"Thank you," Bez said. Then sniffed it. "No poison? Laxative?"

Makeda took a sip from her matching mug, her eyes wide and dark brown and just as stimulating to Bez's senses as her drink.

"I guess those are fair questions since I haven't been entirely welcoming," Makeda said on a sigh.

"You haven't been welcoming at all," Bez corrected. "You threatened me with a Hoover and then a demon cat during our first encounter."

Makeda grimaced. "Your presence is bringing up things I'd thought were in the past. I've been on edge these last few days."

"Is that why you attempted to bash my teeth out with your lips last night?" Bez asked. "Is this a fighting style found on the mean streets of Atlantic City?"

"On second thought, I'll continue being mean to you, because it's what you deserve," Makeda said wryly, but she didn't turn around and leave like she would have before last night.

Progress.

"No need to apologize," Bez said with a casual shrug, though she imagined those things had to do with the call she'd overheard the night before. She'd stayed up late looking through the Ibaranian Embassy's file on Ashley Hicks. She'd perused it before to verify that the claim had been made and rejected and, upon closer inspection, found that the embassy had named Ashley a persona non grata. She was someone to be escorted off embassy premises thanks to her erratic behavior regarding her claim to the throne.

Bez had grown up with a family proud of its heritage but not consumed by it; Henna Jeta often asked her to not care as much as she did. How would she have felt if her grandmother had tried to force her to care about it? If she had made it seem more important than Bez herself?

"I'm not apologizing," Makeda said. "Just acknowledging that I haven't been very hospitable. I think you can understand why having an intruder show up and try to force me into a spotlight that burns would make me irritable."

"That's fine, too. I'm used to people being mean to me."

Makeda's gaze jerked to Bez as if pulled by a string, and Bez saw something familiar in her expression—protectiveness. It was usually Bez doing the protecting, and it was odd to have that look turned onto her. She realized it might lead to another *P* word—pity.

"No, no," Bez said, waving one of her hands. "I'm fine. I'm too much. I always have been, though it took me a while to understand that. I have four older siblings who are also too much, you see, so when I was at home my too-muchness was spread out among them, and my parents, and my Henna Jeta. When I started school and my too-muchness was in its more concentrated form, I learned that the average person can't handle it. That's acceptable to me. It means I end up surrounding myself with above average people in my personal life."

She didn't in fact have many close people in her personal life apart from her family, but like her investigator ranking, Makeda didn't need all of the details about that.

Makeda worked her bottom lip with her two front teeth as she regarded Bez, and her fingers flexed around the mug she held. Bez didn't know why, but she suddenly thought of a dog who'd been trained not to eat a biscuit and was balancing one on the tip of its nose.

"I understand that, in a way," Makeda said, softening a bit. Beznaria didn't want pity but she'd take it if it meant Makeda would be more receptive.

Bez downed the rest of her coffee. "Can I change the subject to what I want to talk about? I don't have much time here, and your background is far more interesting than mine."

Makeda laughed lightly, then leaned back against the counter. "I doubt that."

"It's about your strong anti-princess sentiments," Bez said, barreling past any talk that might bring up certain residual feelings about her time in maritime security. "In my line of work, I've seen people who are willing to do anything—lie, forge, cause grievous bodily harm—to get the chance to meet royalty. To *become* royalty? I've seen people do things you simply wouldn't believe. But you seem angry at the possibility. Why? Please at least let me know why I failed to convince you."

"Because I know what happens when you buy into the fairy tale hype." Makeda lifted the heel of one of her sock-clad feet to rub the ankle of the other. "Sure, the money would be nice, and so would a free trip. But that doesn't change how I feel about everything else."

"And how do you feel?" Bez asked, trying to carefully insinuate herself into a crack in Makeda's emotional fortress so she could settle in for her last siege.

"Like I'm just a regular person," Makeda said. "Look at me. Dropping a crown on my head or sticking me in a ball gown would just be *me* in a crown and a ball gown."

Bez studied her. "And this is a bad thing?"

"It would be silly."

"Ah, the film heroine who doesn't know her worth. Right. Well, I'm going to have to disagree with you. My glasses are clean now, and even when they weren't, I could see there's nothing silly at all about you, in or out of a ballgown."

"Well, you can join my mom in the 'Makeda is a princess' club. Everyone else, and I mean *everyone* else, found the idea that I could be one fucking hilarious," Makeda said. She tugged at the bottom of her shirt with her free hand before shoving it into the pocket of her shorts.

Ah. The opening expanded and Bez shoved the tip of her proverbial lance into it before it could close.

"The royal family generally wore loose-fitting trousers regardless of gender. When a royal family is descended from a pirate queen, their conventions are a bit different than what you've read in fairy stories, and most people aren't fool enough to laugh at them about it."

Makeda's chin lifted and when her gaze met Bez's, interest shimmered in her eyes.

"See, this is why I *know* my grandmother or Prince Keshan is lying. If I was really the long-lost Ibaranian heir, between this Queen Lalla and Grandmore I should be some kind of badass who gives nary a fuck about what other people think, or what they need. I'm not. I'm . . ."

She gestured toward herself with both hands, a sweep up and down her body that Bez's gaze followed intently: the soft curve of her shoulders, the swell of her breasts delicately tugging the buttons of her pineapple-covered Hawaiian shirt, the press of her shorts into those thighs.

Makeda cleared her throat and Beznaria pushed her glasses so far up her nose that her lashes brushed against the lenses. She tried to look like she hadn't just been on an extended tour of Makeda's specific Hicks lines and said, "Caring what people think and need is a form of badassery. Especially when you've encountered people who don't deserve such grace."

That probably sounded like fancy words meant to flatter, but it was true. Bez didn't necessarily care what people thought, and often didn't understand, but she was a Chetchevaliere—a protector. She could fight and she could scheme, but caring for other people, even if it wasn't always in the way they expected her to, was in her DNA, too.

Makeda's fine brows pushed toward one another. "No. I don't think you understand. I'm a pushover."

"Like a clown," Bez said.

"Wow. I guess that's accurate, but that's a bit harsh."

"No, like the toy!" Bez said, laughing. "I had a terrifying clown toy that was my father's when he was a boy. You push it, it falls over, but then it pops back up because nothing can keep it down. A pushover."

"No, that's not what it means." Makeda crossed her arms over her chest and glowered down at Bez. "Nice. *Sweet.* Doesn't stand up for herself. Absolutely *not* a badass."

"I see," Bez said with a solemn nod, suppressing her grin.

The demon cat sauntered into the kitchen and walked straight toward Bez, climbing into her lap and settling there. Bez stiffened for a moment, but then looked down at the small creature and rubbed a fingertip over the wrinkled crown of its head.

"Hello, little friend. Perhaps you can make use of these." She grabbed one of the sleeves she'd cut off and slid it onto the cat. "Excellent. If one has a familiar, it should wear a matching outfit."

"I thought you were scared of Kojak," Makeda said, kneeling down in front of Bez and Kojak, who seemed to be pleased with his new outfit. "I can move him—"

"No," Bez said, reaching out to stay Makeda's hand. "I read up on these cats. Did you know that sometimes other cats reject them, simply because they look different? I am a Chetchevaliere, I do not join in the persecution of the downtrodden, whether they be human or feline. Kojak is now my friend and I'll make sure he always feels welcome. I won't fight animals, of course, but I will send disapproving looks at any cat rude enough to reject him! I will—"

She cut off her tangent.

"Kojak appreciates your passion," Makeda said, flashing her dimple of doom.

As Bez stared at her, Makeda reached out to pet the cat, too, but pulled her hand away when her fingertips bumped into Bez's.

"So far you've only told me what you don't want," Bez said. "Can you tell me what you do?"

Beznaria had said many things that visibly upset Makeda, but this was the first time the woman looked stricken. Her fingers curled into her palm, away from Bez's, and she stood abruptly.

"I should let you finish up with the sink," she said, then tossed off what had come to be a familiar jab between them. "Since you'll be leaving soon."

Bez nodded. "I will be leaving soon."

She'd heard back from her contact and her means home had arrived. Bez should be on it when it was ready to depart, but leaving for Ibarania without Makeda seemed like more than breaking a promise to her grandmother now.

"Oh. Well, that's good." Makeda started to walk away.

"Wait!" Beznaria called a bit too loudly. When Makeda turned around with raised brows, she hurried on. "I was thinking of taking a walk this evening, in case it's my last one here. To catch the sunset from the Ferris wheel before I go. Will you come with me?"

Makeda stared at her for a long moment, and then shook her head. "No. I think it's best for you, me, and my swollen lip if that doesn't happen."

When she left, Bez returned to the pipe she'd abandoned, collecting all the thoughts that crashed about in her head like waves at crosscurrents. She should be doing whatever it took to bring Makeda back to Ibarania, but that wasn't why she'd asked her out.

She had some inkling of the reason why she had, but decided it was just curiosity. She needed to know what Makeda wanted, and fast. If she found that out, she could use it to bribe her into going to Ibarania.

Wanting to know for any reason apart from strategy wouldn't bode well for a tenth generation dame of the guard.

Chapter 8

$\mathcal{M}$akeda tried not to feel anything about Beznaria leaving. She wanted the woman to go, and she was going to.

Problem solved.

Life would go back to normal. Except, there was no normal really. It wasn't that she didn't love her grandmother or get fulfillment from work at the B&B. But Beznaria had asked Makeda what she wanted, and Makeda had no answer that she could share.

So far you've only told me what you don't want.

Because that was how Makeda had lived her life: building contingency plans against the things she didn't want to happen, and searching for troubled waters even when the seas were clear. She always had goals and things to do, and those things generally improved the lives of others. But wants? Desires?

Those were way down deep in the watering can, weighted down with concrete blocks. Makeda couldn't think of what she wanted without thinking of what inevitably happened when she let herself hope, even a little bit. People laughed at her, or, the scarier prospect, they left. Her girlfriends had. Her mother had.

Beznaria hasn't.

It was the investigator's job to hound her into going to Ibarania, but Makeda had been ruder to the woman than she'd ever been with anyone. She'd called her annoying, ripped her clothes, accidentally mouth-butted her—she'd told her no so many times that it felt natural. And still Beznaria remained, cheerful and exasperating.

Except she *was* leaving, and soon.

"Good," Makeda said out loud.

Her cell phone rang and she jumped—her mother had called the B&B a few times that day, and Makeda had avoided picking up, afraid of what her mother might say and how she might respond to it. She'd heard Grandmore speaking to her mother in low tones, and Makeda's stomach had twisted in knots as she wondered what they were talking about.

Would it be Makeda's fault if her mother fell back into her obsession? Would her first attempt at selfishness turn out exactly how she had always feared—would putting herself first mean making someone else suffer?

But the current call was from GrabRite, which was a less existential annoyance.

"I told you I wasn't doing work for you anymore, Lindsey," Makeda said calmly. "Talk to Mr. Romano if you feel you aren't fit for the job."

"Oh, she definitely wasn't fit," Mr. Romano said, teasing vexation in his voice. "Corporate learned the hard way. Things have not gone well over the last few months, and now that we have an actual quarterly report . . . they want you back."

"What?" Makeda's head spun. This was so far from what she'd expected when she picked up the phone. "You're giving me my old job back?"

"I'm giving you mine actually," he laughed. "They're transferring me to the new store opening up—closer to my house—and I recommended you to replace me. Once they saw the mess Lindsey had made of things, well, I got reamed out, but they recognized their mistake. Can you start in a month?"

Pleasure surged through her—no, not pleasure. Purpose. She didn't need to think about what she wanted anymore. She would have a job. She'd make money to pay off the debt from Amber's business. No need for confusion, just work and goals and life sorting itself out for her without confusing feelings like anger and a hunger for Bez's mouth that had resulted in bodily injury.

"A month. Of course. Thank you, Mr. Romano."

"Corporate will email with details," he said. "Congrats, Makeda."

Makeda stood with her phone in her hand. She was so close to being rid of the investigator, a situation she definitely didn't have conflicted feelings about at all. She had a great job lined up, one that she'd worked hard for.

Everything was falling into place for her. Her life could go back to how it had been before—her days planned and orderly. Her skills put toward helping others. Her watering can would refill and she'd be kind and helpful again.

That was what she wanted, she could tell Beznaria, even if some part of her wondered if it would be the truth.

It didn't matter either way; it had to be the truth for now.

Grandmore shuffled into the dining room, expression pensive. "We need to talk," she said, sitting down heavily.

"Is this your last attempt to convince me I'm missing out on Ibarania?" Makeda asked, then tugged her lips up into the smile that had come so naturally to her just a few months ago. "Well wait until you hear who just called me. It was—"

"If it's the same person who called me, it was the bill collector," Grandmore said, and her tone was one that Makeda had rarely ever heard—dead seriousness.

Makeda's celebratory mood crashed into the wall of Grandmore's foreboding look. "What are you talking about?"

"Why didn't you tell me about the debt?" Grandmore asked.

"Debt?" Makeda tried to figure out what Grandmore was talking about. There was no way she knew about—

"The loan you cosigned for Amber Vincent. That she stopped paying so it fell onto you. Who has equity in the Golden Crown B&B."

Makeda felt sick. Absolutely sick. She'd thought she had everything under control, but she hadn't considered that this could hurt her grandmother in any way.

"I've been trying to take care of it," she said weakly. Even if it had just been the minimum payment, it had been something.

"It got sent to collections," Grandmore said. "I'm not mad, even though I warned you about that girl, but I'm not going to lose my home because of one of your little friends."

"I just got offered a job at GrabRite," Makeda said feebly. "It starts in a month."

"Do you think the collection company is going to wait for you to get your first paycheck two months from now? For a house in a prime vacation rental area in the middle of renewal? They'll knock this place down and turn it into a condo full of Airbnbs."

"What about Mom and Bill? Can they chip in and I'll pay her back?" Her mother had the stability she'd never given to Makeda and it would be nice if she could spare a bit of it for once. Makeda had never asked for anything before, and now would be a great time to cash in her guilt chips.

"Your mother and Bill are having a rift because she started talking about maybe going to Ibarania if you don't. He called me to discuss it." Grandmore's expression was weary. "If I ask her for money when she knows that there's money supposedly waiting over there . . ."

Her grandmother made a pained sigh, and Makeda remembered she wasn't the only one worried about her mother even if Grandmore didn't always express it.

Makeda laughed a little, the laugh of a driver who'd successfully weaved their way through a ten-car pileup only for their brakes to give out right as they approached a cliff.

"Keda . . . I don't want it to happen like this, but I don't want to lose the B&B and I don't think you do either." Grandmore rubbed the space between her eyebrows. "This is a mess."

Makeda stood up, shaky on her legs. "I'll be back. I have to think."

There was nothing to think about really, but she felt hemmed in, and maybe the beach and the familiar, limitless horizon would soothe her. She wouldn't be alone for long, she figured; there was blood in the water now and Beznaria would show up eventually.

It took longer than expected; the sun had started to set when a long lean shadow stretched over the sand toward her.

"Do you have anything to do with the lien on the B&B?" Makeda asked bluntly. "You apologized in advance for making me come with you, and now I'm between a rock and a hard place and you're here with the grease."

"I don't know the difference between a rock, which is hard due to its nature, and a hard place, but I assure you I didn't put you there." Bez dropped down beside her in a fluid movement. "I knew about your debt and I'll admit I'm capable of meddling in such a way to get what I want. I didn't this time, even though it would have saved me a lot of trouble. I could have arranged it before I arrived on your doorstep, along with a series of other calamities, and you would have been so grateful when I showed up offering money to save you that you would have—" Bez's gaze dropped to her mouth, then out to sea. "You would have agreed immediately."

Makeda gave her a withering look. "Thanks for enacting the slightly less villainous plan of breaking into the B&B and refusing to leave until you got what you wanted."

"You're welcome," Bez said with a nod and a mock bow.

"I guess I should just believe you then. Of course this was the result of conveniently timed bad luck and not the investigator from a shady organization who threatened to grab me off the street."

"I asked if you wanted me to grab you, I didn't threaten," Beznaria corrected. "And instead of assuming it's bad luck, it might make you feel better to think of it as fate."

"Same difference," Makeda said, wrapping her hands around her shins as she watched the sun drop a bit closer to the horizon and the sky grow incrementally darker.

She'd wanted to have this win, to not cave about the one thing she'd ever stood fast about in her entire life. This was fate all right; some people were destined to do as they pleased and others to do what needed to be done.

"You know where this debt came from?" Makeda asked wryly.

"Your ex-girlfriend, Amber Vincent, resident of Linden, New Jersey, former owner of Party Puppers, a business that was, I suppose, just ahead of its time."

"She kept talking about this business she wanted to try, and asking me about how we got loans for the B&B. And it was never explicit pressure, just little comments here and there, or comments about how she couldn't figure anything out." Makeda shook her head. "And I just dove right in and started doing everything for her, all the things she needed to know how to do herself, because I wanted to be useful. Needed. Things had started to get weird with us, but when we talked about the business planning all she did was tell me how amazing I was."

"I think most people wouldn't be immune to that," Beznaria said diplomatically, and Makeda scoffed.

"I cosigned the loan because I thought . . . it was the kind of commitment that meant she would stay. But she dumped me, and eventually she dumped her loan on me. And I always do stuff like that. Do things for other people like a little lap dog, even when they don't explicitly ask. I wanted this time, with you, to be different. I wanted to say no."

"You did say no," Bez said, kicking her shoes off and digging her toes into the sand. "You didn't change, the circumstances did."

"I don't want to deal with this," she said. "I know this is my own fault for cosigning the loan, but I am so tired of having to *deal* with everything."

Makeda knew she was being dramatic, that she'd been dramatic at nearly every point since her grandmother had brought up the royal heir search, but her frustration boiled up in her, burning her from the inside.

The truth was she wanted something that wasn't being a princess, but that wasn't having her life's path determined by what she did and didn't do for others.

"Did you look at the back of the business card I gave you when I introduced myself?" Bez asked.

"Why would I do that? Information is on the front of business cards," she said peevishly, then sighed. "No, I didn't."

Her eyes stung, and she pressed her lips together as reality started to sink in. Her mother had won. It was a psychological war that Makeda had tried to opt out of for two decades, but Ashley Hicks would get what she wanted: Makeda in a frilly dress, grinning and bearing it as people judged whether she was princess material. Her mother would be jealous as Makeda suffered, not caring that Makeda was doing it to preserve the life her mother made without taking her daughter's needs into account.

She scrunched her nose—not quite a sniffle, but almost—and Bez handed her a tissue, still warm from the pocket she'd pulled it from, and then another copy of her business card.

"Turn the card over," Bez said, and then leaned back, pressing her palms into the sand. A warm evening breeze whipped her hair around her face, the ends of her bob dancing around her jawline as the rays of the setting sun hit her.

Makeda dragged her eyes away and flipped the card over to find an inscription in handwriting.

" 'Beznaria Chetchevaliere, Commendatore, Damsel in Distress Rescue Services, LTD.' What does this mean?"

She turned her head to look at Beznaria, who'd been staring majestically out to sea and whose expression shifted to one of slight annoyance. She leaned over to tap her index finger on each word as she spoke. "Beznaria Chetchevaliere, that's me. Commendatore, that's my rank, sounds much cooler than CEO, no? Damsel in Distress Rescue Services, that's my side gig; I help people who are in sticky situations."

Makeda stared at Bez for a moment. The investigator was calm, sure of herself. Almost comforting. Not rubbing it in her face or making jokes, even though she'd gotten what she wanted.

She jerked her attention back to the card, studying the handwriting that was somehow both loopy and angular. "What, you save people from dragons? Or cut them loose when they're tied to train tracks by a villain twirling his mustache?"

"I've executed one train rescue," Beznaria said. She squinted, then pushed her glasses up onto the top of her head, where it nestled in the strands of her hair. "No, two. Two train rescues. No one was tied to the tracks in either instance."

Makeda carved a line through the cool sand with the card, watching as the grains filled in the furrow it left in its wake, erasing it. She had a million questions, but asked the one that made her heart beat a little faster.

"And you're offering to rescue me?"

She expected Bez to say something brazen or bizarre, in that way she had of making even a direct response as confusing as trying to exit the Garden State Parkway.

But when Beznaria responded her tone was serious. "Yes."

Makeda turned and found those honey brown eyes fixed on her, revealing not a hint of anything other than determination. She realized that because Bez said odd and unexpected things, she'd started to treat Bez the same way others treated her because of her own drive to give—as if she shouldn't be taken seriously. It was one thing to be irritable, to be more easily annoyed, to even be mean—but those things were different from deciding someone wasn't worth listening to.

"How would you do it?" she asked.

Makeda didn't get her hopes up. People often talked a lot of game about what they'd do, whether on neighborhood committees or in more intimate relationships, and in the end she did all the work. But still, she was a businesswoman beneath all the layers of people pleasing. She'd hear her out.

"The solution for one aspect of your situation is simple. You need money. The prospects in the royal heir search get a participation fee. That fee is enough to cover your debt."

Makeda twisted her mouth to the side. "So your rescue gig has the same end result for me as your investigator gig. How convenient."

"This solution certainly works out for me, but it's also the most reasonable one," Beznaria said, sliding her glasses from her forehead back down to her nose. "I can't offer every damsel with money woes a guaranteed fifteen thousand dollars with the possibility of much more. Yes, I want you to go to Ibarania with me, but I'm also offering the only solution to your problem at hand."

Makeda's fingers sank into the sand; the fine grains roughed against her knuckles as her hand curled into a fist. *Fifteen thousand?* She hadn't realized that was the door prize for this—she'd only been thinking about being a princess and how terrible it would be. If she separated the unpleasant emotions linked to the Ibaranian situation, there was money on the table when she needed money fast, and that was the bottom line.

"I don't know," she said, even though she already did, because she knew the investigator would indulge her reticence.

"You're a practical woman," Beznaria said, shucking off her suit jacket. "Turning down this opportunity would be just the opposite."

Her elbow got stuck in a sleeve and she struggled for a moment, and then she leaned over to drape her jacket on Makeda's shoulders. Makeda hadn't realized she'd been trembling. It wasn't from the evening air, that held late spring heat despite the sea breeze, but the sweet grass-scented heat of the jacket's lining wrapping around her still helped.

"You know, I get that maybe I don't make sense. This is what people hope for, right? Someone just parachuting out of the sky with a solution to their problems? Money and fame for nothing, who doesn't want that?" Makeda sighed in frustration. "I don't. I grew up here watching people bleed themselves dry, ruin their lives and their family's lives, just for the possibility of hitting the jackpot. I watched my mother do it to us because she couldn't let go of the idea she was a princess."

She'd never told anyone this, had never really been able to express it, but for her mother, finding out about her supposed royal lineage had been a different kind of gamble. As she'd run into a dead end with each effort to gain royal recognition, she'd had the same dead-eyed hope as someone glued to the penny slots for hours.

"The thing is," Makeda said, feeling the idea become a substantial thing instead of the unease and resentment that always set in when people tried to give her anything, "there's always a catch. You know? No jackpot comes without one, whether it's taxes or family suddenly fighting over money or people giving in to delusions of grandeur and ending up worse off than they started. It never brings the happiness people think it will."

"I've seen your mother's file from the Ibaranian Embassy," Beznaria said in a voice that held no judgment.

Makeda squeezed a fistful of sand like she had when she was young and angry but unable to show it—sometimes she imagined squeezing it into an orb of beach glass. Her watering can was paved with those orbs, with all the things she'd never said and all the comments she'd let slide without clapping back.

"She humiliated herself, begging those people to see that she was a princess. Begging anybody, everybody. She wanted me to care as much as she did, and she was mad that I didn't. My classmates started teasing me because she came to school drunk and made a scene about me being a princess, and sometimes I wondered if she did it on purpose. School was the only place I could get away from that nonsense, and then after her outburst, there was nowhere I could go without being either teased for thinking I was a princess or resented for hoping I wasn't one."

It'd always seemed unfair that entire industries were built on what Makeda had been tormented for: being seen as a girl audacious enough to imagine herself worthy of *once upon a time*.

She glanced at Beznaria and found the investigator looking at her with that intense gaze, like she was solving an equation instead of listening to Makeda's nonsensical rambling. After a long silence, she nodded and finally responded. "I see. My approach had the wrong framing. I played up the aspects of this I thought an American would find appealing—the royal fantasy and fame and spectacle."

"Everything I hate," Makeda said with a chuckle.

"Yes," Beznaria said. "Well you should know real royal life is significantly less glamorous. It's work—even a ceremonial monarchy requires constant work without much recognition, which seems to be the kind of thing that appeals to you. You'll be exhausted and miserable, if that makes it easier for you to give this a shot."

Makeda laughed and looked out to sea, mulling over the offer she'd been rejecting for days. For years, since her mother hadn't let up on forcing the fantasy life she thought they deserved.

"And no one will laugh at you," Beznaria added.

"I don't think you can guarantee that," Makeda said. When she glanced at the investigator from the corner of her eye, Beznaria pulled her knife from her pocket and executed a skilled flourish. She could see that both the handle and the blade were painted with a motif that was similar to the waves and flowers in Beznaria's tattoo, in shades of blue and ivory. Along the blade, the word *promessa* had been hand inscribed.

Bez held the blade up, turning it this way and that so it caught the weakening rays of the sun. "Okay, let's say *one* person laughs. No one would dare it after them."

She flipped the blade closed and tucked it away, looking at Makeda with an almost cheerful expression.

Makeda wondered how she'd never known she had a thing for knives. "Okay then. I won't reject that part of the rescue package. I guess I should do it for the money."

"You should do it for yourself," Bez said. "For the girl who was bullied for being called princess, and the woman who hates that I could think her a queen."

Makeda instinctively shook her head. "No. I'll do it, but I won't enjoy it. There's nothing in it for me except—"

I can break the curse.

The thought came to her with such clarity that she sat up straight, bracing herself as the plan began to form. Her mother would have a royal relapse if Makeda didn't go to Ibarania—she was already coming up with reasons why she had to take Makeda's place. But if Makeda went and had her mother's fantasy confirmed, it was only a matter of time before Ashley Hicks found her way to Ibarania anyway, prayer or no. She'd moved, physically, but you couldn't escape the dream of your heart, especially when it was coming true for someone else.

If you go, you can prove to Mom that you're not a princess after all, and neither is she.

"I'll do it," she said, thrumming with excitement. "I'll go."

Beznaria was examining her again. "You'll go?"

"Yes," Makeda said. "I have to. Didn't you just say it was fate? I'm going to do this for myself, too. Not just the obligation and the money. I'm going to do it because I want to be selfish, and what could be more selfish than traveling across the world to claim I'm a princess?"

And to prove to my family I'm not one?

She would crush the ridiculous fantasies that might still cost her mother her hard-won happiness and Makeda her own peace of mind, and she'd get paid to do it.

"Wait, I don't have a passport," she said, as reality began to dent her plans.

Beznaria reached into the lining of her jacket again and, instead of the knife, pulled out a small blue booklet. Makeda's eyes went wide and she grabbed it from Beznaria's hand. She flipped it open and saw what was clearly a photo from the set she'd taken for her work ID. The signature was hers, too, or she would have thought it was if she knew she hadn't signed it.

"Is this real?" Makeda asked. How many times had she picked up passport forms at the post office, taken photos, and then always found a reason not to turn the forms in, despite being on top of almost everything else? And now here was one in her hands. "How did you get this?"

"Do you think royalty stand in line waiting for passports?" Beznaria asked, raising her chin. The setting sun gilded her in marmalade hues. "They have people who do that for them. I know you've only seen me doing home repairs, but I'll remind you that I'm a junior investigator of the World Federation of Monarchists. If things need arranging, I arrange things."

"Right, right. Top ten investigators." Makeda turned the passport over in her hands. She'd been thinking of this organization as an oddly menacing joke, but if they were out here with these kinds of connections . . .

"So I have a passport. How are we getting there?"

"I got word that the transport to Ibarania leaves in a few hours," Beznaria said.

"And you weren't going to tell me? Rude," Makeda muttered, ignoring the glancing ache at the idea of Beznaria leaving without saying goodbye, even though she shouldn't feel that for a woman who saw her as some combination of meal ticket and mission.

"It was a last-minute thing." Beznaria blinked at her from behind her already re-smudged lenses. "You've been trying to get rid of me for days. I thought you'd be glad to wake up and find me gone."

Makeda rolled her eyes.

"I was hoping it would get delayed a day or two so I'd have more time to woo you, but it departs tonight. This kind of travel requires that you be ready to go at any moment."

"Like standby plane tickets?" Makeda asked.

"Something like that," Bez said. "Standby transportation."

"And is there a seat for me on this standby transportation?"

"There's a . . . provision that allows passage for two." Bez ran a sand-dusted hand through her hair and then began batting at the strands to knock the sand away. "Don't worry about it. Like I said, I'll handle things."

Makeda had watched the sunset on this strip of beach hundreds of times in her life. She'd done it with women she liked and loved and wanted to like and love her in equal measure. But she'd never sat with someone who offered to rescue her and might be competent enough beneath all that chaos to pull it off.

"Yes, you handle it," she said. "I formally accept your offer of rescue services."

"Excellent. I'll print out the contract for you to read over, and we'll countersign before we leave."

Makeda raised her brows. "Contract? That sounds serious."

"There is nothing more serious than honoring someone's request to be saved," Beznaria said loftily, then cut her a somewhat judgmental glance. "Also, legal safeguards protect my business. And boundaries guide my interactions with my clients, making things safer for them, too."

Makeda ran her tongue over the still-healing cut on her inner lip. A contract would be good for both of them.

Beznaria stood up abruptly. "Ah, Henna Jeta is going to be so happy when I bring you back!"

She clapped, raining sand down on Makeda, who felt her first inevitable pang of guilt. The investigator had her heart set on the fact that Makeda was really the long-lost heir just because of a birthmark and a ring. She thought she owed Makeda some kind of familial allegiance. If Makeda proved her wrong, what would that do to Beznaria? Would she resent and leave her, too, like her mother had?

Makeda forcibly derailed her thoughts as they slid easily into the groove of putting someone else's needs before her own—of worrying and weighing how her wants stacked up against other people's.

"We should go sign the contract before you change your mind," Bez said, settling things for her. Bez was happy to use Makeda—they were just two women using each other for monetary gain and personal reasons the other would never know. And Makeda would be okay with that. "And we have to pack. And tell your grandmother. And I have to tell Kojak I'm leaving, too. I believe he'll miss me."

She was already walking away.

Makeda felt the urge to get up and trot after her, but instead she sat and waited for the sun to sink below the horizon. A cool breeze made her shiver, so she wrapped the jacket more tightly around herself and sank her toes into the cool sand. The sun moved quickly, candied orange fire as it arced down below the horizon. There one moment and gone in the space of a breath—that was the speed of change.

When Makeda got up to head back to the Golden Crown, Bez was watching from the boardwalk.

"I thought you left," Makeda said once she'd reached the top of the stairs.

"I don't agree to rescue a damsel and then leave her alone on the beach." Bez reached out and adjusted the collar of her jacket, her finger-tips brushing Makeda's neck. "You're under my protection now. You'll get used to it."

Chapter 9

$\mathcal{B}$ez gripped the handle of Makeda's suitcase tightly for reasons both chivalrous and selfish. It was common courtesy to carry the bag of the person she had signed on to protect, but Makeda appeared to still be confused as to why they were at Port of Atlantic City instead of Atlantic City Airport. When she figured it out, she might try to make a dash back to the Golden Crown.

Bez had the urge to run as well—she'd been so focused on finding transportation and so pleased with herself for managing it that she'd temporarily forgotten her own deep aversion to this particular mode of travel. She wouldn't run, though. She had promises to keep and while she would bend the truth to its breaking point when necessary, Chetchevalieres weren't oath breakers.

Ora Hicks stood with them outside the gate to the port, clutching the keys to the car and ready to run defense if Makeda tried to escape. In the exhilaration that had followed Makeda's agreement and the mad dash to pack and prepare, Bez hadn't found the perfect moment to clarify the *details* of the travel plans she'd pulled together. She'd also been distracted by a call from her sister Dihya, who'd let her know that Henna Jeta was growing despondent as neighbors, journalists, and government officials pressured her to relive Queen Aazi's disappearance again and again. She was quiet and wasn't eating enough.

When Bez arrived with the true heir, all of the attention would turn to her, and the only thing people would think of when they heard the name Chetchevaliere was that one of them managed to find a missing princess. Disgraces, both ancient and recent, would be forgotten. And hopefully, any grievances Makeda held about their mode of travel.

The port was all bright lights and crane shadows, with dim alleyways between the stacked cargo containers and machinery.

"I thought we were flying?" Makeda looked up at Bez from under the hood of the giant yellow sweatshirt she was wearing with blue jeans and canvas high-top sneakers. Her locks were pulled into a side ponytail gathered beneath her right ear, obscuring Lalla's Kiss. On the beach she had seemed resolved and ready to do what was necessary to pay off her debt, but now she looked wide-eyed and vulnerable.

"We will be, in a way." Bez spread her arms and pinned Makeda with a look designed to convince. "Flight . . . over the waves. If you stand at the bow with the wind in your face and close your eyes—"

"'Something like that.' 'Standby transportation.'" Makeda didn't frown, didn't roll her eyes. Her expression was stony and her gaze piercing, seeing right through Bez's evasion. "You really think you're slick."

Bez didn't know what that phrase meant, so she decided to take it as a compliment, as one should when given a choice between perceived insult and perceived praise.

"I am quite slick, though I can also be rough when necessary," she said brightly, then added, "Don't forget, you told me to handle everything, which I have and will continue to do. Handling sometimes means making decisions first and explaining them later."

Makeda hadn't explicitly asked for information yet, so it wasn't as if Bez were lying.

"How long is this trip going to take?"

"About ten days," Bez said. "Twelve maybe? It's quite fast for sea travel, and really, that's like a blink of the eye in the grand scheme of life, isn't it?"

"So almost two weeks? Are you for real right now? And how am I getting home? You know I have a job waiting for me, right?"

"You can fly back," Bez said. "You'll be back in time for the job, though they already fired you once, they'll hardly do it again for being a little late, will they? It would be rude."

Makeda closed her eyes and inhaled deeply. "Does Damsel in Distress Rescue Services have a review page? Because I'm gonna light you up on it."

Bez, again, decided that getting lit up was probably something positive.

"'While her methods are unconventional, she always gets the job done.' That was one of my last oral reviews, though I don't have an online presence. Best not to leave a trail," Bez said. She stood up straighter and pushed her glasses up her nose. "Boats are much safer than planes, you know, so if you're worried about rogue waves or hurricanes or oceanic black holes, don't be."

"Oceanic black holes? I didn't even know that was a thing, but now I do. Thanks for that."

"Blue holes would be more accurate, I suppose," Beznaria mused, thinking about the news report she'd watched on the subject. "I don't think it sucks things down into the center of the earth or an alternate dimension. It's more like an enormous roaming vortex, trapping everything in its path."

"Oh, just an enormous roaming vortex. Wait. That sounds like the Bermuda Triangle," Makeda said. "Are we going to pass through the Bermuda Triangle?"

Bez nodded. "Yes, actually. I made sure the boat we were on had a route that took us directly through an infamous wormhole. It shaves a few days off the trip, you see."

"Why are you inviting trouble?" Makeda knocked on her head three times, her knuckles meeting the soft cotton of her hood.

"It generally shows up unannounced and uninvited." Bez stared out toward the port, tension pulling around her eyes. "Which is why worrying is fruitless."

Bez was nervous, too, and possibly not entirely making sense, but she couldn't stop herself. She'd been carrying out a grueling investigation for months in a foreign and often hostile land. She'd barely slept for the last two weeks and had spent

the last few days repairing an old house and haggling for passage. And her work wasn't nearly
over yet. She kept reminding herself that it'd all
be worth it when she got home with her surprise
for Henna Jeta, and when she erased the stain on
her family's name and maybe in the process,
on her own honor.

Ora stepped close to Makeda and took hold of
one of her hands. "You have the same look in your
eye that Kojak gets when I pull out the cat carrier."

Makeda stopped glaring at Bez to look at her
grandmother. "Why wouldn't I? You lie to Kojak
and tell him you're taking him to the catnip dis-
pensary. You can't just mislead people when they're
expecting things to play out a certain way."

Bez almost interjected that relying on a person's
idea of how something would play out was *exactly*
how you misled someone, but kept that to herself.

Makeda eyed the car keys and Ora dropped them
into her purse.

"You can't make life all orderly like an aisle at
GrabRite, Makeda. Things don't always go how
you think they will. You know this."

"But—"

"You're scared," Ora said a bit more gently. "I
know you're scared. But I remember the trips we
used to plan when you were young. I remember the
way you used to look at the world like it was your
playground, before you stopped seeing all the fun
things and started focusing only on the mess."

Makeda's expression crumpled a little. "That's
because at the playground some people get to play
on the monkey bars, and some get to clean up the

stuff those people drop on the ground while they're having fun up there."

"Then get on the damn monkey bars for once," Ora pleaded, then she shook her head. "What I'm about to do isn't nice, but I'm not a nice woman."

Before Bez's eyes, Ora Hicks began to shrivel—not really, but she hunched and let her expression slacken and her eyes fill with sadness. Bez considered herself a great actor when need be, but Ora was something to behold. She looked absolutely pathetic as she latched her bereft gaze onto Makeda.

"All I want in this life is to see you happy." Her voice shook, and so did her hands as she reached out to her granddaughter. "Will you deny an old woman that? Will you send me to my grave knowing you never lived your dreams?"

"Enough with the emotional extortion." Makeda crossed her arms over her chest and fixed her grandmother with a watered-down version of her glare. "I already said I'd go, and I'm the only one in this family who keeps my word. Just promise you won't get into anything too wild while I'm gone. Don't burn down the B&B before I can pay off the lien against it, or do anything freaky in the common areas."

Ora smiled, her feebleness disappearing. "I promise no such thing, but you'll get your behind on that boat anyway."

She swooped her granddaughter into a hug then, and the sight of it made Bez miss her own henna so much that it was like a fist in the chest. She'd see her soon, and restore their family honor, and make her proud.

Bez's cell phone buzzed in her pocket and she tugged it out:

Knights of the Tangerine Table

Dihya C.: The tourism minister is driving me up the wall with this royalty search! He keeps trying to get Henna to agree to an interview. I'm tempted to tell him yes and challenge him to a duel when he arrives.

Fabrescia C.: Don't stab anyone, it'll be bad for business. "Your grandmother destroyed the monarchy a generation ago" is easier to spin than "your sister skewered her boss yesterday," and I have kids to feed. Speaking of that, has Bezzie checked in yet?

Dihya C.: It says she's online. She's online! Bezzie? Are you lurking?

Bez: I'm at the port. Hi, everyone!

Khalid C.: Are you on the ship? John told me you'd be doing security again? Be careful.

Bez: Boarding soon. It's a safe route and I'm always careful, but I will be extra careful now. You have never seen someone so careful. The world will never know my like again.

Khalid C.: 🙄

Dihya C.: Are you sure about being on a ship? After, ah, you know?

Fabrescia C.: Why are you bringing this up now?

Bez: I'll be fine. Vacation wasn't very relaxing, but I have a surprise for everyone. Will show you when I get back.

Fabrescio C.: Of course, it wasn't relaxing. Who chooses to spend their vacation in New Jersey?

Dihya C.: Hoping the crossing goes safely and you're home soon, Inshallah.

Dihya C.: 🙏

Fabrescio C.: 〰️ 💰

Fabrescia C.: 😔 Inshallah

Khalid C.: Bon voyage!

Bez checked her phone to see if Higginshoggins or anyone from the investigation team had returned her phone call, emails, or texts in their work chat. It had been the middle of the night when she'd sent a message that she'd be transporting a likely heir to Ibarania, but it was almost morning there now. The message had been sent via urgent channels, for a project that was a jewel in their crown, and yet there was no response.

Bez had to assume that everyone was off their game, or perhaps debating how to appropriately grovel after having underestimated her. A lone brain firefly flashed in her peripheral vision, signaling its concerns that something else was amiss, but Bez had to ignore it for now. She was sure when given her allotted email time in the coming days, she'd find a response and it would all work out.

"Okay, you two, get going," Ora said.

Makeda cut Bez a narrow look as she released her grandmother, and Bez tried her own playact of pleading, but it didn't work. For some reason, Makeda's natural inclination toward meek-and-mildness detoured around Bez. There was something infinitely pleasing about that.

"We should get going." From her phone, Bez sent the email she'd saved in her drafts to the Golden Crown's email address. "We won't be able to get in touch for much of the time at sea, because of the lack of Wi-Fi, but we can email occasionally and make short calls via satellite phone. Mrs. Hicks, I just sent you a few links where you can track where we are at all times."

She glanced at Makeda, who didn't seem to use the internet much but might not enjoy the Wi-Fi-free life. Her expression hadn't changed.

Ora hugged her granddaughter one more time, and then, surprisingly, hugged Bez. Her thin arms wrapped tightly around Bez's waist. "Take care of my baby. I'm trusting you."

"Kojak is still at the Golden Crown, though he did repeatedly try to stow away in my luggage."

"I mean my grandbaby!"

"Oh. I pledge to keep her safe," Bez replied. "I will protect her with my life if necessary."

Ora pulled back and looked up at Bez, then laughed. "Well, let's not go there. I don't want you hurt either."

Bez took that into consideration. "Okay, I will keep us both safe then."

"See to it," Ora said, then gave both of their arms a squeeze and turned to leave.

"That's it? I'll be gone for like a month!" Makeda called after her. "Aren't you even going to tell me you'll miss me?"

"Nope! Then you'll be out at sea all forlorn thinking I'm moping, when in reality I have work to do! And before those next bookings start showing up, I'm gonna be eating jalapeño poppers and bingeing the new season of *Destiny's Surrender* that drops this weekend," Ora said with a wink over her shoulder. "Just have fun! I'll see you when you get back."

Makeda's expression was crestfallen, as if her grandmother had just disowned her instead of wishing her bon voyage.

"She'll miss you," Bez said in an effort to reassure her. "She just doesn't want you to worry. I bet she's wiping away tears now that she's safely in the car."

Makeda jumped at the sudden blast of soul music from her car's sound system just before Ora honked the horn and peeled off.

"She will when she gets home," Bez amended. "Let's go. They won't wait for us if we're late."

Bez handed their passports and the paperwork she'd saved on her phone over to the security guard, a young Black man who gave them a friendly smile but didn't make small talk. The man efficiently scanned and scrolled, making notes on his tablet as he did. If Bez had been on a fact-finding mission, she likely would have talked to him about the rules of the port, rather than making jokes, to get on his good side, and likely wouldn't have been able to get him to give up any info.

"So how does this work?" Makeda squinted past the guard. She also looked past the cargo ship looming over the port. "A cruise won't be so bad, I guess. They looked kind of fun on the travel shows I've watched. What line is it? Carnival? Norwegian?"

"Cruise?" the guard asked, his thick brows raising. Bez shot him a quelling glance, and he didn't say anything else before wishing them a good trip.

"I should explain how I've taken care of things." Bez marched toward the cargo ship, watching Makeda from her peripheral vision. "The reason we're traveling by sea is it's free."

"Nothing is free," Makeda said dubiously.

"A cruise certainly isn't," Bez agreed. "And before you get angry, I will remind you that I didn't tell you that we were taking a cruise. I didn't tell you we were taking a plane. Those were conclusions you came to yourself after telling me to handle things."

A crane lifting a huge blue shipping container crossed overhead, and Makeda flinched as the shadow passed over her. She looked up and her gaze followed the container as it was placed atop a yellow one on the deck of a freighter already stacked with them. Makeda began to shake her head as she watched crew members and dockworkers moving busily around the stairs leading up the ship's deck.

"Now hold on a minute." She turned to Bez. "A cargo ship. You have dragged me to the docks, in the dark, so that we can travel by *cargo ship*." Makeda pressed her lips together and then shook her head sharply back and forth.

"You're correct that nothing is free," Bez said, stopping at the base of the steps and looking up toward the deck. "But lucky for us both, I have a background in maritime security. I was informed that a freighter making a stop in Ibarania needed a swing crew member to stand watch and deal with any pesky occurrences like pirate attacks, should they arise."

"I did not sign up for the risk of pirate attacks. No, ma'am." Makeda made an about-face as if to head back to the port exit, but Bez casually stepped into her path.

"There won't be any pirate attacks."

Makeda narrowed her gaze at her. "People always say that before something bad happens. Next thing you know someone will be all 'I'm the captain now' and—"

"Makeda." Beznaria reminded herself that she'd had time to prepare for this while Makeda hadn't. "This is a fairy tale, not a pirate adventure. The *Virginia Queen* is a safe and reliable ship. It has an experienced crew, and we are not passing through waters where pirates roam. I wouldn't put you in danger."

"Do we have to sleep in a shipping container?" Makeda asked. "I'm no princess and the pea, but I hope we're getting more than an air mattress in a metal box."

"If you want to, perhaps that can be arranged," Bez said. "However, this ship has comfortable cabins."

Makeda stared at the ship for a long moment, and then her shoulders drooped in resignation.

"You know what? Fine. Great. The *Virginia Queen* and the high seas it is." There was a resigned acceptance in her voice that Bez found oddly disappointing. She hadn't expected Makeda to be enthused, but she'd hoped she would be a little excited.

"Maybe you'll enjoy yourself," she prodded, feeling a twinge of something like guilt.

Makeda scowled up at her. "Don't try to convince me this is some cute romp. I'm not going to back out—I have my own reasons for agreeing to go to Ibarania, and I told you that I would, so I will. Unlike some people I've met recently, I'm not a liar."

"Who lied to you?" Bez asked, wondering how she could have missed such a thing given her close proximity to Makeda over the last few days.

Makeda's left eye twitched. "You. Did."

"I didn't," Bez said, stopping midstride to look down at Makeda. "I don't lie, except under very specific conditions—to achieve a work-related goal."

Lies made for work didn't count. Her sister Dihya had tried to convince Bez otherwise, but if that were true, then Bez couldn't believe what she'd been told during her brief stint in the military and maritime security: that the things she was told to do were just her job and not something that would be held against her as stains on her ethical record.

"Like your goal to get me to Ibarania so you can claim your promotion or whatever commission you get from this?" Makeda began to pace in a circle at the base of the steps, avoiding two near misses with dockworkers hurrying by. "You withheld information because you knew if you said, 'Hey, we're going to go on a long-ass boat ride on a cargo freighter,' I would have said no. It worked. But don't act like you were up-front about this or like I should be thrilled about it."

Bez pursed her lips, then nodded. "You're right, I suppose. I lied in the same way you did by withholding information about your debt from your grandmother and anyone who might help you."

Makeda started marching toward the ship. "Let's get on board and get this over with."

Beznaria stood and watched her go, trying to puzzle out why the woman's reaction was dampening her pride at having completed the hardest part of the journey—getting Makeda onto the ship. People were disappointed in her all the time, and it mostly bounced off the armor she'd acquired over the years—layers and layers of it, formed like pearl after each episode of her too-muchness being pointed out. If it somehow made it through all that, it was repelled by the self-assurance that had always fortified her from within.

But Makeda's disappointment was like the tip of a thin blade that had slipped through a joint in her armor, cutting deep enough to wound.

Bez didn't know what was more worrying: that Makeda was upset or that it could have such an effect on her. She would have to be very careful, she thought as she watched Makeda, who looked up at the ship with such plain fear that it crossed the line into bravery. Admiring the probable heir to the Ibaranian monarchy was one thing. Wanting to kiss her was another. But dealing with a woman who could actually breach her innate defenses was a problem Bez had never encountered, and a challenge she wasn't sure even a Chetchevaliere could overcome.

Chapter 10

Makeda had grown up seeing cargo ships passing along the horizon as she sat on the beach or walked the boardwalk, or loading and unloading at the port. They were like one of the pictures hanging on the wall in Grandmore's den: in the background, familiar and inextricable from her memories, but nothing she paid close attention to since they were always there.

And sure, she'd seen them up close from time to time, but she'd never boarded one and was beginning to wonder how she'd never noticed just how *huge* they were. She didn't think she was scared of sea travel, but she was at least a little shook as she stood before the seemingly never-ending metal steps that led onto the ship.

"Sorry, we thought you bailed. We don't have time to put the safety net on," a crew member called out in a deep gravelly voice over the noise of the loading. He was short and stocky and wore a saffron yellow jumpsuit and hard hat, but Makeda couldn't make out his face beneath the hat. She could see the urging motion of his gloved hands, though. "Leave your bags for me to carry up. If you're going to get on, you have to get on now."

Makeda nodded and willed herself to move, but her legs didn't comply.

"Don't be scared," the man said. "You just have to put one foot in front of the other."

The words could have been mocking coming from another harried worker who wanted to get a move on, but his voice was supportive even though it was firm.

Okay. Time to break this curse. One foot in front of the other.

Makeda did as he said, clutching the railing, lifting one foot and bringing it down firmly on the step above, and repeating, again and again. Beznaria said nothing, but Makeda felt her presence at her back and, despite the fact that she was pissed at the investigator, it was reassuring. Halfway up the metal steps, a sudden terrible roar shuddered through the boat, and the dark water beneath them began to churn. Makeda shouted and clung to the railing as the stairs swayed back and forth.

"It's the engine," Beznaria shouted from behind her.

"Right."

"Don't worry. Like my annoying presence, you'll get used to this, too."

Makeda nodded and tried to regain her walking rhythm but found herself frozen again. The only movement she managed was to look down over the side at the sinister waves frothing below them. She'd lived along the water all her life and was smart enough to have a healthy fear of the ocean, but at that moment she started wondering what exactly lurked in its depths.

"Are you able to go on or do you need me to carry you?" Beznaria asked. "I'm not sure the view from over my shoulder will be less frightening, but I have a strong grip and won't drop you."

Beznaria pressed against her from behind, as if to wrap an arm around her, and Makeda suddenly mustered the coordination to jog up the remainder of the stairs.

When she stepped onto the deck, she was barely able to take in the bright lights and bustling motion of the crew before a gust of wind swept through the alleys created by blue, yellow, and red stacks of cargo and knocked her back into the annoying investigator.

Beznaria placed a firm hand on each of Makeda's shoulders and squeezed. "First rule of ship life— anchor yourself, keep your center of gravity low, lean into the wind, and don't let yourself get knocked over the side."

"That's four rules," Makeda pointed out.

"Well, the four rules have one reason behind them. If you fall overboard, you'll likely stay there. No one will be able to hear you scream over the noise of the engine, and it's unlikely anyone will see it happen. I suppose 'don't fall into the merciless sea' is the first rule of ship life, actually."

Makeda tugged her hood over her fitted cap and glared up and over her shoulder. "I swear, if I fall overboard and get eaten by a shark, you'll pay for it. I'll possess the shark and make it hunt you down. Vengeance will be mine."

Beznaria looked off into the distance, a habit Makeda was learning meant the woman was probably thinking up some strange scenario.

"What if you get rescued by dolphins and have a once-in-a-lifetime communion with nature instead? I think that would make it worthwhile."

"Communing with dolphins wouldn't make up for falling off a giant boat," Makeda shouted.

Beznaria nodded understandingly, and then her expression brightened as if she'd found a solution to a problem. "What if the dolphins could talk? Would that work?"

"Why are you haggling with me about this?" Makeda laughed in spite of her aggravation. "Are you planning on throwing me overboard to meet a pod of talking dolphins? Not that they exist."

Beznaria's brows rose behind the round frames of her glasses. "You really don't know what military research your tax money is funding, do you?"

"What?"

"Nothing," Beznaria said, looking off again. She seemed distracted in a serious way this time, not her normal all-over-the-place-ness, and despite Makeda's annoyance with her, her help-y senses were tingling.

"What's wrong?"

"There's something else I should tell you before we meet the crew," Beznaria said, and her expression was so somber that Makeda's stomach tightened with apprehension. "Now you might call this 'a lie,' but it fell into the 'reasonable' zone on my rubric. I had to secure us travel, which I'll remind you is part of the rescue package, and—"

"Oh, you made it!" a spritely voice called out. "Welcome aboard!"

They both turned to see a Black woman jogging over from the cargo-loading area of the deck. She was only a little taller than Makeda, with a sturdy, athletic build—thick thighs and generous curves beneath her red coveralls—and a bright smile.

She smiled widely at them, dimples hollowing wells in her cheeks. "I'm Andrea Thompson, first mate of the ship. Captain Del Rosario is up on the bridge, and I'm down here making sure everything goes smoothly with the cargo loading. This is my second trip as first mate. Last time there was a problem with a shipment of live goats, and *some* people won't let you live down a few goats in the engine room."

"Some people don't know how to live," Beznaria said in a tone that reminded Makeda that the investigator wasn't above using charm as a weapon, and First Mate Thompson blinked up at her in delight.

"I'm so glad you were able to make it before we left. We have a solid crew, but we're short-staffed and we'd be stretched thin without someone to stand a few watches and help with security issues that might arise." She turned her megawatt smile toward Makeda. "I'm sorry she'll have to work during your honeymoon, but hopefully we won't take too much of her time."

Honeymoon?

Makeda opened her mouth to speak but was stopped by Beznaria's sudden iron grip on her hand.

"No, thank *you*. We wouldn't have been able to make this trip without your ship's 'crew spouse rides free' policy," Beznaria said in a voice that was so overtly polite Makeda did a double take. "I'm grateful to get to bring Makeda home to meet my family. Meeting her has been life-changing for me, and I'm sure it will be for them, too."

Makeda's face went hot with mortification as she realized what Beznaria had been so worried about telling her before the first mate had come over to greet them.

"That is so romantic. I'd love to think you two are going to bring good luck to this journey, Mrs. and Mrs. Chetchevaliere!" Andrea laughed, an infectiously joyful sound, and Makeda laughed along reflexively even as she was screaming inside her heart.

Mrs. Chetchevaliere?

"I'll do my best to contribute to the safety of the ship, especially because my blushing bride is on board. There will be more than luck involved because I won't let any harm come her way."

Blushing bride?!

Beznaria had gone too far, and Makeda wanted to reach into her newly accessible vault of anger and pull out a baseball bat, but it had selective opening hours it seemed. A familiar paralyzing humiliation clamped Makeda in its fist. Instead of saying something cutting and witty, she stood there frozen, like she always did when caught in the crosshairs of unwanted attention.

"Your ring is lovely," Andrea said, looking at the cursed fish scale ring on Makeda's middle finger.

"So unique. Is it traditionally worn on the middle finger in Ibarania?"

"It was passed down to me, and we haven't been able to resize yet," Makeda managed to grit out through her plastered-on smile, hating how easily the half-truths came out to preserve the peace.

Can't be a bother. Can't make a scene.

Here she was at the start of a journey that was supposed to be the first step in throwing off the weight accumulated by a life-long dedication to taking on other people's burdens. The boat hadn't even left the port yet, and already it was more of the same.

No.

Hell no.

She couldn't think of a way to call out Beznaria's lie without creating even more chaos, but she wasn't going to spend the rest of this trip at the whims of Beznaria's bizarre idea of reasonable.

While her inner scream echoed in that hidden cavern where every people pleaser stored their fury, she smiled teeth and all at the first mate, and then squeezed Beznaria's hand like it was a tube of biscuits she was trying to pop open.

"She's just so full of surprises!" Makeda laughed, the sound a bit shrill but the best she could manage. "I can't wait for the day when I can repay her for everything she's brought into my life."

By proving I'm not a princess and then hightailing it out of Ibarania after securing the bag.

Beznaria smiled down at her, the light flaring off her glasses and hiding what her eyes might reveal. "One thing I love about my wife is that she's so . . .

resilient. And forgiving. And a pacifist. She doesn't even kill spiders, let alone people she's upset with."

"I will destroy a spider if it wrongs me," Makeda said sweetly.

"Thompson!" someone called out.

The first mate's smile faltered and she glanced back toward the containers. A tall brown-skinned man with a goatee held his hand out in their direction, as if he'd just beckoned Thompson and then went back to his work. He wore a hard hat and red coveralls like the rest of the people working on the deck and was talking to a slightly shorter and lighter skinned man in the same outfit. His fingers curled in a beckoning motion, and then he glanced sharply in their direction; Makeda wasn't even in his direct line of sight and she wanted to cower. There was sternness, which she enjoyed, and there was whatever this guy was doling out.

"Ah. Chief Engineer Santos wants to go over some things before we head out, but AK will take over for me." Andrea adjusted her collar and straightened her hard hat. "Our steward, he's kind of like the . . . I guess in terms you'd understand he's like the butler of the ship. He'll show you to your quarters, where you can relax until the kick-off meeting starts after we've left the port and are out at sea."

She gave them a final nod and then walked briskly toward the chief engineer, giving the steward a polite dip of her head as she passed him.

He wore a saffron jumpsuit like the man who'd ushered them aboard and a few people working in the cargo area. His golden brown complexion and dark brown eyes made her think he was likely of Southeast Asian descent.

"Hello, welcome aboard," the man said as he reached them. His voice lilted with an accent that curled warmly around *R*s and *L*s and dipped into vowels like they were cool drinks on a warm day.

His face was angular and might have been severe except for his eyes, which were startlingly kind. His expression was open and friendly, despite the hollows at his cheeks and creases around his eyes.

"I'm AK, the ship's steward. I handle organizing meals, housekeeping, accounting . . . all kinds of things, really. I'm sure I was introduced as the butler, but I'm more the ship's multi-tool," he said, dipping his head in a polite acknowledgment just as Andrea had done when she passed him.

"AK?" Beznaria said, stepping between Makeda and the steward to lean down and examine his face. "AK, you say? Does that stand for anything?"

He nodded, the sweaty strands of his hair sliding over his eyes. "Yes."

"Do I know you from somewhere?" Beznaria was staring him down, but he continued to smile comfortably.

"Possibly. People's paths cross all the time in this world, and in mysterious ways." He wasn't being sarcastic—his words were straightforward even though they took a detour around answering the question.

"You look very much like—"

"I'm a thirtysomething-year-old Asian man," AK said, cutting Bez off firmly but with no malice.

"When I'm traveling in the West, people always think I look like someone who isn't me."

Bez harrumphed but stopped her inquisition.

He turned back to Makeda, and she stepped forward, giving her supposed wife the subtlest cold shoulder she could manage without being detected.

"Hi, I'm Makeda. I'm also a multi-tool, I guess, though not sure I'll be much use on this voyage," she said, briefly dipping her head in greeting. "This is my first time on a ship like this, and my first time traveling far from home."

"Are you scared?" he asked. The question was unexpected—it wasn't something people asked outright. He leaned forward, as if making sure he could hear over the sound of the engine.

"A little," she admitted. "Not as much as I thought I'd be, though."

"You're doing much better than me. I was terrified the first time I was on a ship," he said. "I was with my friend who comes from a land of lakes and rivers, but I'd spent most of my life in the mountains. I was scared of the ocean, of the waves, of the way the ship rolled and the strange sounds it made. Fear is rational, and learning to live with it is part of the journey. For me, at least."

"I'm not scared of anything," Beznaria said blithely. "Definitely not the ocean, or bad things that might happen on ships."

AK glanced at her and gave a nod of acknowledgment, then turned back to Makeda. "We're getting a late start tonight, but there will be a quick eat-and-greet where we talk about how things are going to work on this specific voyage. We'll talk about fun stuff, too, like when you can explore the ship and learn more about it.

"Now let's get you settled. I'm going to give you the basic tour as we go, so you can orient yourself. We're standing on the main deck. That over there . . ." He turned and pointed to what was essentially a several-stories-tall white building a few yards away. It had rows of windows, with the lower ones mostly dark while the top rows were lit up ". . . is the accommodations, where you'll probably spend a lot of time since it's where all your basic needs get met and the safest place for you on the ship. There are several levels; the bridge is at the top, and the other levels are where we all eat, sleep, exercise, and hang out."

Makeda tried to take that all in: main deck, accommodations, bridge. Every part of the ship had its purpose, and unlike Makeda's life, was under the control of experts.

"I'll take you to your quarters so you can get settled and the captain and crew can get us out to sea." He turned and headed toward the superstructure.

Beznaria started to follow after him like a hound on a suspicious scent, but Makeda grabbed her arm. She was no investigator, but she had a question of her own. "Are we just going to pretend you didn't lie and tell these people we're married?"

Bez patted her hand. "While I agree that a honeymoon argument will add to the authenticity of our performance, it shouldn't happen publicly until at least the seventh day or everyone will suspect something is up. Wait until we're alone to unfairly malign my brilliant plan."

Beznaria turned to stride after AK, and after a brief pause Makeda jogged after them.

After entering a weatherproof vestibule between the ship's deck and an inner hallway, they bypassed the elevator to climb several flights of stairs. As they passed each level, AK pointed out the signage for each floor—gym, pool, sauna, and meditation room on Deck A. Galley, mess, and movie theater on Deck B.

"Movie theater?" Makeda blurted despite her simmering annoyance with Bez. "I didn't know ships had all of these things on board."

"The crew live here for weeks or months at a time. We try to make it as enjoyable as possible," AK said. "We also use the theater for karaoke night."

"I've never done karaoke," Makeda said.

"I'm the karaoke champion of Ibarania," Beznaria cut in. "Of my region of Ibarania. Do they have karaoke competitions in Druk?"

AK hadn't said where he was from, but apparently she was right because he simply shook his head as they reached the next landing. "We don't turn things that give us joy into competitions."

"So you *are* from the kingdom of Druk?" Bez asked, challenge in her tone for some reason.

"We're an international crew, with members from the United States, Russia, the Philippines, and yes, Druk."

AK pressed on with the tour, not humoring any more questions of nationality. Deck C had the administrative offices, kitchens, and laundry room, and Deck D, the dining rooms, lounges, and crew quarters. By the time they reached Deck E, Makeda was starting to think that maybe the trip wouldn't be so bad after all. This wasn't a cruise ship, for sure, but it was maybe, just maybe, a really cool first adventure, apart from the fake marriage stuff. She wouldn't tell Beznaria that, though.

They walked down a narrow hallway with mint green walls and steel doors that had been painted a dark teal.

"That's the library and these are the officer accommodations," AK said, pointing at the closed doors they were passing. "You'll be staying at the end of the hall in the cabin belonging to the ship's owner."

Makeda's heart started to beat faster as they continued down the hall.

The cabin? They were sharing a cabin? She had just assumed . . . Okay, Beznaria had been right; Makeda kept assuming things would be a certain way and then being surprised when they weren't. Her brain was still catching up from the last twenty minutes of her already upside-down life being spun like a bottle. Everyone thought they were newlyweds, of course they'd be sharing a cabin.

That was fine. She could handle it.

AK opened the door to reveal a room that was surprisingly nice. It was spacious, with walls painted a creamy orange and dark wood accents for the cabinets and doors. There was a closet with dark-wood French doors and drawers and shelving inside on their left and an adorable kitchenette on their right. Directly ahead was a small seating area with a couch and wooden coffee table. On the wall above the couch hung a large painting of what looked like, to Makeda, a female version of a Buddha figure; she was topless and blue and multi-armed, sitting on a lotus and staring serenely out from the portrait.

An open door revealed the bathroom, which contained a large shower with multiple showerheads, and tucked into the corner between the bathroom and the seating area—

"There's only one bed," Beznaria said loudly.

Makeda stared at the bed, with it's expensive-looking patterned duvet and the dark blue curtains tied neatly at each end; it looked like a bed fit for a princess. It wasn't small but it wasn't nearly big enough for the two of them considering she wanted to evade Beznaria at all costs after the surprises that had been sprung on her. Apart from the fact that she was currently high-key annoyed with the Ibaranian investigator, it also looked much too cozy. Even her anger couldn't stop her from imagining all the ways Beznaria's long limbs might get tangled up with her own.

"There's only one bed and I was told there would be two," Beznaria said in a tone that Makeda hadn't heard from her before. This was a terrible time for the investigator to reveal that she could be stern. If chaos was a wavelength that most attracted Makeda, sternness increased its bandwidth.

AK pulled off his hardhat and ran a hand through his sweaty hair. "This is the equivalent of the honeymoon suite. I've been told this is your honeymoon. Is there a problem?"

"I'll sleep on the floor!" The words jumped out of Makeda's mouth as her disaster diffusion engine kicked into gear.

Beznaria shot Makeda a bewildered look. "Why would you volunteer to sleep on the floor?"

"I don't want to be a bother?" Makeda ventured, though she wasn't entirely sure why she had either. She'd spoken before thinking and now the situation was even weirder.

Beznaria frowned. "Your sleeping on the floor would bother *me*."

Makeda glanced at AK, who was regarding them with a puzzled expression. Oh god, he was starting to suspect something was up. If he realized they were lying and told the crew, Makeda would be stuck at sea with a bunch of people who thought the worst of her; she'd pay the price for someone dragging her into their princess fantasy, again.

"Of course it would. We'll share, of course," she said, glancing at AK to show him that everything was totally normal and super legit.

"I don't like sharing, sea snail. My bed or anything else. You know that." She smiled at her, a slow seductive tilt of her mouth that Makeda hadn't seen before. Makeda's cheeks flushed at the expertly balanced insinuation in Beznaria's singsong voice. Bez *was* aware AK was there, and she was putting on a show. Why else would she look at Makeda like that?

AK looked back and forth between them. "I'm confused. Because you're married so—"

Bez cut him off with a dramatic flourish of her hand. "Even less reason to share a bed. I spend all day with her. I'm going to spend the rest of my life with her. I prefer to sleep alone. How bizarre to force yourself to sleep next to someone *every night*, absorbing their exhalations and having their microscopic skin cells shed on you just because you love them."

Makeda added another item to the list of reasons Beznaria was a no-good life ruiner: she'd probably never be able to sleep next to someone again without thinking about that.

Bez walked back and forth beside the bed and then stopped to stare down at it like she was considering tearing it in half. "I prefer that we both have a refreshing and stress-free sleep and then share a bed when the mood strikes, however many times a day that might be."

She glanced at Makeda and winked.

Anyone watching might think the woman truly wanted her, and Makeda added that to her list, too. Tricking her into a fake marriage was one thing, but looking at her like it was true was almost cruel.

AK gripped his chin between thumb and forefinger and pursed his lips. "You know what? You're right. The world tells us that married couples must sleep in the same bed without acknowledging it can be an act of personal sacrifice done to show love and devotion. I imagine many people don't like it and even feel trapped by this idea that society has created. You've given me something to think about, and I appreciate that."

Then he caught Beznaria's gaze.

"That said, reshuffling rooms at this moment would disturb the crew and start the voyage off with imbalanced energy. I believe one of you can fit onto the couch." He clapped. "Thanks for your understanding, a crew member will come get you for the Midnight Snack Meeting."

"One more question," Bez said. "Your initials, they stand for—"

He stepped out and shut the door.

"The nerve of him. He really thinks he can fool me?" Beznaria muttered to herself. "Top ten junior investigator of the World Federation of Monarchists?"

Makeda glared at Bez, who was also glaring but at the door AK had closed in her face.

"We need to discuss how you share information with me," Makeda said as calmly as she could.

"Well, I have to be one hundred percent certain it's him," Beznaria said, her tone distant, as if she wasn't even paying attention to Makeda. "Right now I'm only ninety-four percent certain."

"I'm talking about us? This ship? This *honeymoon* suite?" The tension in Makeda's voice ratcheted up with each phrase, as the reality of the situation became more apparent.

Beznaria looked down at her, not a shred of contrition on her face. "I share information when it becomes relevant. If I had tried to tell you all of this while I was in the midst of handling things, it would have led to confusion."

"Do you think our current situation isn't confusing somehow?" Makeda just barely kept her voice down.

"It's not confusing at all. We needed free transportation to Ibarania, and we have it. We needed room and board, and we have it." Bez gestured around the cabin.

"They think I'm your wife!" Makeda whispered angrily.

"Yes, we've established that." Beznaria blinked.

"But I'm not," Makeda bit out more quietly, unsure of how their voices might travel in the hall outside their cabin. "It's a lie, and it puts me in an uncomfortable position because now *I* have to lie to support your original lie."

"It wasn't my lie. Not originally," Beznaria said. "An old acquaintance in shipping heard I was looking for passage back and set me up with this job. I asked him if it was possible to bring a guest to share my cabin for free, and he said, 'Crew members are allowed to bring spouses.'"

"And you lied and said you had one?" Makeda prompted.

"No. I said, 'I will be bringing a guest since it's possible under those circumstances,' because if it's possible then, it's possible any time, technically. When he congratulated me on my marriage, I said, 'Thank you for your assistance with my journey back.'" Bez held up her hand when Makeda started to protest. "It was all done in the name of getting you to Ibarania, which is what I promised you I would do."

"I can't believe you think that excuses all this," Makeda said, flailing her hands to gesture at the cabin around them. "I trusted you to handle things, but I didn't ask to be left out of the decision-making process or to have to lie."

Bez nodded sagely. "Consider this one aspect of the adventure. You are on a mission, and lying for work is fine, as we discussed. Besides, if you're taking this lost heir endeavor seriously, there will be more trying tasks than pretending to be married to me."

Makeda scoffed. "Really? I can't think of any. Were there really no other options to pay for room and board? Having to shovel coal in the engine room would have been preferable."

"It's the twenty-first century," Bez said drily. "Ships don't use coal."

"Yes, it's the twenty-first century, which is why we should be on a plane right now!" Makeda realized something that would have occurred to her earlier if she hadn't been so overwhelmed by the sheer improbability of the situation she was in. "Wait, we're doing this so I could ride for free? Why didn't your monarchist bosses pay for our travel?"

Bez's expression didn't change drastically, but for the first time since they'd met, she dropped her gaze instead of holding it until Makeda blinked or looked away.

"There have been some communications issues, as well as a matter of budget restraints."

"Great, so I'm stuck playing your wife because you work for cheapskates." Makeda was trying not to raise her voice, but she was a planner, and every assumption she'd made about the way things would work out had been based on a foundation that, at the very least, the World Federation of Monarchists was a legit organization that would spring for an economy flight.

Bez lifted her chin, as if she was the one who had reason to be upset.

"Do you know how many times I've been castigated for *not* making someone my wife? And here you've achieved it after only having to tolerate me for a few days. You should be happy."

Makeda just stared at Beznaria for a moment, old shame rising to meet new anger. How many times had she accepted scraps while telling herself asking for more was being greedy?

"You know what would have made me happy? If you'd told me what was going on, so we could come up with a plan together. Instead, you put me in this ridiculous situation and expect me to be grateful. You owe me an apology, at the very least."

Makeda stared at Bez, her heartbeat sounding in her ears. She'd never flat out told someone to say they were sorry, and she felt slightly ill.

"I did what needed to be done for us to get to Ibarania, which is my job," Bez replied stiffly. "The alternative was hiding you in my duffel bag and sneaking you on board. I'd say that you owe me an apology for not appreciating my hard work."

Beznaria raised a brow, as if this were all some big joke, but Makeda felt the words like sharp rocks jabbing her in the arch of her foot as she walked over sand. Beznaria had, for a moment, fooled her into thinking that her feelings actually mattered in this whole scheme, but this was a good reminder that to the investigator Makeda was an assignment that needed to be completed.

"You know what? Whatever," she bit out. "Just stay out of my face for the rest of this trip, okay?"

"I'll try but cannot promise anything given the size of this cabin." Beznaria strode over to the couch and dropped heavily onto it, bouncing up and down aggressively. "Harder than the Boulder of Qalbedda," she muttered, then lifted her gaze to Makeda's. "Maybe we should share the bed, like you want to. It's only for a short while and can be counted as one of the hardships of the recovery mission. We can sleep head to foot so I'll be 'out of your face.'"

Makeda was busy opening drawers and inspecting shelves, already planning where her clothing would go. She pulled out the ship's map and stared at it sulkily even though she wasn't reading it. "I don't *want* to sleep next to you, especially if it's such a hardship, and I definitely don't want to sleep next to your feet."

Beznaria chuckled, the sound making a vein in Makeda's temple throb.

"You volunteered to sleep on the floor when even a Chihuahua demands a place on the pillow, so I don't think you have strong preferences on that matter. For what it's worth, I don't find sleeping next to you *specifically* a hardship. I like sleeping alone, and if someone is in my bed, I want it to be because she chose to be there, so there are no misunderstandings."

"Believe me, there won't be any," Makeda said, even as her stomach went tight at the thought of them lying side by side. "Just two grown adults sharing a bed."

"That's wonderful to hear," Bez said cheerfully. "Because I can be quite the octopus. Or perhaps a squid."

"What?" Makeda looked around the room as if the meaning of the woman's strange words could be found. Her gaze landed on the painting, where the goddess's expression seemed to respond, *I don't know what she's talking about either.*

Beznaria spread her arms and legs wide. "I don't like sharing a bed, but when I do?" She wrapped her arms dramatically around herself. "I grab anyone near me with my tentacles."

Her lips pursed and her cheeks caved in as she made a suction cup noise. It should have been off-putting, but caused indecent tentacle thoughts to slither into regions they should *not* have been slithering for Makeda given how angry she was.

She curled her lip, then turned to look out the window. High stacks of containers spread out across the foredeck like a cityscape, and beyond that were the dark ocean and the dark sky with no separation between them. The ship began moving, pushing them forward into what could be everything and nothing—the unseen.

She inhaled deeply and began to do what always gave her a sense of purpose: she started making a plan.

She was still pissed, but Bez had actually given her a fantastic opportunity to practice her new discipline: not putting up with people's shit. She could spend the remainder of the voyage angry and disappointed, or she could finally put all those years of making a way out of no way for other people and apply the skill to herself.

She shut the curtain. "It's going to be an interesting voyage."

Beznaria made another octopus suction noise in agreement. Makeda rolled her eyes and reminded herself that the annoyance was going to be worth it. When all was said and done, putting up with Bez for less than two weeks was worth breaking the curse that had taken her mother from her. Beznaria thought she was transporting a damsel in distress, but she was actually leading the dragon slaying knight right to the dragon's doorstep.

The adventure had started badly, but by the time they arrived in Ibarania, the investigator would regret their fake marriage and Makeda would be ready to prove that she was no one's princess.

Chapter 11

Bez loosened her tie as she watched Makeda open her suitcase and begin to stiffly remove the clothing. Every garment had been rolled like the sweet honey logs her father baked every Sunday, and Makeda stacked them one by one onto the shelves. When she pulled out a sack of smaller rolls, which Bez assumed were underwear, she looked around self-consciously before shoving the sack beneath a pile of clothing.

Bez kicked her own duffel bag into a corner. She was used to living out of her luggage and didn't completely unpack it unless she was home, which meant she hadn't done it in years.

She checked her phone repeatedly while they were still in range of the cell towers. Still no word from the WFM, adding to her general sense of unease. She supposed there was a certain irony in the fact that now that she was finally following protocol and checking in with a request for assistance, her request would be ignored.

No matter. She'd write again.

To: AlgernonSGSB@wfm.com
CC: IbaranianInvestigativeTeam@wfm.com
From: BeznariaC@wfm.com
Subject: I HAVE FOUND THE LOST HEIR

Hello,

I am writing again to inform you that I've found the
lost heir. In my previous emails, requests for travel
expenses were made, but I have managed to secure
passage without WFM assistance. We will arrive a
few days before the official ceremony, if all goes
well. I will have limited internet access but will have
access to email and satellite phone, and request
confirmation that you've received this email.

Best at all things,
Junior Investigator Chetchevaliere

She hit send and assured herself that they'd respond soon. Perhaps it wouldn't be congratulatory,
like she deserved, but it would at least acknowledge
that the WFM was aware of her plans so she could
get past the uneasiness that had started to nibble
at her.

She hadn't considered that Makeda would react so
negatively, because as usual, she hadn't really considered much beyond achieving her goal. But now
Makeda's silence began to itch, a sensation like invisible insects ghosting over Beznaria's skin—guilt
ants in the pants.

Bez wasn't sensitive; she didn't see it as a flaw,
just something about herself that she and those

who loved her had accepted. But for some reason she couldn't ignore Makeda like she generally did when someone was upset with her. She hated this feeling of being a dinghy tossed in the waves of someone else's emotions instead of a megafreighter that barely registered the slaps of other people's anger. She wondered if this was something to do with the fabled connection between al-Hurradassi and Chetchevaliere; perhaps whatever bind tied them together through their family lineage had kicked in with their close proximity. It couldn't be anything else, could it?

"What are you doing?" she asked finally, her voice too loud in the cabin and the question too abrupt.

"Planning," Makeda said without looking at her. "Usually when things happen to me, I just go along with them. I don't think I'll be doing that anymore."

There was something in the calm of her voice that gave Bez pause. Makeda had no qualms about showing her frustration when it came to Beznaria. This coolness was new and made the guilt ants start doing the cha-cha.

"That sounds a bit ominous. Should I be worried about you plotting against me?"

Makeda glanced at Bez, her expression revealing nothing. "You should be worried that you weren't already worried about that. If you really think I'm Queen Lalla's descendant, aren't you concerned what my wedding gift to myself will be?"

"That story is more myth than, say, a template for all royal wedding nights," Bez said trying to sound cavalier, but now she was thinking of Lalla's Kiss.

Makeda seemed like the kind of person who would aim for accuracy, and the thought of that bow of a mouth licking its way up her neck made Bez briefly consider the upside of a gut wound.

Makeda flashed her dimple of destruction. "Don't worry, I have it on good opinion that if you get pushed overboard, there's a good chance of dolphin rescue."

Bez frowned. "That's much less pleasant than the death I was imagining."

Makeda shrugged and went back to her silent planning.

Bez pushed her glasses up onto her forehead and rubbed at her eyes, which were grainy with fatigue, when she was struck with a realization: she had broken Papa Chetchevaliere's Second Rule of Romance: she'd pissed Makeda off and she hadn't apologized. Makeda had even asked her to apologize, but Bez had been too busy explaining why her actions were reasonable to register that request.

She glanced at Makeda

"I apologize," she said. "For not telling you about the cargo ship and fake marriage. I should have apologized when you first asked."

Makeda glanced at her from the corner of her eye. "Why are you doing it now? So I don't hop off at the first port and blow your chance at a promotion or whatever you get for hauling me in to the WFM?"

Bez squinted. "The next port is Ibarania so that's fine with me."

Makeda made a sound that might have been a growl.

"I apologize because you were right. I should have given you more information before we set out," Bez added. "You enjoy the illusion of control provided by data, and I didn't give that to you. I'll be more open moving forward."

She thought that would appease Makeda, but it earned her a sharpened gaze.

"Is there anything else I need to know right now?" Makeda asked. "About our stay on the ship? About what happens when we get there?"

Bez blinked at her. "No. Nothing absolutely pressing."

Makeda didn't *need* to know that the World Foundation of Monarchists hadn't responded yet. It wasn't reasonable to upset her over something that would be resolved before the island was even on their radar.

Makeda shot her a suspicious glance before returning to thinking and planning.

There was a knock at the door, and a crew member who wasn't AK—well, AK himself wasn't actually "AK," but Bez would keep quiet about it for now— showed up to bring them to the ship crew's meeting. It was the ship's bosun, a man named Jay who was in charge of the sailors, and he happily chatted the entire walk to the meeting, easing the awkwardness between Bez and Makeda.

There were only a few people crammed into the mess hall, decorated with the orange and teal accents often found in traditional Drukian design, as well as more modern aspects like a large flat-screen television. Beznaria could see why she'd been allowed onboard—there were only about ten crew in the room, with the other four people at their posts. This was the minimum crew required, though often not enough to actually run a ship for long trips, given the human need for sleep and rest.

Captain Del Rosario, a short man with a square jaw and dark eyes, stood at the front of the room. He was flanked by Thompson and Santos, while the other crew members sat on the long sectional couch or at the few wooden tables.

All three nodded a greeting at Bez and Makeda; Del Rosario and Thompson smiled. Santos did not. Bez didn't take it personally. In many ways she preferred people like Santos, who were unfriendly with everyone. They were vastly easier to interact with because they made it perfectly clear what they expected from people and that no one would live up to it.

"Okay, everyone knows one another, of course," Captain Del Rosario said in accented English, and the room filled with happy assent from the crew in attendance. "But we have a couple of newbies on this ride, so I'm going to do a quick roll call." He glanced at Bez and Makeda, then motioned to the group in front of him. "Representing the ratings, we have Bosun Jay, along with Dema, Chuck, and Tenzi."

The group on one length of the sectional said hello, and smiled and waved. Chuck, who had ushered them onto the ship earlier, gave Makeda a head dip and a smile. They all seemed, to Bez's trained eye, to be Drukian, like the steward, which would make sense given what she suspected.

"Our second mate, Madiha, is on the bridge. Over here we have Jamila, one of our engineering crew."

The woman waved stiffly, decidedly less relaxed than the ratings as they gave their hellos, which was understandable given that she worked under Santos.

"Greg, the second engineer, and Pietr, the oil man, are down in the engine room."

"And then there's the ship's steward, AK, who you already met," Thompson said, gesturing toward the man who stood off to the side helping two people set out trays of baguette sandwiches and baskets of potato chips. "And the galley staff, Chef Rick and Assistant Chef Dana."

"Hi, everyone," Makeda said. "I'm just here to support Beznaria and get to Ibarania, but I look forward to getting to know everyone and learning more about the ship and what you all do. If I can help with anything at all, let me know."

The bitter undertone was gone from her voice. In fact, it was citrus bright, and served as a reminder to Bez that she didn't actually *know* Makeda. She had expected her ward to be shy and unsure of herself in the face of this strange situation and all of these unfamiliar people, but she seemed completely at ease being the center of attention. Was this the innate leadership of the al-Hurradassi line?

"Hello," Bez said, pulling her gaze from Makeda. "I will be handling a daily watch shift and security, if needed, and look forward to working with everyone."

She receded to the back of the room so she could stand against the wall, the better to watch the crew and their behaviors. Makeda moved back with her.

"Congratulations on your marriage," the chief engineer said, then added, "I hope that you know you can't spend your watch shifts entertaining your wife."

Bez slid her arm around Makeda's waist. "You'll find I'm able to manage both with no complaints from the crew or my boo, Chief Engineer."

That earned laughter from both the crew and the other officers, though Makeda stood stiffly at her side. Bez moved to pull her arm away, but Makeda clamped her own arm over it, holding it in place. Little by little—first in her arms, then her back—Makeda began to relax into the embrace.

Bez glanced down at her. Makeda's expression was calm, her focus entirely on the captain as he began to discuss some of the events that had led to the ship's delayed departure from the port, and what the rest of the journey would be like.

They stood that way for several minutes, Bez growing increasingly warm despite the cool air in the room as Makeda relaxed into her. Bez wasn't listening to the captain and crew as they bantered back and forth, though the drone of their voices hummed somewhere behind a wall of frantically flickering fireflies.

As the meeting broke up and the crew started to filter to their tables, Makeda looked up to catch Bez's eye. Her brow creased and she stood on tip toe. The thick fabric of her sweatshirt didn't serve as much padding as she pressed into Bez to maintain her balance.

"What's wrong?" she whispered, her breath a caress over the sensitive skin of Bez's ear.

"I'm confused," Bez replied in a low voice. "You were angry at my subterfuge but now you're . . . not."

Makeda smiled, the sweetness of it making Bez feel like the ship had just listed. It might have been the first time Makeda smiled *at* her and not just in her presence—certainly the first time she'd done it with her face so close and her gaze so determined—and Bez was discovering there was a world of difference. Dimple of destruction, indeed.

"I don't hurt people," Makeda whispered. "And I don't do lies. That's not me, and I've decided that I'm not going to compromise my values before we even reach the damn island."

Bez didn't say anything. For once in her life, the fireflies in her head had stopped blinking—they hadn't gone dark, though. They were full bright, illuminating the resolve in Makeda's smile.

Beznaria swallowed hard.

"On this boat? We're married and we'll act like it," Makeda continued. Her expression was soft but not yielding, and anyone who looked at them would think she was whispering sweet nothings when really she was giving marching orders. "I'm not going to have anyone question our devotion to one another. It will make everyone upset if they find out, it will mess up the energy of the crew, and it will make me feel bad. You may lie for work, but I'm going to make *your* lie work because cleaning up other people's messes is my superpower. If we're going to do this thing, we do it all the way."

She sank back on her heels and leaned her head on Bez's shoulder as she returned her attention to the crew's conversation. Her grip on Bez's arm didn't loosen and, in fact, tightened a bit.

Bez had been wrong; Makeda didn't enjoy the illusion of control. She enjoyed *actually* being in control, and that was something Bez hadn't accounted for when she'd grabbed the brightly blinking firefly messaging *pretend we're married*.

She'd made a rather large misstep. She was a dame of the guard, by lineage. She was a junior investigator of the WFM, by contract. She was the commendatore of Damsels in Distress Rescue Services, by choice. Those three spheres of her life all overlapped, and at the point of overlap—which would helpfully be labeled People You Absolutely Should Not Have Romantic Feelings For—was Makeda Hicks, distressed damsel and possible heir to the Ibaranian throne.

Bez had found Makeda attractive from the beginning, and when the opportunity had arisen, had leaned in for a kiss and been met with a bash in the teeth. Lesson learned. But seeing this fierceness in Makeda awakened a new sensation that wasn't simple duty or desire.

It was a problem, was what it was.

"Right," Bez managed hoarsely. "Make it work."

She understood what Makeda must have felt like now, being told they were married and being unable to ask questions immediately. Because she suddenly needed to know what Makeda meant by *do it all the way*. What did "all the way" entail? What was "it"? Clearly, she wanted to perform acts of affection—only in public? What about in their room? What about in that single bed?

She'd teasingly told Makeda she was an octopus, but what kind of sleeper was Makeda? How would she respond if Bez accidentally ensnared her? She'd thought she would push her away, given how angry she was, but now she was pressed against Bez as if it was entirely natural.

As if she enjoyed it.

Makeda tugged her toward their table.

Dema and Captain Del Rosario sat across from her, Makeda beside her, and AK and Thompson at either end of the table.

"Is there no hierarchy on this ship?" Bez asked after swallowing a mouthful of crisp, chewy baguette, pork belly, and vegetables. "The officers don't have their own lounge?"

Usually a chain of command required enforced separation, a reminder of who was in charge and who was not. At the WFM, it meant people like Lord Higginshoggins sat in a teal costume on a fake throne while other people did what he told them. On cargo ships, it meant some people ate in the fancy officer's mess and others ate in a mess with cheap chairs and tables and even cheaper silverware.

"No," Captain Del Rosario said. "One of the reasons I feel lucky to be captain of the *Virginia Queen* is that it's owned by a shipping company that actually cares for its employees."

"It's based out of Druk, where most of the ratings are from," Thompson said. "You know, the kingdom where happiness is seen as the most important human right? Those values are part of the company's values."

"Oh yes, Druk is the gold standard of kingdoms," Bez said. "Apart from their prince, who's been shirking his royal duties for the last decade or so while his sisters manage things."

"Our prince is on a quest for enlightenment," Dema said with an edge to her voice. "One must see the world and know all it contains, good and evil, before one can hope to be worthy of the sun throne."

AK took a conveniently large bite of banh mi that prevented him from adding his thoughts to the conversation.

Captain Del Rosario pointed a fork at Bez. "I've worked for some bad companies. Terrible. From the way they treated us, it was obvious they didn't see staff as human. Here, we are offered good pay, great benefits, onboard mental health services, and no one is better than anyone else."

"But aren't you the captain?" Bez asked. "You're supposed to believe you're better than everyone else."

That was how the world worked, and once, Bez had thought it was supposed to. Those at the top of the hierarchy were either divinely better or believed themselves to be.

Dema laughed, then ran a hand through her short hair. "Captain Del Rosario has more experience than most of us and has a different pay grade because of that, but that is different than being a better person."

"We try to eat breakfast and dinner together every day, and group activities are mixed," AK said, his gaze moving from Makeda to Bez and then back. "When I first started out, I also worked on ships where the ratings were treated as inferior. People believe what they're told every day, don't they? They react to what they're told their worth is. This shipping company tries to do out at sea what doesn't always happen on land—help everyone understand that they are as good as every other person, and that all people have the potential to be good."

"I love that!" Makeda was suddenly animated in a way she hadn't been when sulking around the B&B and Bez tried not to look startled. "I tried to do something similar at my last job, because there was this weird rift between the managers, the cashiers, and the stock people, but my manager said 'that Kumbaya crap isn't gonna fly with everyone' so we didn't even try."

"That's the thing—you have to try. It's an experiment in how people might live and work together in a society without one person being superior to another, I suppose," AK said before tucking back into his sandwich.

Bez took note that everyone was deferring to the ship's steward instead of the captain.

"We do usually have lunch separately, though," Dema added around a mouthful of sandwich. "And we have our own private lounges as well as a mixed one. Because this *is* a workplace, and we're in tighter quarters than any office. Sometimes we need space away from one another so that we don't blow up at each other."

"Right," Thompson said. "Even people you truly care about can get on your last darn nerve after days at sea, especially when the crew is stretched thin."

"I'm sure you two will understand after a few days on the open seas in that cabin together," Captain Del Rosario said.

They all laughed, but Bez felt Makeda's fingers slip around hers.

"I think we'll get along just fine, won't we, honey?" she asked, and Bez blinked several times.

"Of course." Bez tried to think of something to say, but Makeda's fingers were warm and distracting.

"How did you meet?" Thompson asked.

Makeda shrugged. "It's all happened so fast. I guess you could say she just kind of strong-armed her way into my life and I've been stuck with her ever since."

Captain Del Rosario barked out a laugh and nudged Bez jovially. "You know, people try to romanticize it, but that's exactly how it works sometimes."

Bez said . . . something, she wasn't sure what, but it made everyone else laugh some more. The conversation receded as her focus honed in on their entwined hands; each brush of skin and flex of finger sent undulating waves of good sensation through her. Their hands were under the table, and so weren't integral to the act they were putting on, but neither let go. Bez hadn't informed Makeda that she didn't like holding hands—another one of her relationship flaws, she'd been told. After a minute or two, it made her want to gnaw her hand off at the wrist. Or it usually did. Maybe her sense of professionalism was what allowed her to enjoy what was happening. She was on the job after all.

It was a quick meal, with the crew eager to get to bed after a long day of loading. When Bez and Makeda got back to their cabin, Makeda went into the bathroom, chattering away about everyone they'd met—as if her anger from earlier had disappeared entirely.

"Do you get weirded out by people talking to you while they pee?" she called out.

Bez sat down on the couch, her head back against the cushion. The soothing scent of the nearby incense cones filled her nose.

"No," she said. "Though I'd rather not be involved in any other bathroom-related functions. Wait, vomiting is fine. I don't mind a between-retch conversation if it helps you."

"Hmm, okay. Everyone is so nice, aren't they? I told Thompson about the face masks I brought with me and we're going to have a facial night tomorrow when she gets off shift. Dema was telling me about the cinnamon buns the chef makes for breakfast. Do you like cinnamon? That seems like something your wife should know."

It was like someone had slipped a wind-up key into Makeda without Bez's notice, and one side of her mouth lifted in a tired smile. She preferred this species of sea snail; not because she was better in any way, but because for the first time since Bez had met her, Makeda seemed excited about something. Happy, even.

Another question echoed from the bathroom, though Bez hadn't been able to remember if she liked cinnamon yet so she could answer the last one.

"Do these toilets just evacuate into the ocean?"

"Are you always so chatty while you're on the toilet?" Bez asked, her words slightly slurred by fatigue. "Maybe this was one of the issues of your past relationships. Not everyone is as open-minded as me."

The toilet flushed, the sink water ran for a moment, and then Makeda appeared in front of her, a blurry figure with crossed arms. "You know what? We're not sharing the bed after all. You can sleep on the couch."

"I can sleep?" Bez's eyelids drifted shut—in that moment all of the travel and research and investigating she'd been doing for months, and all of the relief she hadn't yet allowed herself to feel since they'd boarded the ship, pushed her down into the rock-hard couch and made it soft as sea grass beneath her.

Henna Jeta had told Bez for years and years that she should live her own life, that she was not beholden to the past glory of the Chetchevalieres and al-Hurradassis, or to a promise she'd made when she was a child.

But Bez was currently on her way back home with Queen Aazi's heir, and she would prove everyone wrong.

The hardest part—convincing Makeda to go with her—was done. Now she could sleep. The rest of the trip would be easy, even if she could still feel the imprint of Makeda's small hand in her own as she drifted into a dreamless slumber.

Chapter 12

The next morning Makeda awoke to the scent of coffee brewing and the sound of a guest singing in the shower as if they wanted everyone in the B&B to hear them. The house was also moving—bouncing?

She opened her eyes in a dark room with the barest bit of light peeking through the blackout curtains.

Not house—cargo ship.

Not guest—Beznaria.

Makeda was out at sea.

She was going to claim her possible princesshood, and then reject it. She was going to save her mother. And to do that she was going to have to be in even closer quarters with Beznaria than she'd tried to avoid at the Golden Crown.

The night before, the investigator had passed out cold on the couch, and no amount of tugging or prodding had been enough to wake her. Makeda, exhausted herself and not trying to throw her back out or sleep in a bed with someone with their outside clothes on, had draped one of the extra blankets over the investigator, showered, and curled up in the bed. She'd thought the rocking of the ship, unfamiliar setting, and nerves about the adventure she was undertaking would keep her up all night, but she'd dropped into a deep sleep as soon as her bonnet hit the pillow.

Now she lay in bed as warbled lyrics in an unfamiliar language erased the last vestiges of her dream, an anxiety adventure in which she'd mistakenly added a nude photo of herself to GrabRite's weekly sale circular and had to collect them all as customers tried to flip through them.

Beznaria's voice wasn't angelic by any means, but there was something endearing in the way she was off-key one moment and pitch-perfect the next. It took Makeda almost a full song to realize that she was listening to Bez sing in the nude, which jolted her fully awake.

The singing stopped and the sound of running water tapered off. Soon Beznaria would come out into the living space and they would have to talk about what exactly they were doing.

Makeda lay back down and pulled the sheet over her head. They had avoided sharing the bed the first night, but even having avoided that awkwardness, she was living in close quarters with a partner, of sorts, for the foreseeable future. What was she supposed to do? How was she supposed to act? Usually she would be up and out of bed first, straightening the room, preparing coffee, making sure she was useful. The night before, she'd resolved that things would be different going forward, but now she wasn't sure what *different* was supposed to be. She didn't want to just be mean or selfish. That wasn't the opposite of being help-y, and even if it was, it didn't make her feel good.

Wait—would Bez be naked? Back at the Golden Crown she'd talked about walking around in her underwear like it was no big deal, and they'd been total strangers. What would happen now?

Sweat broke out on her brow even though the room was cool.

The bathroom door opened and she heard Bez walk out. Even her stride sounded confident. She'd only seen the investigator show a lack of composure once—when Makeda had whispered in her ear that they were going to act married for real.

Makeda's cheeks went hot and she frantically scrambled for a crumb of the bravado she'd felt the night before with her arm wrapped around Bez and her plan settling into place.

A light flipped on.

When she peeked from under the blanket, she saw Bez wasn't nude—she was dressed in tapered charcoal gray sweatpants and a black Henley that was one size too small and so exactly the right size. The sleeves were pushed up to her elbows, exposing the smooth skin of her forearms and that tantalizing tip of her tattoo.

"Bonmera," Bez said, pulling her hair up into a bun at the top of her head, revealing an undercut. That felt like another intimate revelation, the close shaven sides of Bez's head that Makeda hadn't previously noticed despite being within lip-busting distance.

"You're not wearing your suit," Makeda said, her voice scratchy from sleep and the sudden throat-drying understanding that she had to share quarters with *this* woman for ten days.

"My suit is a uniform for a different job. Do you prefer it?" Bez cut a glance at Makeda as she walked to the kitchenette.

"I don't care what you wear," Makeda said, sitting up as Bez pulled down mugs and poured coffee and hot water for her own tea. It was technically true. The woman looked good in both a suit and sweats.

"Ah, I forgot you're a grumpy lobster in the morning," Bez said, grinning as if she'd seen right through Makeda's indifference. "You slept through breakfast, and I didn't want to wake you. I brought back some food for you and there are pastries and other snacks out in the mess. Here."

"Don't you mean crab?" Makeda asked, taking the cup. "Thank you."

"Crabs are generally good-natured creatures. Lobsters can be quite rude, though."

"Mmm-hmm," Makeda said, sipping her coffee and deciding not to delve more deeply into how Beznaria was privy to the temperaments of crustaceans.

Bez sprawled on the couch with a cup of tea and pinned her with a bright gaze. "Are we going to talk about the definition and parameters of 'making it work' as a faux married couple? I'm glad that you're no longer angry about the situation but I didn't think you'd be so . . . *eager*. Didn't you say you'd prefer shoveling coal to pretending to be my wife?"

She sounded a bit too pleased with the change in the situation.

Makeda rolled her eyes. "Don't get a big head. I decided that I'm going to use this as practice."

"Practice?" Bez glanced at her, interest dancing in her amber eyes.

Makeda felt her lips press together, her body instinctively fighting against revealing anything like vulnerability. But she'd laid down the rules of their relationship herself, and talking about the practice would be practice in itself.

"Practice pretending to be something I'm not, like a princess," she said.

"Right. I told you that you seem more like a queen. I do believe I'm the one with actual professional experience here."

Makeda would have pulled the sheet over her head again if she wouldn't risk spilling her coffee.

Bez squinted at her. "What else? That doesn't explain your change of heart."

Usually it was Makeda asking the intrusive questions. Being fake married to an investigator was going to be a problem.

"Relationship practice," she said almost defiantly, her chin lifting. "All my past relationships have been me giving and someone else taking. A lot of that was my fault, if I'm honest, but after getting dumped and fired I tried to do things differently. I decided I wasn't going to let myself be used ever again—and then I found myself pulled into a fake marriage I had no say in on a ship I was misled into getting onto and heading toward an island I've been trying to forget existed."

Bez blinked several times. "Go on."

Makeda let out a long breath, sorting through motivations that were still somewhat unclear. Every instinct urged her not to share what she'd been thinking, fodder for ridicule, but she could feel the ship's engine in her bones and feel the waves bumping along its hull. Like the Ferris wheel, this wasn't solid ground; it was a place where she could indulge her fantasies because they wouldn't affect her life at all when her feet landed firmly back on the solid ground of reality.

"I've decided that we—you and I—have to act like a real couple outside this room because I don't want anyone to find out we're lying. But I also want to do the things I wish I'd done in past relationships. Like . . . being independent. And not brushing aside things that upset me. And asking for what I want and need without feeling guilty."

Just saying it out loud made her feel like she'd stripped nude, and not in a fun way. She waited for Beznaria to laugh or make fun of her, but she was still looking at her with that serious expression, like Makeda wasn't making a fool of herself.

"And you want to practice that with me?" Bez asked, and Makeda rolled her head to the side.

"You're the only person I can practice it with, for now. Even if it's just ten days, I can use this time to do what I've never managed in real life," Makeda said. "If I'm going to pretend I care about being royalty, I can pretend to have standards for myself."

Bez leaned back on the couch, propping her long legs up on the coffee table before taking a pensive sip of her tea.

"That seems like a reasonable plan," she said. "I love playing a role—it's one of the best parts of being an investigator."

Makeda internally winced, thinking of their near kisses after Bez had said herself that she intended to charm Makeda into giving her what she wanted. And now here they were on the ship.

"This would also be covered under the rules of our contract, since your past relationship style has caused you distress," Beznaria continued. "I think we should keep up the act *inside* the room, too. It will be less jarring than having to change arbitrarily because we cross a threshold, and leave less chance of one of us slipping up."

She held Makeda's gaze, unblinking this time.

Makeda was glad she had just swallowed her coffee because she would have definitely choked on it. She nodded. "That's a good idea. Inside the room, too."

Neither spoke for a moment, and Makeda thought about the tension that seemed to sometimes burst into life between them. Could all of that be an act? And even if it was, did she care?

"There are limits to how far our act can go, for those same reasons," Beznaria added. Her gaze lingered on Makeda in a way that felt like it was expanding possibilities instead of shutting them down.

"Oh?" That should have been good news for Makeda, but she felt an odd sense of frustration. "Why? I'm asking because I explained the rules I'm operating by, so you should do the same. Not because I *want* to go past certain limits."

She tried to maintain Beznaria's all-seeing, un-blinking gaze, and hoped the woman couldn't tell that her cheeks were hotter than the beverage she was drinking.

"Well." Bez worked her lower lip with her teeth, and Makeda ran her tongue over the healing cut that was the indentation of one of those teeth. "There are cultural reasons, but I have agreed to transport you as an investigator of the WFM and I have sworn to rescue you via the contract we signed before we left."

"There was nothing in that contract prohibit-ing relations between you and a client," Makeda pointed out. Was Beznaria making stuff up to let her down gently?

"It's in the fine print," Beznaria said.

"No. The fine print only said, 'Romantic entan-glements shall not be encouraged or pursued by either party except in specific extenuating circum-stances.' That's not forbidding anything. More like gently discouraging."

Beznaria looked up at her through long lashes. "You read the fine print?"

She might have been flirting if Makeda didn't know she was judging her for past deeds that had made going to Ibarania necessary.

Makeda huffed. "I do. Always. When I cosigned that loan for Amber, I knew what I was getting into. I was eager to please, not ignorant."

Beznaria nodded. "Generally, the people under my protection are in need of my strength, wisdom, and guidance and are perhaps not at their best decision-making capacity. This hasn't explicitly come up before, but throwing in any kinds of feelings or fucking could be problematic. Can a client say no to me? Can I say no to a client?"

Makeda was so close to asking Bez to say *fucking* again—apparently she *was* an accent ho—but that wouldn't help the situation. "So you do have some shame," she said instead.

"I do," Bez said quietly. When she spoke again, it was in her usual singsong, upbeat tone. "Are you disappointed? I can be shameless. There's lots of shameless fun to be had before feelings or fucking enter the situation."

Makeda shifted on the bed so that her back was against the wall and Bez couldn't see her face. "You know, you really are fascinating. I would call you careless, but you toe the line of impropriety too well not to know exactly what you're doing."

"I'm an expert navigator of fine print and fine lines," Bez said, her voice taking on the slightly distracted tone she used when she was talking just for the sake of it. "I don't know much about how a married person should act, unfortunately, so I think I'll be good practice for you if it's some sort of relationship resiliency boot camp you're seeking."

Makeda laughed ruefully. "I believe that."

Bez's head popped up. "I'll have you know that my complete lack of relationship skills doesn't stop me from being in high demand. Even on our small island, with everyone and their father knowing I am rude, careless, and easily distracted, I'm quite the pita straight from the oven."

"Of course, you are," Makeda said, reaching for a pillow with her free hand and tucking it behind her. "It makes you even more appealing. To be the person who fixed a walking trash fire of red flags is a badge of honor to some people."

"By 'some people,' do you mean yourself?" Bez asked. She raised her eyebrows and her glasses slid down her nose.

"Maybe." Makeda thought of the women who'd shared her home, her bed, and her life, but had never really ever shared her heart. She liked doing things for people, but how many of the things she resented having done for others had been attempts to be indispensable? She'd thought making herself needed was *normal*. Necessary. Otherwise, what would keep someone around?

Being a doormat hadn't led to success, but it had seemed logical at the time.

She sighed. "I guess trying to fix disaster people and hoping they appreciate it isn't the best basis for a relationship."

"Did it ever occur to you that disaster people don't want to be fixed?" Bez asked. "I wouldn't know from experience, but I'd hazard that when the right person comes along, we fix ourselves."

Just like that, Makeda remembered why she hated opening up to other people. It allowed them to land blows when they didn't even realize they were swinging in her direction.

"Okay, great talk team," she said, slapping a hand down on the duvet. "What's the plan for the day?"

"I have to meet the captain about my schedule, and then our safety walk starts in half an hour, so I'll meet you at the door to the portside stairwell on the main deck, okay?" In the blink of an eye, her expression shifted from friendly to stern.

"Go directly to the meeting point, please. Don't leave the stairwell, don't make any deviations. I don't want you falling off the ship before you learn how not to fall off the ship. Because it's not dolphins who'll be plunging into the ocean to rescue you, it will be me, and I've already checked that particular item off on my bucket list."

Then she grabbed a sweatshirt from a hook and strode out the door.

The coffee Makeda was sipping was strong, and she figured that was why she felt a little light-headed in the wake of that last declaration. The way Bez could swing from unbridled chaos to chaos bridled by responsibility might also have played a small part in the sensation. Her methods made no sense, but as Makeda snagged a cinnamon roll from the platter she had to admit that Beznaria had done everything she said she would.

After showering—the multi-head setup was so amazing that she understood why Bez had been singing—she threw on a white T-shirt, black leggings, and a yellow hoodie and headed out.

She paused when she entered the stairwell, a bit of rebellion surging up in her. While Bez's orders had been kind of hot, Makeda didn't actually have to listen to them.

She headed in the opposite direction, up to the highest part of the superstructure—it was a deck with a guardrail around it and a few large pieces of equipment that Makeda assumed fed information to the deck below. It also had a few benches and provided a three-sixty view of the ship and the ocean.

Both apprehension and awe filled her as she stepped fully onto the open deck and wind whipped at her locks—even though she'd always told herself ocean was ocean was ocean, she definitely wasn't in Atlantic City anymore.

When they'd boarded the ship, the sky and sea had been various shades of shadow outside the bright lights of the port. She'd also been nervous, overwhelmed, and barely able to process that she was really going to make the journey. But this—it was beautiful, too beautiful almost.

All around her was nothing but blue sky and bluer sea and golden morning sunlight skipping all over the waves like magic she'd stopped believing in much too young.

Her eyes couldn't fix on any one detail as she gripped the railing and shuffled cautiously around the perimeter of the deck, taking in the view bit by bit. It felt like all the possibility in the world was spreading out around her from beneath her feet; like she was the center of everything, and that was fine and natural.

She'd thought she would be afraid when the light of day arrived, might regret ever agreeing to this ridiculous plan, but in that moment she felt something she hadn't in months: optimistic. Like maybe those golden waves could refill her watering can with something that wasn't her old saccharine sweetness or the newfound bitterness that'd been bubbling up. Something that had been there before the loneliness and the fear—before the whole shining sea of her own hopes and dreams had become a watering can that served as a reservoir for others.

Her eyes stung as the wind whipped at her face, and she blinked back tears she didn't know the cause of.

Being out at sea must make you suddenly prone to deep thoughts.

After a few minutes, she carefully made her way back to the door and headed down for the safety walk.

When she got to the bottom of the steps, she saw Beznaria through the window of the stairwell door, speaking to someone. It was strange, coming across her in a situation where they weren't in the B&B or somewhere they had arrived together. Beznaria could have been any woman Makeda happened to spot on a ship in the middle of the Atlantic—the problem was that, if Beznaria had been any woman, Makeda would've thought she was exactly her type.

Bez was looking at whomever she was talking to intently, nodding, staring, but not quite in the same way that she did with Makeda, which made her feel both smug and annoyed with herself. Jealousy had never been her style and it shouldn't kick in while she was *pretending* to be married.

When she stepped through the door onto the deck, she saw that the other person was a woman dressed in a deck officer's uniform. She was slightly shorter than Bez with an olive complexion, rosy cheeks, and curls mostly covered by hijab except for a few that escaped to frame her round face. Bez didn't look away from the woman as they chatted, but reached her hand out toward Makeda expectantly, like she'd been waiting for her to arrive. When Makeda took her hand, Bez pulled her close to snuggle her under her arm. She stiffened for a moment, then remembered it was all pretend and wrapped both arms around Bez's waist. She decided in that moment that they were the kind of couple who occasionally crossed the line of annoying public displays of affection.

"This is Second Mate Madiha Alvi," Bez said. "Officer Alvi, this is my sea snail."

Makeda glanced up at Bez dubiously. "You really need to chill with that."

"It's lovely to meet you," Madiha said in a surprisingly quiet voice with hints of a Midwestern accent. "I was on watch last night when you arrived and during the midnight snack. So this is your first time on a ship?"

Makeda nodded. "I thought I would be scared but I actually kind of like it? I was just up on the top deck—"

Bez squeezed her harder. "Were you now?"

"—and it was so peaceful. I'm glad I went, even just for a minute. Because I could. I'm going to try to live this experience to the fullest. When will I be on a cargo ship again?"

Bez's grip relaxed.

"That's good," Madiha said. "Some people end up hating it and they're stuck slowly going mad for weeks." She laughed, but not as if what she'd said was funny.

If a person hated being on the ship, there'd be no hiding that from everyone else on board. Discomfort probably made a voyage tough for everyone; Makeda was glad she'd decided to go along with things, even if it had felt too much like giving in.

"I know your wife has spent time in the Ibaranian Maritime Forces and worked in shipping, so this safety instruction might be redundant for you if she's already given you the tour."

"I haven't told her too much. My plan was just to keep her close to me," Bez said. "Not have her go gallivanting on the flying bridge without saying a word to anyone."

Madiha nodded. "Right. Well, it'll take us about half an hour to walk fore and aft."

"Cool," Makeda said cheerfully, having no idea what that meant, but interested nonetheless.

"I guess the most important rule is the 'one hand' rule," Madiha said as she held up a palm and wiggled her fingers. "One hand for you, one for the ship. Always have one hand free so if you slip, trip, or tumble, you can grab onto something solid."

"Like me," Bez said, flexing a little, and Makeda glanced up at her. Bez winked.

The tour moved quickly, with Makeda quickly understanding that she'd underestimated how long it would take to walk across the ship. They walked what seemed like miles as Madiha explained the rules in rapid-fire fashion. She also pointed out the location of the lifeboats, and on the return trip stopped to show Makeda how to release one if necessary and how to climb inside.

"They're fun to hang out in actually, as long as you don't move anything around or mess around with levers so that you accidentally launch yourself into the sea." Madiha opened the entrance hatch to the orange pod and let Makeda crawl inside for a minute; Beznaria didn't follow her in. Bench seats lined the walls and both sides of the metal panel that ran through the middle of the boat.

Every item was labeled, and everything was in its place. The lifeboat wasn't pretty, but the organization comforted her. She noticed that the steering wheel was up high, so the driver could see out of a windshield at the top of the boat; the driver's seat was a U-shaped piece of plastic secured to the ceiling of the boat that didn't seem nearly secure enough to Makeda, but she figured she just didn't understand how it was used.

"There's water, rations, and survival supplies beneath each seat and in these cubbies. Each boat can hold thirty people, way more than our crew," Madiha said as they clambered out. "But that's fine because they're not just for emergencies for us—they're also for helping others who might need it if we're in the area. We look out for each other on the open water, because if we don't, who will?"

"Honestly, I kind of want to make a tiny house from a lifeboat now. It's all so orderly." Makeda glanced at Bez to see what she thought of tiny houses, but she was frowning out at the crest-capped water. "Are you seasick?"

Bez's queasy expression drew up into one of indignation. "You're asking *me* this, landlubber? I was just thinking."

Bez held out her hand again, and Makeda took it as she hopped down from the lifeboat. Makeda knew the gesture was because she'd asked her to take their fake marriage seriously. It shouldn't have given her any kind of warm fuzzy feeling, but she appreciated that the investigator was trying.

That bar was so low the long-legged Ibaranian could clear it without changing her stride, but *trying* hadn't even been something Makeda'd requested of a partner before. She had never been treated horribly, and she was well aware that others had been through worse, but that was what had made it easier to settle for not-so-bad. She'd locked her expectations away in the vault with her anger and hopes and dreams. Bez had somehow picked the lock; Makeda wasn't sure what to do with a fake marriage to someone who'd activated real feelings of every kind from the moment they'd met.

"Well, I need to power walk back, but you two take your time," Madiha said, grinning as she glanced back and forth between them. "I'm the one on the clock, not my honeymoon. If you decide to, ah, explore the lifeboat, make sure you close the door tightly after you so no sea birds get in."

The woman hurried away, leaving Makeda peering at the lifeboat with renewed interest.

"What do you think of life at sea so far?" Bez asked, starting to stroll back toward the accommodations. She released Makeda's hand, but only to switch positions so that she was the one closer to the guardrail as they walked back. Then she took up Makeda's other hand.

Makeda felt a brief spike of panic but wrangled it before it could get ahead of her. She wasn't a teenager on her first date at the mall, wondering if the girl she was with really liked her or just wanted a shopping buddy to help her pick out flannel shirts at JC Penney. She was a grown ass woman strolling with her fake wife; there was nothing to worry about because the end of this relationship was predetermined.

"I feel surprisingly good so far," Makeda said, "Though I haven't seen too much."

"What would you like to do? I was thinking of taking an afternoon exercise class in the gym before my next shift, if that's okay with you," Bez said, and then looked down at her expectedly.

"Is this like some royal bodyguard thing?" she laughed nervously. "You don't need to ask my permission."

Bez's brows furrowed. "I'm aware of that. But I did bring you onto a boat without any notice. The least I can do when I'm not on shift is check what you'd like to do before making plans."

"Oh, yeah."

Bez squeezed her hand, the action somehow both reassuring and embarrassing. "I'm not the best at relationships, but I think moving forward you should perhaps take whatever behaviors you associate with a royal guard, whose role is to make sure their charge is comfortable and safe, and believe that you deserve them from anyone—friend, romantic partner, or otherwise—whom you allow into your life."

Makeda caught her bottom lip with her teeth as she absorbed Bez's words, and then nodded. "That's pretty good advice. Maybe you're not as bad at relationships as you think."

Bez laughed. "Oh, I'm bad. I'm great at giving advice to other people about theirs, though. I worked in the royal marriage matchmaking division for a while and observed a lot of things."

"Observed, but didn't learn anything yourself?" Makeda asked.

"Hm." Bez looked out toward the ocean, where a sea bird was winging alongside the ship. "I guess I haven't had much practice in the last few years, now that I think about it. My last girlfriend was . . ." Bez's stride slowed as she got lost in thought, then resumed its regular pace. "Well, that is not important. But perhaps you're right and I've learned as much as I've observed. Though I will say that there are plenty of things I cannot do myself but can still critique via observation. Decorative cake baking, application of makeup, animal coiffure."

Makeda was tempted to ask more about Bez's last girlfriend, but that seemed too real for their pretend relationship.

"Well, this will be good practice for you, too, then," she said, though something about that didn't feel right either. She decided to change the subject.

"Speaking of practice—are you going to give me any royalty lessons now? Teach me to waltz and then give me a makeover?"

"I thought you didn't want to do those things," Bez said.

"Well I don't, but I guess that's what we're supposed to do now."

Bez squinted down at her. "I think you could walk into any ballroom dressed exactly as you are and you would still look like a queen to me."

Makeda's ears burned even as they were buffeted by the sea breeze.

"I accept this compliment, but I also suspect that it's deflecting from the fact that you don't know how to waltz," Makeda said, her smile pulling her cheeks tight.

Bez lifted her chin.

"The waltz means nothing culturally in Ibarania outside of ballroom competition. We are a rhythmic people with our own dances." Bez pushed her glasses up by the bridge and continued talking, but Makeda was momentarily distracted by that small action. She'd sniped at Bez about her fingerprint-covered glasses for days, and now Bez had stopped touching the lens.

She wasn't sure the investigator had even noticed. She felt a strange happiness soar through her, like the birds that kept pace with the ship. Bez had noticed something that bothered Makeda and stopped doing it. But her elation was followed by a twist of unease. She'd been rude when she said those things to Bez. Maybe her behavior at the time had been warranted, but she didn't like thinking that some part of Bez's subconscious had reacted to her attempts to be unkind.

Bez was still talking. "I can teach you the traditional knife dance that's been passed down in my family for—"

She stopped when Makeda reached up her free hand and pressed her index finger against Bez's glasses lens. This was the second time she'd seen the investigator shocked into silence. She found she preferred surprising Beznaria more than she did changing her.

"What was that for?" Bez asked, her voice wavering between delight and dismay.

"Just an urge I had," Makeda said.

"I suppose that's fine then," Bez said, then pushed her glasses up by the lens, her fingerprint overlapping Makeda's.

When they reached the accommodations building a few minutes later, they hesitated for a moment at the door before releasing each other's hands.

"I guess I'll go check out the library and see if they have anything to keep me busy," Makeda said. "And you'll go to your class?"

Bez nodded.

"Don't walk around on the deck without me," she said as they went up the stairs, then added, "Please."

The library was empty when Makeda went in and she walked around it slowly, trying not to think about the fact that she and Bez had spent a morning together where she hadn't had to plan or predict—everything had just happened naturally.

Something about how smoothly things were going made her uneasy.

As she looked over the tightly packed shelves of dark wood, with the books stacked seemingly any which way, she decided a book wouldn't keep her busy enough. She started pulling books out and stacking them—alphabetical order would keep her busy while Bez was occupied with work and exercise, and make things easier for the crew.

And maybe it would get rid of the lingering sensation of warm strong fingers closed firmly around her left hand, a sensation that was much too real.

Chapter 13

*B*y the third day, Bez had fallen back into ship life easily—friendly conversation, helping where needed, and being where she needed to be when she needed to be there. She'd almost forgotten how enjoyable it could be, since everything good had been shrouded by her last, traumatizing moments on a cargo ship.

Captain Del Rosario had been right about the atmosphere of the ship. The difference between that work experience and life on the *Virginia Queen* and her last job at sea was like an olive and a grape—she'd expected something salty only to find it was sweet.

She wondered if that had anything to do with Makeda, as she searched for the woman. She'd gotten off her watch shift and found their cabin empty.

"Bez! Do you want to play a match, or do you prefer getting your beat down in the gym?" Tenzi called out from the Ping-Pong table on the far side of the room. She and Chuck rocketed the ball back and forth, despite the fact that the ship was rocking on rough seas. The woman turned to grin at Bez over her shoulder, but still managed to swing her paddle out and catch the serve Chuck had tried to sneak through, smashing it into the corner of the table where he dove just short of reaching it.

It wasn't a fluke—it was a lifetime of training, muscle memory, and reflexes that made even Bez feel slow and uncoordinated.

"Can't you let me win just once?" Chuck groaned.

"You'll win when your mastery exceeds mine," Tenzi said. "Though I suppose if I let you win once in a while, it would let you know what victory feels like and motivate you to work harder."

"I believe I'll pass," Bez said. "I'm far more likely to hurt myself lunging for a tiny plastic ball than I am getting flipped over your head. Plus, I need to find my wife."

Bez tilted her head a bit, wondering why she hadn't just said she needed to find Makeda. Everyone knew her name. Everyone believed they were married. She told herself that she was just instinctively leaning into the role of smug newly married person.

"I saw her heading to the library," Chuck said, trying to aim his shot toward the unprotected corner of Tenzi's side of the table.

Tenzi launched herself up and sent the ball careening back, then landed lightly on her feet, then added, "She's been in and out of there a lot."

"Thank you. I'll go see if she's there," Bez said, wondering if she had somehow overlooked the fact that Makeda was a prolific reader. She surely didn't know as much about the woman as she might have wanted to, but she would have noticed that.

When she sneezed while standing a few feet away from the door to the library, she understood what was going on.

She opened the door to find Makeda kneeling on the ground surrounded by stacks of books on nearly every surface except the shelves they were supposed to be on.

"Keeping yourself busy?" she asked, and Makeda startled and dropped the book she'd been holding.

"Oh! Hi." Makeda smiled like she'd been caught doing something she wasn't supposed to do. She was dressed in a black tank top and jeans with her hair pulled up into a ponytail so that the long column of her throat was fully exposed. She ran a fingertip back and forth over her collarbone, which might have been nothing more than a sheepish gesture if anyone else had done it. Bez found herself imagining her own fingertips over the soft skin there, tracing it down toward that hollow between Makeda's breasts.

"Bez?" Makeda's voice was high-pitched, drawing Beznaria out of the erotic direction her imagination had taken.

"I was just admiring your stacks," Bez said, gesturing toward the books piled near her. "Though I have to ask what exactly you're doing?"

Makeda looked up at her with eyes that were slightly wild.

"Well, I was going to read but then I saw that the shelves were a mess, so I decided to organize them.

I've been at it while you work your shifts, but today I didn't notice how much time had passed."

"And why did you decide that?" Bez asked, frowning. "To do hours of work on a ship that you're not paid crew on?"

She sensed motion and turned to find AK coming out of a room down the hall; likely his office. He caught her eye and then walked over to her, his steps light but sure.

"We're about to do satellite phone calls. Do you two want to go first?"

Bez saw the moment where he first understood what was happening in the room and the moment where he tamped down his initial reaction of frustration. "Oh hey, what's going on in here?"

"The shelves were a bit messy so I thought I would reorganize them," Makeda said.

AK rubbed his fingertips back and forth through the short hair at the nape of his neck. "They actually were already organized, using my personal system I've developed over the last few years."

He said this as nicely as he could, but there was really no totally judgment free way to point out to someone that they'd just wrecked something you'd worked hard on.

"I was just trying to—" Makeda squeezed her eyes shut. "Help."

"I get it," AK said.

"I just—I thought I would try to do something useful."

AK blew out a breath, not in frustration, but as if he were processing what he was seeing. "Okay.

Well, maybe this is a sign that I needed to change some things up in here. Why don't you just leave all these out and—"

The ship hit another rough wave and listed a bit—not much, but enough to knock over one precarious stack that then toppled over several others.

"—and I'll take care of them later."

"I can help put them back," Makeda offered, gathering books that had fallen.

"No, you can't actually," AK said. "Because that would require being inside of my head and knowing where I want them placed. But it's all right, I'll do it later."

He smiled.

"Sorry," Makeda said.

AK nodded his acknowledgment. "I'd say it's partially my fault for not realizing that you would need something to do."

Bez stiffened. "And why would you realize that?"

The steward was acting like he somehow knew Makeda when Bez had known her for at least several days longer.

AK turned his grin on her. "It's my job to know what fulfills people."

Bez grudgingly nodded; she still didn't like his presumption, but given who she thought he was, figuring out what made people happy was likely muscle memory for him in the same way being able to complete feats of dexterity was for Tenzi.

"I'm really sorry," Makeda said, drawing their attention back to her. Her expression was taut. "I should have asked instead of thinking it was a nice surprise."

"I accept your apology," AK said. "I appreciate that you were working so hard to do something for the crew, and in the end we've both learned something. Don't dwell on it because I won't."

Makeda frowned, but then nodded and stood.

"Do you want to call your grandmother?" Bez asked. "I'm sure she'd love to hear how you're doing."

"Yeah. She'll love hearing that my adventure thus far has been ruining someone's library, so she can shake her head and wonder where she went wrong." She grimaced. "I do stuff like this all the time and never learn when it doesn't work out."

"Look, I'm sure it works out more often than not, at great cost to you and no one else. If that wasn't the case, you would have stopped. You're too practical to do things that never work." Bez took Makeda's hand, was holding it before she realized what she'd done. "You saw a situation that needed to be fixed and tried to fix it. It wasn't necessary, but the fact that you tried is . . . good leadership."

Makeda smiled weakly. "I told you you were good at this," she said in a low voice.

They headed over to the communications room, where Makeda went first while AK left to gather other crew who needed to call their friends and family. After her allotted five-minute call was over, Makeda came out of the room with her mood lifted. "Grandmore is doing fine. She said that Kojak has been wearing his fashionable sleeve dress and is feeling himself."

Bez laughed. "I kind of miss that little demon."

And it was true—she was used to traveling and always being on the move but she rarely made connections or befriended small wrinkled felines. She wondered how she would feel when Makeda claimed her prize and returned to her job at GrabRite. She reminded herself that even if Makeda wouldn't be in Ibarania permanently, she'd have to come back from time to time to do royal events. It wasn't as if she'd never see her again, not that that would bother her.

Such was life.

"I'll go make a few calls," she said, brushing aside the dour mood that had coincidentally started to close in on her.

She left Makeda and AK talking in the hallway and quickly input the number to the WFM's main office. She'd checked her email in the computer room the day before and had received no response and was starting to worry.

"Office of Lord Higginshoggins, how may I help you?" came the response from one of the secretaries and Bez almost sighed in relief.

"This is Junior Investigator Chetchevaliere," Bez said, pacing back and forth around the small room. "I'd like to be connected to Lord Higginshoggins's cell phone."

She waited a long moment, and when there was no response glanced at the phone's screen—the call had cut out.

"Odd," she muttered, then decided to try her grandmother. Higginshoggins had visited her, maybe he'd given her a contact number.

Her grandmother didn't pick up—she was possibly screening calls since so many journalists had reached out to her—so Bez called her parents.

"We are not doing any interviews," her father said in English when the call picked up. "Please leave us alone. Thank you!"

"It's Bezzie," she said quickly before he could hang up.

"Bezzie!" She could hear her father's smile in the way he said her name. "I thought you were coming home, where are you? Things are a mess here. I had to give the tourism minister a piece of my mind yesterday because he wants your grandmother to do a live TV interview."

"I'm traveling by sea," Bez said. "It will take a while."

"Your siblings told me this and I have to ask, why didn't you just let us pay for a plane ticket? We can afford it."

Bez blinked several times.

"I didn't think of it," she admitted sheepishly.

"No, because you always do things without asking for help and find the most bizarre way possible." He laughed. "You are truly my daughter, and I love this about you, but I wish you were here already. That boss of yours has been trying to talk to your grandmother too, and asking me and your mother if we know what really happened. He's lucky I'm a pacifist."

There was a knock on the door, signaling her time with the phone was up.

"Did he leave a number where you could reach him?" she asked quickly.

"No, he just keeps showing up unannounced. He rented a Rolls Royce and keeps showing up like he's some bigwig. He even made them move the date of the announcement up by a week."

Bez gripped the phone more tightly. "What?"

Moving up by a week meant that they would arrive the day of the announcement ball. Not with time to prepare and have Makeda properly recognized.

"It makes no sense! We've waited years and years, and now they have to rush everything? For what?"

Her father's voice was getting more and more high-pitched, but another knock meant Bez didn't have time to give him even her meager comfort.

"I'll try to figure out what's going on," she said. "I have to go now but I'll talk to you soon."

She didn't tell him not to say anything to Higgins-hoggins before she hung up—he was a Chetchevaliere and knew not to share their business with someone who couldn't be trusted.

Her brain fireflies were flashing warning signals as she exited the room, but she tried to pretend nothing was amiss.

"Everything okay?" Makeda asked.

"Splendid!" Bez pushed her glasses up. "Nothing to worry about at all."

Makeda raised her brows. "Okay. Glad to hear it."

Bez knew she was acting strange, and Makeda was one of the few people who seemed to be able to discern the levels of her strangeness.

"I have to go change for my martial arts class, I'll see you in a bit," she said, and then hurried off down the hall.

She had made a mistake in grabbing at the first option that had jumped out to her. What had she been thinking? She relied on the fact that things generally always worked out for her, but this was cutting it much too close. If she failed now she'd be breaking two promises, to Henna Jeta and Makeda, and honor aside, the thought of failing either of them disturbed Beznaria in a way that reminded her of the last, and biggest, error of her life.

When she got to their cabin she closed the door and realized something else—she was hiding. She wasn't supposed to be scared of anything, but the thought of telling Makeda that things might have gone disastrously wrong terrified her.

She'd figure out how to fix this—not because she was a Chetchevaliere, but because she had to.

Chapter 14

Day 5

$\mathcal{M}$ akeda and Bez lounged in their room after breakfast, doing a jigsaw puzzle they'd found in the lounge room. It was a group illustration of characters from what was apparently a popular mobile game—something called *One True Prince*. Apparently all of the tablets on the ship had the game loaded, and in the library she'd seen multiple spin off novelizations. Makeda had seen some of the younger workers at the supermarket playing it obsessively but hadn't expected the crew of a cargo ship to be stans as well, though time at sea was the perfect opportunity to play long, immersive dating simulations she supposed.

She was doing the same in real life, in a way. Apart from a couple of hours of weirdness after they'd made their calls, the few days on board with her fake wife had been the best relationship Makeda'd had thus far. She and Beznaria talked about their families, their jobs, past embarrassments and successes. Now that she'd grown used to the investigator, the strange outbursts weren't so strange and the way she could go on a tangent about almost anything kept Makeda endlessly entertained.

She'd also discovered that Bez, for all her talk of not understanding relationships, was the type of person who cried at the climax of romantic comedies. She'd had to assure her multiple times that the couple in the film they'd watched during movie night would definitely get back together, though when Tenzi had teased her afterward, Bez had blamed allergies for her loud sniffling.

They still hadn't shared a bed, but everything else felt much too real. Makeda had called it pretending, but hard as she looked, she couldn't find the line delineating real and pretend. It would have made sense if they'd been banging all over the ship, but it was in the mundane moments, like Bez currently trying to force a puzzle piece that was clearly the wrong shape and skin tone, that were confusing everything.

"Just try another piece," she said gently.

"I'm sure this is right. This has part of a crown. This crown is missing a part." As she pushed, the rounded edge of the puzzle piece broke off. "Oh."

The PA system fuzzed, and then AK's voice filled the room. "All available crew and passengers please report to the main deck for immersion suit training. Thank you."

"Ah, yes." Bez clapped. "A task that will heal my bruised ego."

She grabbed Makeda by the hand as she'd been doing for the last few days, leading her down to the main deck.

There they found Jay, Tenzi, Madiha, AK, and a gangly white man with brown hair and a long beard who Makeda somehow hadn't met before though they'd been on the ship for almost a week. He was wearing a T-shirt and smoking a cigarette even though it was chilly, given the lack of sunshine and the strong breeze off the ocean. Like Beznaria, he emitted a particular vibe that spoke to chaos and unpredictability, though it was on a wavelength Makeda wasn't sure even she could get down with.

"I'm Greg," the man called out in a thick Russian accent. "I'm the mole in the tunnel who keeps this ship from sinking."

Makeda blinked. "Um, hi?"

She looked at the other crew members, and none of them seemed bothered by his strange introduction. Jay rolled his eyes and shook his head, but in a way that seemed indulgent, not annoyed—or frightened that the ship was being sabotaged from belowdecks.

"Yes, Greg here is the world's best cargo ship engineer, and he also has a lovely singing voice," Jay said.

Greg's posture straightened and he stroked his beard, preening. "This is all true."

"We have to do our immersion suit practice," Jay said, stepping into the middle of the small circle and dropping a bright yellow duffel bag that matched everyone's safety jackets, and then looking at Makeda. "This is a waterproof emergency survival suit. We hope to never have to use these, but if the situation arises, we need to get the suits on quickly. Two minutes is this ship's requirement, but Greg can get it on in one minute twenty seconds."

"I slide in there like an eel," Greg said, making a smooth motion with his hand.

"I can do it under a minute," Bez said, releasing Makeda's hand. She pulled off her glasses and handed them over.

Greg squinted at her and exhaled a plume of smoke. "I would like to see you try."

"I have a stopwatch," Tenzi said, tapping at the digital watch on her wrist, then looking to Bez. "Ready when you are."

Bez strode toward the duffel, then turned to face Makeda. "Pay attention, sea snail."

Everyone chuckled, but there seemed to be actual worry in Bez's gaze.

"Go!" Tenzi called out, and Bez flew into motion.

Makeda knew that Bez was strong—that was evident in her physique, and the fact that she'd caught her doing one-handed push-ups in the B&B's foyer. But seeing her in action put Bez's *I'm an investigator for a weird organization and save strangers in distress on the side* schtick in perspective.

Bez swooped up the sack and gave it a hard shake so that the yellow suit rolled up inside of it slid out. It looked like a yellow Gumby creature had been smooshed by a steamroller. She spread the suit out on the floor, folded back the material on either side of the front zipper, and dropped herself flat on the ground to slide inside of it.

"Oh my god," Makeda gasped involuntarily as Bez shimmied into the suit with forceful hip gyrations. Once her shoes were firmly in the suit's booties, Bez hopped to her feet in one smooth motion without using her hands.

"Okay, I can't do that," Greg said, pulling out another cigarette while watching Bez with appreciation. "I would break my back if I tried that. Did you see that? She has the core strength of an oak tree. How can I compete?"

As Greg provided the play-by-play, Bez slid her arms into the suit's sleeves, which ended in mittens, and then zipped the suit up over her mouth and closed the safety flap, her wide-eyed gaze on Makeda. In fact, Bez had made eye contact at each step of her lightning-quick suit-up, as if saying, *See? This is how you do it.*

"Fifty-seven seconds!" Tenzi called out, waving her watch-clad wrist, and everyone hooted and hollered.

"Impressive," AK said, grinning.

Bez's gaze hopped to him. "I'm sure you can do it faster."

AK shrugged, but his grin deepened a bit. "I'm not a proponent of doing anything quick that can be done slow, but I make an exception for the immersion suit. My record is forty-nine seconds."

Bez gave a nod of respect, and then turned back to Makeda, sporting her gap-toothed grin. "Do you want to try, sea snail?"

Makeda wasn't generally one for competition but she was all about contingency planning and if this was something she needed to know so she wouldn't be a hindrance in an emergency, she would do it. "Sure."

Bez slid out of the suit and returned it to its storage sack. When Tenzi started the timer, Makeda struggled to get the suit out of the bag for what felt like as long as it had taken Bez to get zipped up in it. She carefully unrolled it, pressing out wrinkles, and startled when Bez shouted, "There isn't time for all that in an emergency!"

"Right! Sorry!"

Makeda dropped to the ground, shoved her feet into the too-long legs of the suit and rolled over to her side to push herself to her feet. She stuck one arm into a sleeve and zipped the suit halfway before bringing her arm in and struggling to finish zipping it up with the giant mittens on her hands. The suit smelled like rubber and Beznaria. When she was done what felt like an eternity after she'd started, Tenzi called out, "Three minutes thirty-two seconds!"

Makeda winced.

Bez approached her with a grin. "Good job. I particularly liked your worm wiggle at minute two."

"No, it wasn't good. I would've gone down with the ship in a real emergency," Makeda said with a chuckle, trying to shake off the fact that she'd done so badly. Logically she knew it was her first time, but everyone had just watched her wriggle like a fool and not come close to a minute.

"Did you forget?" Bez asked in a voice that was soft but with an underlying tautness that made Makeda's gaze jump up to meet hers. Beznaria's honey eyes had darkened to maple, and Makeda felt the strange urgency in that gaze pour over her, warm and sweet and alluring. "I'm here with you. And your safety will always be my first priority. I would never let that happen."

Makeda's breath caught in her throat, trapped there by her heartbeat that seemed to be hammering the breath out of her. The beast at the bottom of her watering can surged out of the depths, hungry, so hungry, and unable to resist the feast of possibility laid out in Beznaria's words.

I'm here with you.

"Thank you," Makeda said, trying not to show how much the words affected her. Bez was just being herself. She probably always made people feel like they were covered in syrup—and like she'd volunteer to lick it off if they played their cards right. Makeda needed to get her body out of the suit and her mind out of the gutter.

"I mean it. You did so well for someone who had never set foot on a ship before, let alone had emergency evacuation training. Be proud of that."

"Okay," Makeda said. The word came out almost as a whisper. She didn't know how to respond to such blatant praise. She was used to doing all kinds of labor for barely a pat on the head, but Bez's words made her feel like she was wearing five immersion suits, made of pleasure instead of polyurethane, and they were swaddling her in goodness.

A warning siren went off in her mind. Feeling this good was a predecessor to disaster. Makeda tried to drag her expectations down from the elevations they'd rocketed off to from a bit of simple praise, and then Beznaria said, "Let me help," reached for the zipper of the suit, and tugged.

It was ridiculous—Makeda was fully clothed beneath the suit and they were in the middle of a group of people on the very exposed deck of a ship. Exhibitionism wasn't her thing *at all*, but Bez was looking down at her like no one else was around—like no one else existed—and Makeda happily joined her in that alternate reality just for a moment because it felt so good.

A surge of anticipatory pleasure rushed through her as Bez slid the zipper down to its base, just above Makeda's waistline. Her fingers slid in between the plastic and Makeda's clothing, a firm caress from Makeda's neck down to her elbows, searing even through the layers of hoodie and T-shirt, as Bez pushed the suit off until it pooled to the ground at her feet. Each move was made with deliberation and care—as if she was touching her real wife, without any awkwardness or hesitation. Bez touched her like she knew her.

Makeda wanted to kiss her.

She'd already almost done it twice, acting on some emotional impulse, but now she felt it like a need cascading over her skin. She wanted to press her mouth up against Bez's, to take and take, like giving was a concept she'd never been introduced to. *This* was what it was to want something for herself, for real, and it was as terrifying a thrill as any boardwalk amusement park ride.

"Oh," she said, or tried to say, but it came out too breathy—more like a moan.

Someone cleared their throat.

"I know it's their honeymoon but do the rest of us have to be subjected to this?" Greg asked, shattering the illusion of privacy. "No canoodling on the ship!"

"You're the one who brought your wife with you last year," Jay said. "And accidentally activated the PA system when you sneaked into the main office to—"

"Okay, okay, let's not talk about that," Greg said.

Makeda looked away from Bez and found the crew watching them, their amused expressions snapping her back to reality. She had just almost kissed Bez *again*, this time in front of an audience.

"Sorry," she mumbled.

"Don't apologize!" Thompson said. "Of course newlyweds will occasionally forget themselves. It's fine."

Makeda should have nodded and smiled, going along with the ruse as usual, but instead she felt slightly sick. She didn't want this to be a ruse. She realized with an ache in her chest that she wanted it to be real.

"And you were worried they would figure us out. I'd say they're pretty convinced," Bez said in a low voice, efficiently sniping every one of Makeda's buoying hopes.

She was so bad at this fake marriage thing; she'd basically commanded Beznaria to act like she actually cared about her for the benefit of the crew, and when the investigator went along with it Makeda was foolish enough to believe the feelings were real.

I'm here with you. And your safety will always be my first priority.

Of course, a person who saw Makeda as both a package to be delivered and a damsel to be rescued would say that. It wasn't romantic; it wasn't some seismic shift. It was Makeda reading between the lines of the literal contract she had signed, searching for the same thing that always screwed her over in the end.

She was wrong, actually; there had been a seismic shift. Somehow, knowing that Beznaria's false attentions could affect her like this changed everything. It hurt worse than Steph leaving, like someone had punched her in a bruise that she had mostly forgotten.

Makeda, who'd vowed to be more careful about who she gave her heart to, had been ridiculous enough to fall for a person she already knew didn't care about her. Bez was pretending for work, and out of some twisted sense of honor. Bez had even warned her, in word and in deed, that she'd left a trail of women pining after her and wasn't planning on changing.

Humiliation seared her.

This was why the fine print had the entanglement clause—and why Beznaria herself had specified that both feelings and fucking were off the table. Was Bez doing this because she had to or she wanted to, and if Makeda had to ask, did it matter?

Bez was still looking at her the same, but the maple syrup gaze felt like a trap, not a treat.

"I'll do the rest myself," Makeda said, stumbling back to shuck the suit off her feet and step out of it.

Bez's brows drew together in confusion, but then Madiha came over to them, smiling as if she was interrupting newlyweds, and not just one person holding up her end of an arrangement and another setting herself up for disaster.

"Beznaria, Captain Del Rosario wants you to come to the bridge."

"Do you want to come with us?" Beznaria asked, holding her hand out to Makeda. "I can show you the bridge; I'll even let you look out of my binoculars."

"I think I'll go up to our room," Makeda said, hoping no one heard the pathetic tremor in her voice.

"Good. Our room is on the way to the bridge. I'll escort you." Bez stepped closer to her, her expression shrewd, and Makeda stepped back.

"Um, actually, I'll go see the engine room, with Greg," she said.

"I'm the best engineer and the best singer, not the best conversationalist," the man said, flicking his cigarette. "Wait for Pietr to be on shift, he likes that tourist stuff."

"Best singer my ass," Jay said, and Greg mock-sneered at him and gave him the middle finger, which Jay grabbed in his own fist and pretended to break off.

"Oh, well, I—" Makeda didn't have any excuses. She had no duties or responsibilities, and she didn't know anyone apart from the one person she desperately needed to avoid.

"You can come to the kitchen with me if you want," AK offered. "I can give you the exciting tour of the pantries, and maybe Chef Rick will let you get a preview of his lunch menu."

"Yes! Yes, I'd love that." Relief washed over her.

Beznaria pushed her glasses up her nose but followed Madiha up the stairs and accepted Makeda's weak wave when she and AK left for the galley.

The kitchen was gigantic—or it seemed especially large with only two people working in it. Rick and Dana moved in a kind of whirling synchrony as they prepped for lunch.

Makeda glanced at the growing pile of dishes in the sink.

"Should I load those into the dishwasher? Or I can wash by hand." It would feel so good to wash a dish, to actually do something that had a tangible result—and would keep her away from Bez.

"That's okay," Dana called out. "Thanks for the offer."

When AK showed her the meat storage, fish storage, veg storage, and dry storage, Makeda took note of all the ways they could be streamlined.

"You know, I worked in restaurants for years, and I helped my grandmother start a B&B," she said, an idea starting to stir in her head. "I can help—"

"No, you can't," AK said gently. "You haven't signed a contract and you are a guest on the ship. Working would endanger you and would also threaten our insurance rates if you got injured doing something unauthorized, like using knives in the kitchen or creating dangerous stacks of books."

"Oh," she said, reluctantly retracting her help-y claws, which had been desperate to find purchase in something other than her own ridiculous thoughts.

The shining sea she'd felt glint on the surface of her watering can had gone dull. She'd spent most of her trip doing the same things she'd always done—getting hung up on an emotionally unavailable woman and trying to help where it wasn't needed—only now she was trying it on the high seas.

"You told me before you were a multi-tool," AK said, leaning against the door to the dry storage pantry. "Do you think being out of use for a few days will rust you?"

Makeda chuckled a little miserably. "I'm not used to doing nothing," she said, then thought of the downtime she'd been spending with Bez. "Or . . . only doing things for myself. It isn't relaxing."

"I understand that. You need to feel useful. To be serving a purpose outside of yourself?"

"That sounds more majestic than how I'd describe it, but basically."

AK nodded. "For some people, happiness is sitting down and not doing anything all day. For others, happiness is keeping so busy they don't have the time to sit down. But both can simply be methods of avoiding reality."

Damn this man and his affirmations.

"What's happiness for you?" Makeda asked, turning the conversation away from herself.

AK smiled ruefully. "I've been seeking my happiness for years, but I might also be avoiding the reality that I had it, lost it, and I won't be able to reclaim it."

"Ouch," she said.

He looked away from her. "Yeah."

"I haven't found mine yet," Makeda admitted, lulled into honesty by AK's nonjudgmental demeanor and the fact he was a stranger she'd never see again once she left the boat. "Finding it and losing it sounds awful."

"It is, though I guess I'm supposed to say the experience made it worthwhile." He exhaled deeply. "I won't be presumptuous, but I didn't know what my happiness was until after I gave her up. If you want to take stock of something, there are more important things than the pantry."

"Are you a therapist?" she asked, laughing.

He pointed at himself. "Useful multi-tools generally have an unlicensed therapist attachment."

They laughed.

"You can't work, my friend," AK said. "But you can shadow me if you want. I'll show you all the things I do on the ship. Maybe I'll even let you file some paperwork."

"Will you?" she asked brightly, knowing he wasn't being condescending.

"I try to look after the well-being of the crew. I can't assume other people feel like having an intern, but if it helps you pass the time—and distracts you—I'm happy to do it."

"Thanks," she said. It calmed her a bit, knowing she had some other purpose to focus on for the rest of the voyage. If she'd spent the rest of the trip solely as Beznaria's wife, it would have been too much.

Complete panic was averted, but as the tour continued, Makeda couldn't help but think about happiness. It wasn't something she'd really thought about in relation to herself. She'd thought about giving, and the opposite of that, which she'd thought was selfishness. She'd thought about passiveness, and now, taking action. But happiness?

Even thinking of it possibly existing for her seemed like she was getting too big for her britches. She decided that expecting that after all these years was pushing it. She'd watch from the corner of her eye and see if maybe it approached, but she'd focus on more realistic goals, like undermining her chances at winning the Ibaranian crown.

She knew one thing for certain: she wouldn't expect it to arrive in the form of an exasperating investigator.

THE DAY AFTER the safety walk, Makeda found herself still unable to shake the shame that, even for a moment, she'd believed Beznaria's act. It was a simple mistake, and a natural one—she knew that on some level—but it slashed open old wounds that, turned out, had never actually healed.

As a girl, she'd been amazed when Grandmore had revealed the story of Prince Keshan, and pulled the fish scale ring out of the small pouch she kept in her delicates drawer. It had felt magical, like something from the movies—Makeda, an ordinary girl with scabby knees and too-big teeth, was something special. Then her mother had taken that magic and twisted it into something ugly as she tried to make it do her bidding.

She'd felt that spark of hope and magic again as Bez had looked into her eyes, but this time she was going to stomp it out herself. She was traveling to Ibarania to pay off a debt that wasn't hers and end this princess farce for good. Not to get swept away by Chaos Vibes de la Biceps.

She'd already helped AK do some admin work that morning, and then strained her way through lunch, skittering her hand away when Beznaria tried to hold it.

"Are you going to do anything else today?" Beznaria asked.

"Didn't you say I should try sitting around doing nothing?" Makeda's words came out with more attitude than necessary, but she didn't know how to act when they were alone now. It had gone from easy comfort to the tension caused by her own foolishness. "Or do you want me out of your bed?"

That was the other humiliation-that-shouldn't-have-been—Beznaria had chosen the rock-hard couch over sharing a bed ever since that first night on the ship. Makeda hadn't taken it personally, but the problem with her new awareness was that she was taking everything personally in a way she wouldn't have if they'd just posed as two buddies taking the scenic route to Ibarania with no romantic overtones to confuse her newly reawakened libido.

Or if I'd just stayed at home and found some other way to get the money. I probably could have worked out some kind of plan until my GrabRite paychecks came through . . .

"I'm going to the gym for the afternoon martial arts course, so I relinquish the couch to you," Bez said. She gave her the curious look she'd been giving her since Makeda had fled to the kitchen, which added to Makeda's edginess.

She'd told Bez to be affectionate. She'd made a plan for them, and *she* was the one deviating from it, but she couldn't help it.

"There's yoga, if you want to try that," Bez said brightly.

Makeda lowered the book she was reading. "Is there any particular reason I would go to yoga while you do martial arts?"

She was picking a fight now, but it was a way for her to interact with Bez without all her other feelings surging to the surface to make her feel miserable.

"Do you want the true answer or the nice answer?" Bez asked, and when Makeda shot her a look, she added, "I'm communicating. Like you requested. Stop clacking your lobster claws at me."

"I want the true and the nice." Makeda put the book down and crossed her arms over her chest.

"The nice answer is that yoga taught by a Drukian monk is something most people will never get to experience."

"Monk?"

"Yes. Several of the crew were trained in a Drukian monastery if I'm correct—it's why I'm taking as many of the martial arts classes as I can. Frankly if anyone is foolish enough to try to board this ship, they'd have all their bones shattered before I even made it to the deck. My security services are definitely not necessary."

"Okay, you're doing that wild information drop thing again. You don't just sprinkle the presence of bone-shattering monks into a conversation and act like it's normal."

"It is normal. It's not like I said they did it with their minds. They use their fists and feet." Bez shook her head as if Makeda were the strange one.

"What's the true answer?" Makeda ventured before Bez revealed that she *did* know monks who could crush people with their minds.

"The true answer is that you're so tense right now it's difficult to be around. Your jaw is clenched, your shoulders are hunched, you're gripping that book like a brick you want to lob at me. And you're lobbing your words instead, which is less pleasant than a mass market paperback would be."

Beznaria was right, of course. Makeda had been a ball of tension since she'd been zipped out of that immersion suit and suddenly wanted Beznaria more than she'd allowed herself to want anything in years.

In ever.

It would pass.

"Yoga will help you relax," Beznaria added, interlacing her hands and stretching her arms over her head. Makeda's gaze ran over the long, muscular length of her—she knew what the flex of those muscles felt like under her palm and she ached for it.

Beznaria peered at her through her glasses and then stretched to the side. Makeda might have thought she was purposely posing for her if she didn't know better.

"Is yoga what helps you relax?" Makeda sounded parched as hell, but maybe it would pass for moody.

"No, pretending to kill people is what helps me relax, sea snail," Bez said with a devious smile. "I'm naturally balanced, and my chakras flow like the waters of the Iber River so I have no need of yoga. You, however, require . . . loosening, and it's the only technique I'm allowed to offer to you at the moment."

Makeda swallowed. "What other techniques would you offer? If you were able?"

"For you, specifically? Those fall outside of our current arrangement, so I'll refrain from answering. See you at the gym, yes?"

Bez loped out and Makeda got up and slipped into her workout clothes. She wasn't a workout person, really, so they were just regular clothes. Much of her exercise had come from running back and forth doing things for people. Grandmore had been bugging her to try yoga for years—it seemed she would get her wish that day.

When she reached Deck A, she stepped through a door that led to a three-walled space with a fenced-off area that opened out to the ocean. The brisk breeze carried away most of the smell of sweat and dampened the sound of people beating the hell out of each other. At least that was what it looked like to Makeda. On one side of the room, Chuck and Pietr watched with wide eyes as Tenzi and Beznaria re-enacted the climax from some Marvel movie. Both were covered with sweat, despite the cool air flowing from outside. Bez unleashed a roundhouse kick with one of her long legs and Tenzi did a backbend to duck underneath it.

"What in the *Mortal Kombat*?" Makeda's heart beat wildly in her chest.

From her backbend, Tenzi moved into a handstand, where she launched a foot in Bez's direction before flipping backward fully and landing on her feet. Beznaria dodged the kick and dropped into a crouch, sweeping her leg out to hook Tenzi's feet with her own and topple her over.

Tenzi hit the floor lightly, and then burst out laughing. "Damn. I haven't been taken down in months. Do you usually travel the world snatching people's pride like that?"

Beznaria helped Tenzi up and then they began practicing the backbend move like they hadn't been in full attack mode a moment before.

"Are you going to challenge Tenzi next?" AK stood beside Makeda. He wore a tank top and basketball shorts; it was the first time Makeda had seen him outside of the crew coveralls. He had the lean, muscular body of someone whose work required constant lifting. Both of his arms were covered with sleeves of intricate tattoos down to his wrists. These weren't the terrible kanji offered at the boardwalk tattoo shops that were often lifted from restaurant menus. These characters were impossibly fine-lined calligraphy interspersed with mountains, dragons, and, adorably, goats.

"Oh no," Makeda said. "I'm not trying to get my bones crushed. I'm here for the yoga. Nice, relaxing yoga."

AK laughed. "We'll see how you feel about that when the class is over."

"You're the yoga instructor, too?"

He pointed to himself and waited a beat.

"Multi-tool," they said at the same time.

She followed him close to the fence and watched as he laid out two mats.

"We'll take it easy today," he said as he knelt on one of the mats and gestured toward the other.

"And I'm not actually an instructor, but where I come from we all do yoga together, often taking turns leading, kids and elderly alike. So don't expect this to be like something from a yoga studio in the US."

"I have zero expectations. I've only done a few yoga videos here and there over the years," she said, sitting facing the ocean. "So easy is good."

AK started her out in child's pose—sitting with her knees underneath her and spread a little, bending forward with her arms stretched in front of her. It was relaxing enough to make her start to drift into sleep as the boat swayed and her muscles unclenched. After that, she wished she had joined Tenzi and Beznaria, because at least with a high-speed martial arts fight, you know you were about to get your ass kicked.

Although they never even did any standing or balancing poses, and the positions mostly consisted of not moving for a few minutes, each new move that AK guided her into stepped up the sensation that she was being pulled apart at the hips and shoulders and heart, but in a good way.

"Can I ask you something?" she whispered while they stretched their upper backs with a twist. "Since you have this lifetime knowledge?"

"Yes," AK whispered back.

"Is there a yoga move that will like, align something in me, and make me a different, better version of myself?" she asked. There had to be, given how people had been on her case to try the exercise for years and years. At the very least, her edges had better be flourishing after this initial session.

"Oh, yeah!" He said something in his language that she didn't catch. "We'll do that move next."

"Really?" Makeda squeaked, untwisting a bit to look at him.

He glanced at her with raised brows and a grin, and she sighed.

"Fine," she whispered. "I just thought maybe all this pain would be worth it in the end."

"Is that ever the case with pain?" he asked.

Makeda made a disgruntled noise.

"What is the better version of yourself?" he asked a couple of minutes later as they came out of the pose. He looked poised and composed, but sweat had beaded on his temples and he'd been doing this for most of his life. Makeda didn't feel so bad about her drenched T-shirt. "What are you doing to get there?"

She thought for a moment. "I'm building rock-solid boundaries. I want to stop giving everything I have away. I want to be selfish like everyone else."

Even as she said it aloud, it felt childish. Infantile.

"Has trying to create those boundaries made you feel better?" he asked, tone light.

"No," she said. But something had; those brief moments where she'd imagined that Bez wasn't acting, that something might really exist between them. "I think I didn't build them strong enough, though."

"You don't have to build boundaries. You already have them, Makeda, and using them doesn't make you selfish." AK slowly shifted into a new pose as he spoke, crossing his legs so they were stacked at the knees and his feet rested on the ground on either side of his butt. "You may not be listening to them, or respecting their delineation, but you have them. We all do."

"Well, I'm about to respect the boundaries of my knees because I cannot do what you're doing right now." Makeda positioned her legs as close to AK's pose as she could manage, and the pressure along her outer thighs and into her hips ratcheted up. She inhaled deeply.

"You can't force yourself to take on boundaries that aren't natural to you and expect happiness," he continued, not allowing her to redirect the conversation. "You're talking about boundaries like they're walls to keep people out instead of instincts to keep *you* safe."

The pulling sensation intensified the longer they sat, and seemed to throb as his words sank in. "I hadn't thought of it that way."

She felt that old shame stir in her—she shouldn't have told him what she was really thinking. Now he thought she was a fool, too, one who didn't know herself.

"I'm not judging," he said gently. "Hell, I might not even be right. But I've struggled for years with feeling out what I'm willing to give to others. I'm not trying to be yogi master here, just a guy who spends way too much time thinking about this because of my job."

She didn't know why a ship's steward would need to be well-versed in this, but she supposed he did do a lot for others, and time at sea made a person contemplative.

"Any advice?" she asked as they switched their crossed legs and restacked them.

"I'd say start with understanding your own boundaries better, why you have them, and how much energy it costs you to ignore them. Sometimes it's worth it. Giving does not always mean being taken advantage of, and sometimes you're getting more than the person you're giving to. Sometimes they don't want or need what you offer, and you're taking from them."

Steph's parting shots popped up in her head, and she dropped her gaze to her hands resting on her knees.

"Thank you," Makeda said. "I appreciate you talking through things like this with me even though I'm a stranger."

"You're a friend. I think everyone can be a friend, but us multi-tools have to stick together," AK said with a laugh, though the brightness in his eyes had dimmed. She wondered what he had offered, and who hadn't needed it, and whether that had anything to do with the happiness he sought.

She didn't ask, though. She simply sat in the pose, sweating and on the verge of a kind of panic as she wondered how much longer she'd have to hold it. The sensation was growing more intense. She was shocked to suddenly hiccup out a sob and feel tears on her cheeks, cooled by the sea breeze.

"Are you in pain?" AK asked.

"No," she assured him, then sniffled and used the hem of her shirt to wipe her face. "Sorry. I don't really know why I'm—" Her throat went rough and she stopped talking. She was embarrassed by the ugly crying face she knew she was making, but the crying felt good—cathartic.

"Nothing to be sorry about. Some of these moves can release repressed emotions," he said. "Some of them release repressed gas, so I think we lucked out here."

"You might've mentioned that before we started," she said with a wobbly chuckle.

"Do you want to breathe through it or stop?" he asked.

She was on a ship in the middle of the ocean heading toward an island that represented her greatest shame. She had fallen for the woman pretending to be her wife because she thought her duty to her family and her job required it. She'd thought getting on the ship would change her somehow, but she was still the same person—and maybe that wasn't such a bad thing.

"Let's breathe through it," she said.

She inhaled the salt air as she stared out toward the blue horizon, sniffling, sore, and still ignoring the fact that their destination was getting closer and she had no real idea what would happen when she got there.

Chapter 15

In Bez's mental ship's log, it was day seven on the *Virginia Queen* and day two of Makeda's sudden retreat from the bonds of fake marriage.

Makeda had been keeping busy otherwise—during the day she'd started an informal apprenticeship with AK, learning the ins and outs of ship management, which was exactly the kind of thing she'd do instead of relaxing in their cabin and eating delicious food. She'd been doing afternoon and evening sessions of yoga, and had even learned a few moves from Tenzi. When there had been an informal doubles table tennis competition, Makeda had paired up with Dema.

The one thing that didn't interest her at all was interacting with Bez. Not more than necessary to keep up their ruse, at least. She didn't even call her annoying anymore. Bez had bunked with people who didn't like her, often, but Makeda's withdrawal was the first time it felt like rejection. For some reason, the idea that Makeda, who had once tried to kiss her, had possibly found her to be too much after a few days in close proximity wasn't soul crushing, but it did cause a deep dismay that Bez had only experienced when one of her family members was angry at her.

At the moment, her supposed wife had just finished alphabetizing the discs in the crew's bootleg DVD binder, even though they'd all been saved on a thumb drive, and was now clearing up storage space by deleting unused apps.

"Why are there so many sim dating things on these tablets?" she asked aloud. *"Byronic Rogues from Mars*? That sounds amazing, but every tablet has individual copies of the same five games!"

"People get lonely at sea," Pietr from engineering said, peeking over his tablet at Makeda with a grin. "And AK is really into games from that company and always buys copies for each tablet as soon as they drop. Except for *One True Prince Two: More Happy, So Ever After*. He bought it, but told us not to talk to him about it. I mean, I get it, the prince from his country is never included as a dateable character in the games and the other characters always shit-talk him, so he has a legitimate reason to dislike it."

Bez watched Makeda as she talked to Pietr without any of the awkwardness that was between them now and tried to figure out what she was doing wrong.

She had already followed three out of four of Papa C's Rules of Romance: *One, if something pisses her off, do the opposite of that. Two, if YOU piss her off, apologize. Four, when she talks, pay attention to the details.*

Everything should have continued to move smoothly but she'd gone amiss somewhere.

Makeda still participated in the pretense—the hand holding, the cuddles, the joke-making during their meals when Bez wasn't working—but that was all: pretense. An air of reserve had sprung up between them after immersion suit training and hadn't faded. When they were alone in their cabin, Makeda said things that were friendly, but not quite right. She didn't even lose her temper with Bez anymore.

That should have been fine. It was an act, after all, but it didn't sit right with her that Makeda had closed herself off after that brief openness between them. It was a matter of pride in Bez's work but also the simple fact that she had enjoyed the tingling warmth that came from focusing her attention on Makeda. She wasn't sure she'd experienced it before, outside of her dedication to her work and her family, the latter of which had faded years ago.

The fireflies in her brain were transmitting the message that it would be lovely to feel that connection—that was what it had been—again. The fireflies also transmitted messages from other regions of Bez's body, but she thought it best not to decipher those.

"Who's up next on the sat call?" AK leaned into the door frame of the crew lounge.

"Do you want to call Ora again, Makeda?"

Makeda's eyes brightened, and she finally fully looked at Bez. "Yes!"

AK led them to the communications room and Bez cut in front of him to input her grandmother's number and hit Send. Then she stepped out, where AK leaned against a wall, taking notes in the small notebook he carried in the pocket of his boiler suit at all times.

She was slightly irritated by the way he was calm and collected, and how much Makeda must like that since she now spent a good chunk of her time with him. She hadn't bothered him for a few days, but her brain fireflies were flashing the code for "petty" and she obeyed.

"I just need to know if you think you're fooling me or if you know that I know."

"Whatever gives you contentment works for me," AK said, still scribbling.

"The call I'm about to make is to the World Federation of Monarchists," she said, and for the first time since boarding she got a reaction from him. His gaze flew to hers. There was no panic or anger, just watchfulness.

"I'm not calling about you, and I won't mention anything about your ship, but after my tenure in the royal match division, I have to know."

"Know what?" he asked, and in those two words he assuaged the frustration that had been bothering her like a fishbone stuck in her tooth. He was who she had suspected him to be; anyone else would have asked what she was talking about.

"Why you rejected every match sent your way?" She shook her head. "Do you know how much effort I went through? Refining and refining, and you rejected every one of them. It became personal to me."

"One of life's simple lessons, which I learned the hard way, is that when someone rejects something they didn't ask for, it means they don't want it." He went back to his writing.

Bez watched him, knowing that he wasn't pretending to write nor was he waiting for a response. Despite the puff pieces in the news and the belief that he was a *soft boi* in royal fandoms, the Prince of Druk was both self-possessed and able to knock someone out with little effort. Bez felt a little spark of jealousy; he and Makeda were friends now. Maybe this was the kind of personality her faux wife preferred over Bez's grabbing at fireflies.

"You are required to take a marriage partner," she said, and even she knew it was silly for her of all people to suddenly care about societal rules.

"Perhaps you should be more concerned with your own *marriage*?" AK said, his writing hand not slowing.

"Is this the mythic ability of the Sun Prince to read minds, or are you just making assumptions about my relationship?"

"I can't read minds," he said. "European voyagers started showing up to Druk a couple hundred years ago all wanting the same thing—our resources and labor—and when successive kings guessed what they had come for, the voyagers assumed Drukanese royals were magical mystics, not that we had deductive reasoning skills. Funny, huh?"

Bez studied him. "You know, people make you out to be all sunshine and smiles."

"Another simple life lesson—even the most basic organism is a miracle of complexity. Why would a human be any different?" He glanced up at her from under his eyebrows with a look that didn't speak to benevolence, grace, and peace. "I could have rejected your request to work on the ship and I definitely could have rejected your request to bring a *spouse* for free. I'd appreciate it if you don't make me regret that decision."

Beznaria mimed zipping her lips.

The door to the room opened and Makeda walked out smiling—at AK. She walked right past Bez, and AK shot her a second glance.

"How is Ora, sea snail?" she asked, placing a hand on Makeda's arm.

Makeda's smile faltered and for a moment Bez thought something had happened, then she realized, yes, it had—Makeda was having to interact with Bez.

"Oh, she's great," she said with a smile that was not at all authentic. "I think she has a man friend over, so she's making full use of my absence and the B&B's many rooms. Andrea wanted to call her sister. I'll go tell her the phone will be free soon."

She pulled away to seek out the first mate. It wasn't pointed, but it felt like it because Bez knew what it was like when Makeda leaned into her instead.

Bez turned on her heel and marched stiffly into the communications room, punching the number into the giant phone that looked like something out of the nineties. Instead of calling her family, she called her job.

She still hadn't heard back from the WFM and it was adding to her agitation. Rule number one of Papa C's rules stated that if someone pissed your woman off, you should do the opposite. Makeda would be angry if they arrived in Ibarania to find that the royal heir had already been chosen, and she was determined to fix this preemptively.

After several rings, the call was picked up. "Direct line of Algernon Shropsbottomshireburrough, Lord Hig—"

"Yes, it's Junior Investigator Chetchevaliere, and don't hang up on me," Bez interrupted. "I don't have long. I'm following up on—"

"You were supposed to report back weeks ago," the woman interrupted in a clipped British accent. "Your ticket to London went unused, and we will expect that to be reimbursed. Your next assignment has been passed on to another agent and you *will* be reprimanded for going AWOL. After your unsatisfactory review, this will likely end your contract."

"Well, you see, I found the possible heir to the Ibaranian throne and had to track her down and verify, so you can understand why I was indisposed. We're currently—"

"That wasn't your assignment." The secretary spoke as if she hadn't heard Beznaria at all. "Lord Higginshoggins expressly stated that an American candidate would not be desirable."

"Should I jump in a time machine and instruct her grandfather to spread his seed on another continent more pleasing to the director? Does the WFM possess that technology?"

"Junior *Investigator*." The woman's voice was frigid. "You will be written up for improper language as well."

Bez growled in frustration, not understanding why the woman was ignoring the point of her call. The fact that she had found a possible heir should have been the priority, not Bez's bad behavior. "And the heir?"

"I will pass the information on to the director and he will do with it as he sees fit. You report back to headquarters immediately for a debrief."

"But we're already en route. They need to delay the—"

"Goodbye," the secretary said, and then hung up.

The call ended and Bez sat there for a moment.

"But I didn't give you the information," she said to dead air, then put the phone down.

She still had three minutes left, so she called her family. Her mother picked up, the sounds of raucous conversation greeting Bez before her mother's greeting, "Beznaria! I know it's you calling from this strange number. Always the strange numbers, and the secrets." Her mother giggled. "Are you almost home, dear? If you let me know when you'll arrive, I can make your favorite foods. Now, what are your favorites again? Hard to say since you never come home so we can cook them. I was telling your father—"

"Hi, I love you, I only have one minute," Bez said quickly. "Yes, I'll be home soon. I want fried fish. How's Henna Jeta?"

"She is still upset about the search for the heir. She says they shouldn't look, shouldn't stir up old memories. Your father is trying his best to calm her, but I've never seen her like this."

"But if we find the heir—wouldn't she be happy to know the queen survived?"

"You would think so," her mother said. "Do you want to talk to her?"

Tenzi walked into the room then.

"No, I have to go. I'll try to call her before I arrive."

Nothing was going as Bez expected, and now she felt doubt—usually an absolute stranger to her—begin to chip away at her resolve. Perhaps she should have borrowed money for plane tickets. Perhaps she should have paid more attention when her grandmother said she didn't have to solve problems no one had asked her to.

Perhaps this was all going to blow up in her face.

All she could do now was make sure she got Makeda there and was able to claim her money.

LATER THAT AFTERNOON, Beznaria stood on the bridge listening to Makeda get a tour of the bridge from Second Mate Alvi.

She'd turned down tours from Bez for two days, but here she was as friendly as could be with Alvi. Complimenting her hijab. Asking her about the weather instruments.

Bez wanted to explain the weather instruments. Bez wanted to make Makeda laugh. Instead she got a stiff hug before Makeda headed to the top deck to get some sun, even though it had been overcast for two days.

Bez stood with the binoculars pressed to her glasses, surveying the sea for danger and wondering if Makeda was safe and why, though she'd known her longest, Makeda seemed to prefer everyone's company to hers. When she handed over watch to Chuck, she bolted up the stairs without changing out of her boiler suit and found Makeda sitting on a bench facing the back of the ship and the turbulent wash trailing behind it. Her legs were crossed in front of her, knees resting against the metal safety grille. Her locks danced against her back in the wind.

"Hello," Beznaria said, sliding onto the bench beside her, with her back against the grill, and crossing her left ankle over her right knee.

"So," Makeda said. "We need to talk."

"Communication." Bez fiddled with a short coil of rope she'd carried up onto the deck with her. "Are you dissatisfied with my marriage performance? You can be frank. I'm used to less than satisfactory evaluations."

"What?" Makeda whipped her head in Bez's direction, brow wrinkled. "No. It's great. Perfect. Maybe a little too good? I have no complaints. I wouldn't complain even if it was bad. I mean, you shouldn't *have* to act like you like me." She cut off the flow of words and looked back out to sea.

"But I do." Bez uncrossed her legs and crossed them in the opposite direction, then began tying a knot with the rope. Doing something with her hands helped distract her from what she was admitting. She liked Makeda Hicks. That was perfectly normal, wasn't it? People liked other people all the time, and just because Bez hadn't liked someone in this way before didn't mean this change was of particular import. "Of course, I'll act like it. What else would I do in this situation?"

"Oh." Makeda frowned, which wasn't at all the reaction Bez was expecting.

"Oh?" Bez asked, fingers deftly pulling the rope over and under.

"Sorry," Makeda said, then sighed and placed her hands over her face. "This is just so weird. I don't mean to make things awkward."

"There's nothing awkward at all," Bez said. Her voice sounded strange and she cleared her throat. "We are two adults on a mission. There will be misunderstandings occasionally."

Her knot fell apart and she coiled the rope and shoved it into her pocket.

"Speaking of mission, that's what I wanted to talk about," Makeda said, clearly trying to revive the conversation Bez had killed with her confession. "We haven't talked much about the whole princess thing."

Bez pursed her lips. *Because we haven't talked much at all.* "Is there anything more to discuss?" she asked.

"Well, yeah." Makeda shifted. "I mean, this is a really huge thing, heading across the world to claim a crown. I feel like I've been really underplaying it. It's starting to feel overwhelming as we get closer to Ibarania. Like everyone's suddenly going to be scrutinizing me."

"If it helps you to feel any better, you're not the only royal in the world. You're not even the only royal on this ship. I'm personally invested in the al-Hurradassi line, so I might have skewed how much attention this will get."

Makeda's brow furrowed. "Wait, what? Not the only royal on this ship?"

"It was just . . . an example," Beznaria said, remembering the warning look AK had given her. "To give you some perspective. I mean, I deal with royals all the time for work."

"That's the other thing," Makeda said, having been sufficiently redirected. "What exactly is the World Federation of Monarchists? Why do you work for them?"

"It's a tale as old as time. Girl fresh out of the Maritime Forces signs a contract with a maritime security company. Girl disobeys a captain's orders and gets fired. Girl receives job offer from monarchist and thinks it's fate, given her family's rich history, but discovers the WFM isn't an organization that studies monarchies, it's one that tries to control them." Bez kicked her feet out and sprawled a bit more insouciantly. "It's a job."

"No, working at GrabRite is a job. You travel around the world investigating monarchies and finding royal heirs and"—she fixed Bez with a speculative gaze—"what else?"

"Handling things that need to be handled," Bez said. "At the end of the day, most royals are just rich people with too much time and money on their hands getting themselves or their kingdoms into trouble."

"So you clean up their messes?" Makeda's mouth twisted.

"I spent much of my time in the archives when I first started, as a researcher. When I was promoted to mess cleaning, as you say, I learned that the monarchies *were* the mess. When I met you, you told me there was a specific way to clean up the rooms at the Golden Crown, yes?"

"Yes," Makeda said, turning on the bench so she was facing the same direction as Bez. "And you paid me not a bit of mind and did what you wanted."

"Correct. I have my own ways of doing things. I'm not my superiors' favorite investigator because my methods are unorthodox and we have differing opinions on whether to use bleach or a deadly cocktail of household cleaners."

Makeda rolled her head to the side, and Bez could see tension around her eyes even though she was trying to keep things light. "This sounds like a streaming drama that my grandmother would watch."

Bez grimaced. "No one wants a show about what monarchies are really like."

"But the WFM . . . That sounds so regal and fancy. How are they controlling monarchies when they couldn't spring for plane tickets for us even if we had like five layovers before we got there?"

Bez's fingers stopped moving. She should tell her what was going on now. But telling her would cause her distress with no remedy, and she was contractually mandated to remedy her distress, not cause it. She'd wait until she heard from Higginshoggins.

A very reasonable cop-out.

"Are you hiding something in our fake marriage?" Makeda prodded. "That's against the rules."

"You're one to talk," Bez said, her tone more frayed than she would have liked. "You asked me to act like things are real and then started shutting me down every time I try to."

She hadn't meant to admit that, but there it was. She expected Makeda to respond with another jab, but the woman frowned and looked away.

"I told you. You're too good at the 'acting like it's real' part. And I'm silly enough to forget it's practice."

Bez was reaching for her when a siren blared through the public address system.

"What's that?" Makeda asked.

Bez kept reaching, grabbing Makeda so they could head down to the muster point as the length of the siren had indicated. She didn't let herself worry, just focused on quickly, but not recklessly, getting Makeda inside the stairwell, mingling with the other crew as they headed down. She was the only one in a hurry she realized about three flights down after elbowing her way past Jay and Thompson.

"A drill," she said, slowing her pace. "An unannounced drill."

"It was put on the announcement board today," Chuck said from behind them. "We are doing a practice stowaway hunt."

"People stow away on these ships?" Makeda asked, huffing a little after the jog down the stairs. "And you hunt them?"

"Not hunt," Thompson said with an eye roll. "Search. Anyone desperate enough to sneak onto a ship might be in need of food, medical care, mental health services."

"And it's dangerous," Santos cut in. "For them and for us if they were to get into the engine room or get hurt by cargo or stuck between pipes."

"It's fun," Tenzi said. "The drill is, not having a stowaway. The ultimate game of hide-and-seek!"

"Who's it?" Jay asked, clasping his hands together when they reached the muster point. "Not me this time, my knees are still hurting from when I decided to hide in the life preserver niche."

"Makeda can be it," AK said. "She's the only one of us who has the mindset of someone who doesn't know the ship very well looking for someplace to hide."

Bez would have preferred that Makeda explain what she'd been saying when the siren had sounded, but Bez didn't have time to disagree. Makeda was already jogging away from them.

"Don't run!" Bez called out over the noise of the engine. "One hand for the ship! And put on your safety jacket. And don't hide in the cargo area or belowdecks!"

She stared after Makeda, who slowed to a power walk as she shrugged into her safety vest, then held both hands out as if ready to catch herself if she fell. She smiled full-on at Bez, the first time she had in days without the strange distance between them.

Bez nodded in approval.

It was only when Andrea giggled that she realized everyone was looking at her. She crossed her arms and examined the label on a wall beside her.

"We'll count to one hundred and then fan out," Santos said. "Meet back here in half an hour if victory isn't announced on the PA system first."

The calm, steady countdown was carried out by AK, who seemed to know that Bez's ghost ants had turned into ghost wasps as she waited for him to be done.

Makeda might have slipped and fallen. She could have tried to hide in a dangerous crevice with an exposed wire or a gas leak, or—

"Ninety-seven, ninety-eight . . ."

Bez was off, figuring that by the time her foot hit the ground, he would have reached one hundred, so she technically wasn't cheating.

While the rest of the crew split up into teams, Bez worked alone as she always did. First, she searched the nooks and crannies where a short person could hide, then looked over the guard rail to make sure Makeda wasn't clinging to the side of the ship, where Bez would have hidden since she took these kinds of drills very seriously.

The ghost-wasp sensation grew more intense as time dragged on and each possible hiding place turned up empty and no announcements were made on the PA system. Bez retraced her steps, basically the route they had taken on the safety walk, and found herself outside the lifeboat. The lifeboat that had its hatch slightly propped open, the move of someone daring enough to go inside of it but forward-thinking enough to plan against the possibility of a lock mechanism that would trap her.

Bez pulled the hatch open, hopped inside, and closed it behind her, leaving it propped on the food ration packet as Makeda had. She didn't see her at first glance, and wondered if she could possibly fit in the space under the bench, and then she caught sight of sneakers near eye level.

Makeda was sitting in the U-shaped pilot seat connected to the ceiling of the boat, gazing down at Bez. She had piled her hair up on top of her head in a bun secured with the snail hair elastic. Though she would resist the comparison if Bez said it aloud, she looked very much like a queen.

Brightness bloomed in Bez's chest at the sight of Makeda safe and sound, burning away the sting of the wasps, which had been nothing more than simple worry. Apparently Makeda had worked her way into the small cluster of people whose well-being mattered.

"Of course it was you who found me."

Bez tried not to be offended by the displeasure in the way she said *you.*

"Well, yes," Bez replied. "Do you think I'd let anyone else do it?"

"I guess you had to," Makeda said, swinging one of her feet back and forth. "Just like you have to pretend to like me. Because of the contracts on contracts and guard oaths and all that." She cringed. "Wow. Apparently the salt air really pries every pathetic thought out of my head. Now it's like I'm guilting you because I keep pointing out that I made you act like you like me when you really don't, which could add more pressure to make you act like you do, which is even sadder and, shit, I'm just going to stop talking now." She slammed her mouth shut with an audible click of teeth.

"Talking is good. Clarity is what we strive for—"

"—at Damsel in Distress Rescue Services?"

"No. In our relationship." Bez stepped up onto the bench seat in the middle of the ship and walked across it toward Makeda, the metal clanging under her boots with each step. She understood now what had been misunderstood on the upper deck in their previous conversation.

"Remember when you discussed communication, and how we had to have it in this fake marriage?" Bez asked, coming to a stop at the edge of the bench just in front of Makeda, who was now slightly taller than Bez thanks to her perch on the pilot seat.

"Of course." Makeda's leg began to swing faster. "I made rules for our situation that ended up making me break your rules."

Bez caught Makeda's frantically swinging leg by the calf, palming the tense muscle through her leggings. "What rules?"

"No feelings and no fucking," Makeda said quietly.

"Those aren't my rules," Bez lied. "Why would I, master of planning for the future, create such shortsighted and prohibitive rules?"

Makeda rolled her eyes. "They are. The entanglement clause? We talked about this just a few days ago."

"Ah." Bez nodded. "Right. No feelings and no fucking. Those were more *suggestions* than set-in-stone rules, I'd say. I think 'some feelings and some fucking.' That was the spirit, if not the letter."

Makeda moistened her lips—they were lovely from any angle, but Bez loved being able to look up at her, to see the full bow of her bottom lip and the tender curve where her neck met her jaw.

"What about the fine print of our contract?" Makeda pressed, ever a stickler.

"The fine print says 'except in the case of specific extenuating circumstances.' I would say our situation is the height of extenuating, whatever that means. I just put it there because it sounded good."

Makeda tried to pull her leg away. "Look, I get it. You're doing your whole 'at your service' thing and because of circumstances you think this is part of being of service. Just because you're good at it doesn't make it okay for me to have asked."

Bez stared at Makeda for a long moment, trying to make sense of what had just been said. She was still thinking of sometimes feeling and, more important, sometimes fucking, and now Makeda was talking about being of service?

"Oh!" she cried out, rediscovering the thread of the conversation that Makeda's contract talk had distracted her from. "I was trying to communicate. I didn't let anyone find you because I *wanted* to be the one to do it," she said. "Just like I have to act like I like you because I *do* like you."

"Please just stop this." Makeda fixed a serious gaze on Bez. "Enough. I asked you to live up to the lie you roped me into, and you're going all in with it but I'm telling you that you don't have to do this anymore. It's not funny anymore."

"Have you noticed that you keep coming up with different reasons to dismiss the thing that I have admitted to you three times over now?" Bez asked.

"Your stubbornness would be admirable if it wasn't so frustrating."

Makeda inhaled sharply and looked away.

"Pretending to like you for a contract is one thing, but because I think it's funny? What kind of logic is this? There's nothing humorous about that," Bez said, and when Makeda didn't answer she continued figuring it out on her own. "Wait a moment. The complex you have. You think I'd laugh at you. I see."

Makeda groaned.

"Why wouldn't you? *I'm* laughing at me. I'm on a supposed quest for independence and I developed a full-blown crush on you. I thought I was taking charge, and the minute you did what I asked, I started getting ideas. I thought . . . that maybe . . ." Makeda's mouth twisted and she shook her head ruefully. "I guess this trip *has* been a learning experience, in one way. I now know for sure that I'm always going to be a watering can with a hole in the side, leaking common sense."

Beznaria wasn't fully listening to what Makeda was saying. She tried, but frankly the woman wasn't making sense, and also the weak light streaming in from the window was highlighting her cheekbones and wide brown eyes.

Something occurred to her then.

"I haven't applied rule three yet," she said.

Makeda squinted at her. "What?"

She lifted Makeda's chin with the knuckle of her index finger, looking into her eyes. "I skipped that one entirely. Maybe that's why we keep misunderstanding one another."

"Rule number three. Is that the one about not moving around on the deck when cargo is loading?" Makeda asked, clearly confused.

"No," Bez said. The brain fireflies were blinking wildly. "We have too many sets of rules to sift through, but this one is the most important at the moment. I'm fairly certain I know the answer but I'll ask to be sure. Do you like kissing?"

Makeda was holding onto the arms of the U-shaped pilot seat with both hands, and gripped them harder as she leaned forward a little. "What?"

"Kissing. Pressing mouths together." Bez grazed her finger up Makeda's jawline and reveled in the tremor that it elicited. "Do you like it?"

"Um. Yes." Her gaze dropped to Bez's mouth, and that heat Bez had seen flare up in the depths of Makeda's brown eyes flamed on. "I guess it depends on who the kissing partner is. Would be. You?"

With her free hand, Bez pushed her glasses up to rest above her hairline. "Me."

"Oh, yeah. Yes."

"Well then. Rule three states that if she likes kissing, then kiss her. I know that you prefer I adhere to rules, so I'm afraid I must." She stepped to the very edge of the bench, closing the scant space between them, and pressed her mouth to Makeda's.

It wasn't an earth-shattering kiss, or a smoldering one that made Beznaria's clit throb to life. It was, instead, like a key working into a lock and opening a door, revealing a treasure that had always been there, waiting to be discovered. Each brush of their lips pushed that door open farther, allowing more of the jewels and gems hidden inside to catch the light until their glinting made Beznaria feel aglow from the beauty.

The feeling that thrummed through her body was the same one she'd felt when she'd knelt in front of Makeda in the dining room of the Golden Crown. She still wasn't sure what it was, fealty or something to do with the bonds of guard and queen. It was a quickening in her chest and tingling pleasure all over and the urge to bring Makeda closer, kiss her more deeply, to touch and caress her in the hopes that she could give her a fraction of the goodness she was feeling.

Makeda tasted like tart strawberries with a hint of deep sweetness—Chef Rick had made his famous cheesecake. Her lips were slick with gloss and so damned soft—but Makeda herself wasn't, oddly. Bez had thought the woman would be timid, but she brought both hands to either side of Bez's head and held her in place as she licked into her mouth, moaning like she was starved. The kiss was hard, demanding, without an ounce of reservation; Makeda took what she wanted from Bez with no apologies and made her delight loud and clear. It seemed there was one area in which Makeda didn't naturally default to giving or self-doubt, and the knowledge sent a thrill through Bez.

Makeda used the heels of her feet to pull Bez closer, running her tongue over Bez's lips at the same time. Her hands caressed Bez's neck and shoulders and—there, in the possessive spread of her fingers through her hair and the slight tug, tilting Bez's head back to kiss her more deeply—*there* was the clit throb. Bez had wanted Makeda since she'd walked into that half-cleaned room at the B&B, but now that want coalesced into an aching desire.

Bez had only thought to kiss her, but she wanted to touch her, to feel her skin under her palms. She slid her hands up Makeda's thighs, reveling in the flex of muscles through the thin material of her leggings, before moving under the hem of her sweatshirt and T-shirt to grip her by the waist.

"Are you—" Makeda pressed a kiss to Bez's lips, and then another "—are you making sure I don't fall out of this seat?"

Bez caressed one hand over the sweep of skin where torso met waist, curving around to spread her palm over Makeda's back, mapping the hills and valleys.

"Yes," she panted between kisses. "If you fall and break anything, we'll have to pay for it, and if you damage the steering there will be one less lifeboat in case of emergency."

Makeda pulled her head back and looked down into Bez's eyes. "Practicality is sexy as hell."

"You could also hit the release lever and send us plummeting into the sea, and that's not the *O* face I want to see right now." Bez squinted, wanting to see Makeda more clearly without her glasses. "Most important, I'd have to stop kissing you if you fell. I'm both practical and horny."

"The best combination," Makeda said, laughing and leaning down into the kiss. "You know. We're in a small semiprivate space with a time limit until someone finds us. I've heard that some people find that kind of challenge a turn-on."

"By some people, do you mean you?"

Makeda wrapped her legs around Bez's waist, her thigh muscles flexing as she dragged her forward.

"I don't know. No better time to find out, though."

"I imagine that both of us work best under pressure," Bez said. "Well, that sounds like a line a Bond villain would say so perhaps we should just kiss before I embarrass myself further."

Makeda laughed quietly, and it transformed her face, like a photo filter except it was natural joy and mischief and lust. The laughter caught as Bez slid her hand from Makeda's back to rest at the creases of her thighs. She leaned forward, pressing her lips to the birthmark beneath Makeda's right ear. She licked lightly while brushing her thumbs back and forth over the leggings molded to Makeda's inner thighs.

Makeda's exhalation trembled past Bez's ear—the sound of someone trying to be so quiet. Bez had thought she liked wringing loud cries from her lovers, but this was a different kind of pleasure, knowing that Makeda wanted to be loud but wouldn't.

"Do you want me to get you off?" she asked in a low voice as she brushed one of her thumbs over Makeda's mound. When Makeda lifted her hips the slightest bit, angling up to press more firmly against Bez's thumb, that was the answer, wasn't it?

She gripped one of Makeda's thighs firmly and then laid three fingers of her other hand over the imprint of Makeda's folds beneath the clinging material of her leggings. And then she rubbed.

"Oh," Makeda whispered, dropping her head so that her forehead rested against Beznaria's. "Harder, please. More."

Bez grinned and gave the woman what she wanted.

Makeda still had one arm looped around the driver's seat, for safety, but she reached down with the other to reach down into Bez's shirt and cupped a breast, palming it before lightly pinching the nipple.

Bez shuddered beneath the sensation and pressed more firmly with her own fingers, circling deep and slow, or rubbing hard and fast—doing whatever made Makeda pant quietly and throw her head back as she rode Bez's hand—the tight controlled motions of someone who doesn't want to fall but just wild enough to show she trusted Bez to catch her.

"Does it feel good, Makeda?" Bez asked.

"Yes, so good. But . . ." She briefly released her hold on the seat to position Bez's hand a centimeter to the left. "Oh fuck."

A moan ripped from her throat, and she pressed her mouth back against Bez's, kissing her deeply and muffling her cries at the same time. She gave up her hold on the captain's seat, using one hand to hold Bez's face as their tongues clashed.

Bez repositioned her hand, using the heel of her palm to knead deep, hard circles against Makeda's clit, and got what she wanted—an orgasm surged through Makeda, jerking her body from limp to tense to limp. Bez was glad she had a tight grip on her lover, and excellent core strength, because Makeda bucked right off the edge of the perch seat, clinging to Bez with arms, legs, and mouth. Bez held her fast as the aftershocks shook through her, their tongues slowly tangling. Her own body begged for release and was already close to it just from watching Makeda get hers.

She stepped down onto the floor of the lifeboat and Makeda broke their kiss and laughed into her neck.

"I didn't even think," she said, laughing and shaking her head and looking up at Bez with shining eyes. "I could have died from falling from a perch midorgasm, but you caught me."

"You knew I would," Beznaria said and felt something unclench when Makeda didn't refute that claim. She nodded and gazed at her eyes that were still glazed with lust, then rocked her hips forward, sending a sharp bolt of lust through Bez.

"Really rethinking my feelings on princess dresses," Makeda said, then tilted her head toward the captain's seat. It was directly in line with Bez's face now that she stood on the floor of the lifeboat. "Because the things your tongue could do from this angle—"

"Found the stowaway!" a voice called out suddenly. "And company."

Bez turned and saw Santos and Thompson. Thompson was halfway through the hatch, doubled over laughing, but Santos frowned from outside the door. He also quickly removed his hand from Thompson's butt.

"I found her first," Bez said.

"And didn't say anything," Santos said. "Making the rest of us waste time as we continued the search."

"I'm sure it was a hardship for you," she said, glancing suggestively at the hand he'd pulled away.

"Come on, Thiago, ah, Chief Engineer," Thompson said, then turned to Bez and Makeda. "And you two. There is absolutely no fraternizing in the lifeboats, understand?" She winked as she retreated from the hatch.

"Um." Makeda shimmied down Bez's body to the floor below, leaving a trail of sensation and tantalizing ideas in her wake. "Was that . . . Should we . . . Maybe we shouldn't do *that*, even if it felt good as hell."

Bez could almost see the thoughts colliding in Makeda's head as she adjusted her hoodie; her own was still spinning and she wasn't sure what to do either.

"Alternatively, maybe we should," Makeda said after a moment had passed.

"I'm in favor of option two, based on the fact that I want you to ride my fingers like a jockey at the Annual Seaside Preakness," Bez said as casually as one could say such a thing. "I want to touch you everywhere, taste you specific-where, and know what you sound like when your fourth orgasm hits."

Makeda covered her ears with her hands, then her eyes, then her ears again. "Oh my god. That is unfair."

"It's the truth," Bez said. "You like the truth."

"But you can't just say things like that!" Makeda looked up, and her expression made it apparent that she was open to hearing more.

"I can say all kinds of things. But we can do option one if you like. At least until we're off the lifeboat. Let's go inside," she said, holding her hand out. "The rest will work itself out."

Makeda's fingers clasped Bez's and they closed up the lifeboat and headed back to the accommodations.

Bez kept her stride confident, but she had no idea what she was doing. She'd just kissed the possible princess, which would be a violation of the Oath of the Guard. If Makeda became princess, even just ceremonially, had Bez just risked the Chetchevaliere reputation she was trying to save from dishonor?

Chapter 16

The next morning, after breakfast with the crew, Makeda stood by the door to their room, watching Bez fold the blanket she'd slept with on the couch the evening before. The ship was hitting the waves a little harder than usual due to a storm system somewhere hundreds of miles away from them; she placed a hand against the wall as she waited, trying and failing not to analyze their new situation from every angle.

Makeda had been sure that after what had happened in the lifeboat Beznaria would finally share the bed, but even though they'd made out in the stairwell, and the hallway, and up against the door to their cabin, she'd settled into her usual spot on the couch at the end of the night.

Makeda wasn't sure how to read the decision to take it slow, but she decided that she couldn't worry about what would happen when they were off the boat—whether Bez liked her or *liked* her liked her.

The rules of engagement, or fake marriage rather, had changed, but this was still practice for her, no matter what her heart and other body parts were telling her. Part of that practice, and maybe the hardest part, was going to be dealing with the fact that she had no control over how Beznaria felt about her, how Beznaria expressed whatever it was she felt, and what they would both do with those feelings in a couple of weeks, since they lived very different lifestyles.

Bez was an international investigator, while Makeda had a job as a supermarket manager awaiting her when she was done with the princess escapade that kept falling to the wayside. She was proud of that job, but it didn't seem like the kind of life someone like Bez would want to settle into. If she didn't even want to share a bed, she wouldn't want to hear about the latest sale on quinoa and drama from the meat department.

Makeda sighed, annoyed with herself.

This was her problem. She'd been kicking herself for letting her crush get out of control, and now after a few kisses and an illicit orgasm, she was already thinking about how they would spend forever together.

I need to stop getting ahead of myself, she chided herself.

Bez turned, her gaze already locked on Makeda's, as if she'd known she was being watched. Makeda tried to look away quickly but, in an extremely smooth move, turned to face the wall on her right instead of the kitchenette on her left.

"Ready?" Bez asked in a knowing voice.

Makeda nodded, and they headed down the hall and into the stairwell. "I'm going to take the elevator down to AK's office," Makeda said. "Today I'm going to go over the books. I thought it was going to be some super difficult job, but it's not that different from what I've been doing for years at GrabRite and the Golden Crown, just on the high seas."

"Of course, it wouldn't be difficult for you. I think you could do anything if you put your mind to it," Bez said, then reconsidered. "Well, not anything. You're too short for certain jobs and don't have a natural aptitude for others—like, you'd be terrible as a lobbyist for an evil enterprise. But you'd certainly be able to master more than the average person through competence alone."

Makeda's face and neck heated. "Thank you."

She'd almost written off Bez's compliment as nonsense talk meant to make her feel good, but it felt like more than that. Makeda didn't need someone who thought she could do anything; she wanted someone who saw her well enough to know her strengths and weaknesses.

The ship rocked from side to side—the sea had been rougher than usual since they'd woken up—and Makeda's balance almost didn't kick in on time.

"I'll ride down with you," Bez said, taking her hand to keep her from falling. "My watch shift doesn't start for a few minutes."

Makeda felt like a teenager as Bez's hand enclosed hers, trying to decipher each caress and change in pressure. Was Bez holding her hand because she wanted to? Because she liked her? Or was it a public display meant for anyone who might walk by? Did Bez even care what other people thought anymore?

"You're not allowed to be tense right now," Bez said in a low voice, squeezing her hand to draw her attention. "I'm about to go on shift and I don't have time to provide a full-service loosening."

Makeda allowed her annoying thoughts to be replaced by more entertaining ones of just how loose Bez could get her. If she was going to stress about a future she was in no way privy to, she might as well aim for having her toes curled instead of her heart broken.

"Don't think I'm reliant on you for that," Makeda said. "With this yoga I've been doing, I'll be so loose I'll be able to get my feet behind my head before we arrive in Ibarania in a couple of days. That can be my special talent to prove I'm worthy of the crown." She held an imaginary mic to her mouth. "'And here we have the prospect from Atlantic City and oh—oh, her knees are behind her ears. Never has Ibarania witnessed such a display of grace and royal majesty.'"

Beznaria's smile faltered and she pushed up her glasses. "They won't see that coming."

Makeda could feel it—the way Beznaria redirected every time the subject of what would happen after their arrival in Ibarania came up. She didn't think Bez was lying, exactly, but something was off.

"Should I be worried?" she asked. "About what happens when we arrive? I like details, and so far you haven't really given me any."

"I'm waiting on word from the WFM," Bez said, and this time there was no hesitation in her tone. "With life on the ship, communication has been rather difficult. I'll go check my email after the shift to see if there's word from them, and if not I'll surely be able to make contact with someone tomorrow to see what the holdup has been."

"Sounds good," Makeda said cautiously as the elevator arrived. When the doors opened, Beznaria stepped inside, pulling Makeda in with her.

She hit the button for the admin offices, and slipped her hand around Makeda's waist as the doors closed, tugging her so that their bodies were pressed up against one another. She looked down at Makeda, studying her face, her expression more sober than usual. "I don't think I've adequately prepared you for what awaits us there."

"Um." Makeda reached up and linked her hands behind Beznaria's neck. "Is there some terrifying secret you haven't told me about the royal family? Combat to the death? Unpleasant rituals? I mean, I know some wild shit has happened in the Mediterranean, historically, and bacchanalian orgies aren't on my bucket list, but—"

Bez smiled, a soft and unprecedented tilt of just one corner of her mouth, and squeezed Makeda more tightly to her. "No. I was talking about my family."

"Your family." Makeda nodded, though her stomach did a little dip that had nothing to do with the bouncing waves.

"Of course," Bez said finally. Because she was staring up at Bez, Makeda could see when her expression shifted from open to . . . not distant, but discomfited. It reminded her of the look Kojak gave her when he walked up to her to demand pets and then seemed shocked and uncomfortable when he received them. "I'm sure they'll be thrilled to meet the heir to the throne! And Henna Jeta will be so relieved."

"Oh, right, royalty," Makeda said, feeling the elevator brakes engage and the car begin to slow. "Missing heir. Yes, I'm sure they'll be happy I can clear your family name."

She tried not to get sucked into overthinking things again, but she thought of something that she'd mostly ignored since they'd boarded the ship. Makeda wasn't going to Ibarania to be the heir—she was going to prove she wasn't. She had her own family ledger to balance, and for her plan to succeed she'd have to crush Bez's dream.

She hadn't taken Beznaria's feelings into consideration, and when she had, she'd only wondered what it meant for her own emotional well-being. Even if Bez did see her as something more than the solution to her family's problems, would she still feel that way when Makeda refuted being princess, no matter what the truth was?

The elevator doors opened noisily behind her, and she started to pull away from Bez's embrace. "I'll see you at dinner?"

That sounded nonchalant, and not like someone who suddenly had a refined palate when it came to relationship goals, as if she hadn't subsisted on stale crumbs for years.

Beznaria's hold around her waist tightened, clamping Makeda up against her with one arm and reaching out with the other—a moment later the doors closed again.

"I don't know what's bothering you, but I won't be able to concentrate during my shift if I have to worry about the way your eyes look right now," Bez said. "I also just want an excuse to do this."

Bez kissed her; a hard press of lips and insistent swipe of tongue that dropkicked every thought out of Makeda's head except for how soft Bez's lips were, how good she smelled, and how much Makeda wished she wasn't going on watch so they could ride the elevator back up to their cabin and finally share that bed. She'd share the rock-hard couch at this point. Anything to ease the ache between her legs. She was one tongue tangle away from riding the woman's thigh in the elevator.

"You said there are no pirates on this route, right?" Makeda asked against Bez's mouth. Then she dropped her head to the side and let her nose gently graze Bez's neck, receiving a brief shiver for her trouble. "If you missed your shift, how bad would it be?"

"Well, with the weather and the fact that we're getting closer to land, watch is actually important today." Bez smiled. "Though I guess I can say loosening accomplished. I've gotten you, of all people, to encourage me to commit dereliction of duty. And that was from one kiss. Imagine the possibilities."

She waggled her brows.

"Oh, I've been imagining," Makeda said, feeling bold. "Next time you make me come, I might suggest a crime spree. And when I make *you* co—"

Bez clamped a hand over Makeda's mouth, her gaze serious even as her glasses slid down the bridge of her nose. "Save it for tonight, sea snail."

She dropped an awkward kiss on Makeda's eyebrow, an act that should have been benign but drew a tremor of anticipation from her.

Tonight.

Bez hit the button to open the elevator doors, and Makeda stepped out blinking into the hallway, emerging from the alternate reality she fell into every time she was with Bez now.

"Makeda?"

She looked over her shoulder, expecting to find Bez leaning insouciantly in the elevator car, but the woman was ramrod straight, like a cadet reporting to a drill sergeant. "I should clarify something, in the name of communication since that is a priority in our, ah, situation. I think my family will like you for reasons unrelated to the royal heir search, just for who you are. And my evidence for that is that I like you for reasons unrelated to the royal heir search. Just for who you are."

Then she reached forward and jabbed repeatedly at a button, what Makeda assumed was "Close Door." Bez waved goodbye, one hand on her hip and a pleased expression on her face.

Makeda stared back, hands clasped in the pocket of her hoodie like an anxious marsupial, processing what she'd heard.

The elevator doors didn't close, and Bez laughed nervously and pressed the button again. And then again.

"Ah, do you believe this? This elevator? How can a door be so slow to close at moments when one needs them to close quickly? I need to tell Chief Engineer Santos to have someone take a look at this," Bez said, her words tumbling out almost too quickly for Makeda to understand. She poked her glasses up and then gestured in frustration toward the elevator panel. "Imagine this was an emergency. Imagine there was a—a serial killer chasing me down the hall, and the elevator was my only means of escape, and the doors refused to close like this! This is unacceptable. Of course, I would never run from a serial killer, I would fight them and I would be victorious, but this is a hypothetical situation and—"

The doors finally slid together, cutting off Bez's rambling, and Makeda laughed quietly to herself. As she headed to AK's office, she placed a hand over her chest, taking a moment to savor the sensation that rippled through her watering can.

Happiness.

That was something that took practice, too, and she was going to savor it. Everything else, the things accumulating between her and Bez that could ruin that happiness? She'd ignore them until they got to Ibarania. Like the Ferris wheel, she'd let herself have this fantasy until she set her feet on the solid ground of reality.

A FEW HOURS later, it was dark outside the window of Makeda and Bez's cabin despite it being the afternoon. AK had cut their session short because the storm was stronger than earlier forecasts had predicted, and he'd had to leave to help with securing the ship. Though it wouldn't hit them directly, it was apparently going to be a rough night.

Makeda had put away all the dishes and any items that might pose a risk if they flew across the cabin at high speed. Her and Bez's toiletries had been packed away carefully, and the cabinets and drawers secured with safety locks. She'd stopped peeking out at the pouring rain and the huge waves cresting against the cargo on the deck as the ship rocked back and forth like the Flying Dutchman at the boardwalk amusement park, rolling from one side to the other. A few stray objects slid across the floor, but she could barely hear them knocking into the furniture over the roar of the ocean.

The PA system in the room emitted static and then Captain Del Rosario's voice came through. "This is the captain. We are in rough seas, as you're well aware, but this ship was built for rough seas. I'm not worried, and if anyone on board is, don't be. Just hold tight, and I'll get us through this."

Makeda smiled, knowing the message was likely for her, and then climbed onto the bed and wedged herself into the corner of the alcove. She should have been more frightened, given that it seemed like the ocean and the *Virginia Queen* were in the middle of a fistfight, but nothing gave her a sense of steadiness like impending disaster.

It wasn't that she was calm and collected; her body was tense and her stomach wasn't doing so great. But her worry and planning had met their first insurmountable obstacle. She couldn't do *anything* about this. Any sense of control she'd imagined she had in this world was being smashed against the hull of the ship by pounding waves. She was nothing. Her problems were nothing. She could die here, and all the giving and self-effacement and the belated attempt at being selfish would mean nothing.

There was something comforting in the macabre realization.

A peal of thunder louder than anything Makeda had ever heard pressed into the cabin from all sides—she felt it in her body like she was sitting on an amp at a concert. She yelled and squeezed her eyes shut as lightning flashed outside the window.

Okay, it seemed the peace she'd found at her loss of control had pushed past the threshold from *serenity now* to *shit what now?*

"Jesus? Lord? Okay, I haven't spoken to you much lately but please, please talk to your boy Poseidon, or any deities in the area who can help." She glanced at the goddess portrait on the wall so as not to leave her out. "I don't think I can do this all night."

The door swung open, and lightning illuminated a hooded figure. Makeda wondered what her grandmother would say if she survived to tell her that the Savior himself had shown up to do a rescue at sea. But then the door slammed shut and Bez stumbled in, soaking wet.

The stumble should have been the first sign, given that the investigator usually moved with a lithe, assertive confidence.

"This was definitely not in the itinerary I received," Makeda half-jokingly shouted over the wail of wind and the crash of waves. "This better not be the entry point to the Bermuda Triangle."

She waited for Beznaria to joke or call her a landlubber, but she didn't respond. She peeled off the yellow security vest over her sweatshirt, and that was when Makeda registered that Bez's teeth were chattering. Her eyes were wide and wild behind her steamed up glasses lenses.

"Bez?"

The wild gaze flew to Makeda, but Bez didn't seem to register her. She steadied herself, bending with the sway of the ship like an experienced sailor, but her stance was otherwise slack, lacking her usual energy.

"Are you okay?" Makeda asked, sitting up abruptly. Her stomach heaved as she ran into the wrong side of gravity in the ship's tossing.

"Not at all," Bez replied, her words shaky.

Makeda felt it spark to life in her—that desire to help, to rush into action and manage things. Her already quickly beating heart picked up the pace in anticipation of the opportunity she'd been unknowingly waiting for with Bez—to fix things. Wasn't that how all of her relationships fell into place? Some hardship that drew them together inextricably?

Makeda fought the urge, instead asking with modulated concern, "Did something happen?"

"Yes. Not recently." A shudder passed over Bez's body and her eyes squeezed shut. "I haven't thought of it, because I made myself not think of it, but now it's all I can think of. I think I'm having some kind of . . . psychological crisis. I think that's normal. It will pass in a moment." She stood there, her years of experience keeping her upright as the ship listed, seeming to wait for that moment to arrive.

She looked so helpless that Makeda felt it like the stormy sea, but inside of herself, in that internal watering can as the hunger, the loneliness, lunged.

She needs me right now, Makeda thought. *When people need you, they don't leave.*

When her mother had needed her, things had been terrible, but her mother had stayed.

The thought added to Makeda's growing seasickness, but she stored it away for later. She remembered that she was supposed to be practicing here, exploring her boundaries and, now, thinking about how they rubbed up against the boundaries of others. She was a helper—a multi-tool. That wasn't bad, if she kept it in check. Instead of impulsively leaping to give—as much as one could leap on a boat that was twerking its way across the ocean—she tried to think of what she knew about Bez.

The woman saw herself as a protector. Coddling her would make her feel worse. It would be giving that was taking—Bez's pride.

Makeda waited for the ship to temporarily right itself. Then she released the bar on the wall next to the bed, grabbed the balled-up blanket from the couch, and made her way to Bez on wobbly legs.

"It's okay," she said calmly, reaching up to wrap the blanket around Bez's shoulders.

"It is *not* okay," Bez corrected, sounding mildly offended despite her panic. "I'm supposed to be taking care of you. I'm . . . I'm . . ."

"You are taking care of me," Makeda said, grabbing the metal bar on the wall next to the bathroom door, riding out the ship's roll to the other side. "By letting me help you. It helps keep me calm. Maybe how protecting people makes you feel. Can I help?"

Bez nodded.

"Let's get you into something dry." With her free hand, Makeda grabbed the robe hanging from the hook on the door and held it out to Bez, looking away from her. It was snatched from her hand, and when she turned around another ship roll later, Bez was tying the belt with shaking fingers, her wet clothes in a heap with the outerwear she'd shed.

Makeda looped arms with her and pulled her toward the bed. "Let's get under the blankets. You're freezing."

Bez pulled up short. "You said you changed your mind about sharing beds," she said over the roar of the storm. "That first night."

"You heard that?" She'd heard, and followed the directive. Had she been waiting for an invitation all this time?

"I'm an investigator," Bez said, jutting her chin out. "I don't always let people know what I hear or see."

"Yes. Top ten," Makeda said, tugging her toward the bed.

"Out of ten," Bez admitted, still resisting getting into the bed. "I told you, if I'm in someone's bed, I want to be there because they want me there. Not by chance. And not out of pity."

Makeda might have rolled her eyes if Bez didn't look so vulnerable. She really thought there was a question about this?

"You are formally invited to the royal alcove," Makeda said, and tugged Bez's sleeve. "Please. Come to bed."

"If you insist," Bez said, looking at least a little pleased with herself, then they were tossed onto the bed by the next bounce of the ship over the waves. It wasn't a cute fall, where they tumbled onto one another and looked into each other's eyes. The jolt of the boat lifted them from the floor. Makeda grasped Bez and Bez grasped back. Gravity tossed them both against the back wall of the alcove, which didn't help a body already sore from days of yoga and exercise.

"Are you all right?" they both asked at the same time but neither answered, or laughed, or said jinx. Neither moved except to grip one another more tightly.

"This bed should come with straps or something," Makeda said, pulling the blankets over them. "I mean, like straps that could hold us down so we don't fall off the bed not, you know. *Strap* straps. Do you need a drink?"

She pulled a thermos of tea she'd tucked between the mattress and the wall during her storm setup. Bez took it and sipped quickly, closing the cap before it could spill.

"I can hold you down," she announced, her voice a bit stronger. "Since there are no straps. I'm supposed to protect you after all."

Makeda thought that might mean that Bez needed to hold her, and to be held. That whatever had prompted her wild-eyed entry into the room was still going on in her head.

"Okay. I guess those tentacles of yours can be put to use."

Bez pressed herself back against the corner where Makeda had lodged herself a few minutes earlier, holding the bar on the wall and spreading her long legs so that they pressed against the wooden frame the bed sat in, adding extra security against being tossed around. She patted her lap.

Makeda had never dated someone so much taller than her. She wasn't sure if this was the kind of condescending shit they pulled all the time, but it was endearing in a way, too, she supposed. She wasn't going to sit like a child, though. She nestled kitty-corner to Bez, her back against the other wall and her legs thrown over Bez's. Then she slid both arms around Bez and cuddled against her.

"Is this good?" she asked.

Bez wrapped the arm that wasn't holding the bar around Makeda, hauling her more tightly against her. "It was, but this is better."

"Do you want to talk?" she asked, and felt Bez shake her head. Some part of her wanted to talk anyway, to override Bez's sense of what she needed with how Makeda was used to offering comfort, but she just took a deep breath instead. "Okay, let me know if that changes."

She repositioned one of her arms so she could hold onto the bar, too—Bez shouldn't have to support their weight alone. They sat like that for a long time, with their bodies tensing and flexing against one another as the rolling ship tried to eject them from the bed. There was a comfort in the way their bodies worked in unison, without either of them having to speak a word, or without Makeda having to point out her own discomfort being overlooked. They could be careful with one another, she realized, could form an interlocking shell of protection made of a hundred tiny flexes and contractions— the evidence of their desire to keep each other safe and comfortable.

This was the first time they'd sat like this without kissing or touching or exploring, and it felt good. Natural. She felt still, despite the terrifying situation they were in. It was like Beznaria's general aura of chaos met the perpetual help-y motion that had been propelling Makeda through life, and they canceled each other out.

This was the yoga pose she'd been looking for that could make everything feel better: the Beznarian snuggle.

Sleep was impossible, despite their silence, so Makeda was wide awake when Bez stirred in that particular way of someone steeling themselves to say something.

"I—" Bez sighed deeply, and Makeda rose with the expansion of her chest. "I saw a body in the waves. While I was on watch this afternoon."

Makeda stiffened. "Did someone fall overboard?"

Bez shook her head. "No. There was no body. But . . . I haven't been in a bad storm at sea since that last time I was on a cargo ship. And there were bodies, that time."

Bez was shaking again. Not continuously, but in fits and starts.

"Do you want to talk about what happened?" Makeda asked. "Was this in the military?"

"I joined the military because I thought it was something that would have the same honor as the Ibaranian Royal Guard. And honor is important to me. But military life was difficult. My too-muchness annoyed everyone. My superiors always thought I was talking back when I thought I was simply answering them. And we didn't do anything, except repair our ship and run drills. After I served my term, a family friend got me a job in maritime security. I thought it would be a way of doing what I wanted to do. Protecting people."

Makeda tightened her hold. "Wanting to protect people is good."

"It was a Mediterranean route, between Tangier and Crete." Bez released a shuddering exhale. "People in overcrowded boats started appearing more and more, trying to make it to Ibarania, or Greece, or anywhere that wasn't the place they were fleeing from."

Preemptive dread filled Makeda. She didn't always have time to watch the news, but when she did, she'd seen images like what Bez was describing—desperate people driven to flee their homes.

"The shipping company wouldn't let us help them, you see. They told us that the military would handle it, but my friends in the military were told that someone else was handling it. And while people passed off responsibility, the ships, some of which could barely be called that, kept appearing along our route. I'd just have to sit there with binoculars and watch these people on their boats, people who might have been me or my family if we hadn't been born in Ibarania."

Bez repositioned herself a bit, and her fingers slid between Makeda's as they clasped the bar more tightly. "I tried to do as I was told. But I was standing watch and there was a ship, barely a raft, as the worst storm I'd seen on the Mediterranean started to roll in. I just had to watch as they tried to bail water, with the rain and the waves adding a hundred times more than they could get rid of."

"Did the ship sink?" Makeda asked around the dread lodged in her throat.

Bez managed a weak laugh of bravado. "I'm a Chetchevaliere. I ignored the orders of my captain and commandeered one of the lifeboats. I didn't think of what I was doing until I was plunging into the sea and heading for the boat that was going under."

Makeda's breath caught in her throat. She'd stared out at the ocean as she waited for someone—for Bez—to find her in the lifeboat during the stowaway search. She'd thought about how terrifying it must be to just be launched into the sea from such a height, and she'd been looking out at calm waters. Bez had launched herself into seas like this. She held her more tightly, wishing she could stop this storm. "Oh my god, Beznaria. What happened?"

"I was fired, had all kinds of fines levied against me, but I saved many people. We had to pass the storm in the lifeboat with the waves hurling us every which way, but we were rescued eventually when conditions were safer."

Makeda rubbed her cheek against Beznaria's. "That's incredible. Do you understand"—her throat closed up with emotion and she cleared it—"do you understand that you're incredible?"

"I saved many people, not all of the people. Because I waited. Because I listened to rules that made no sense to me, but were supposed to prove that I was a good employee." Bez dropped back against the wall behind her and then down to rest against Makeda again. "There is a difference between knowing you can't save everyone and experiencing it firsthand. I had spent my life thinking failure was impossible if you tried hard enough but . . ." She shrugged. "I forced myself to forget. Just like people who get on those boats force themselves to forget if they make it to land. But right now, it's damned hard, sea snail."

Makeda's eyes were hot with tears even though Bez seemed to be returning to herself the more she talked. She thought of the back of the business card she'd been handed, with Damsel in Distress Rescue Services written as neatly as Bez could manage in her scrawling handwriting.

"Beznaria," she said, and she thought it was too quiet to be heard above the roar of the storm, but Bez must have felt it where their bodies pressed together.

"I'll be all right," she said, rolling her shoulders but still holding Makeda tightly. "I just want the storm to pass. It carried these memories with it, and it will take them away."

They sat in silence for long minutes as Makeda ran through things she could say to make it right.

Makeda's entire body was tense with the desire to fix this. To make Bez feel better, or to talk and talk and drown out whatever thoughts were in Bez's head with caring and kindness. But that wasn't what the investigator needed.

"You're right," she said. "You'll be all right. But I'm proud of you. You did a good thing and you still do good things."

"It's in my blood," Bez said. "I'm a Chetchevaliere."

Beznaria had said this so many times before, but this time Makeda couldn't let it stand. She loved her family, too, but so much of her life had been lost to the idea that the people she came from should dictate who she was and what she wanted in life. She was Grandmore and her grandfather, even if he hadn't been biologically related. She was her mother for better or for worse. But she was her own person, even if she still didn't know who that was, and Bez was her own person, too.

"No." Makeda pulled her head back so that her nose was almost pressed against Bez's. She wanted to be sure the woman heard this part, not just assume the message had gotten through. "If that was true, I'd be someone different—I'd be brave and careless and want to be a princess. Doing good is just who you are, apart from your family and their history. I'm proud of *you*."

Makeda saw the usual mischief that illuminated Beznaria from within begin to brighten her eyes, like a dawn in shades of honey brown. Bez still looked shaken, but not overwhelmed.

"Thank you," she said, a little haughtiness in her tone. "I am rather incredible. But so are you."

Makeda began to shrug and look away but Bez's grip tightened around her. "Don't do it. Don't act like you aren't, or I really will fling you out into the sea and you'll have to hope the dolphins rescue you."

Makeda smiled, mostly because if Bez could joke about this right now, it meant her crisis was passing. "I didn't even say anything," Makeda replied, rocking forward a little since her arms were busy holding onto Bez and the boat for dear life.

The *Virginia Queen* skipped across a large wave just then, jolting their faces together. This time their noses bumped and their lips pressed together, but there was no pain and split lips, just a shock of awareness that they were pressed close in the corner of the sleep alcove, that Makeda was mostly in Bez's lap. That their bare thighs touched where the hem of Makeda's shorts ended and Bez's robe had hiked up. Need awoke in Makeda, with this new acknowledgment of proximity—mouth to mouth, thigh to thigh, a clench at her core and an ache in her clit.

"Well, it looks like Mother Nature wants to keep it that way," Bez said against Makeda's mouth, and then her tongue pressed between Makeda's lips.

They'd kissed a lot in the last twenty-four hours, but so few times in total. They were still at the stage where every kiss was new, a different facet, a heightened emotion. Bez's kiss—deep, beseeching strokes of her tongue—seemed to be a request for connection. Her usual mischief shone through in the way she nipped at Makeda, but her kiss was demanding and the hand that had been holding Makeda closest to her started to roam.

The rough skin of Bez's palm sent tingles of pleasure over Makeda's back as she stroked, and Makeda mirrored the action through the fabric of Bez's robe. For the first time she was annoyed at high-quality fabric; it was too thick.

Bez's hand tightened around hers on the bar, and the other slid up between her shoulder blades. Makeda arched her back so that her head dropped back and Bez could leave a trail of kisses down her jawline to her neck, where she licked and sucked.

"That feels good," she said, and Bez slid her nose up her neck on a return journey that left sparks of pleasure in its wake, until her mouth was at Makeda's ear.

"The storm is loud," she said. "If you want me to hear you, you're going to have to *scream*."

Makeda angled her head to catch Bez's mouth with her own almost before the last word was spoken. Need rose up in her, furious as the storm, and even as she ravaged Bez's mouth, she was thinking of how she could get them what they needed without having to let go of the bar keeping them from flying off the bed. As they kissed, she took advantage of a lull in the listing boat to pull her legs under her and reposition herself so that she lay atop Bez, their legs interlaced so she was straddling a thigh. Bez's robe was half undone, and Makeda's upper thigh rested atop the trimmed curls between the investigator's legs. She licked hard into Bez's mouth, relishing the gasp when she rocked forward, sliding her aching clit along Bez's leg and more firmly pressing her own thigh against Bez's warm slick heat.

"So will you," she said, grabbing the bar on the wall above Bez with both hands and gyrating her hips. Bez picked up her rhythm immediately, their bodies having already been in sync, and they ground to the rolling of the waves.

"Fuck," Bez grunted, her hand sliding down to grip Makeda's hip as she met the slide and roll with her own. Makeda cried out, not worrying about being heard this time, when Bez leaned forward to lap at her nipple through the fabric of her nightshirt, catching the pebbled flesh between her lips and sucking hard.

"Shit," Makeda gritted. The sounds of the storm receded even as the ache in her clit deepened and spread. Sweat beaded on her back and in her hair but it was pleasure that slicked Bez's thigh as she rode. She dropped one hand to reach into Beznaria's robe, thumbing the nipple and then squeezing, watching with an unbefore-known greed as Bez gasped and bucked up beneath her.

She wanted her beautiful, exasperating investigator to break, just for her. She wanted her to writhe, to cry out, to lose her damn mind. Makeda knew what real greed was, in that moment.

"What?" Bez asked, sweaty hair curling over her forehead and eyes dark with lust. "What are you thinking with that expression?" She arched back with desire, dropping a kiss along Makeda's jaw before her head briefly rested against the padded wall.

"I'm thinking that maybe, I'm an oceanic black hole," Makeda said.

For the first time she had the pleasure of seeing Beznaria be the one who was confused by a non sequitur. Makeda's response was to slip her hand down over the ridges of Bez's abs, undulating as need shook through her, to slip her hand between her own thigh and cup Bez's mound, her fingers pressing against her clit and rubbing deep circles.

If Bez wanted further clarification, she didn't ask. She whimpered and moaned, catching her lush bottom lip with her teeth as lightning emblazoned the image on Makeda's memory.

Makeda ground against Bez's thigh harder, teasing herself to draw out the sensation that made her breath catch in her throat and her legs tremble. She was so close, but . . .

Bez nipped her earlobe, her slick heat rocking up against Makeda's fingers as she found their rhythm again. "Look at you. You're about to come while riding my thigh in the middle of a tempest. I'd say that's rather brave and careless, sea snail."

"I'm not careless. And I don't want to be anymore," Makeda breathed, reveling in the pleasure battering at her willpower, growing more intense as she tried to hold back. "You come first. Come for me, Bez."

Beznaria's eyes squeezed shut as Makeda curled her fingers so that she rubbed both Bez's clit and her slick pussy. She quickened her pace with short, controlled thrusts of her hand, teasing her.

"Now." Makeda rubbed her thumb over Bez's clit with more pressure. "Come for me *now*."

"*Mutanna min diu,*" Bez cried out as warmth spurted over Makeda's fingers. The orgasm ripped through her, and she shuddered beneath Makeda. They both slid down the bed as her grip on the bar momentarily gave out.

Makeda's hold tightened as her own climax overwhelmed her, rippling through her and then surging, surging, so that she didn't even realize she'd shouted Bez's name until it rasped against her throat.

Bez regained her hold on the bar and they lay as they'd come, Makeda atop Bez, both of them drowsy and storm tossed and blissed out.

"I think this proves my theory that you're also incredible," Bez said with such reverence that they both burst out laughing. Makeda nestled her face into Bez's neck, not caring about the sweat-damp hair against her cheekbone.

"If this were a movie, the storm would end now, and we'd sail under a rainbow," Makeda said. Something tickled the back of her mind—hadn't Grandmore dreamed about a ship?

Then Bez's tongue curled along the shell of her ear. "Unfortunately this isn't a movie. The storm won't pass for a few hours, so I suppose we'll just have to keep ourselves occupied."

"Do you think we can do a jigsaw puzzle with the ship rolling like this?" Makeda asked with false earnestness, and Beznaria hugged her tightly.

"Possibly, but we'll have to find out next storm. I have other plans for my hands."

Chapter 17

Most of the crew was exhausted the following day, so after a breakfast where they were regaled with stories of all the terrible storms the *Virginia Queen* had passed through, Bez and Makeda had spent the day napping.

When they arrived at the dining room for dinner it was empty, except for Pietr, who was charging one of the tablets.

"Did your hot date go long?" Makeda teased.

Pietr flushed and pushed a hand through his hair. "I chose the wrong route and had to start the romance over from the beginning. I got so engrossed I didn't realize the battery was dying on the tablet, and it shut off just before they accepted my declaration of love."

"The wrong route?" Bez asked.

"Yes. I was playing *Byronic Rogues from Mars* and I chose the option of keeping a secret from Percylion, the alien I was romancing, because I thought it would add to the drama, but in the end he dumped me!"

He flushed more deeply, but Bez had the opposite reaction—she went cold.

"Lesson learned," Makeda said. "At least you get to charge the tablet and try it again."

"Where is everyone?" Bez interrupted, not liking this topic, which had a troop of guilt ants roaming over her body.

Pietr's expression suddenly shifted, and his gaze dropped. "Oh, you didn't hear? Dinner was moved to the main deck."

"Outside?" Makeda asked, her face scrunching up.

"You can't barbecue inside," he said with a wink, and Bez's worry was at least temporarily pushed out of the limelight by delight.

"Oh excellent! I've missed grilling at sea. Everything tastes better out in the ocean air."

"I'll have to test this theory," Makeda said quietly, then made an octopus suction noise, and Bez burst into shocked laughter. Each time she learned some new and incongruous facet of Makeda's personality, she liked her more.

It occurred to her then that they would be in Ibarania the following day, and everything would change. The comforting schedule of the last few days would be lost. The connections they'd made with the crew, the daily rituals they'd formed— what would become of them? She was worried about Makeda's reaction to the news of the WFM's behavior when they landed, but now she worried about her own. She didn't plan for the future, but at the moment it was all she could think of. Makeda was American; Ibarania wasn't her home, even if it was her heritage. What would happen when everything was settled and she had claimed her participation fee?

She tried to think of a solution, but her brain fireflies were conspicuously dark.

THE THREE OF them headed down to the deck, the scent of frying seafood filling the stairwell. When they stepped out, Bez was momentarily confused.

Someone had strung Christmas lights just outside the entrance to the main deck. They blinked bright and cheerful, creating a festive mood. On deck, the crew milled around a buffet table set with heaping platters of shrimp, veggies, and fish. Chef Rick stood over a long half-barrel barbecue and was happily tending to a slab of spiced meat searing on the grill.

Then she saw it—the large confection shaped like the bow of a ship, with two small figures standing on its deck, posed like Jack and Rose from *Titanic*. One tall, and one short, one with a black bob and one with locks—both wearing the red coverall of the crew of the *Virginia Queen*.

"Oh my god," Makeda said. "Are we cake? Are those cake versions? Of us? And this ship?"

Tenzi looked their way, her expression brightening. "They're here!" she called out, and everyone looked toward them, shouting, "Surprise!"

"We're celebrating surviving the storm," Greg said drily. "I deserve a party for that after being tossed all over the engine room."

"I was the one who worked a double," Pietr griped.

"We're celebrating your last night on the *Virginia Queen*," Jay said, shooting Greg an annoyed look.

Just like that, Bez had an excuse to not tell Makeda the bad news until later.

"And your wedding," Thompson said, wrapping her arms around Chief Engineer Santos. "Our wedding party was so wonderful, but it's been two years. We all thought it would be fun to celebrate yours, since you'll be leaving tomorrow."

"You're married? I thought you were scared of him!" Makeda clamped her hand over her mouth and Bez laughed.

Makeda hadn't been privy to Santos's hand on Thompson's butt in the lifeboat hatch the other day, and Bez herself had forgotten. She'd assumed they were simply shipboard lovers trying to keep things professional, but she was in no position to judge role-play in a relationship so she took the news in stride.

"Yes," Santos said, actually smiling for once—and that smile was directed down at Thompson. "We try to maintain a certain distance while on duty, but we're married. That's why I warned you about not paying too much attention to your wife. It can have, ah, serious consequences."

Thompson laughed and took a pull of her beer, apparently not wanting to comment.

AK stepped through the doors behind them and onto the deck, likely from the galley given the tray of sliced fruit he was carrying. He looked like he hadn't slept at all, but after the storm, most of the crew was exhausted. Despite his clear fatigue, he smiled as he passed them.

"We once had a problem in the engine room and couldn't find our chief engineer because a certain couple enjoys finding unpopulated corners of the ship for their trysts."

"You're the one who insisted we seek out happiness and fulfillment," Santos said, still staring down at Thompson. Bez had mistaken his intensity for hard-assedness, and surely that was there, too, but she realized now—understood now—that it was the strain of a person constantly fighting against pouncing on their partner. She filed a new idea away in her Rolodex of sureties: there were many ways to care for someone. Her past relationships had made her think she would be bad at every relationship, but maybe she just hadn't learned how to be good at them yet.

Greg scoffed and took a pull of his beer. "Just rub it in, the luck that you get to work on the same ship with your person. I'll be fine here by myself. No need to worry about my feelings."

"Most of us don't get to," Chuck said. "This is supposed to be a celebration of love, not a reminder that our partners are thousands of miles away."

Beznaria felt those words like a blade; Makeda might soon be thousands of miles away from her, too.

She was being ridiculous, she told herself. She'd spent approximately 99.999 percent of her life away from Makeda and been fine. She'd spent the last few years away from her family and been fine. She liked being alone, not having to report her comings and goings to anyone, not having to share a bed.

She glanced down at Makeda, whose eyes were bright and glossy.

"It's—this is so—thank you, everyone!" She burst into tears and the crew all cried out at once, gathering around them.

Bez lifted Makeda up, one arm beneath her back and one under her knees, something that Americans seemed to enjoy at wedding-related festivities if film and television were accurate.

"My wife has been overcome by emotion, or hunger, and I will valiantly carry her to the buffet," she announced.

"I can walk, you know," Makeda said, wiping at her eyes. "You can't just go around picking people up."

"I can. I'm quite strong." She scrunched up her face, lowering and raising Makeda a few times, as if she were an adorable barbell, before nodding. "I don't think I'll lift anyone else, but I like doing it to you."

"How romantic," Makeda said. "If you let me sit on your back while you do one-handed push-ups, I'll know it's true lo—ack!"

Makeda startled and threw her arms up to shield her face; Bez held her more firmly, blinking at the fistful of rice grains hitting her in the face, most of them rebounding off her glasses. She spit a few grains on the deck and then glared at Greg, who took a self-satisfied drag of his cigarette.

"Sorry," he drawled on the exhale. "I didn't mean to ruin your perfect little romantic moment over there, I was just trying to join in the festivities."

"You are such a hater," Makeda said, laughing, and then Bez laughed, too, and everyone joined in. "Put me down so I can make you a plate," Makeda commanded, voice warm.

"I can make my own," Bez replied, confused.

"Let her make it for you," Thompson said, nudging Bez, so she let Makeda go and took a seat at the long table, saving space beside her for her fake wife on their last night of fake marriage.

Bez tried to enjoy the moment, and not to think about what would happen when Makeda found out Bez had never received official confirmation from the WFM, and had led her to Ibarania under false pretenses.

Makeda sat down beside her, placing a heaping plate in front of Bez and then a plate with slightly less food at her own place.

"Thank you, sea snail," Bez said.

"Why do you call her sea snail?" Tenzi asked from across the table. "Back home we have some funny nicknames, but this one is new to me."

"Yes, why do you call me sea snail?" Makeda asked, a grin lifting one corner of her mouth and her dimple creasing her cheek. "Tell them."

"It's a funny story actually," Bez said, dragging Makeda's plate over to her and picking up a kebab of meat and vegetables. "When I first met her, I compared her to a sea snail, but it was a language mix-up. I was thinking of something else."

She carefully cut the food away from the wooden stick, checking for splinters, and then handed the plate to Makeda, who beamed up at her. Bez loved that such small acts gave Makeda joy; Makeda should have been treated like a queen even if she wasn't an al-Hurradassi.

Makeda speared a chunk of meat. "What did you mean to call me? Was it something cute?"

"Oh yes, very cute. Sea *slug*." Bez bit into her own kebab contentedly as Tenzi and the surrounding crew members burst into laughter.

"That's even worse!" Tenzi said, her eyes filled with mirth. "Though I guess she doesn't mind if she married you."

"I have to tell my wife this when we talk on the video phone later," Chuck said. "She got mad at me for calling her Goat Hooves." Tenzi burst into laughter again and Chuck shook his head. "I meant that she could manage everything so easily, like a mountain goat scaling a sheer cliff. She takes care of the household and kids and restaurant while I'm at sea."

"And you return home and call her Goat Hooves?" Makeda shook her head. "Oh, buddy."

"Maybe I'll call her Sea Slug next time," Chuck said with a mischievous grin.

"I know Bez means it with affection," Makeda said, though she looked slightly affronted. She didn't like people laughing at her, and maybe she thought Bez was.

Bez wrapped an arm around her shoulder and jiggled her playfully.

"Have you ever seen a sea slug?" Bez asked. "They're cute creatures. But if they come across a fish, they'll go from cute to carnivorous and devour it in a feeding frenzy."

"Is that supposed to be better?" AK asked.

"Keep going," Greg prodded. "At this point you'll end up sleeping in the engine room and my envy will be assuaged."

Bez tried to find another way to explain since people clearly weren't getting the point. "My wife is small and cute. She minds her business, doing the small things that need to be done to maintain the equilibrium of her environment. People underestimate her. But she is also vicious if she needs to be, even more so because people don't see it coming. She almost attacked me with a vacuum when we first met. You should hope that someone would ever regard you so highly as I regard sea slugs, and *my* sea slug, specifically."

There was a silence around the table and Bez wiggled her glasses up her nose.

"That is . . ." Santos said, shaking his head. Thompson finished for him, ". . . so romantic!"

Greg stroked his beard and mock-glared at her. "Core strength, beauty, and knows how to make a sea slug into an object of affection. You really do win."

Bez lifted her chin a bit, pleased, but then glanced down at Makeda. Her eyes were glossy again, but she smiled as she ate.

A few hours later, after cutting the cake and a trip to the theater for karaoke, they returned to their cabin.

By the time the door closed behind them, Bez was in a state of what she assumed was dread. Throughout the night, every time she looked down at Makeda, she wanted her more, not less. She didn't know what would happen once they were off the ship, but she wanted to imagine *something*—that was the problem.

"This was the best night of my life," Makeda said dreamily, pulling Bez by the hands into the cabin. She'd only had one drink—the champagne toast, so she seemed to be drunk on emotion if anything. "Can you believe I thought this trip would be bad?"

Things had reached a critical point. Bez had to tell Makeda. She knew she had to because it was the thing she wanted to do least in the world. Bez stood rooted in the doorway.

"What's wrong?"

Of course, Makeda would be able to tell something was going on with her. She'd been on top of Bez's reticence, every time. She had to tell her.

Now.

"Wait." Makeda held up her hand just as Bez opened her mouth. "Wait. I know something is up, and I can probably guess what it is, more or less. One of the reasons I'm good at helping is that I'm good at figuring out what's wrong—like some investigator told me once, compassion is a skill. It's detective work, but I don't want this case solved just yet. Tell me afterward. Tell me in the morning."

Bez felt a moment of relief. Maybe all would be saved. Makeda was forgiving, maybe she wouldn't be angry?

"You're not upset?" she asked.

"Oh, I am. Future Makeda is hurt and furious at you. But Present Makeda is going to use that compassion she always had for others, and she's using it for herself. I deserve a night that's just good things, with no surprises. You can ruin things in the morning." Her voice shook, and when she smiled that shook, too. "I am *so* good at pretending everything is okay when it's not. Let's do that, okay?"

"Yes," Bez said, then sighed and shook her head. "No."

"Please," Makeda pleaded, squeezing her eyes shut. "Aren't you supposed to save me from distress? I was having such a fun night."

"I don't want to ruin things. I want to—" Bez couldn't believe the words that were coming out of her mouth. "I want to communicate. So we can put things off until morning, you can use me to have a good night, for anything you want, but I don't want you to do it because you think things are ruined. That they're irreparable."

"Of course you don't," Makeda said, sounding tired. "You did the possible ruining, so it's convenient to not want it to affect me. Trust me, I know, no one wants to think about the role they played when things blow up. And I'm sure it would mess up your idea of yourself—you see yourself as the protector, not the perpetrator. One thing I've thought about a lot while here at sea is that sometimes, people are both."

That blow landed firmly in Bez's chest, but she didn't let it slow down the momentum of ideas that were gathering in her head, needing to rush out now or forever be lost.

"I ruin things all the time, and I'll own up to that—sometimes I do it on purpose. Not this time, though." She held Makeda's shoulders firmly. "I don't want you lowering yourself if you think

I have done something beneath you. I'll wait, but I don't want you to spend the night with me because it's practice at being selfish, the same way I don't want to share a bed unless you invite me, even if there's only one on the entire ship. I want . . . I want . . ."

Makeda's hard gaze softened. "You want me to choose you, is what you're saying."

Bez cleared her throat, turning that thought over in her mind for a moment.

"Well, yes, I suppose that's the sentimental way of phrasing it," Bez said. She ran her hands up and down Makeda's arms. "I'm a disaster person, clearly. You are, well, you're not perfect, but you're the kind of person who thinks disasters need fixing. But I don't want you to fix me. I told you, when the right person comes along, we fix ourselves. And I want to fix myself for you."

Makeda frowned. "Bez, that's not—"

"Oh, don't get me wrong. I'm magnificent as I am, I know that," Bez pressed on, grabbing at fireflies that blinked once, then four times, then three, a message she hadn't ever received before. "Fixing myself doesn't mean *changing*. Fixing myself can mean that I accept my disaster status and accept your itch to fix it, and that I believe we can find ways to work through problems that pop up. And it means that I haven't told you everything that I needed to because I thought it was reasonable, but I didn't explore why I thought that."

"And why is that?" Makeda asked.

"It was reasonable because I, selfishly, didn't want you to hate me. It was reasonable because you hating me felt unacceptable, even as we boarded the ship."

"What did you do?" Makeda said, leaning in so that her cheek rested against Beznaria's chest. "Let's get it over with now, Beznaria, Destroyer of Good Times."

"The WFM hasn't been responding to my emails, texts, or phone calls, so they haven't officially acknowledged you. And because they haven't, there's a chance you won't be eligible as a princess prospect."

"That wouldn't be the worst thing," Makeda said, an odd thread of relief in her voice.

"That means there would be no money," Bez said. "And that's why you came. Though, about that—"

"You know, I've been thinking about that, too," Makeda said. She pulled away from Bez and sat down on the couch. Bez sat down beside her, cautiously, not because Makeda was a likely al-Hurradassi, but because she was a sea slug.

"I was panicked when I found out about the bank going after the B&B. And there was money right there. But if you know anything about me, I always have a contingency plan, especially because your details were sketchy as hell. Did you think I was entrusting my entire future, my grandmother's future, and my credit report to a total stranger?"

She laughed and Bez suddenly understood how anxiety-inducing it was not knowing if someone was laughing with you or at you. So many years had gone by since someone's derisive laughter could sting, but this passed over her like a tuna's scales, abrading the conception she'd had of the last few days.

"Oh," Bez said, trying to muster up a smile. "Of course you wouldn't."

"I can save Grandmore's house without the money from the royal search. That would be the easiest solution at this point, but I can go harder after Amber to pay. I can take out a loan with better interest. I can ask my mother for help because one thing I've learned is I shouldn't have to shoulder every responsibility in my family just because I'm a multi-tool. Plus I have a job waiting." She looked away from Bez in a jerky motion. "I've had fun and learned things on this trip. I never wanted to go to Ibarania really, and if it doesn't work out, well, that's that. But there's more than one way to solve this problem."

"There's still a chance that I can get you in," Bez said, not ready to give up yet. "And I can help pay the debt, if contingency plans don't work."

"Why would you help pay?" Makeda asked quietly.

"Because I misled you and I've failed to uphold my end of the contract," Bez said quickly, knowing it was the wrong answer even before it passed through her lips. She would help pay because she cared about whether Makeda had to struggle and that had nothing to do with damsel saving.

"Well, I haven't been entirely truthful either. Let's call it even," Makeda said, then yawned. "If it works out, it's fine. If you can't, it's fine. One thing about me? I always figure out how to fix things by myself."

Makeda said it almost cheerily, but those last words—*by myself*—hit Bez in the throat, choking any response out of her. She had one more admission to make, no two, but the moment for them had passed.

Makeda wasn't angry.

She should have been upset. She should have felt betrayed. Instead she was resigned and already figuring out how to do things alone.

Bez knew in that moment that she had failed, and, worse, that Makeda had always expected her to. All this time, Makeda had been humoring her, even as Bez felt pride in solving both of their problems in one swoop.

Bez sat there, bound by her own thoughts, as Makeda showered and prepared for bed.

"Are you coming to bed?" she asked.

"Oh, I'm comfortable here. I think we both need a good night's sleep after last night, since tomorrow will be busy."

"Oh. Okay. Good night."

If her fake wife noticed something was wrong, this time she didn't ask what it was. Bez, having learned that communication didn't solve everything and sometimes created additional problems to boot, pulled her blanket around herself and went to sleep.

She dreamed of a sea snail in a crown who stripped her sword from her and rode off on a kraken, a scenario that should have been funny but left her with a deep sadness she couldn't shake when she awoke in the middle of the night.

Sleep had apparently fled on the back of that kraken, too. Bez lay awake, thinking.

Her instincts had guided her to Makeda and back to Ibarania. Now, when she should be excited—contest or not, she could clear the stain on her family's honor and make her grandmother proud—she felt nothing but worry. Why had the WFM been ignoring her? Why had her grandmother been ignoring her?

When she couldn't come up with any reasonable answers, she was left with a rare sense of foreboding. She was sure bringing Makeda home was the right thing to do, but something told her the next few days might not turn out how she'd imagined.

She had to hope that for once, her instincts were wrong.

Chapter 18

$\mathcal{D}$on't cry," Makeda said, feeling her own eyes
well up in response to seeing someone else's
tears.

"It always passes too quickly," Greg sniffled, his
voice wavering. "Now who will I direct my petti-
ness at?"

The crew had assembled on the main deck as
Ibarania drew closer and closer, a rocky island that
stood sentinel in the blue sea, its beaches strips
of white sand beneath cliffs nestled with white
houses. Light green tiled roofs accented the darker
green of shrubbery and trees. The picture was
so familiar from the photos her mother had kept
around the house, framed images from a calendar
she'd ordered and repurposed.

A small boat motored toward them from the island and Makeda's stomach lurched. She looked
toward Bez to find her staring at the boat, too. She
had been reticent since they'd woken up—it was
hot, in a way, but also worrisome. She hadn't said
much all morning, almost as if she were upset.

They'd had their clarifying talk the night before and it had gone fine, Makeda thought. She hadn't gotten angry—she hadn't demanded anything of Bez, hadn't made her beg, and hadn't smothered her in forgiveness either. She'd thought it went well and had honestly been a bit relieved to have her suspicions confirmed, since she'd started to feel guilty about her goal of *not* being Princess of Ibarania. The thought that it might be true was still laughable, but now her desire to prove she wasn't the royal heir might have an easy fix in someone else claiming the title. Then she could break her family's curse, and crush her mother's dreams, without having to hurt Bez.

But somehow, despite Makeda making it clear that she didn't expect Bez to solve her problems, something was wrong. There was a new distance between them that made her anxious, which was silly given they weren't even in an actual relationship.

She reminded herself that she couldn't guess what Bez was thinking. Makeda could come up with the reason Bez was mad at her as well as a five-point plan to fix it, and it could turn out that Bez was just nervous about returning home or had indigestion or sleeping on that hard-ass couch had finally gotten to her.

Instead, she returned her attention to the crew lined up to say their goodbyes, with AK last in line. He gave her a warm hug and when Makeda sniffled, he said, "Hey, it isn't goodbye. We'll see each other again, especially if you really are a princess. Though I hope for your sake that you aren't."

Makeda pulled away to look up at him. "You know?"

"Multi-tool," he said, crossing his arms, then added, "And Beznaria told me while trying to pry information out of me about my own situation. Anyway, this has turned out to be my last voyage as AK, and I'm glad I was able to share it with you. If you and the investigator are ever in Druk, stop by the palace and ask for Prince Anzam Khandrol. *King* Anzam Khandrol, I guess." He exhaled slowly, breathing through it as he'd shown her how to do.

AK, the "butler" of the ship, the multi-tool, the one who did so much of the grunt work of organizing and keeping the ship running, was a king?

Bez's words came back to her. *You're not even the only royal on this ship.*

When he'd taught her things about running the ship, she'd noticed it seemed like he was discussing a worldview more than a managerial manual. Now she understood that she wasn't the only one who had been practicing on the ship.

Makeda was sure she'd be more shocked later, but in the moment she saw a friend struggling; a friend who had helped her better understand herself. Whether he was royalty or not, he was upset and she wouldn't suddenly start being formal with him.

The meaning of his words started to sink in, if not their import. He was going from prince to king. "Wait, are your parents—"

"They're fine," he said. "More than fine. It's . . . complicated."

"Is your happiness in Druk?" she asked, already knowing the answer, but still sad for him when he shook his head. "I hope there's some way for you to find it."

AK smiled, one she was familiar with—a pretense that everything was going to be fine when it wasn't.

"And if there's something I can do to help," she added, feeling a bit silly since he really was a royal but saying it anyway, "just let me know."

They quickly exchanged email addresses and then the small ship arrived next to the *Virginia Queen*.

"Well, I have to go hop over the side of the ship now," Makeda said, even though her stomach had started to compact into a ball of nerves.

"It's okay to be scared," he reminded her.

She and Bez were strapped into harnesses attached to a winch. She waited for Bez to make an inappropriate observation as they held onto one another, but all she said was, "Hold on tight."

The fit of the harness lowering her and Bez onto the boat was like the atomic wedgie Makeda had received from a classmate who'd taken their bullying playbook from a Nickelodeon show. Still, she couldn't be too nervous as they swayed in the breeze with the Mediterranean's clear blue depths below them. She was too focused on how wrong everything felt. She wanted to shimmy back up the rope, back to the cabin that had started to feel like home and back to the people who had become her friends.

She looked up at the smiling friendly faces lined up along the guard rail of the *Virginia Queen*, the wind whipping silly tears from her eyes, and then into the expressionless face of the woman pressed up against her.

Makeda might as well have been a package Bez was ferrying between vessels. In reality, she supposed that was what she was: a princess to be handed off to the WFM to clear Bez's family name. Bez had liked her on the cargo ship, sure, but they were heading to her home turf now. She'd achieved her objective.

Bez's words from the Ferris wheel came back to Makeda again, a moment that seemed like years ago but had really only been a couple of weeks.

. . . when in a small semiprivate space, fornication becomes a challenge of sorts . . .

Ah, maybe that was it. Makeda couldn't be sure, of course, but here they were leaving their semiprivate space and Bez would barely look at her.

They landed on the boat before she knew it. At one point, she would have thought this ferry large, but after life on the ship, it seemed minuscule.

A short barrel-chested man with deeply tanned skin and a crown of dark curly ringlets shot through with gray popped his head out of the wheelhouse. "Bezzie!"

For the first time that morning, Bez smiled, taking a few long strides to the man. She pulled him into a rough side hug and planted a kiss on each of his cheeks. "John! Excellent to see you. Thanks for the ride, and for getting us the space on the ship."

"No trouble at all," the man replied in an accent like Bez's but without the British lilt shaping his words. "For you, anything, my dear."

John started the idling ship and began pulling away from the *Virginia Queen*, and Makeda was momentarily too busy looking back at her friends to pay attention to what awaited her.

The crew began to drift away from the port railing—they were used to goodbyes, on some level, having to say them to friends and loved ones for part of each year. But it was new for Makeda. She hated losing people and hadn't anticipated how off balance it would make her feel, having to say goodbye to people she'd only just met.

It felt like grief, and she couldn't wait to be at her hotel or wherever she wound up so she could respond like it was. She tried to swallow the burning in her throat and sadness suddenly weighing her down.

"Ah, so this is the lucky lady?" John said, pulling her attention away from the cargo ship. "Your wife?"

Makeda glanced at Bez. Their fake marriage had ended when they left the *Virginia Queen*, hadn't it? That was another part of her grief. But this man was acting like it hadn't, and Bez wasn't disputing it. In fact, she was staring at the crowd gathered on the shore, pretending she hadn't heard him.

"Is that my family?" Bez asked, changing the subject.

"Of course," John said. "You've been gone for ages, so they were tracking the ship to see when you'd arrive."

As the shore drew closer, Makeda began to make out the forms of several people standing along the shoreline, holding up a banner.

"Did you tell your family about, ah, why you were bringing me back?" she asked.

Bez tensed. "I didn't. I wanted it to be a surprise and . . ." She held onto the railing and dropped her head and *this* wasn't anything Makeda had ever seen from her before either.

Resignation.

"I suppose it's what you expected of me," Bez said, her voice so low it was almost lost to the sound of the engine.

"What? I just wanted to know if they knew?"

"That you're married?" John asked, one brow cocked. "Of course they do."

"Mutanna min diu, you told them?" Bez asked and it shouldn't have hurt that she didn't sound thrilled about it.

Makeda stared out at the crowd as the boat drew closer to land and the faces of the people on shore became more distinct.

"Ih, I told them," he said. "They kept asking what this surprise was, and then they were asking if it was about the royal heir, and you know Dihya can be scary when she wants an answer! So I said maybe you finally settled down, and then when their guest arrived, they put two and two together."

One face in particular pulled Makeda's attention then, a familiar jawline and slope of shoulders that gave her pause. A frantic awkwardness to the way the person waved their banner.

Well, if she was a quarter Ibaranian, then she was going to see some people who looked like . . .

"Oh no," Makeda said loudly, completely unable to modulate herself as terrifying recognition gripped her. Now she gripped the railing, too, uncertain if her knees would hold out against the surge of reality.

"Her mother arrived to welcome her, so I told her, too," John said, concern and confusion vying for dominance in his tone. "Your wife, is she okay, Bezzie?"

"Just a bit seasick," Bez said, as she came to stand beside Makeda and speak in a low voice. "You didn't know she was coming."

"No," Makeda said. "No, and this is terrible. My plan was to make her want to never come here. I'm too late."

All of the ways in which her mother might have blown up her life in order to be standing on that shore played in horrifying clarity in Makeda's mind. She seemed to be alone, no Bill in sight. Had he left her, unable to deal with her obsession with royal power turned up to eleven? Did he even know she was here? What about her job?

Tears burned the back of her eyes and clogged her throat as they pulled up to the pier, surrounded by questions Makeda had hoped she'd never have to ask herself. She'd been able to forget while on the boat, but this was the reality of Bez having come into her life. She'd thought to break the curse, but it might have broken her in the end.

"You know she's an adult," Bez said as her family approached, Ashley Hicks chatting away happily with them. "She is the one who should have this worried expression on her face, not you. I hate this expression."

"You're the reason it's there!" Makeda whispered harshly. "You said that the WFM tried to recall you before you came to the Golden Crown. You should have followed your orders and we wouldn't be in this mess!"

Beznaria made a sound like someone who'd been hit with an arrow. Through her worry and anger and frustration at seeing her mother smiling like all was well, Makeda understood what her words had boiled down to: she'd just told Bez that she wished they'd never met.

As awful as it felt, part of her had meant it.

Her mother's eyes were bright with that foolish determination as she approached—she would be at home if Bez had never shown up. Makeda wouldn't be filled with a rage that made her want to shout at her mother and humiliate her. She wouldn't be buried under layers of hurt, old and new, and not least of which was that she'd hurt Beznaria and couldn't say it was a misunderstanding.

Another sweet thing her mother's obsession had turned sour.

"Don't worry. I'll take care of things," Bez said.

"Bez?"

As the group approached—people in varying shades of brown complexions, height, and musculature—they began to call out in a mix of English and Ibaranian, excited and happy and completely unaware of the gulf that had just opened up between the two people they thought were in love.

"Bezzie, this is a big secret! A wife? You brought home a wife? My romance rules worked! I told you they would," a tall older man called out as the crowd drew near. He was clearly Bez's father— DNA had hit Copy and Paste on his genes with a few tweaks to the code. Their faces were almost the same, with the same luminous dark brown skin, full circle of a mouth, and wide nose, though his hair was gray and close-cropped and his glasses rectangular. Their long bodies were almost matching heights. But their eyes—Bez's father was also a chaos agent. Makeda could tell, even though he strode slowly and looked like a kind grandpa.

A woman who seemed about his age stepped in front of him. She was shorter, her skin a light brown, but she had the same gap in her teeth when she smiled and the same amber eyes—and her chaos vibe was even stronger. Bez was descended of two chaotic people, which was probably why Makeda had found her irresistible. She was chaos double concentrated.

"Welcome to the family. You can call me 'Big Mama' like they do in your American movies," the woman said, pulling Makeda into a crushing hug. "She will call me Big Mama if none of you ingrates will!"

Bez's father cut in for his hug. "Well, if you call her Big Mama, I'd like it if you call me Big Papa, so we match."

Makeda would have laughed if she weren't caught between grief and overwhelm.

"Omm and Papa, cut it out and let us meet our new sister," said a woman who was like a pocket version of Bez with a pointy nose and long curling hair. Makeda was released, and the woman said, "I'm Dihya, Bezzie's oldest sister, and you absolutely don't have to call my mother Big Mama. There was one movie that kept playing on television, and she won't let it drop, and now my father is in on it! Do you even like hugs?"

Makeda nodded, and was pulled into another hug that squeezed the breath from her. Then she was handed off to Fabrescio and Fabrescia, the twins, and then to Bez's slightly older brother Khalid, who was medium height with light brown skin and looked about as overwhelmed as Makeda was.

"They can be very loud, but they mean well," he said with a sheepish smile.

When Makeda had passed through all of Bez's siblings, the hugging assembly line continued with their partners, their kids, their neighbors, until she was face-to-face with her mother, her head spinning and her anger reigniting as the familiar face came into view.

"What are you doing here?" Makeda asked in a low voice, not hugging her.

"I came here to support you," her mother said, that frustrating expression of hurt on her face. "I came because I started following things online and saw that the process had already started and you weren't here yet. Your name wasn't even mentioned anywhere. It was like we were a secret again, like they'd gotten our hopes up just to ignore us again."

Her wide brown eyes were pleading. "I came because you were on a boat, and by the time you arrived, you might have missed everything! I didn't know where you were or how to reach you. We might have missed our chance, so I came to be your backup. Just . . . you finally seemed to care. If you missed it, I would have felt . . ."

Her mother threw up her hands helplessly, and Makeda's anger, which had for a millisecond been a towering inferno, sputtered out like a pilot light when the gas got cut. She would never understand her mother's obsession with royalty, and she knew her reasons for being here were for the most part selfish. But somewhere in that pool of selfishness, which had left Makeda with her watering can, she'd been trying to intervene on Makeda's behalf. To prevent her from experiencing the same rejection and shame. Her mother couldn't imagine that Makeda didn't care like she did, despite having been told so a hundred times, and so here she was.

Makeda sighed and crossed her arms over her chest and asked her mother the questions she'd always been afraid to.

"What will change for you if it's true? If we are from some royal line? What will it change? Are you going to leave Bill and go find a new man worth your status? Try to get a reality show? What?"

Her mother blinked in confusion. "Well, it will change everything. About me. And you."

"And what if we aren't?" Makeda asked, her stomach in knots.

She waited for her mother's expression to crumple, for her to deny it was even possible, but it remained the same. "Well, that will change everything, too. About me. And you." She reached out tentatively, not to comfort Makeda but to see if she was allowed the intimacy of giving comfort, and smiled when Makeda didn't shrug her hand off her shoulder.

"We'll know. After tonight, we'll know. That'll be good, right?"

Bez stepped beside her then, slipping her arm around Makeda's waist. The difference in the hand on her hip and the one on her shoulder—how one was giving and one was taking, just by the nature of the people they belonged to—almost tipped her composure over, spilling emotion everywhere. She kept it upright, though.

"Nice to meet you," her mother said politely. "You're the investigator?"

"I'm Makeda's wife," Bez said so smoothly that Makeda's composure wobbled again.

"Oh! Right. Yes. Marriage at sea sounds so romantic," her mother said, clearly trying to maintain interest then failing. "You do know that the ceremony is tonight, though, and there are already apparently three possible heirs? Because you traveled by boat and they moved up the dates so—"

"I'll take care of it," Bez said, then looked at Makeda. "I want to introduce you to Henna Jeta, but she isn't here. Apparently she went to pray at the tomb of the king, like she does when she's upset."

Things were still weird between them, but Makeda knew that Bez was hurt. If Makeda was just a package to her, Henna Jeta was the recipient, and she'd apparently turned her nose up at her gift.

Makeda slipped her arm around Bez, unsure exactly what the hell they were doing, but holding onto her in the chaos. "I'm sure she'll turn up soon."

"She'll turn up tonight, to crown the winner!"

Makeda's mother said. "They reveal the results of the test tonight, so there's still time to prove Makeda is a princess. We both know she is. My mother told me what you said. But it's your fault she's late. What if she loses her life dream because of you?"

The same childhood embarrassment that had always sealed her mouth shut when she was younger rose up in her, and Makeda shut her eyes. She would let her mother get it out of her system, and then—

"To my knowledge," Bez began, and Makeda's eyes flew open because she was using the sexy stern tone again, "Makeda's life dream is to never hear the word *princess* again. Since we're here to see if she is owed the money the heir will receive, I will find a way to get her inside the event, by normal or creative entry. You need not worry about a thing, and you need not pressure Makeda about anything either. You are her mother, but she's under my protection now."

Makeda kept her eyes closed, this time savoring the fantastic sensation of that Damsel in Distress contract kicking in. Bez might not care about her in the way Makeda had imagined, but she was still willing to protect her.

"Okay," her mother said in that tiny hurt voice, but it seemed to have no effect on Bez.

"Good. We understand each other," Bez said, then added cordially, with an elaborate bow, "I hope we'll get to know each other better while we eat, Mother."

Ashley Hicks couldn't stay upset after being literally bowed to, so she giggled and went on her way. Always able to bounce back from being called out and act like it had never happened.

"Okay, we are all heading to the house for lunch to meet our new Chetchevaliere," Dihya called out, holding up an arm from a suit of armor like a tour guide holding up a bright umbrella. "We are having fish stew and fresh baked bread. All manner of beverages will be provided! Single file so we don't clog the sidewalks!"

"You're all like this," Makeda said, trying to lighten the mood.

"Disappointments?" Bez asked, and when Makeda looked at her, the firm charm she'd been wielding was gone. "Your mother was right. I did mess everything up, and I know you expected me to not handle things, but I told you I would. If you want to 'light my ass up,' you can."

"What?" Makeda's head was spinning from everything going on, but she was sure she had no idea what Beznaria was talking about.

"I failed you. But it hurts realizing you never trusted me to take care of things to begin with. And that you wish I'd never come for you." Bez glanced at her, her expression confused. "I didn't think those kinds of things *could* hurt me."

Various Chetchevalieres straggled by, but everyone seemed to understand they were speaking privately, and speeded up so that they could bring up the rear.

They walked on cobblestone streets, passed

restaurants and tourist shops in buildings that had been there since medieval times. Makeda only saw them in her peripheral vision since her focus was on Beznaria.

"I wish I could take that back; in the moment, I meant it. But I meant it in a way that wouldn't change everything else that happened between us. Things with my mother . . ." She shook her head. "You only know a bit of the story, more about the teasing than anything else. You don't know how bad things got at home with her. She loved me, but she really started to resent me. All because I didn't want to be a princess in the same way she did."

"Makeda."

"Thinking it was cool to daydream about or fun to pretend wasn't good enough. I had to be obsessed like her, and when I wasn't, she just left. I mean, she remarried and moved, but she'd left me before that. For alcohol, and gambling, and anything that soothed the sting of having a little tomboy daughter who hated dresses and who had a plan to save them both."

It was strange, but it felt freeing to say it here, in the streets that had hung in photographs on their walls. Sometimes, when she had still yearned for adventure, she'd imagined stepping into those pictures. Now she was here, and her mother was here, and nothing had changed between them. But maybe something could change in her.

"She hurt you," Bez said. "And her being here hurts you."

"Yes," Makeda said.

"You couldn't count on her, I imagine," Bez continued. Makeda shook her head, and Bez wrapped an arm around her. "I have always only trusted my family. It was us against the world, with our too-muchness and the rumors about Henna Jeta."

She had a certain lilt in her voice that let Makeda know she was in communicating mode—like she had been on the ship, when they were pretending to be married.

"I was hurt when I realized you always had a backup plan after I told you I would take care of things," Bez said. "But you are the—what did An-zam Khandrol call it?—the multi-tool. He is that way because he knows the work that awaits him and has been training for it until it became second nature. You had to become one because you had no one to depend on."

Makeda's eyes heated and she blinked away tears.

"Okay, I'm good on talking through my sad childhood," Makeda said, squeezing Beznaria's side. It was comforting, having someone understand all this without her having to say it. "That was very insightful, though."

"Well, I was an investigator," Bez said.

"Was?" Makeda stopped walking.

"My brother had mail for me. It was my official termination for untoward behavior and a history of pathological lying, which isn't how I would characterize things but to each their own."

Makeda started to comfort her, but Bez threw back her head and shouted, "I'm free!"

An old woman popped her head out of a storefront and shook her head, but with a warm smile. "Welcome back, Bezzie."

Bez returned the greeting with a nod, and they started walking again.

"So what do we do now?" Makeda asked. "Should I just go back home with my mother?"

She wondered if her mother *would* go back.

"No," Bez said, her voice back to its old familiar chaotic bravado. "A Chetchevaliere keeps their promise. And I, Bez, want to help you with this. Can you tell me what you meant when you said not having to do the princess thing would make things easier?"

"You heard that?"

"I hear everything. I remember later. My brain has me on a need-to-know basis as well, if that makes you feel better when I don't tell you things in the future."

In the future. Could it really be as simple as that?

"I wanted to prove I wasn't a princess," Makeda admitted. "So I had my own ulterior motives, and unlike you, I wasn't trying to find another way around them. You contacted the WFM every chance you got. I was figuring out how to make sure I wasn't a princess even if I technically was one. I was going to betray you."

Makeda tried to feel bad about it, but even though there was some guilt, she couldn't regret her decision.

"If you're not princess, then your mother will be able to move on," Bez said. "Is that the plan?"

"Well . . . yes. But it means your grandmother's name doesn't get cleared."

Bez pushed her glasses up. "I have a plan. And you have a plan. Let's talk about our plans, and we'll see what there is to see." Bez took her hand. "I think we could talk about some side quests as well, but we will try your straightforward thinking for now. One step at a time."

Chapter 19

ℬezzie, come on, you're asking me to risk my job. Are you kidding or are you kidding?"

The DNA testing laboratory of Ibarania was a small-scale operation, like the island itself. Given the population, it was bound to be run by someone Beznaria knew—unfortunately it turned out to be one of her exes.

"I'm not asking you to change results or anything like that. All I ask is that you include the results for this late participant so that it can be read aloud with the other results. Look, I told my boss I could get this in last minute because I have connections here. Please, I'll do anything."

"This has to do with your henna losing the queen, doesn't it? You're trying to be sneaky, showing up in your tuxedo looking all suave. I'm not going to be the crab under the trap when the stick gets pulled. No."

Bez turned the charm up a notch, keeping it within the platonic sector of her personal meter. "No, Mariane. There is no trap. There will be no ramifications for adding extra information. You're not taking anything away, just adding an additional data point."

"And you'll do anything?" Mariane asked sweetly.

"Within reason." Bez beamed at her, adjusting her bow tie.

"Well, get out then." Mariane gestured toward the exit. "And tell your boss next time to make sure he has all the samples in when he says he will."

Bez bowed at her and caught Mariane's hidden smile as she turned to head back into the lab.

When she walked out, Dihya honked the horn of the van she'd rented to ferry everyone to the ceremony. Henna Jeta still wasn't around, and seemed to be avoiding Bez, even though she was answering calls from her siblings. Bez told herself that her grandmother was overwhelmed with pride and that was why she hadn't responded.

She slid into the back seat with Makeda, who was wearing a gown she'd borrowed from Dihya—a simple dress in vivid teal, blue, and purple pattern that made her look more goddess than queen. She'd grumbled before putting it on, but after looking in the mirror, she'd decided this particular dress didn't count as frilly. With her locks pulled up into an updo and a bit of makeup, she looked as beautiful as she always had to Bez, just in a different package.

"Did you make the delivery, Ms. Bond?" Makeda joked as Bez slid in beside her.

"Yes. The game is afoot," Bez said.

"That's Sherlock Holmes!" Dihya called out from the driver's seat, and everyone laughed, but

Makeda clutched Bez's hand with her own shaking one as they approached the resort where the ceremony was being held.

"There's no way in hell this is going to work," Makeda whispered.

"It will," Bez reassured her even though she had no idea if that was the truth. "One way or another, something will change tonight."

BEZ FOUND THAT a royal ball wasn't at all as glamorous as they made it seem in the films. Finding parking had been hellish, and they'd had to walk half a mile to get to the front entrance only to then find themselves in a swarm of people trying to talk their way into the event. When they'd finally gotten inside half an hour later, they'd ended up seated at three different tables as the one Dihya had reserved had been taken by strangers.

The room itself was beautiful, but the decorations were of lower quality than many weddings Bez had been to, in a gaudy color scheme of purple and bright yellow. The hors d'oeuvres being circulated were either over- or undercooked, and the wine had clearly been purchased for economy, not taste.

"This is not how they make it seem in the movies," Makeda said as she shifted from one foot to the other in front of one of the wine stations set up around the room, clearly uncomfortable in her borrowed high heels. "I feel like I'm at the prom. I hated prom."

She kept scanning the room—her mother was supposedly watching from her hotel room but Bez understood Makeda's fear that she would pop up at any moment.

She was also searching the crowd—her grandmother was supposedly on the premises, though Bez hadn't managed to find her yet.

Bez stroked Makeda's shoulders, the soft brown skin exposed by the dress's straps. "I would be surprised, but when it comes to royalty, nothing is as good as stories make them seem to be. Dihya is going to have her boss's head though. He went behind her back and downgraded all of the fancy things she ordered."

"After tasting that mini-quiche, I think he deserves it," she said lightly, and Bez grinned.

"I see your bloodthirsty nature is rising to the surface," Bez joked. "Maybe being on the island has activated your pirate queen genes."

Makeda smiled, flashing her dimple, and then Bez caught sight of a familiar gray-capped skull bobbing through the crowd. Her grandmother wore a simple black suit, usually reserved for funerals, with her ceremonial knives hanging from her hips.

"Henna Jeta!" she called out, and the old woman turned her way. Her grandmother wasn't an expressive woman, but she didn't even pretend to be happy to see her as she strode over.

She walked up to Bez and looked her up and down, then turned and did the same to Makeda. "Nice to meet you," she said to Makeda. "You married my starfish brain granddaughter, so I give you my condolences."

Bez's breath caught in her throat.

"You're the woman she traveled halfway around the world trying to please?" Makeda looked her up and down. "It's a pleasure to meet you, but please don't call her starfish brain again."

Bez took a step forward in alarm.

"Makeda—"

Makeda swept her arm out, herding Beznaria behind her.

"And you think you are the princess?" Henna Jeta said. "That's why you act like this?"

"No. I don't think I'm a princess, but Bez does. That's why she went through so much trouble to bring me here. Because she wanted to clear your name. The least you could do is give her a proper greeting."

Henna Jeta stared at Makeda for a long, long moment, and then, to Beznaria's surprise—she blinked.

"I'm mad at you," she said, turning her gaze to Bez. "Look at all this fuss!"

She shook her head and then grabbed her granddaughter into a rough embrace. Bez's stress ratcheted down a few notches.

"I didn't have anything to do with this," Bez said and Henna Jeta shook her head.

"It doesn't matter. I handled everything, okay? This will be put to an end soon. I have to go make the announcement, and then it will be over." She sighed deeply.

"I hope we get to speak more afterward," Makeda said in a friendlier tone, and Henna Jeta nodded. "Maybe, if I'm still alive. These people are trying to annoy me to death. But yes, yes, talking is great, we'll do that."

She shuffled off toward the stage.

"You talked back to my grandmother while she was sporting her blades," Bez said, her heart thumping wildly in her chest. "She might have stabbed you."

"I would have deflected with one of these burnt flatbreads," Makeda said with a grin.

"You are—"

"Hungry," Makeda said, then leaned up to kiss her on the cheek.

A blast of fanfare screeched out through the speakers, and they both winced and brought their hands to their ears. The music was quickly turned down to a less excruciating volume, and the lights in the hall dimmed.

The tourism minister, Mr. Buttielgiorno, stepped out onto the stage nervously, perhaps feeling Dihya's death glare fixing on him from somewhere in the crowd.

"Ah, hello everyone, hello," he said, blinking against camera flashes. "Thank you for joining us this evening for the official results of our heir search."

He began to clap, urging the people in the crowd to join him.

"This is a new and exciting chapter in Ibaranian history—we are keeping our feet planted firmly in the future while honoring our glorious past. Uh, we are an island of people known for our fierceness and our independence, but also for our missing queen. It's a mystery that has gone un-answered until today. We hope with the crowning of a ceremonial monarch, we will open an excit-ing chapter, ah not chapter I already said that, an exciting avenue that lets us and people around the world, learn more about our royalty, in a direct line from Lalla to whomever we select tonight."

He nodded a few times as the audience clapped, then fumbled in his pockets. He looked offstage and a woman trotted out holding an envelope.

"And now for the results of the DNA test."

He began opening the envelope like he'd never received mail before, picking at the edges with shaking hands as the tension in the crowd rose.

Bez held Makeda against her. "It will be fine," she said.

"It will," Makeda said. "I know it won't be me, but I'm still nervous. It's not every day you get to break a curse."

The minister finally ripped the envelope open and grabbed the slip of paper inside as it fluttered to the ground.

"And the new . . . princess! Is Makeda Hicks! Makeda Hicks? Who is Makeda Hicks?"

The crowd burst into applause that faded as confusion set in.

"It—it can't be." Makeda gripped Bez hard. "Bez. Oh—I—I don't know how—"

Bez heard Makeda's confused attempt to com-fort her, but her ears were ringing and she felt slightly ill.

"I will take care of it," she said.

"No, let's think about this. You don't have to do anything right now."

She gently pulled Makeda's arms away, giving them a squeeze, and then her legs carried her to the stage. The crowd parted before her, perhaps because she looked like she was about to vomit, and her shoes felt like they were filled with lead.

Mr. Buttielgiorno looked at her with wide eyes. "Beznaria? What are you doing?"

She took the mic from him and gripped it tightly while looking out into the crowd. "Hi. I am not Makeda Hicks. But I am—I am . . ." Her thoughts were all over the place, but she took a deep breath and did what needed to be done to keep her promise to Makeda and, in a terrible way, to Henna Jeta.

"I am Beznaria Chetchevaliere, as many of you know. And I provided the sample that was submitted to the DNA testers under the name Makeda Hicks. *I* am the one who is a princess of Ibarania."

The noise level in the room went from curious murmurs to an explosion of shocked voices.

Bez couldn't make out what people were saying because her own head was full of the chatter of her thoughts. The plan had been simple—she'd swab her own saliva for the test, Makeda would be ruled out. Her name wouldn't be mentioned, but they'd have the results to share with her mother to prove Keshan had lied.

Except they'd discovered that it was Henna Jeta who had lied. Everything Bez had believed in had been based in lies.

"This woman makes a mockery of the ceremony," a familiar fake English accent called out as Higgins-hoggins stormed the stage. "She is a known chaos agent, a thief, and she was recently fired from the World Federation of Monarchists for being a liar. Those are not the correct results!"

Bez stared at him as he snatched the microphone from her.

"It is a well-known fact that Queen Aazi sought refuge in the former Kingdom of Hogginshiggins. I am the heir to the Ibaranian throne."

Another, even louder outburst from the audience filled the room and Mr. Buttielgiorno looked back and forth between them, utterly lost.

It fell into place for Bez why he had sent her away on a wild seagull chase, why he had been ignoring her calls and emails, and why he had been pressuring her grandmother. He was a kingmaker who wanted to be a king, and he'd orchestrated all of this for the chance at even a ceremonial crown.

She glared at him. "You knew. You knew all this time. That's why you recruited me, isn't it?"

He sneered, but didn't respond, instead turning to the audience. "I know what those results were supposed to be. Where did this Makeda Hicks even come from. Clearly this is an attempt to besmirch the name of the World Federation of Monarchists and Ibarania itself."

He took a deep breath, but before he could speak again, he cried out in pain and folded to the ground. As he collapsed, Bez saw her grandmother on the other side of him, gazing back at her with sadness in her eyes.

She sighed and picked up the microphone. "Hello everyone who is about to hear my personal business that I have managed to keep a secret for over fifty years."

"Henna, did you stab him?" Bez stage whispered, worried that her grandmother had committed murder on camera.

"No, I just incapacitated him. I never taught you that move for a reason," she said, stepping over the prone man, who was starting to stir. "Now. To publicly display my shame, which this man was attempting to blackmail me with and would have succeeded if not for my beloved starfish brain." She sent a look to Bez that made it clear that she thought her anything but. "Many of you expect me to say I killed Queen Aazi, because that is what you all have said behind my back for years. And sorry, no, it is nothing that boring."

She motioned to someone in the audience. "Bring me a chair."

The man hurried and passed the chair on stage, and she sat heavily in it. "I think it will be good to get this off my chest before I die, actually. So I did not kill Aazi, but I did betray her. King Angelo and I were friends from childhood; the best of friends. But I was a Chetchevaliere and he was an al-Hurradassi. Our love was forbidden, and we both lived by those rules for so many long years.

"When he was married to Aazi . . . it was not a good match. Both of them knew this but there was not much they could do. You are royalty, you marry who you are told. We remained friends, but when wartime came, he was not the man to stay in the castle. He decided to fight, and he knew he might die." She inhaled deeply. "It was one night. One night to pretend that he was not king and I was not his guard. And then he died so quickly. And I was pregnant."

There was dead silence in the room as Henna Jeta spoke, the pain in her voice carried through the speakers. "So yes, I deserved all the gossip and rumors. I broke the oath of the guard. I betrayed the queen. I will forever hold that guilt. But when she found out? She was happy. She said that it meant she was free— she didn't want to rule, and I was carrying the next hereditary heir. She is no longer alive, but she lived for a very long time, quite happily, in Australia. But I couldn't ever bring myself to shame Angelo, who had died a hero. But yes, yes, my son is the lost heir of Ibarania, and his children are too."

Bez heard the clattering of footsteps as her family stormed the stage, but her eyes were on her grandmother.

"Sorry, Bezzie," she said.

Bez wanted to run away, but instead she walked to her grandmother, knelt beside her, and grabbed the first firefly that flitted by in her mind. "So you mean, I'm a Chetchevaliere and an al-Hurradassi? I am the product of the two most prestigious families on the island? My belief that I am an above average human, that all of us are, is now backed with evidence? Henna, that's wonderful."

"What are you talking about?" the old woman said.

"I'm saying that I now know that I am both princess and warrior and will be entirely insufferable."

She laughed, tears welling in her eyes. "Don't be sad, anymore, okay?"

Her grandmother started to laugh, too, and when their family joined them onstage they piled into a hug of confused laughter. Bez caught Makeda's eye and beckoned her onto the stage.

She hesitated, then kicked off her high heels, lifted her gown, and clambered up.

Bez pulled her into her arms. "I have some bad news for you."

"What," Makeda said, apprehensive.

"Everyone thinks we're married," Bez said.

"I'm not sure that's bad news," Makeda said. "Unless you think it is."

"Well, I'm a princess now. And if everyone thinks you're married to me . . ." Bez sighed.

"Oh god, then I'm a princess too." Makeda's eyes went wide and then she burst out laughing, and Bez did too.

"Your mother will like me better now I think," Bez said, wiggling her nose so her glasses inched back up where they belonged.

"Remember when you said this might be fate?" Makeda asked as she caught her breath. "I'm starting to think you were right."

"I know you hate the idea of it, but have you considered the pure petty joy in all of the people who teased you finding out that you are in fact a princess now?"

Makeda held her gaze. "I think I could get into that kind of vengeance. Maybe I'll go harass Amber wearing a crown and tell her to run me my money."

Bez tilted her head to the side. "Ah that. I already did."

"What?" Makeda gripped her by the arms. "What!"

"I swear, this is the last thing that I was supposed to tell you that I hadn't yet. I thought that you coming and getting the money to pay off the debt would be nice, but it would be nicer if you returned home and found that someone had scared Amber Vincent of Linden, New Jersey, into remembering her obligation so you could keep it for yourself."

Makeda's eyes were bright as she stared up at her. "You are—"

"—a Chetchevaliere-al-Hurradassi, possibly the most dangerous woman known to mankind. Apart from Tenzi."

Makeda laughed. "I was going to say practical and horny, but that works, too."

Bez laughed and ran her hands over Makeda's shoulders. "What do you think about me coming back with you, or you staying here for a bit?"

"I think we should make that decision in the morning. Tonight, we have to celebrate your coronation, or possibly bury your boss." Makeda grinned. "But don't forget I'm a planner—I tried to resist, but I already have three options for us to consider if we do this thing."

"We're doing it, and we're not going to stop," Bez said. "Can you also make me a plan for better seductive one-liners?"

"On it," Makeda said.

The speakers had started spouting cheesy dance music for the ceremony after-party and guests in the crowd who were high on drama began to dance as they blew up their group chats with photos and updates. Makeda and Bez joined her family at center stage, where they'd already begun squabbling over what kind of crown her father would wear and how they'd split the prize money.

"This feels like my kind of happily ever after," Makeda mused, and Bez kissed her, just to seal the deal.

Read on for a sneak peek of Alyssa Cole's
New York Times bestselling thriller

WHEN NO ONE IS WATCHING

Rear Window meets *Get Out* in this
gripping novel, in which the gentrification
of a Brooklyn neighborhood takes
on a sinister new meaning . . .

Welcome to the OurHood app, helping neighbors stay connected and stay safe. You have been approved as a member of the GIFFORD PLACE community. Please use the site responsibly and remember that each one of us can make our neighborhood a better place!

Chapter 1

Sydney

$\mathscr{I}$ spent deepest winter shuffling back and forth between work and hospital visits and doctor's appointments. I spent spring hermiting away, managing my depression with the help of a CBD pen and generous pours of the Henny I'd found in Mommy's liquor cabinet.

Now I'm sitting on the stoop like I've done every morning since summer break started, watching my neighbors come and go as I sip coffee, black, no sugar, gone lukewarm.

When I moved back a year and a half ago, carrying the ashes of my marriage and my pride in an urn I couldn't stop sifting through, I thought I'd be sitting out here with Mommy and Drea, the holy trinity of familiarity restored—mother, play sister, prodigal child. Mommy would tend to her mini-jungle of potted plants lining the steps, and to me, helping me sprout new metaphorical leaves—tougher ones, more resilient. Drea would sit between us, like she had since she was eleven and basically moved in with us, since her parents sucked, cracking jokes or talking about her latest side hustle. I'd draw strength from them and the neighborhood that'd always had my back. But it hadn't worked out that way; instead of planting my feet onto solid Brooklyn concrete, I'd found myself neck-deep in wet cement.

Last month, on the Fourth of July, I pried open the old skylight on the top floor of the brownstone and sat up there alone. When I was a teenager, Mommy and Drea and I would picnic on the roof every Fourth of July, Brooklyn sprawling around us as fireworks burst in the distance. When I'd clambered up there as an adult, alone, I'd been struck by how claustrophobic the view looked, with new buildings filling the neighborhoods around us, where there had once been open air. Cranes loomed ominously over the surrounding blocks like invaders from an alien movie, mantis-like shadows with red eyes blinking against the night, the American flags attached to them flapping darkly in the wind, signaling that they came in peace when really they were here to destroy.

To remake.

Maybe my imagination was running away with me, but even at ground level the difference is overwhelming. Scaffolds cling to buildings all over the neighborhood, barnacles of change, and construction workers gut the innards of houses where I played with friends as a kid. New condos that look like stacks of ugly shoeboxes pop up in empty lots.

The landscape of my life is unrecognizable; Gifford Place doesn't feel like home.

I sigh, close my eyes, and try to remember the freedom I used to feel, first as a carefree child, then as a know-it-all teenager, as I held court from this top step, with the world rolling out before me. Three stories of century-old brick stood behind me like a solid wall of protection, imbued with the love of my mother and my neighbors and the tenacity of my block.

Back then, I used to go barefoot, even though Miss Wanda, who'd wrench open the fire hydrant for kids on sweltering days like the ones we've had this summer, used to tell me I was gonna get ringworm. The feel of the stoop's cool brown concrete beneath my feet had been calming.

Now someone calls the fire department every time the hydrant is opened, even when we use the sprinkler cap that reduces water waste. I wear flip-flops on my own stoop, not worried about the infamous ringworm but suddenly self-conscious where I should be comfortable.

Miss Wanda is gone; she sold her place while I was cocooned in depression at some point this spring. The woman who'd been my neighbor almost all my life is gone, and I didn't even get to say goodbye.

And Miss Wanda isn't the only one.

Five families have moved from Gifford Place in less than a year. Five doesn't seem like much, but each of their buildings had three to four apartments, and the change has been noticeable, to say the least. And that doesn't even count the renters.

It's gotten to the point where I feel a little twinge of dread every time I see a new white person on the block. Who did they replace? There have, of course, always been a few of them, renters who mostly couldn't afford to live anywhere else but were also cool and didn't fuck with anybody. These new homeowners move different.

There's an older, retired couple who mostly have dinner parties and mind their business, but call 311 to make noise complaints. Jenn and Jen, the nicest of the newcomers, whose main issue is they seem to have been told all Black people are homophobic, so they go out of their way to normalize their own presence, while never stopping to wonder about the two old Black women who live next door to them and are definitely not sisters or just friends.

Then there're the young families like the people who moved into Miss Wanda's house, or those ready to start a family, like Ponytail Lululemon and her Wandering Eye husband, who I first encountered on the historical tour. They bought the Payne house across the street—guess they *had* been casing the neighborhood.

They don't have blinds, so I see what they do when they're home. She's usually tearing shit apart when she's there, renovating, which I guess is some kind of genetic inheritance thing. He seems to work from home and likes walking around shirtless on the top floor. I've never seen them actually interact; if I had a man walking around half-naked in my house, we'd be more than interacting, but that's none of my business.

The shrill, rapid-fire bark of a dog losing its shit pulls me from my thoughts.

"Goddammit, somebody put him in his cage before the guests arrive! Terry!" a woman yells, followed by a man shouting, "Christ, calm down, Josie! Arwin! Did you let Toby out of his cage?"

Terry and Josie and Arwin and Toby are Miss Wanda's replacements. They've never properly introduced themselves, but with all the yelling they do, I figured out their names quickly.

Toby barks incessantly while they're at work and school and whenever he damn well pleases because he needs more exercise and better training. Terry wears ill-fitting suits to work, leers at the teenage girls in the neighborhood, and doesn't pick up Toby's shit when he thinks no one is watching. Josie wears tailored suits to work, spends her weekends dividing her backyard garden into exactly sized plots, and obsessively posts in the Columbusly titled OurHood app about people who don't pick up dog waste.

Claude, my first post-divorce friend with benefits, used to call my new neighbors "Becky and Becky's Husband." We laughed at how they'd peek suspiciously at him through the curtains when he waited for me in his car out front, or how they'd hurry past when he stood at my front door in sagged jeans and Timbs instead of his tailored work suits and loafers.

Claude is gone now, too. He texted right before Valentine's Day:

Not feelin' this anymore.

Maybe there'd been another woman. Maybe I'd spent too much time stressing over my mother. Maybe he'd just sensed what I'd tried to hide: that my life was a spinout on a slick road and the smart thing to do was pump the brakes while he could.

When Drea had opened her apartment door and found me sniffling as I clutched a pint of Talenti, she'd hugged me, then given my shoulder a little shake. "Girl. *Sydney*. I'm sorry you're sad, but how many times do I have to tell you? You won't find gold panning in Fuckboy Creek."

She was right.

It's better this way; a warm body in bed is nice in the winter but it's too damn hot for cuddling in the summer unless you want to run the AC nonstop, and I don't have AC-nonstop money at the moment.

I notice a group of people approaching from the far end of the block, down by the garden, and scratch at my neck, at the patch of skin where a few months ago three itchy bites had arisen all in a row. *BEDBUGS* had been the first result of a frantic "what the fuck are these bites" internet search. Plastic-wrapped mattresses on the curb are a common sight now, the bedbugs apparently hitching rides on the unwashed legs steadily marching into the neighborhood. Even after weeks of steaming and bleaching and boiling my clothes and bedding, I can't shake the tainted feeling. I wake up in the middle of the night with the sensation of something I can't see feasting on me—I have to file my nails down to keep from scratching myself raw.

Maybe it's too late; maybe I'm already sucked dry. Sure as hell feels that way.

I drop my head and let the morning sun heat my scalp as I sit hunched and hopeless.

The group I'd spotted, apparently this week's batch of brunch guests, clusters a few feet away from me on the sidewalk in front of Terry and Josie's outer stairs, and I stop slouching: shoulders back, chin up. I pose as the picture of unbothered—languorously sipping my bodega coffee and pretending sweat isn't beading at my hairline as I blatantly watch them. None of them even glance at me.

Terry and Josie come outside—her rocking an angular *I'd like to speak to the manager* platinum-dyed bob and him with a tight fake smile. They keep their heads rigidly straight and their gazes fixed on their friends as they greet them, like I'm a junkyard dog who might growl if they make eye contact.

I don't think they even know my name is Sydney.

I don't want to know what "funny" nickname they have for me.

"The place looks great," one of their friends says as they start up the stairs.

"We used the same company as Sal and Sylvie on *Flip Yo' Crib,*" Josie replies as she stops just in front of the doorway so they can admire the newly installed vintage door and stained glass in the transom window above it.

Their contractors had started their early-morning repairs right after the new year, waking Mommy up each time she finally managed to get comfortable enough to rest. In the spring, I'd been jolted awake a full hour early before I had to head to the school office and smile at annoying children and their annoying parents all day—everyone was annoying when you just wanted to sleep and not wake up for years.

Or ever.

"You just would not believe how these people don't appreciate the historic value of the neighborhood," Josie says. "We had to completely renovate. It was like there'd been a zoo here before!"

I glance at her out of the corner of my eye. Miss Wanda had been of the "bleach fumes so strong they burned her neighbors' lungs" school of cleaning. Josie's a damn liar, and I have the near-death experience with accidental mustard gas to prove it.

"The other houses look nice to me, especially this one," says the last person in their line of friends, a woman of East Asian descent with a baby strapped to her chest. "It looks like a tiny castle!"

I smile, thinking about the days when I'd sit at the window set in the whimsical brick demi-turret, a captured princess, while my friends scrambled on the sidewalk out front, vying for the chance to rescue me from the evil witch holding me captive. It's cool to say the princess should save herself nowadays, but I don't think I've experienced that sensation outside of children's games—of having someone willing to risk life and limb, everything, to save me.

Mommy protected me, of course, but being protected was different from being saved.

Josie whirls on the top step and frowns down at her friend for apparently not being disdainful enough. "The houses look nice in spite of. No amount of ugly Home Depot plants can hide the neglect, either."

Oooh, this bitch.

"Right," her friend says, anxiously stroking the baby's back.

"All I'm saying is that I can trace my ancestors back to New Amsterdam. *I* appreciate history," Josie says, turning to continue into the house.

"Well, family trees have a lot of missing leaves around here, if you know what I mean," Terry adds as he follows her inside. "Of course they don't appreciate that kind of thing."

Maybe I should hop over the banister of my stoop and give them a lesson on the history of curb stomping if they like history so damn much.

The chastised woman's gaze flits over to mine and she gives me an apologetic wave of acknowledgment as she files into the house. The door closes firmly behind her.

I was already tired, but tears of anger sting my eyes now, though I should be immune to this bullshit. It isn't *fair*. I can't sit on my stoop and enjoy my neighborhood like old times. Even if I retreat to my apartment, it won't feel like home because Mommy won't be waiting upstairs. I sit trapped at the edge of the disorienting panic that strikes too often lately, the ground under my ass and the soles of my flip-flops the only things connecting me to this place.

I just want everything to stop.

"Hey, Sydney!"

I glance across the street and the relief of seeing a familiar face helps me get it together. Mr. Perkins, my other next-door neighbor, and his pittiehound, Count Bassie, stroll by on one of their countless daily rounds of the neighborhood. Mommy had gone to the ASPCA with Mr. Perkins after his wife had passed a few years back, and he's been inseparable from the brown-and-white dog ever since then.

"Morning, Sydney honey!" Mr. Perkins calls out in that scratchy voice of his, his arm rising slowly above his bald head as he waves at me. Count lets out one loud, ridiculously low-toned bark, a doggie *hey girl*; he loves me because I give him cheese and other delicious human food when he sits close to me.

"Morning!" I call out, feeling a little burst of energy just from seeing him. He's always been here, looking out for me and my mom—for everyone in the neighborhood.

He's usually up and making his daily rounds by six, stopping by various stoops, making house calls, keeping an ear to the ground and a smile on his face. It's why we call him the Mayor of Gifford Place.

Right now, he's likely on his way to Saturday services, judging from his khakis and pressed shirt. Count usually sits at his feet, and Mr. Perkins jokes that when he howls along with the choir, he hits the right note more often than half the humans singing.

"You gonna have that tour ready for the block party next week? Candace is on my behind about it since you put it on the official schedule."

I want to say no, it's not ready, even though I've been working on it bit by bit for months. It would be so easy to, since I have no idea if anyone will take this tour, even for free, much less pay for it, but . . . when I'd angrily told Mommy what Zephyr had said to me about starting my own tour, her face had lit up for the first time in weeks.

"You always did have the History Channel on, turning to Secrets of World War II or some mess while I was trying to watch my stories. Why shouldn't you do it?"

It became a game for us, finding topics that I could work into the tour—it was something we could do while she was in bed, and it kept both of us occupied.

"This is the first time I've seen that old fire in your eyes since you got home. I'm glad you're coming back to yourself, Syd. I can't wait to take your tour."

"How's your mama doing?" Mr. Perkins calls out, the question causing a ripple of pain so *real* that I draw my knees up to my chest.

"She's doing good," I say, hating the lie and ashamed of the resentment that wells up in me every time I have to tell it. "Hates being away from home, but that's no surprise."

He nods. "Not at all. Yolanda loved this neighborhood. Tell her I'm praying for her when you see her."

"I will."

Count lunges after a pizza crust left on the sidewalk, suddenly spry, and Mr. Perkins gives chase, bringing the painful conversation to a blessed end.

"Come to the planning meeting on Monday," he calls out with a wave as he walks on. "I've got some papers for you."

He could just hand them to me, but I think he's making sure I show up. He knows me well.

I nod and wave. The window of Josie and Terry's living room slams shut, punctuating our conversation.

I take a sip of my coffee and hear the slapping of two sets of feet against the sidewalk.

"Good morning!" Jenn and Jen say. They're holding hands as they stride down the street in sync, matching smiles on their faces. Even their flourishing plots in the garden complement each other: Jen's bursting with flowers and Jenn's with vegetables.

"Morning! Have a good day, you two," I say as they march past, sounding like an auntie even though they're probably only a few years younger than me.

I'm not faking my pleasantness. I want them to know that if their presence bothers me, it's not because they're holding hands. It's because of everything else. I wish I didn't have to think about everything else, but . . . Miss Wanda is gone. The Hancocks. Mr. Joe.

Sometimes it feels like everything rock-solid about my world is slipping away, like the sand sucked through my fingers when I'd sit in the breaking waves at Coney Island.

I suddenly remember one of our mother-daughter beach days, when I was four or five. Mommy had treated me to Nathan's, and a seagull swooped down and snatched a crinkle-cut french fry out of my hand right before I bit into it. The biggest fry. I'd saved it for last. The sudden shock of the fry theft, the unfairness of it, had made me start wailing. Mommy shook her head and laughed as she wiped my cheeks with thumbs gritty from sand and smelling of ketchup. "Baby, if you wanna keep what's yours, you gotta hold on to it better than that. Someone is always waiting to snatch what you got, even these damn birds."

I'm trying, Mommy. And I hate it.

A shiver runs down my spine despite the heat, and when I look up, I see Bill Bil coming. His name is William Bilford, real estate agent, but I call him Bill Bil because it annoys him and why should I be the only one suffering? I'm alone, my new neighbors are assholes, and this con artist is roaming the neighborhood, trying to bring in more of them.

I grimace in his direction. He's wearing jeans that are too thick and too tight for the heat index and the amount of walking he's doing. There are sweat stains around the armpits of his tight gray T-shirt, hinting at the swamp-ass horror show that must be playing below. His face sports carefully contoured stubble and eyes that are red-rimmed from too much booze or coke or both. His light brown hair is carefully styled, though, so he's not entirely a mess.

"Hey, Ms. Green," he says with a wink and a grin that probably goes over well in a dive bar in Williamsburg but has no effect on me at all.

"Hey, Bill Bil," I chirp. His shark's smile doesn't falter but the brightness in his eyes dims. I pick up the loosie and lighter I bought from the bodega and make a big production of holding the flame to the tip of the cigarette. The smoke that floods my mouth is disgusting—I can *taste* the cancer, and hey, maybe that's what makes it enjoyable—but I've been smoking one with my morning coffee every now and again anyway.

"That's bad for your health," he says.

I exhale a cloud of smoke toward where he's standing at the bottom of the stairs. "Nothing has changed from the last ten times you walked by here. We're still not selling the house. Have a blessed day."

His shark smile widens. "Come on. I'm just being friendly."

"You're just trying to create a false sense of camaraderie because you think it'll make me trust you. Then you can convince me to sell so you can pocket that sweet, sweet commission."

"You really think that?" He shakes his head. "I'm out here trying to *help*. A lot of people don't even know that they could earn more than they've ever had in their entire life, just by moving."

"Moving where? Where are people supposed to go if even this neighborhood becomes too expensive?"

I suck at my cigarette, hard.

He sighs. "The struggle is real; I feel that. Why do you think I'm out here hustling? I have bills to pay, too, but I don't have a house to sell for a huge profit. If I did, I could pay off school loans, medical bills." He shrugs, like he couldn't help but point out those two specific things.

"Well, there are plenty of vultures circling, so if I do give up on the neighborhood, I have lots of realtors to choose from." My hand shakes as I lift the cigarette to my lips again, and I try not to fumble it.

He drops his affable shark mask.

"You act like I'm some scumbag, but you just proved my point. There are lots of realtors interested in this area, especially with the VerenTech deal as good as done. It's the hottest emerging community in Brooklyn right now."

"Emerging community?" I tilt my head. "Emerging from where? The primordial ooze?"

His brows lift a bit, and I know it's not because he's registered my question but because the motherfucker is surprised I can use *primordial* in a sentence.

"Look." He runs a hand over his hair backward and then forward, not messing up his look. "I'm not some villain twirling my mustache and trying to push people out onto the street. I'm not even one of the buyers carrying around bags of cash and blank checks to tempt people into taking bad deals. I'm just a normal guy doing a normal job."

Just doing my job. How many times have I heard that while arguing with people over my mother's health, money, and future? Everyone is just doing their job, especially when that job is lucrative and screws people over.

"And I'm just a homeowner who's told you repeatedly that I don't want to sell," I say.

"You don't have to sell," he says, walking off in search of someone more receptive to his bullshit. "But you can't stop change, you know."

I don't think he's even trying to be threatening, but I mash out the cigarette against the bottom of my flip-flop and stand, suddenly full of nervous energy. After stepping into the hallway to grab my gardening bag and slip on sneakers, I lock the door and make my way to Mommy's community garden. I could never manage to keep even a Chia Pet alive, but I'm doing my best. I go every day; I put in work, even if I don't have much to show for it.

It keeps me close to her, and that dulls away the sharp edges of the guilt that's always poking at me. I sigh deeply, then pull out my phone and call her—it goes to voicemail. And when I hear her voice say, "You've reached Yolanda Green. I'm away from my cell phone or otherwise indisposed. Leave a message, unless you're asking for money, because lord knows I don't have any," my throat goes rough as usual.

"Hi, Mommy," I say after the beep, even though I usually don't leave messages. "Things are hard, but I'm holding steady. Just wanted to hear your voice, but I'll see you soon. Love you."

*G*ive in to your Impulses!

These unforgettable stories only take a second to buy and give you hours of reading pleasure!

Go to *www.AvonImpulse.com* and see what we have to offer.

Available wherever e-books are sold.

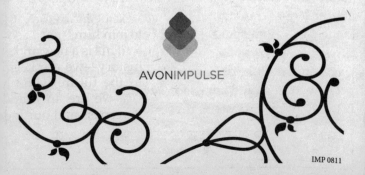

AVONIMPULSE